LOUISE PENNINGTON

Louise Pennington worked in advertising for five years before devoting all her time to writing. She was born in Bristol and lived in Vienna, where her diplomat husband was posted, and now lives in Brighton. She is the author of *The Dreambreakers* and *The Diplomat's Wife*.

GW00707717

SINS OF ANGELS

Louise Pennington

ARROW

Arrow Books Limited
20 Vauxhall Bridge Road, London SW1V 2SA

An imprint of Random House UK Ltd

London Melbourne Sydney Auckland
Johannesburg and agencies throughout
the world

First published in 1992 by Century

Arrow Edition, 1993

1 3 5 7 9 10 8 6 4 2

Printed and bound in Great Britain by
Cox & Wyman Ltd, Reading, Berkshire

ISBN 0 09 987920 4

For my brother, Adrian, with love

My thanks to Cameron Mackintosh
for his time and valuable advice

ONE

'Flesh like fresh peaches, oozing sweetness and sexual promise.'

Angela scanned the line again and began tearing up the beautifully typed pages, one by one, and little white paper squares fell and scattered over the three-hundred-year-old Persian rug.

'Mother – are you still there?'

Angela's attention flashed to the telephone and the sound of her daughter's irritatingly pleasant and very English voice; she picked up the receiver from the table where she had left it.

'I don't like it and I don't want anything to do with it.'

There was silence for a moment, then the voice again, touched by surprise. 'But it's brilliant – and I'm not the only one who thinks so. Are you sure you haven't just flicked through the pages, I mean, you have actually read it?'

'I'm not a complete fool, Jacqueline,' Angela said sharply, 'and in my opinion it has no buzz, and it's been done before a thousand times.' But it *was* good, even very good.

Jackie stiffened. 'Well, the only thing you have to do is release the money.'

'I'm not willing to do that.'

'Why not?'

'I've just told you.'

'That's not enough.'

'I am starting to lose my cool, Jacqueline.' Her mother's voice began to rise ominously and Jackie closed her eyes, sensing disaster.

'I think I deserve at least one good reason why you will not advance me the money.'

'The word "no" should be good enough.'

'Mother – don't treat me like a child.' Jackie tightened her grip on the telephone, anger turning her knuckles white.

'And don't call me "mother". How many times have I told you?' Her daughter had an uncanny knack of making Angela feel her age, reminding her of the camouflaged lines on her carefully

1

made-up face and the soft flesh which grew softer each day no matter how many work-outs she did. 'I gave birth to you, that was more than enough.' Envy, hot and ugly, constricted her throat, Jacqueline had talent, beauty and youth – glorious, delicious, reckless youth, which had passed through her own hands so fast she could hardly remember it.

She had never wanted her daughter. Finding herself pregnant had been one of her worst nightmares come true. Angela's 'stage career' had just started, and she had every intention of making sure that there would be no backsliding to her soul-killing Mid-West roots and the hundreds of miles of flat godforsaken corn-land she had run away from, but with a baby strapped to her back it was impossible to climb where she wanted to go. And she had been so afraid, even now she could still remember the fear.

The 'abortion' had taken place in the dismal rooms above a back-street bar, the man's hands had been shaking and she could remember making a nervous joke, a stupid break-the-ice kind of a joke, but he had said nothing in return, only staring back at her when he took the fifty dollars from her clammy, eighteen-year-old hand, and she had been beaten down by that gaze.

Except that whatever he had tried to do hadn't worked and she had ended up lying flat on her back for two weeks when the haemorrhaging started. The bleeding was followed by a burning fever from the not-so-clean instruments the humourless son of a bitch had used. And the baby had stuck in there, refusing to budge.

When she was better she had been too afraid to go back and try again, even if she had had the money. Fifty dollars had meant a lot way back then.

Angela had resented the growing child in her stomach prob-ably more than anything in her life – hating it, damning it each time she caught sight of her reflection because men no longer looked at her in that 'I want' kind of a way. When Jacqueline had been born – after twenty-six goddamn hours of agonizing labour – she had already managed to persuade a doting aunt to take the baby, but the aunt had died and the by then three-year-old child had been returned to its constantly roving mother.

There would have been a children's home sooner or later, but David had found out about Jackie during the course of their eventual, and naturally very bitter divorce, and wanted her sent to him. Angela had refused point-blank, there was no way she would ever let her ex-husband have anything that he might, indeed, *really*, want. So David had simply done what he could and that was pay, which was little enough at the time.

He had been no big-shot movie star back then, only another out-of-work actor with a drink problem, and she had made him wait and wait to see his daughter, four long years, until his marriage to the rich and lovely Clare had made it difficult for Angela to go on refusing access. David was respectable by then, of course; she should have guessed that sooner or later he would come up reeking of the sweet, sickening smell of roses.

'Call me "Angela" goddamn you.'

Jackie felt the unlovely echoes from her childhood sound in her mind and was tempted to put down the telephone there and then.

'I just don't understand why you are doing this?' She asked carefully, but hating her mother for her selfishness, her neurosis, her vanity and, most of all, for making Jackie beg.

'Like I said before – it will never work – better people than you have tried and failed.'

Jackie winced at the stinging remark. Bullseye, mother.

'And I don't see why I should release over a million dollars from Lloyd's trust fund so you can flush it down the john.'

'The money is mine – and Lloyd would never have stopped me.'

'Lloyd was an old fool, and the money won't legally be yours for another five years.'

'You've never objected to the way I've used my money before. Why now, for God's sake?'

'Because I have an international reputation to think of and I don't want to be associated with any sort of failure, musical or otherwise, particularly one about a dumb blonde who was also a screwball and who happened to strike it lucky too many years ago to recall.'

'I know you're wrong. Marilyn Monroe's life story is a fabulous basis for a musical . . . and have you considered that maybe she simply had that little extra something that all the other starlets lacked?'

'Or maybe she simply knew how to screw around better than anyone else . . . if you know what I mean.'

Jackie closed her eyes. Now that was rich coming from her mother.

'I don't care about all of that – what I do care about is the fact that I believe I can really make something out of this.'

'Obviously.' Angela yawned. 'But you won't get one cent out of me – and who do you think will want to back an idea that's been done before and flopped so badly that no one who matters can remember it anyway?' She sighed heavily. 'And what sort of schmuck would back *you*? You've never even had a musical in the West End of London, let alone here on Broadway. You've got no experience worth having and no one has ever heard of you. Do you want any more reasons, for chrissakes?'

'I may not have produced a great musical yet, and may not have received much attention from those almighty sons of bitches on the Broadway merry-go-round who you seem to love so much, but I do know what I'm doing and I've been working in the theatre since I was eighteen – nearly twelve years,' she paused, trying to control her temper. 'Okay, I've had a few failures, but who hasn't? I got damn good reviews for my fringe production of *Wuthering Heights* and for *The Holy Grail* at the Hackney Empire.' She realized, even as the words slipped out of her mouth, that Hackney did not exist for her mother.

'Hackney *where*?'

'It doesn't matter.'

There was a silence for a moment before her mother spoke again. 'Well, I think we've said all there is to say.'

'Thank you for your help and encouragement.' Sarcasm was wasted on Angela, she was too good at it herself.

There was another pause and for a brief irrational moment she thought that her mother had changed her mind.

'I'm doing it for your own good.'

Jackie shook her head in disbelief. 'No, you're not – you're doing it for yourself and I just can't figure out why.'

'There's nothing to figure.'

Jackie made no answer as a strong image of her mother, her very beautiful mother, formed in her mind. She would be alone in that lavish New York apartment, probably standing by the window, a cigarette in an ivory holder in her free hand, looking beyond the glass to the black beauty of the Manhattan skyline and the millions of tiny, brittle lights looking back at her. None of her often very young lovers had ever been allowed to stay at the penthouse, not one – at the mansion in Virginia and the retreat in Martha's Vineyard, yes, but not New York. After all, she had her reputation to think about.

'So there really is nothing more I can say to make you change your mind?'

'No,' Angela said meanly, 'but why don't you try asking your saintly father for a few dollars . . . or his equally saintly and fortunately very rich wife. Fortunate for him, that is.'

'Goodbye, mother.'

'Angela, goddammit.'

But her daughter had already put down the phone.

Jackie moved over to the window trying to press the ugly moment down; there was always something grey and relentless left in the air from any communication she had with her mother, but their conversation and her decision to withhold the money had come as a complete and unhappy surprise.

It was ironic that at that moment she felt that she had been rich all her life. Filthy rich. Vulgarly rich. She drew a circle on the misted glass of the window and looked down on to the green expanse of Hyde Park. But it hadn't always been like that. When her mother had been struggling, when she had only been yet another Hollywood starlet waiting for 'the big break', there had been dubious night-clubs and smoke-filled rooms where her mother had been called Pinkey Jones and peeled her clothes slowly and slickly from an almost perfect body.

Jackie had generally been left to stand in whatever space she could find backstage, or in a dressing room if she was lucky. She had always known when her mother's star-spangled brassière had come off because there would be hooting and hollering, and thumping on tables which shook dust from the ceiling and rattled all the lights. Yet, more than anything else, it had been the heavy silences which followed that she had loathed; the creeping quiet when she knew her mother's hands were sliding across the white, white skin and the men out there were eating her alive with their eyes.

Jackie swallowed and turned back into the room. Pinkey had met Lloyd shortly after her daughter's fifth birthday; she had been a magician's assistant that night, called in at the last moment by her agent, Oleg, to help an ageing magic man pull live white rats out of a stinking, but nevertheless, dazzling gold turban. The act had been at one of the better venues, way down the list, and Lloyd was sitting at a table right at the front. When Pinkey palpitated into view wearing shimmering harem pants and very little else Lloyd had almost fallen off his chair.

He had been very, very rich, a retired television mogul, and crazy about redheads. So it had been easy for her mother to decide to marry him three weeks later, before he found out about the stripping and could change his mind, and in a dress that Jackie could only describe as breathtaking – a white satin sheath, skintight, studded with rhinestones and with a neckline that plunged the depths of her mother's ample cleavage like the Grand Canyon. Lloyd had hardly been able to control himself – at least, that was what her mother had told her much later, with a smile of triumph that made that full, beautiful mouth suddenly greedy and unkind. Her daughter had never doubted it.

Jackie glanced down at her watch and went into the adjoining bedroom. She picked up her jacket and briefcase and moved to the door of her suite because she was already due at the studio for more auditions. Later she would have dinner at their Hampstead home with her father and stepmother, who were blissfully unaware that she now intended to ask them whether they would be prepared to act as 'angels' and invest in the show, something which had suddenly gained rather more importance than it should have done.

Jackie seethed and wondered vengefully how her mother would react now if she were to call her back and remind her of that first, unmentionable wedding; wondered what she would say if she were asked what had happened to that gaudy, unforgettable dress and the rhinestones which had glittered so prettily in the eyes of her five-year-old daughter. The idea almost made her want to laugh out loud because Angela would deny it, of course, or suggest in that sweet, husky voice of hers that Jackie hadn't been much more than a baby, really, and babies don't remember very much, very well. Do they? Angela Shriver, now Angela

Cassini, alias her mother, alias Pinkey Jones stripper *extraordinaire*, darling of the international gossip columns and New York society hostess.

Jackie felt the beginnings of a headache and swore softly. Lloyd Shriver had been the first human being she had learned to love; he had been a friend as well as a stepfather. There had been no children for the ageing statesman of fading television legend, no one to inherit the Shriver fortune except his newly adopted family, but when he died on that gloriously sunny July day seventeen years before, her mother had been in New York as usual. It had taken Pinkey four days before she had made it home, she had almost missed the funeral. Jackie had never forgiven her for that.

'Oh, God,' Lucy stared back at her white face in the mirror, 'if I don't get this part I'll probably do something stupid like get myself a proper job . . .'

'At least you're close, really close – down to the last four.' He wondered if she heard the trace of envy in his voice.

'Like last time.'

'You're the one who always tells me not to be negative.'

She sighed heavily, dramatically. 'Sorry, Richard.' She turned to look at him. 'I just want it so much . . . more than anything.'

'All you can do is keep yourself together and sing your heart out.'

'I know, I know . . . ,' she said and drew a sharp, weary breath, her voice suddenly lower, almost sad. 'I've tried to get inside her somehow, but she's so elusive . . . so hollow.'

'We've been through this,' he said patiently, 'Marilyn Monroe *was* elusive as a person because even *she* didn't know who she was.'

'But there was a vulnerability, an innocence . . .'

'She was a product of a horrendously deprived and disturbed background – damaged goods by the time she was three years old.' He looked at her sharply. 'She was a child in a woman's body.'

'She was also the greatest sex symbol of modern times.'

'Okay – she was schizoid – or at the very least tragically mixed up,' he sighed heavily, 'but she was a human being, after all, with

7

human frailties, not just this amazing legend the media keeps forever shoving down our throats. Sure, she was complicated, insecure, lonely, sweet and dreamy, but she was also ambitious, ignorant, boring, slovenly, narcissistic and probably psychotic. Luce, at the very best you can only give a glimpse of her, only capture her at moments and create a convincing illusion.' He gave her a searching look, for her own sake willing her to believe him. 'Maybe the lyrics and the songs themselves will help give you that extra bit of inspiration.'

'A couple of them are real weepies, tragic, you know – sheer emotion . . .'

'I wish you didn't sound so wistful about it all, as if the part was already out of your grasp,' he said impatiently.

'Well, I thought it *was* in New York.'

'We all have bad days, and obviously *they* didn't feel you performed as badly as you think you did, otherwise you wouldn't have been shortlisted.' He stared at her, suddenly exasperated. 'You have a fantastic voice and a body that is probably as good as, or even better, than Monroe's – all you need is a blonde wig.'

She matched his stare, the faintest of smiles tipping the edges of her mouth. 'You say the sweetest things sometimes.'

'And just suppose, just suppose,' he continued, as if she had not spoken, 'you don't get the part, there'll be something else in that production for you – you know that, don't you?'

She nodded.

'And you'll be able to give up your job at the casino.'

'I know, I know.' He was probably right about everything, but she didn't want just any part, she wanted Marilyn.

'God,' Richard exclaimed with a trace of irritation, 'I wish I could bloody well sing, at least it would broaden my options a bit.'

She glanced back at him, suddenly touched by guilt.

'Sorry, sorry, sorry – I didn't mean to go on, but getting the lead would also mean more money . . .' A hell of a lot more, at least a thousand pounds more per week, the thought almost made her swoon.

'I had already worked that out for myself, Luce.'

His eyes reproached her and she wished she hadn't spoken.

'Do you have any plans for today?' But she already knew the answer to her feeble question.

Richard smiled wearily. 'I suppose I'll give my dynamic agent a call and see if he has any amazing offers lined up.' But if there were an offer, any offer, Ned would naturally call him, not the other way round. He sighed inwardly; seven months with not even a single, solitary ad to chalk up. 'I shall also be a good boy and pick up *The Stage* and *Plays and Players* from the newsagents and see what auditions are going.' He slumped into a chair and said in mock sorrow, 'God, it seems a long time since I walked the hallowed cobbles of *Coronation Street* and propped up the bar at The Rover's Return.' He shook his head. 'To think I didn't even get to say a bloody word, all I did was leer at Bet Lynch and give an inane nod as she handed me a plastic pint of beer which tasted like pee . . . ' his voice trailed off, '. . . one bloody episode.'

'You did that American Express ad in January.'

'Thank you, Lucy, my darling, my sweet, for reminding me of the best-paid job I've had in four years – all thirty seconds of it.' For a moment he wished that she would go because in this mood he was no good to her.

She examined his partly bowed head carefully, knowing that there was nothing more to say, but then he looked up at her and she was surprised by a surge of pleasure, and thought that he had a wonderfully endearing face, somehow sad, tender, loveable.

'Love you.'

'I know,' he said quietly. 'You'd better finish getting ready.'

'What will you do?'

'What will I do?' he repeated. 'After trotting gaily to the shops, I expect I shall make some of my not-to-be-missed sandwiches, probably cheese and Branston, and a smattering of ham and tomato with a touch of mustard, and try and flog them in that big office block down the street and earn a few bucks – and then I shall return to my battered old Olympia and write a few tired lines about the glamorous life of an out-of-work actor.'

'Think of me.'

'I always think of you.'

'Something will happen, Richard . . .'

'. . . something always does,' he finished for her, 'sooner or later, but why is it always later rather than sooner?' He snapped his eyes shut with impatience. 'Don't answer that. And now – don't you think you'd better hurry?'

She disappeared into their bedroom and he turned reluctantly to the piece of paper he had picked up from the table and the tedious shopping list he had written that morning. It was getting to him finally, he could almost feel the depression sinking deeper into his bones as every day passed, and it was becoming harder and harder to wake up each morning to nothing except that familiar anxious feeling in his chest and the empty promises of the telephone. Lucy's forced cheer jagged his nerves even more, but he didn't know what to do about that; after all, he had been through the same dismal times before, had heard and read enough about the perils of a Thespian existence to know that he was only walking the lonely path of the resting actor, but it didn't help because no one could tell him when the road would end – *if* the road would end.

Richard glanced at the ageing typewriter sitting on a table against the wall: somehow it did help to write it all down. Like therapy, he supposed, with a snort of contempt, or literary diarrhoea – a vast, bitter enema of words. A dry smile slid across his face and he thanked God that he still had his sense of humour.

Lucy left Richard staring out of the window, and as she stepped out into the street she turned and waved as she always did and he blew her a kiss. Then her thoughts switched to the audition and she swallowed nervously; the competition for the role had been unbelievably fierce and even if she was in the last four it counted for nothing in the end. No one was interested in an 'also ran' or a 'might have been' and there had been too many of those lately, although her luck had not been as bad as Richard's.

Luck was often all it was unless you knew someone in the right place at the right time, but neither she nor Richard came from theatrical families nor had the necessary connections; they simply had themselves and whatever talent they had been given, which was considerable, but that was often not enough. She screwed up her eyes as a gust of wind blew into her face. And there was also Max Lockhart, of course. She had met the director of *Marilyn* in another time, another place – an audition three years before. He had asked her to stay behind after the other girls had left, apparently 'to discuss the part in more depth', and she had agreed although his motive had been transparent – his eyes had stripped her naked more than once. But she had desperately needed the job, hadn't she? She remembered gritting her teeth so hard her jaw almost locked as Lockhart's greedy hands had squeezed her breasts too hard, her head tilting back in silent agony as he had made her kneel in front of him, and then the unforgettable sound of that zip on his trousers and the bile climbing into her throat as he forced himself into her mouth. Lucy closed her eyes. She had vomited all down his pale spindly legs.

She smoothed away a wisp of hair and caught sight of Primrose Hill on her left. There was a man with a kite, a vast laughing blue face which was rising and falling as the wind tossed it across the sky. For a cowardly moment she wished she were taking the narrow path through the wrought-iron gateway, up the steep slope and away from the fickle and sometimes corrupt world she had chosen to enter. Instead, she turned her face away and thought again of the audition. Lucy caught a sharp breath as her stomach churned alarmingly, but at least the songs were beautiful, at least there would be some joy in singing them, she told herself. Her doubting spirits seemed to lift a little and she tried to hum. And Max Lockhart could go burn in hell.

'I'm sorry you haven't had much time to study the score, but it's only recently been finalized – ' Jackie smiled encouragement. ' – I hope!'

Lucy gave a small nervous laugh in response. They were standing in the studio, a wide gaunt room with a piano and an ominous row of chairs waiting to be filled along one wall.

'They're wonderful songs – you must be very excited.'

'Yes, I am, but it's been a long, long process to get them just right and I don't doubt there may be more changes as the production takes shape.'

'I suppose so.' Lucy swallowed and then said abruptly, 'It's a marvellous role.'

'Marilyn? – Yes, it is.' Jackie gave her a searching look. 'And I sometimes think that casting is the most difficult and frustrating time of all.' She smiled. 'You want the part very much, of course?'

'Oh, yes,' she said. Oh yes, oh yes, oh yes.

'Then let yourself go this time, Lucy,' Jackie said gently. At the audition in New York, Lucy had seemed stiff and uncomfortable which they had put down to nerves. Max, who had heard her sing before, had been distinctly disappointed, but she had persuaded him to give her another chance despite his protests and reluctantly he had agreed, not only because physically Lucy was what they were looking for, but also it was very clear from her first interview that she had studied Monroe's life with particular care and interpreted it well.

'I'm always tense at auditions, but somehow this part has got under my skin more than usual.'

Jackie touched her arm, warming to her honesty. 'I know it's hard, but try to push that aside and rise above all of this – ,' she waved her hand impatiently at the room, ' – the studio and the people in it.' She sighed inwardly, knowing there was little more she could say because it really was up to Lucy now. 'We're going to sit down and Aldo, the musical director, who you've already met, will take you through a couple of the songs. Sing like you know you can . . . just think of the lyrics and what they're trying to say.'

Lucy nodded as Jackie walked away and the fears she knew so well began to dance inside. She envied Jackie suddenly, and the other members of the production team who already had their sure and seemingly inviolate places in the making of the musical. For a long moment she let her eyes rove about the studio – to the wall blanked out by heavy velvet curtaining, to another with a door marked 'Exit', and inevitably to the far wall and the five people waiting in judgement.

She blinked and cleared her throat, willing the nerves to die, willing her voice not to dry up and betray her as Aldo Morris began the opening bars of her song: a first act piece, 'Ladies of the Chorus', named after a low-budget picture at the beginning of Monroe's career in which she had played the part of a girl rising from poverty to stardom, echoing her own experience. Lucy followed this with a contrasting song, a beautiful ballad from the second act, 'Bennie, the Camera and Me': the lyrics conveying Monroe's slide into pill-popping or 'Bennies'. Benzedrine was a trade name for amphetamines, or stimulants, which suppressed a starlet's appetite and kept her slim, kept her awake and gave her a small, swift high in exchange for metabolic chaos and depression. Marilyn Monroe had been one of many blossoming young stars encouraged to pop pills by studio bosses to keep them working. It was a deadly road of uppers and downers and alcohol. A very short road.

Even as her voice began to soar Lucy found herself touched not only by the words of the song and the tragic life of the star she had never known, but by real melancholia as the memory of Poppy came creeping out of a closed corner of her mind. Poppy who had been at RADA with her and won the coveted Bancroft Gold Medal – brilliant, wild Poppy who had blazed and dazzled, and Alex her beloved boyfriend and drug-pusher *par excellence*, who had taken it all away and slowly sucked Poppy dry until her soul was gone.

Lucy's voice died slowly as the song faded, but she didn't want the music to stop, to hear the final note followed by abrupt gaping silence, and then the conclusions of the five people sitting in judgement at the back of the room. Getting this part had taken on mammoth proportions, and she was suddenly afraid of herself and how she would react if they said that she had failed.

This would be goodbye, but she would make it the best and that was why she had invited him here, to her apartment – her cosy little nest in the sky, something she had never done before and would not do again.

Angela steered her thoughts carefully and without emotion: he could keep the hotel room at the Mariott for another month if he wanted, she would leave him a fat cheque, there was the car . . . She lay back on the bed and let her eyes travel across the pristine whiteness of the ceiling to settle on the crystal chandelier. Drew would survive; after all that was what his life was all about and, besides, their affair had gone on too long and she could feel herself becoming involved, which was dangerous.

'Do you know what you look like?'

She turned her head: he was standing in the alcove leading to the bathroom and she had not realized he was there.

'No. What?' she asked quietly.

'A goddess.'

She laughed.

'A beautiful, exotic goddess.' His gaze moved over her almost naked body: the long tanned legs, the breathtaking shape of her waist, her wide but succulent hips . . . and the magnificent breasts; yet he wondered what she had that made him want her so much more than other beautiful women he had known, and to keep on wanting her.

'Come here.' She lifted one of her hands and offered it to him.

He looked down into her face: there was hardly a line and he still found it difficult to believe that she would be fifty sometime over the next two or three years, and he only knew that because of Jackie – sweet, unsuspecting Jackie who had almost found him out.

'Pull me up,' she said.

'I want you lying down.'

'Not yet.'

She swung her legs away from him and stood up, moving leisurely across the room, tiny scarlet panties smoothed perfectly, like slick red paint, over her superb backside. She disappeared through the alcove, only pausing to dim the lights, and he could hear her opening a drawer, then another, then the sound of the dressing-room door opening and closing. He stared at the empty space where she had stood and wondered what she was doing, sat down on the edge of the bed and reached for the fresh bottle of champagne he had brought from the ice-box.

Angela stared back at her reflection in the mirror, ran her fingertips from the bridge of her nose to her cheekbones and was pleased by the tautness of her skin; she could forget about a facelift for quite a while.

She began renewing her foundation with deft skilful strokes and then proceeded to accentuate the beauty spot just beneath the left side of her mouth with a black make-up pencil. Using the same pencil she brought it to the edges of her eyelids and drew a thick slanting line, upwards, so that immediately her eyes were darkened and tilted at the corners. She pulled her large mouth tight and then repainted her lips with vibrant red and added gloss so that they shone slick and wet.

On the stool beside her she had dropped the costume she intended wearing, something she imagined Drew would like very much, and something he would not forget in a hurry. Her parting gift to him. She had toyed with the idea of keeping him on hold, but it would never work; Dougie had begun to suspect something and Drew was becoming too possessive to accept being a play-thing. She wondered if it was his first time at love, wondered reluctantly about his background, but she didn't want to know about that because it would mean going too deep and soiling her hands with his past which she knew was a far from pleasant place. A dark pit. Drew dreamed and the dreams, the nightmares, made her skin crawl.

Angela began brushing her hair, hard, so that the thick auburn tresses began to swell and run wild. She put the brush down and buried her hands in her hair, shrugging with pleasure as she tugged at the roots. He would relish what she was about to do, all of it, just as she would, because their thoughts ran along the same wild lines when it came to sex. It had been a very long time since she had met any man who could make her feel the way Drew could: that heat, that sudden draining of breath, the blood shoot-ing through her veins.

When she was finally ready she took a step back and almost smiled; it was like old times.

He was lying spreadeagled across the bed as she stood on the edge of the dimly lit room and she wondered if he were sleeping. To her left and fixed in the wall was a small control panel which channelled music through the speakers from the salon: she reached for the volume control and turned it slowly so that a sax solo began to ooze like syrup into the room. She moved a broad low table into the centre and angled a lamp so that its light made a glowing circle on the carpet, then poured herself a glass of champagne and stepped up, on to the table, and drained the glass. For a moment she simply stood there, watching him, caught suddenly by how beautiful he was, then her hand was tightening around the glass and in one swift movement she had thrown it against the wall so that it smashed and Drew jumped.

'What the hell . . . ?'

'Look at me.'

He looked, and looked good and hard as his eyes awoke to the little scene she had created.

'Jeeesus . . . ,' he murmured, gaping at her, mouth partly

open, taking in every amazing detail. He had never seen her like this, not acting the whore, and it seemed to him that it could be someone else standing up there, someone he had never known. He felt sweat break out on the back of his neck as she closed her eyes and began to sway, move, rotate her hips.

She stretched her arms over her head and strained her body, then the arms dropped to her sides and hunching her shoulders she let her head fall back, the black leather biker's jacket slipping down her arms to the floor.

Her breasts were squeezed into a tiny jewelled brassière and the opulent white flesh trembled as she began to rotate her pelvis slowly, tantalizingly, the crotch-hugging black G-string leaving very little to the imagination. In the heavy heat-filled silence Drew could hear his own breathing.

She jerked her head forwards, opening her eyes, and began peeling off black elbow-length gloves, letting them fall one by one to the table. She turned around and bent over, running her hands over her buttocks and thighs, down to her high-heeled shoes and back again, all the time swaying languidly. She turned back to look at him and her mouth moved into a smile, and then she stepped off the table and began to move towards him, very deliberately – strutting, parading, teasing – narrowing the gap between them all the time.

There was an aroma of perfume mixed with her own scent, a heavy sweet fragrance which made his head swim. She planted a long-stemmed red rose between her breasts, tucked casually into the jewelled brassière and leaned down towards him, whispering huskily, 'Do you want to go flower pickin' in the hills?'

The words hung in the air, hot and humid with meaning, as he nodded slowly, sick with desire. She ran her tongue across the edges of her upper teeth as if tasting anticipated pleasure, took a deep breath and her left breast began to quiver and then the right, until the tiny brassière literally popped right open and he caught her in his mouth.

Drew knew, even as he suckled her, that the strip was that of no amateur, he had seen too many in all those sho-bars and sleaze clubs to know the difference.

He rolled her across him on to the bed, brought his hand

16

up between her legs so that the G-string tightened and rubbed, creating a delicious friction.

'That wasn't the first time you've stripped . . . was it?' he murmured in her ear.

She moaned.

'Tell me.'

'Oh, God . . .'

'Tell me – ' His fingers began to play and she writhed beneath him, and he wondered how long he could play this game with her.

'Fuck me . . . or go to hell,' she gasped.

He sighed with resignation and yielded because his control was going fast, but what followed seemed worth the surrender. Their lovemaking was much more than just screwing, it was skill and decadence and brutal passion.

All the same he knew, oh, yes, sirree, he knew.

'I'm leaving tonight.'

Drew sat up in bed. 'What do you mean?'

'What I said.' Angela did not look at him as she threw clothes on to the *chaise longue*.

'Where are you going?'

'You don't need to know that, Drew.'

'None of my goddamn business, you mean.'

'If you must know I have a gala to attend in Chicago, a charity ball to organize, and a lot of other things besides,' she said, thinking of Dougie. 'Is that enough for you?'

He watched her steadily as she walked to and fro across the room, white silk robe exposing thighs and legs as she moved.

'You're dumping me.'

'I told you, I have a lot of things to do.'

'Which don't include me.'

She stopped abruptly and sighed. 'We've had a good time,' she said, looking back at him, 'a really good time, but it has to stop somewhere.'

'Why?'

'You know why, Drew.'

'No, I don't.'

She swung round and walked away from him, out of the room.

'Bitch,' he said under his breath, then pushed the covers back from the bed and followed her.

She was standing at the picture window lighting a cigarette.

'You haven't answered my question . . .'

'I don't have to answer your question,' she snapped, 'I'm not your goddamn wife.'

'Let me come with you.'

'You're crazy.'

'For chrissakes . . .'

'No, Drew,' She turned around, 'and for God's sake put some clothes on.'

'I'm not leaving.'

Angela blew a cloud of smoke into the air. 'That's up to you,' she said, 'but I am. Now, if you don't mind, I have to get dressed.'

He caught her arm as she tried to walk past him.

'You can't . . .'

'I have to,' she said, 'now let go.'

'You don't *have* to do anything,' he said, ' – you're Angela Cassini, remember?'

'Let go.'

'I want to make love to you.'

'And I don't want to make *sex* with you. I have more important things on my mind.'

'You bitch.'

He gripped her arm more tightly and with his free hand picked up a nearby statuette, a figure of a young woman, and lifted it into the air. She froze as he held it above her head.

'You're afraid, aren't you?' he said softly, 'I've never seen you afraid before.'

'Bastard.'

He did not move for what seemed a long time, but then his arm lowered very slowly and he placed the figurine back where it had stood.

'You really thought I'd break it over your head . . .' he said and switched his gaze to the statuette, 'but it's much too beautiful to waste on a whore like you.'

'I'm not the whore, Drew,' she said, pulling free from him, 'I pay *you*, remember?'

*

18

There was a shriek in his throat. Drew sat up abruptly, still half-sleeping, sweat lying like gloss on his skin, and as the dream, the nightmare, died away he brought his hands up to cover his face.

'Shit.'

He lifted his head, dropping his hands into his lap, and switched on the light, groaning at the sudden brilliance.

'Shit.'

He shook his head in disbelief as his mind dragged back the dream to re-examine it, to make some sense of its relentless repetition. But he knew, didn't he, what it meant? The dream was his keeper: a spectre who came at night to rake his spine with feral fingers. Except that when he was allowed to see the fingers they were only pale, slim, unappetizing – almost delicate – leaning over the arc of his neck to trace the line of his shoulders, running down the curving hardness of his chest muscles, tugging at the sensitive mat of black hair coating his torso and then sliding to the firm belt of his belly, and beyond and beyond and beyond . . . Tantalizing, teasing, driving him mad with desire and a need he did not – ever – wish to have, a need that made his gorge rise, made bile climb into his mouth.

There was water, too, a great wall, rolling ominously towards him from a sea that should not have been there, not in that familiar room with the paint peeling off the walls and the big tin bath with the one gaunt tap hanging out of the plaster. He knew that the water would drown, no smother him when the fingers, the pale unfed fingers, forced his climax to spew forth, explode, rupturing him and splitting him in two as the water crashed out. Sometimes, when he mercifully awoke, the bed would be wet with sweat and semen, sometimes there was only sweat.

Oh, he knew what it meant all right, he didn't need one of those high-rolling therapists to tell him what his particular private hell-hole was all about.

Drew cursed and then swung his legs out of bed and sat in silence, immobile, brooding, looking at the phone. Angela would be tucked up now, no doubt, getting her beauty sleep, lying all spread out between slinky satin sheets. She was still good, despite her age, really good, and besides, the age thing had never bothered him; he *liked* older women. An unbidden thought flashed into his brain, but he pressed it down, repelled, not wanting to examine it too clearly. No sir, not that shit again.

Once he had had Angela Cassini almost eating out of his hand, at least that was how it had seemed to him, but it had been the other way around. She was after bigger fish, big fat political fish, like the Governor of California, Douglas Hicks the Third, crap-artist of the year. Drew cursed again and ran an impatient hand through his thick black hair. She loved his hair; she had buried her hands and her mouth in it, curled her thighs around his head so that she could feel its softness on her juicy hot spot. Crazy. He sighed wistfully, remembering a line of horny poetry he had read in an upmarket men's magazine, something about 'the liquid gold of heaven's gate' . . . Def-in-ite-ly.

Then she had dropped him, just dropped him, as if he were nothing, and could crawl right back under that stone where he had come from. He felt tears start in his eyes and, like a small boy, he brought his fist up to wipe them away.

'Bitch,' he said wearily and then took a deep, shuddery breath, looking around the empty hotel room which only served to remind him of his loneliness.

Because she had dropped him with such cold calculation he would deliberately resume his relationship with Jackie. She might have left him and gone to England, but he knew with certainty that given the right opportunity he could persuade her that she had made a mistake and they could start again.

Angela would go crazy when she found out, but she'd had her chances and blown them right into orbit. During his fling with Jackie at Cape Cod she had been worried enough about his relationship with her daughter to want him back for a while, but she hadn't been able to keep it up, too worried about Dougie kiss-my-ass Hicks and his add-height shoes. Drew smiled meanly as an unkind picture of the Governor of California formed in his mind and then he stood up and stretched, feeling better than he had done a few minutes before.

He padded over to the mirror above the washbasin and scrutinized his face; he looked pretty good, and he still had plenty of cash in the bank and a wardrobe of neat designer clothes all chosen and paid for by Angela. She loved dressing him up. He stood quite still for a moment, staring at himself in sullen silence.

But she had rejected him. He thought of his past, a shit-hole, and all those moments of anguish, hatred and resentment when other people had made him suffer.

He had always been an outsider – a pimply, gangly kid with no friends and a weird, weird mother who had insisted on meeting him from school so that he had wanted to crawl away and die.

At high school his social high point had been when a girl he idolized took him to the prom so that her boyfriend would get jealous, and he did, and she had dropped Drew immediately, like so much hot shit. Just like that.

For years afterwards all his sexual encounters had been fuelled by a sort of revenge and, as his physical attributes had grown, so had his confidence and he began to specialize in taking women, usually older women, away from their husbands. Drew developed a sixth sense about the women he came into contact with, examining them for any indication that they would be, if the occasion were right, unfaithful. He had become so good at it that he made it into an 'art', a profession, and except for a couple of inexplicable non-starters, it had worked beautifully, until Angela.

It was ironic that they were so much alike and yet so far apart on the goddamn social ladder she cared so much about, and yet she had allowed her high-society mask to slip at the penthouse by doing that very professional strip.

Drew blinked and rubbed his cheek: he hadn't shaved since leaving her and his skin was sandpapery with a beard two days old. He would get his own back. Not only would he make up with Jackie, he would also do some digging on Angela. There had been a few interesting things Jackie had mentioned about her mother which had puzzled Drew, and when he found some free time he promised himself that he would follow Angela Cassini right back to where she came from.

For the time being he would settle for Jackie. It might take a little persuasion, but she would come round. After all, he was very good at deceit; he had spent his whole adult life creating lies and myths about himself and his background. There was always someone, somewhere, waiting to believe him.

Rose leaned her head back and looked up at the pale-blue sky,

21

way above her clouds were being torn by a wind that remained unfelt on the ground. The sun was shining now, the rain having magically cleared, and it felt like summer rather than an autumn day. She shifted her gaze to her legs which were still clad in the leggings she had worn for her aerobics class; the muscles ached from the work-out she had given them and if she stood up she knew that her knees would feel like jelly. Jules had liked her legs. Had. Her mouth drooped just perceptibly and she began to bite her nails.

'One spritzer coming up . . .'

Rose smiled automatically at her flatmate, Babs, as she set their drinks down carefully on the pine table.

'It's lovely out here, I don't even feel cold,' she said, sitting down. 'I'd almost forgotten this pub had a garden.'

'Are you out tonight?' Rose asked, darting a glance at her over the rim of her glass.

'I've got an art class,' Babs picked up her drink, knowing what the next question would be.'

'So you won't be home?'

Babs shook her head. 'I thought you were working at the club?'

'I am, but I don't have to be on until eleven,' which would mean spending the evening at the flat on her own.

'Isn't that director guy coming to see your act?'

Rose nodded.

'Didn't you say it was something to do with a musical?'

'Marilyn Monroe's life put to music, apparently – they still haven't settled on the lead.'

'You mean Monroe?'

'Yes.'

'Rose – that's fantastic!'

'It'll be a waste of time,' she prodded her sports bag with a petulant foot. 'I always get nervous and screw up if I know there's an agent or whoever in the audience.'

'Oh, come on – ' Babs said with disbelief, ' – I've seen you in action, you're like a different person when you're on stage.' Amazing came close to the appropriate word.

'I still feel nervous as hell.'

'I thought all great artists are supposed to feel nervous?'

'I'm not a great artist.'

'You could be.'

'I don't know how to push myself . . .'

'But you *will* try?'

'I just wish I wasn't feeling so depressed.'

Babs stared at her, feeling irritated, but said nothing further.

'Are you sure there were no calls for me last night?' Rose asked, switching to the subject that mattered to her most.

'Quite sure,' Babs replied; Rose had already asked her more than once.

Rose sighed with something like despair and resumed the assault on her fingernails. Then, 'I don't understand why Jules hasn't rung; everything was fine.'

Babs made no answer.

'It's been well over a week, you'd think he would have contacted me by now,' Rose continued dolefully. 'I mean – we were getting on so well.' She glanced at the tips of her fingers and frowned, then forced her hands into her lap.

'The telephone bill arrived this morning,' Babs said abruptly.

'What?'

'The telephone bill.'

'I was talking about Jules.'

'I know, Rose,' Babs said. 'I was trying to change the subject.'

Rose looked hurt.

'Sorry . . . ' Babs said tiredly, 'but for the past ten days your whole conversation has been wrapped around Julian, or Jules, and it's driving me slowly insane.'

'He means a lot to me.'

'When you brought him in that night, all he could talk about was his band.'

'It's healthy to have a hobby.'

'If you say so.'

'Anyway, Jules is different,' Rose mused, 'and I know he really likes me. He told me he did,' she said, as if trying to convince herself. She had imagined seeing him every day, every night – living together, and weaving intricate dreams of her future life with him.

'You hardly know him, Rose.'

'You don't need to go out with someone a long time to know

them, it's something that happens naturally between the right people.'

'You said more or less the same thing about Frank.'

'Frank had problems.'

'He was a waste of time – you know he was.'

'He was a nice guy.'

'Standing you up three times is nice, borrowing money and not paying it back is nice?'

'It wasn't his fault.'

'He was *gross*, Rose,' Babs said impatiently, and then wished she could call the clumsy word back because Rose was sitting very still now and her eyes glistened ominously.

'I liked him,' her friend responded in a small voice.

Babs sighed and said softly, 'I know you did.' But Rose liked all her men, no matter how they treated her, and there had been many in the three years they had shared a flat.

Babs had known Rose since school, had helped her through her parents' divorce and watched her go from the arms of one boy straight into the arms of another as soon as she was able. The thought of being alone, or single, seemed to fill her with dread. She had played around with drugs, meditation and veganism and was presently into astrology in a big way. Rose was a mess emotionally, but she was sweet and kind and very generous, and Babs hated to see her hurt.

'What do I do wrong?' Rose said suddenly.

'Oh, Rose,' Babs closed her eyes for a moment.

'Say something,' she persisted, 'I know you want to. Go on.'

Babs looked at the paving stones beneath her feet. 'Maybe you're a little too nice, a little too eager to please.'

'What's wrong with that?'

'There shouldn't be anything wrong with that,' she shrugged, 'but there is.'

'What should I do?'

'I don't know, Rose.'

'I hate being on my own, that's all,' Rose said, 'everything seems sort of pointless and empty when there isn't a man in my life.'

'*Any* man?'

'I need to know there's someone there.'

24

'Even if he makes you miserable?'

'I'm miserable now.'

'What are we talking about then?'

'I just wish something would turn out right.'

'You mean some*one*.' Babs shook her head gently. 'Try and stop thinking about it, them, so much. Men are only people, Rose, not gods, and have you ever thought that if you put as much effort into your career as you do trying to please all these guys, you might actually be walking the boards of the West End by now?'

'Some hope.'

'With a voice like yours? Believe it,' Babs stood up, 'and you have a chance tonight, don't you?'

'I suppose so.'

'Well, then, give yourself a break and think about yourself for a change.'

Rose looked up at her and gave Babs a tentative smile. 'I could try.'

'Go for it, Rose, it's called positive thinking.' Babs looked into her friend's pale, pretty face, and felt that her words were probably wasted. 'Another drink?'

Rose nodded, then added quickly as her flatmate began to walk away, 'Babs?'

'Yes?'

'You don't really think I can, do you?'

'What?'

'Put myself first.'

Babs said nothing.

'You just watch me,' Rose said with a touch of defiance.

Babs wanted to believe her, she really did, but they had had similar conversations before and nothing changed. Rose did not seem to like, or respect, herself very much and spent her whole life doing everything in her power to avoid being alone – desperate to love and be loved in return. She had yet to realize that the only person she had to live with forever was herself.

TWO

Jackie leaned her head back and let it rest on the back of her father's old wing chair; he was finishing a letter in his study, but had promised that he would not keep her long. She smiled, because her father had never had any real sense of time passing and would probably not appear until she began to grow restless and blasted the house with some music to wake him up.

She took a sip of the gin and tonic she had made herself and thought of the show, *her* show. The dream, the musical of the life of Marilyn Monroe, had everything: pathos, glamour, success, failure, even politics and history if she brought the Kennedy angle in at the precise moments she wanted, particularly the famous Birthday Salute in honour of the President, at Madison Square Garden.

The scene couldn't fail, in fact, to be fabulous, even memorable, if it shaped up just as she planned – the finale of finales for a tormented, fading star who had had only three months to live . . .

Marilyn – a skilfully hand-picked 'Marilyn' would live, and walk and talk and sing again from the glory of a West End stage and then Broadway. The world had done a great deal to the legend of Monroe, but no one had successfully made her seesaw life of sensation and sadness into an unforgettable musical. Others had tried and failed, but for almost five years Jackie had nurtured the idea, finally breathing life and love into the long months of research which preceded the finding of a jewel like Aldo Morris to be her composer and musical director, and then hiring Gordon Mackey and Joe Newby, two young lyricists she had 'discovered' after seeing an off-beat musical play based on the life of Janis Joplin.

Ironically, it had been her mother who had unwittingly kindled her daughter's dreams when Angela had had a role in the chorus of a small-time production of *South Pacific*. That show had lit the spark, giving Jackie a love for the stage, the only gift from her mother which had ever been worth having. It began an enduring passion for the theatre, and musicals in particular, which had gripped her ever since. But *Marilyn* – *Marilyn* was special.

Even Drew had said as much. She closed her eyes, feeling a tightness in her throat. Even now. She had met him at one of her mother's glittering parties on *The Angela*, her precious private yacht. It had been one of those nights when the sea was like a sheet of black velvet and the sky incredibly low and thick and soft. Jackie took a deep breath, trying to push away the memory, but it only came back more strongly, seizing her in its gentle and unrelenting grasp. Dream-like that night. Heady. Potent. She had not meant to let him take her, not there, not so soon, it had just happened, but she had wanted it more than anything else. More than anything.

Jackie shuddered in self-contempt as she recalled how easy she had made it for him, how eagerly she had followed his suggestion of a swim. Just a swim in that warm, languid, silky water. They had been moored off Port Antonio, only a hundred or so yards from an outcrop of rocks beckoning to her like a curling, coaxing finger.

'Just a swim . . .' he had said.

She could remember looking down for a long moment and then reaching wordlessly for the clasp of her dress, feeling the fragile crêpe fall with a soft sigh. The water had slid exquisitely up her thighs like caressing fingers and she had gasped with mild shock, laughing as it engulfed her, and she had struck out for the rocks. Drew followed at a leisurely pace and she had watched him, one hand tightening its hold on the black wet rock as he had drawn closer and closer and she was suddenly uneasy.

He came for her from below, sliding upwards out of the water to overwhelm her and then driving into her so quickly that she screamed until his mouth silenced the scream, but not her useless struggles against the power inside and the weight of him, and against herself most of all – because she had wanted it: the expectation, the sudden possession – her head jerking back, her body squirming against him to prolong that searing, impossible pleasure which was never long enough. Hadn't she? But for that treacherous inner response, it would have been rape; but Drew

27

had been gentle later, even tender, as if he had guessed her thoughts.

Their affair had lasted the whole of the summer in Cape Cod, all through the time she was working on the draft for the production, and she supposed that she must have been in love with him. And he had made the loving easy with his clever, faultless attention to her – and the gifts, the boat-trips, the promises, and that way he had of pulling her back into bed because 'he couldn't get enough of her . . .'

'Hello?'

She swung round, startled.

'You must be Jackie.' He would have known her anywhere because she was so like David.

'Yes . . . ' she said, 'and you're –?'

'Jamie.'

'Of course, I'm sorry. I was miles away.'

He smiled and gripped her outstretched hand, looking back at her with frank interest.

'I think you're early.' He was still gripping her hand.

'Yes, I know.'

'You're quite lovely,' he said, 'but you must know that.'

Heat flooded her face. 'Are you always so . . .'

'Blunt?'

'Actually, that wasn't the word I was going to use,' she said, retrieving her hand.

'Blunt or otherwise, I don't seem to know how to be anything else,' he said. 'My father never taught me how to be subtle.'

She thought that there was still the air of an eager, innocent boy about him. How old was he? Her father had mentioned it when he told her of the impending visit of her stepmother's godson. Twenty-four, she was certain. He looked both older and younger at the same time.

'I have to go,' he said. 'Clare's waiting for me.' He lifted his arm slightly indicating the piece of scarlet folded over it. I only came back for her shawl.'

'You're going for a walk on the Heath?'

He nodded.

'Well, I'll see you later then.'

'I very much hope so.'

'Say hello to Clare for me.'

He was already at the door, but he turned back. 'Of course.'

Jackie watched him from the window. He ran the length of the drive effortlessly and with the elegance of an athlete; there was no doubt about it, Jamie was beautiful to watch. She wondered if he knew.

Twenty-four, six years younger than she was, yet the age gap seemed so much more than that; just lately she was beginning to feel like everyone's mother.

Jackie sought out her gin and tonic as her thoughts returned reluctantly to Drew and his 'other woman', torturing herself. She still wondered how she could have been so stupid, how she had not even sensed the tension or smelt the other woman's sex clinging to him like a second skin. Eventually he had made one really big mistake because the other woman had managed to get hold of her telephone number and, unbelievably, she had called and told Jackie everything in sweet, sordid detail; there had even been a little weeping at the end, a little whining and coarse emotional blackmail. Jackie had put the telephone down and then she had started to pack.

She sat for a moment, wrapped in silence. At least Drew had not been a fortune hunter; he was apparently connected to the Caroccis, a powerful and wealthy Italian-American family, and had a private income of his own. He had even talked of taking her to his family home near Capri, on 'the island', for a *real* vacation. She had believed him, there was no reason not to and besides, her mother never had anyone at her parties who wasn't 'someone' and someone who had been checked and double checked. Despite that, Angela had warned her against him, but she had stopped listening to her mother a long time ago, almost fifteen years to the day, in fact.

Tony Cassini, her mother's third husband, had been the final breaking point. It had been her fifteenth birthday and he had hugged her a little too hard, kissed her a little too long, so long that his lips had skilfully moved from her soft cheek to the trembling mouth which was partially open, to the dry, fear-filled throat. Her mother had come then, as if she had known, and Jackie had actually been thankful to see her standing rigid in the doorway, her face turned a murderous, livid red, but then she had taken a step towards her daughter and slapped her: a swift, savage blow which had knocked her sideways and left a mark for days afterwards. She had been in England by then, with her father.

She could still hear the sound of that slap, like the crack of a whip, a severing of something, and the final deadness in the room as they stared at one another.

The memories were stark and ugly and she wished she could forget them, put them away somewhere and simply forget. She stood up and walked over to her father's baby grand and the collection of old theatre programmes scattered haphazardly over the shining, polished lid; his face was on the front cover of most of them, spanning the years of his acting career. Nothing changed here and it seemed to her that it never had and perhaps that was the beauty of it.

'What about the independent producers like Lloyd Webber and Cameron Mackintosh?' David asked. 'I suppose you've tried them?'

Jackie nodded as she looked back at the tall, greying figure of her father and smiled wearily.

'And there's Robert Fox, don't forget – and Thelma Holt might be able to help.'

'They've all been very sweet and polite, but basically none of them are interested, they don't think *Marilyn* can work,' she replied flatly. 'It's been tried before and flopped badly. Besides they're all tied up in other projects.'

'I expect they're simply being cautious and you can hardly blame them for that. After all, ten musicals closed prematurely last year, losing their backers several million pounds.'

'I know,' she said, 'but others like *Miss Saigon* and *Phantom* continue to reap fortunes.'

'Is that what we have here – one of those rare, magical shows touched with gold?' David asked with a dry smile.

'Oh, I know what you're thinking – yes, it's a big gamble and much more of a gamble than a straight play, but there's a great story here and one that everyone can identify with. It has all the vital ingredients for a hit. In my opinion *Marilyn* is commercially almost a sure thing.'

David smiled wryly. 'A lot of people think that about their pet productions.'

'Daddy, I've been working towards this for over five years.'

'I know, Jackie.'

He looked into her face which was flushed with determination and he was reminded of himself, suddenly, a long time ago.

'Have you tried the Arts Council?'

She responded with barely concealed impatience, 'You must be joking. Any money they are willing to part with is hardly likely to be given to a producer they have never heard of and for a show – and a musical don't forget – that no one else is willing to touch.' She frowned. 'And it's not a star show either, so I don't have any big names to offer as bait.'

'When do you open?'

'February or March of next year.'

He raised his eyebrows. 'And you need to raise something in the region of two and a half million pounds?'

She nodded. 'Perhaps slightly less if we're lucky.'

A breath caught audibly in David's throat.

'But you've managed to find over two-thirds of that amount, including the money you've already put in yourself?'

'Aldo Morris, the composer and musical director, has contributed one hundred thousand and his brother fifty thousand. We've got ten and fifteen thousand from Gordon Mackey and Joe Newby respectively, the lyricists, and a further seventy-five thousand from Max Lockhart, the director. Two Australian entrepreneurs have promised another three hundred and fifty thousand and a Japanese backer, who has a permanent love affair with the Monroe legend, a further three hundred and fifty thousand. I've also persuaded Baroness Grayshott, who backed my *Holy Grail* to contribute another fifty thousand.' Jackie drew a breath. 'There are a few other, smaller, backers, but basically, yes, that leaves us with less than one-third to find, approximately three-quarters of a million pounds. I've already put down a deposit on the Adelphi of seventy thousand pounds which is in addition to production costs. But I'm wiped out now, the core of my capital used up or accounted for.'

'I could probably give you something in the region of one hundred thousand,' he said, 'your stepmother considerably

31

more.' He paused, examining her rather sharply, 'You won't accept the opinion of the top producers?'

She shook her head. 'I think I'm still considered too young to attempt such a large project, particularly as the subject matter itself has never worked in the past.' Jackie sighed and then continued, 'But that doesn't surprise me in the least because I don't believe it has ever been treated seriously – some people seem to have thought that the Monroe legend alone could sell a musical. For instance, the 1983 production of *Marilyn* was notable for its amazing lack of depth. Sheridan Morley remarked that it was "cobbled together from the pages of old movie magazines".'

David frowned quizzically and she returned his gaze, begging him silently not to turn away from her now and cursing her mother for putting her in such a position. When had Angela ever cared about wasting money or, in particular, what her daughter was doing with her life, let alone her money? If she had known what her mother intended, she would have made the last in-put from the trust-fund last longer – somehow.

'But, more important,' she continued quickly, 'I don't think anyone has ever succeeded in finding the right person to play Monroe. It might seem relatively easy – a sexy blonde who can sing is the crudest bottom line, but you know and I know there was rather more to her than that.' She shook her head. 'In any event, I am starting from scratch, from birth and her traumatic childhood and the person who was Norma Jean. We open with a scene which features her mother and her inability to cope with herself, let alone her child – an inability which dooms Norma Jean's future life to the care of foster parents . . .'

David watched her face with fascination, caught by her enthusiasm as he always was.

'Our stage designer, Brian Wells, suggested a revolving stage to symbolize the passing of time and the people the young Marilyn's childhood passes through. It works brilliantly.' She gave him a searching look and then plunged on. 'We are attempting to create a musical play of her whole life: warts, manic disorders and all, not just the film star and the piece of public property the world has come to know.' Jackie swallowed slowly. 'We have a fine score, too: Aldo has composed some outstanding and exciting numbers and the lyrics are superb.' Jackie reached for her briefcase. 'I've brought you a tape of the songs and a detailed scene-by-scene breakdown of the proposed dramatic structure. I also want to add another dimension to the production, something I haven't really sorted out in my head yet, but the more I think about it the more I like it.'

'What do you mean?'

'A narrator.'

'Are you sure that will work?'

'Not totally, but there are some aspects of Monroe's life that need expansion and emphasis and if that could be supplied through some sharp and sensitive phrases from a narrator – only at appropriate intervals – I think it could add an interesting edge to the production, particularly if this narrator were to provide both a certain style and a striking contrast to the dazzling Monroe image.'

'What sort of contrast?'

'I do have a rather unusual idea, but for the time being I'd rather not say until I've had a chance to talk it through with Max and Aldo.'

'But the person to play Marilyn – you've found her?'

'I thought I had, but Max called me last night to say that he'd seen the right girl, the only girl to play her . . .'

'Who is she?'

'A singer/impressionist at Madam Jo Jo's.' She sighed. 'She was part of the cabaret.'

'You haven't seen her yet?'

'No.'

'Do you really think there can be two girls in London who have the talent and the voice to become Marilyn Monroe eight times a week – isn't that stretching credibility just a little too far?'

'Don't, Daddy.'

'Jackie,' David said and his voice was low and insistent, 'notwithstanding the time, money and effort you have put into this project yourself – you need *me* to invest a very considerable sum of money in your musical and Clare substantially more – yet you still haven't found the right person to star in it.'

He walked across to the window and the view she knew so well, overlooking Hampstead Heath, and her mind was flooded by echoes from her childhood. The first real conversation she had ever had with her father had taken place in this room and she had been shy, awed and tongue-tied until he had crouched down from a great height to stare directly into her nine-year-old eyes. And she had looked back into the handsome face and the startling blue 'Paul Newman' eyes with something like adoration. Father and daughter, two strangers, meeting for the first time.

'This is a very, very special part . . . ' David was continuing carefully, 'it's the life of a real person, someone we all, in a sense, knew and someone who had many sides, many contradictions, if you like. I suppose you realize that you have given yourself a harder task finding such a person than if you were, for instance, casting for *Miss Saigon*. Even so, I understand that Cameron Mackintosh and his team scoured a good part of the world to find, shall we say, an imaginary person to play the lead. And now you tell me that you've found *two* girls to play Marilyn Monroe – and in London?'

'Lucy Wilding attended the first auditions in New York, she was attending a workshop there . . .'

'And now we have a second "Marilyn" magically turning up at Madam Jo Jo's.'

'Daddy – we auditioned in practically every English-speaking country . . . ,' she said with exasperation.

'I'm sorry, Jackie, but I have the right to ask, don't I?'

'Yes, of course.'

'Are you sure you're not being too hasty in your choice – are you really convinced that this Lucy Wilding is capable of being Marilyn Monroe?'

'Yes.' And she was; from merely a promising performance at the first audition in New York, Lucy had grown in stature amazingly by the second and had even taken on some of the vulnerability of Monroe. Max and Aldo had both agreed: with time, the right direction and some work on the appropriate accent, she could be perfect. It had only been Max's unexpected call that had unsettled her and the fierce conviction in his voice that had prevented her from calling Lucy that morning and telling her she had got the part. He had insisted she wait.

'All right, then.'

She stared back at him. 'You mean it?'

He smiled wryly. 'Did you think I'd forgotten your three previous ventures? Two of which were very successful, although much smaller. I know they didn't make the West End, but *The Holy Grail* in particular got excellent reviews, and it has to be said that you managed very well and with a great deal of professionalism. Neither have I forgotten those weird and wonderful touring productions you mounted year after year.' He grinned. 'I adored that Edinburgh fringe thing you did – *Wuthering Heights* with a truly frenzied Heathcliff and frantic Cathy; you even managed to get away with the nude scene.'

'Well, I wasn't tied by the stifling rules and regulations of Victorian society as Emily Brontë was. It's a story of powerful passions – and they must have made love.'

'Yes, I'm sure you're right . . . ' he said, trying to sound more serious than he felt, 'and I'm sure Emily applauded from the grave . . .'

Jackie smiled a little sheepishly.

'Anyway, getting back to the present – I've always rather fancied myself as an angel.' He paused. 'A musical based on the life of Marilyn Monroe can only be extremely appealing and undoubtedly very popular with the masses. Perhaps I'll make a killing on my investment, like all those lucky beggers who backed *Cats* . . . but above all *you* are very convincing, my dear, and obviously totally committed to this project, almost passionate like our friend Heathcliff, or perhaps "formidable" would be a better word.' He smiled again. 'Not unlike your mother.'

'Oh God, Daddy . . .'

'You may look like me,' he continued, 'but sometimes there is a look of Angela about you.' And then he added to soften the blow, 'At least you can be grateful that you haven't inherited her utter selfishness and an ego the size of Texas.'

Jackie raised her eyebrows a little, unaccustomed to such revelations from her father.

'I take your point, but I'd rather not think about mother at the moment; she's deliberately made things difficult for me and I don't have the faintest idea why – she's never given a damn how I spent my money before. It staggers me sometimes how ruthless she can be.'

'Your mother, my dear, is one of Nature's wonders, you

should know that by now.' There was a small smile on his lips. 'She met her once, you know.'

'Who?'

'Marilyn Monroe.'

'How?'

'Oh, God knows – at some beauty parlour in LA if I remember correctly. The whole place closed for the afternoon to cater for Monroe when she turned up unexpectedly. Angela missed out on a 'vital' facial which she claimed cost her an audition. She blamed Monroe, of course, despite the fact that she would have been totally unsuitable for the part, and made the whole story larger than life. She never forgot, never.'

'I can believe that quite easily,' Jackie said, 'and because of her I now have to come crawling to you to raise some money.'

'That's what fathers are for.'

'I didn't want to do it this way and I know you haven't that much capital of your own.'

'I shall never have any money as long as I have a hole up my ass, my darling Jackie . . .' he said and then snapped good-humouredly, 'of course you must have the damned money.'

She crossed the room to kiss him tenderly on the cheek. 'I have sometimes wondered what I would do without you.'

He shook his head. 'No, it is *I* who have often wondered that.' He brushed her nose lightly with his lips. 'When I left your mother and came back to England to those dark, boozy years of professional oblivion, it was only the knowledge that I had you that finally pulled me together.'

It seemed incredible to him now that he had not known of Jacqueline's existence for so long, but once he left the memory of the Hollywood studio sharks and the pathetic line of contract hopefuls behind him, he never wanted to return, and he and Angela had not parted on the best of terms by any stretch of the imagination. He cringed inwardly at the image of his ex-wife doing the rounds of the 'sho-bars' and strip joints. And with Jackie – a child – that was the worst, the most obscene part.

David closed his eyes for a moment. Taking her clothes off had never meant very much to Angela: it had been her habit to stroll naked around their shabby apartment. In the end the nakedness had become insignificant, even embarrassing. They had hated each other finally – fighting and screaming abuse in the stifling confines of those small grey rooms so that the neighbours had thumped on the walls and banged on the ceiling.

They had both made a terrible mistake by marrying. Passion and infatuation had swept common sense aside, but burnt themselves out so quickly once the novelty of living together day after day had worn off. She had hated and despised him for not wanting to stay in Hollywood, accusing him of being too stupid and too stubborn to see that the well-worn pavements of tinsel town had been paved with gold. But the booze was getting to him by then, lots of it; Angela had preferred Dexamyl, a pretty little pill which gave her the perfect high.

One day he simply walked out, leaving her behind, because she had refused too often to come with him and he wasn't able to stand it any longer. The only communication he received from her after that was the divorce papers.

'And then you met Clare.'

'And then I met Clare,' he smiled gently. 'Shortly after our meeting, I landed the first decent role I'd had in over four years. Everything seemed to turn around all at once.' David coloured slightly as if he had said too much. 'Would you like another g and t?'

She nodded and watched him as he walked to the various bottles sitting on a vast silver tray in the corner of the room. He was much taller than his daughter and yet she was considered 'statuesque' for a woman and like him, blonde and blue-eyed. His face was lean and still handsome despite the ravages of drink and the fact that he was now in his sixties. His hair was peppered with streaks of gold amongst the grey, but he was much too thin and although he had decreased his alcohol intake over the years he still drank substantially and his appetite was erratic to say the least. David just didn't give a damn about it and Jackie knew that nothing she could say would change him.

'How is Clare?' Lovely, Bohemian Clare who made the most sensational pieces of ceramic art: sensuous bronzed torsos which claimed a place in the art galleries of the world. Even Angela had a 'Clare Arnold' piece, just to prove that she bore no grudge against either her famous husband, or his famous wife. And people actually believed her.

'Oh, fine,' he said, 'should be in any moment with Jamie.'

'I had a brief encounter with him, actually.'

'Really?'

'Came back for Clare's shawl.'

'What do you think?'

'Took my breath away rather.'

'Yes,' David smiled. 'He seems to have that effect on people.'

'It must all seem rather strange for him here after spending most of his life in Kenya.'

'*All* of his life in Kenya.'

Her eyes widened. 'How is he getting over the death of his father?'

'I don't think there was a lot of love lost, but it's hard to tell.'

'No other relatives?'

'Not really – not close, anyway. Apparently there was no one Clare knew from the family at the funeral and no whites from the surrounding areas as they avoided his father, thought him some kind of eccentric. Mind you, they lived in the middle of bloody nowhere. Quite a few local people turned out.'

'What was he doing there?'

'He left England years ago with his wife, couldn't stand what he called "the greed and blindness of the so-called civilized world" and set up in the wilds of Kenya as a cross between a missionary and an early version of a conservationist.' David waved disparagingly. 'Sounds crazy as a coot.' He crossed the room and poured himself another drink. 'His wife died shortly after Jamie was born of some kind of infection; they lived so far into the bush that by the time a doctor arrived she was already dead – and buried.' David took a gulp of his Scotch. 'A body rots so damn quickly out there.'

Jackie grimaced. 'I suppose he must have been terribly lonely all those years.'

'Perhaps,' David drew an impatient breath, 'but, after all, he chose to live that way; he could have returned home or moved nearer to a city, even for his child's sake, and yet he refused. When James was only thirteen he decided to send him to a Jesuit school with a view to a seminary afterwards.'

'You obviously don't approve.'

'Well, would you?' he said. 'It's inhuman. Good God, Jamie

wasn't much more than a child.' David moved back to the window. 'But he kept running away . . .' he lifted his glass into the air, 'and good for him.'

'What did his father do?'

'Beat him.'

'Poor Jamie.'

'He said it didn't hurt.'

'What?'

'His father had arthritis in his hands – no strength,' he said.

'Lucky for Jamie.'

'And then he grew too big for beatings, but he was twenty before his father finally gave up on the idea and Jamie was allowed to return home. Battered but unbowed you might say.'

'And then?'

'There was a sort of truce apparently. The old man gave him some land to develop, but Jamie was far more interested in the local wildlife than following his father's wishes, and that didn't go down too well, as you might imagine.'

'Then his father died?'

David nodded.

'What does he intend to do now?'

'Clare wants him to go to university, but he says he's not sure.'

'It will be difficult for him to make a fresh start: an ex-student priest, no real qualifications, no work experience, not even any experience of living in a city.'

David looked back at her warily as a thought struck him. 'Perhaps you could help?'

'Me?'

'I'm sure Clare would more than show her appreciation if you gave him a job – in this new musical.' He saw a shadow cross her face.

'He can't know anything about the theatre, or musicals.'

'True, but he's very intelligent and willing to try anything within reason.'

'He might not like the idea.'

'I'm sure he won't refuse a stab at it; he doesn't seem to have any plans of his own.'

'If I agree.'

'Come on, Jackie . . .' he said, 'Clare would be thrilled and

39

I'm sure would return the favour by becoming one of your most generous backers. Remember that she is very wealthy in her own right, apart from her income as an artist.'

'I know, Daddy.' Clare was the niece of the seventh Earl of Cattistock, one of Britain's largest landowners, and his only living relative.

'You would be doing her – and me, come to that – an enormous favour.'

'I don't think I have much choice.'

'Don't put it like that.'

Jackie closed her eyes for a moment. 'Okay – that wasn't fair and I suppose it's not so much to ask after all you've done for me.'

'Just think of Jamie and what you would be doing for him.'

She sighed, not wanting the responsibility of a young man who probably had enough problems of his own.

'I could only offer him a production assistant's role, and a trainee at that.'

'A sort of glorified tea-boy?'

'Not at all, Daddy – he'll have to work bloody hard for his twelve thousand a year, which is all I can afford at the moment.'

'Of course, of course,' he said, with a trace of sarcasm.

'Anyway, making tea is very important.' She started to smile.

'For God's sake don't mention anything about making tea when they get here. I can just see them turning into the drive.'

Jackie stood up and joined David at the window.

'He is the least likely candidate for the priesthood I have ever seen,' David said with laughter in his voice, ' – reminds me of that chap I saw in a bloody awful film – *Tarzan in New York* – or something equally ludicrous.'

Jackie followed his gaze and saw the slight, familiar figure of her stepmother walking towards them and beside her big, blonde Jamie who had his arm draped casually across his godmother's shoulders.

When they reached the bottom of the stone steps leading into the house he looked up as if he had sensed their eyes on him and his mouth moved into a smile of astonishing warmth. Jackie could only wonder at the number of hearts this man, this almost-priest, would have quite innocently broken if he had pursued his dead father's dream.

She was wearing black leather, her dark hair was spiked into dangerous points and she was being Tracey Ullman. Somehow she disappeared behind a screen on the small makeshift stage and came out looking like Joan Rivers. Then she was Cher, then she was Madonna. Finally Rose Lyle was Marilyn Monroe.

'I told you,' Max whispered.

Jackie made no answer as the girl began to sing 'Diamonds are a Girl's Best Friend' – and she waited one minute, two minutes, but then she knew he was right. Absolutely right. Lucy Wilding had just missed. Even amongst the ridiculously cramped conditions and the smoke and the coughs and the laughter there was no contest. Rose finished her act with the famous Monroe pose from *The Seven Year Itch*, the one with her legs slightly splayed, a white skirt billowing above her thighs as she stands over a wind blower on a subway grating. As a clever finale she blew the mostly male audience a kiss – pouting and delightful – and the applause boomed.

Jackie wrapped her fingers around the long-stemmed glass which held an almost untouched champagne cocktail and looked into Max's small, white face; it was glowing with triumph.

'Is she interested?'

'Oh, yes.' Then he laughed. 'That was for you . . .' he gestured towards the stage. 'I told her you'd be here.'

'I'd like to give her an interview, see if she can make ten tomorrow morning – and I'll see her with Aldo.'

'Naturally.'

But it was only a formality. Jackie stood up in readiness to leave.

'Thanks, Max.'

He touched her arm.

'We both know the Wilding girl has great potential – but this girl has a sort of luminosity . . .' he struggled to find the right words, '. . . different . . . you understand what I'm trying to say?'

'I understand.' But what she didn't understand was herself and why she had almost been prepared to argue with him about Lucy.

41

'We can give Wilding the understudy . . .' He smiled and shrugged as if he were saying 'that's life', and 'you, of all people, should know that's what this business is about'.

She sighed inwardly, suddenly feeling tremendously tired, and he was right, there was little doubt in her mind. Then why did the decision disturb her? Perhaps she had instinctively liked Lucy and had sensed what this role had meant to her; maybe it was as simple as that. Nevertheless her second audition had been excellent – and so close, so damned close.

Jackie wove her way through the tables to the back of the crowded room and out into the narrow, neon-lit streets of Soho. It was late now and all she wanted to do was get back to the hotel and sleep. She would tell Lucy tomorrow morning, after the interview with Rose Lyle. But she would hate the telling.

A soft amber lamp glowed in the corner of her suite and, with a sigh of relief, Jackie slipped off her shoes and padded over to the window. It had been quite a day one way or another beginning with a call from Max first thing, worried about the potential length of one of the scenes because he felt that one song was far too long. He had implied, and not with much subtlety, that Gordon and Joe, the lyricists, were not concerned enough about it to do anything concrete – like make some changes. His voice had risen ominously, but she had managed to calm him down, finally. Once rehearsals got under way they could trim the lyrics and probably without harming the message to the audience.

Max Lockhart was renowned as a very good director, but finicky and uncompromising at times. There was talk of a *prima donna* streak, and he had a reputation as a womanizer, which surprised her because he certainly wasn't the world's most attractive man. Jackie shrugged it off: that was his business. At least so far their association had worked well, but she knew there would be moments when her patience would be stretched to the limit. Yet they did share the same view with regard to casting and tomorrow morning Rose Lyle would audition officially, and with Aldo's presence as musical director to add weight to the final decision. If the girl performed as well during the interview as she had that evening, she knew they would all be in total agreement about offering her the role.

Jackie pushed a stray strand of hair back from her face and sat down, leaning against the soft cushions of the chair and feeling hot and slightly irritable. Her talk with her father had solved one problem and created another. Perhaps she could persuade Jamie Thurley to try acting and a good theatre school: he certainly had the looks and the presence to draw the right sort of attention to himself. Or modelling. But even as the thought took shape in her mind she could not see the blonde, beautiful boy willingly giving a hollow, fixed smile to a camera lens. That would not be his style at all. She had a mental picture of him in priest's robes and found herself smiling. That was not his style either.

The telephone rang and she frowned, wondering who could be calling her at this time of night.

'Miss Jones, there's a Drew Carocci to see you in reception.'

Jackie froze for a moment.

'Miss Jones?'

'Let me speak to him, please.' She glanced at her watch.

'Jackie?'

'What are you doing here?'

'I need to see you.'

'I think we've seen just about enough of each other, don't you?'

'You didn't give me a chance to explain.'

'Look Drew, I'm tired and it's one-thirty in the morning, why don't you write me a letter.'

'I didn't fly half-way across the world to write you a goddamn letter and I'm not leaving this hotel until I see you.'

She paused and stared around the room: she felt a reluctant eagerness despite all her fine words.

'All right, but don't get any funny ideas.'

'Look, I'm trying to book myself a room – okay?'

She raised her eyebrows a little. 'As long as I've made myself clear.'

'You've done that all right, Jackie.'

She deliberately fell silent, making him wait. 'Like I said, I'm very tired.'

'I won't keep you long.'

'Okay,' she said, 'I'm in the Bennett suite.'

As soon as she had put down the telephone she moved quickly

into the bathroom, determined that he would not see her looking hot and tired, yet hating herself for caring at all.

As she emerged there was a light tap at the door and she took a deep breath before opening it. And there he was, just the same, just as devastatingly good-looking.

'You're not going to keep me waiting out here in the cold, are you?' he said softly, and there was that smile, that certain way he had of tilting his mouth.

Drew.

She swallowed slowly, feeling slightly foolish, and let him pass into the room.

Once inside he stood quite still for a moment and looked at her carefully. 'You look great.'

'Do I?' she said dryly.

He sighed. 'Come on, Jackie.'

She shook her head. 'I don't need you to flatter me.'

'I wasn't.'

'Let's forget it.'

'It wasn't what you think.'

She looked away from him as anger and self-contempt began to surge back.

'Jackie . . .'

'Do you want a drink?'

'A Scotch.'

'Of course.' It was etched into her brain.

'You don't want to listen to what I have to say, do you?'

'You're here, aren't you – I let you into my room, didn't I?'

He watched her as she crossed the suite to the drinks cabinet, let his eyes scan the sumptuous room while the Scotch was poured. 'Does that mean you'll actually listen?'

She swung round and looked back at him.

'How's your other lady friend?'

He shook his head vigorously. 'What do I have to say to convince you that it's over – I mean – what do I have to do, crawl?'

'I don't like deceit, Drew,' she said quietly.

'It wasn't meant to be like that.'

'But that's what it was.'

He shrugged and looked down at his hands. 'Okay.'

'So what do you want?'

'A second chance.'

She sat down. 'What guarantee do I have that you won't do what you did again?'

'If I gave you one, you probably wouldn't believe me.'

'Right first time.'

He raised his eyes to heaven and put his glass down. 'Shall I go?'

'You'd better see if they have a room free first.'

Drew reached for the telephone with barely concealed anger and slowly put it down again once the reservation desk told him there were no rooms free, only lavish suites which were currently way out of his league.

'Nothing?' Jackie asked.

He shook his head. 'I'll try elsewhere.'

She examined his face sharply as he moved to pick up the telephone again. 'I could have the sofa-bed made up for you.'

'Are you serious?'

'As one friend to another, you understand.'

'You don't give up, do you?'

Her mouth tilted upwards just perceptibly, but she ignored his remark. 'It's very comfortable, so I've been told.'

He flashed a glance at her. 'Don't play games with me, Jackie.'

'Why would I want to do that when you're so good at them yourself?'

He matched her stare. 'You really want to make me pay, don't you?' At that moment she seemed more like Angela than he had ever noticed before, and how simple life would be if she were.

He wondered how Jackie would react if she knew that 'the other woman' had been her own mother? And there was nothing he could do about wanting Angela.

'You lied to me,' she said. 'I hate lies.'

'And I said I was sorry.'

Her thoughts tumbled backwards and she tried to go over all those moments in her mind when she had doubted him, when he had hurt her. She flicked a glance at him and then picked up the telephone and arranged for someone to make up the bed.

It was 2.30 by the time everything was ready and Drew's luggage had been brought up. She stood in the doorway studying him for a moment as he removed his jacket and hung it very carefully over a chair, took a black Gucci toilet bag from his case and placed it on the same chair. So neat, almost sweet, but she switched her attention safely back to herself and the hot shower she intended to take before bed.

When she returned the room was in darkness except for one lamp and she could just see him sitting silently on the side of his bed.

'Bathroom's free.'

He looked up. 'Thanks.'

'Goodnight.'

His eyes darted hopefully to her face, but Jackie's expression was veiled and he was left with a deepening sense of disappointment. He echoed her 'Goodnight' in a lacklustre way as she moved past him and out of his reach.

Jackie paused and stood still as he went into the bathroom and waited for the door to close behind him before switching off the light, slipping out of her robe and climbing between the cool, silky sheets. She heard the shower burst into life and imagined him stepping under the myriad jets of water, but he was quick, barely a few minutes before there was quiet again and then the sound of the door opening to tell her he had finished.

Drew turned out the light automatically and moved into the darkened, unfamiliar room, almost stumbling against the foot of the bed. She heard him swear and wanted to laugh out loud, but then he was turning back the covers and sliding into bed and his foot was touching hers.

'Jackie . . . for chrissakes!'

'Did I startle you?'

'Yeah,' he said slowly, 'you could say that.' But before she could reply his hand was gliding up, up her body.

'Before you get completely carried away,' she said with a gasp, 'I want you to know that this is your last chance, Drew – your very last chance.'

'Okay, okay . . .'

'I mean it.'

'I know you do.'

She closed her eyes tight with pleasure as his hand found her again.

'There's something more, something you won't like . . .' but she was weakening and her caution almost gone.

'Tell me, hon,' he said huskily, 'just tell me.'

She took a deep breath. 'I want you to wear a condom.'

He stopped what he was doing. 'A what?'

'A condom, a sheath, a Durex – whatever you want to call it.'

'Jackie,' he groaned.

'I've left one out for you on the table beside the bed.'

'You had all this planned, didn't you?'

'No, actually I didn't,' her voice began to grow cold, 'but under the circumstances I think it's wise, don't you?'

He lay back on the bed in exasperation.

'Perhaps I should just go if you find it so difficult to understand,' she said.

His arm shot out across her. 'No.'

He rolled on to his side and looked at her. 'You're right, I know you're right. I just hate those things.'

'Those things, as you call it, wouldn't be necessary if . . .'

'Okay,' he broke in, 'okay.'

Her eyes were getting used to the darkness, and she could see his face more clearly and the sullen frown which did nothing to dampen her desire; if anything, it was heightened because she would have him on her own terms now.

His hand was resting on her stomach and he began to move it gently in small, gradually widening circles until his fingers grazed her breasts, her thighs, the sensitive core between her legs. She cried out and he quieted her with his lips, relieved that the talking was past and the tension over. He closed his eyes as he worked upon her body and each time she made any sound his hot open mouth would close over hers.

Time slowed as her voice faded from his mind and a vision of Angela took shape, the strip in the penthouse, when she had been drunk and hot and horny and loving. He ached towards the memory and the warm pillowy softness of her breasts – the holding, the rocking, the caressing, and the blinding ecstasy. Even the memory was almost enough to drive him out of his mind.

The world seemed to swirl and he took a deep gulp of air, fighting to control his breath because it seemed to him that it was

Angela who moved beneath him, not Jackie – Angela whose voice cried out to him, not Jackie.

Drew made a soft, despairing sound, rough like a sob and began to rake her face, her eyes, her lips with kisses in a fury of desire and possession.

THREE

Jamie lay down on the bed and closed his eyes in the darkness. His hand slid slowly to his neck and fingered a long strand of hair which, until a few month ago, had always been kept short. He continued letting his fingers run down and then across until he found the bulge of his Adam's apple; keeping his forefinger on the fleshy nodule he swallowed and let it bob and fall and then trailed his hand onwards to the skin of his chest and to the sensitive nipples which waited. The darkness and silence seemed thick and heavy so that he could imagine he was back in Kenya in the small room that had been called his own in the seminary: the aloneness was the same, the nightly touching ritual was the same, and the ultimate betrayal of himself if he let his fingers reach for the once forbidden area below his naval.

Blood rushed into his face as he heard his godmother's voice on the stairs wishing him goodnight and then his own voice, like someone else's, coming out of the darkness to answer her. In an instant his hands had withdrawn and were lying at his side. Thou shalt not touch. He thought of David's daughter and that cool, white skin which would be whiter underneath. Jackie had laughed at him and there had been something intoxicating in that laughter and the way the silky blonde hair had fallen across her face and been swept back again by one swift, practised brush of her hand. She had leaned a little towards him and for a fleeting second his eyes had settled on the opening of her blouse and the creamy swell of her breasts. He had hardened just by looking at her.

Jamie winced and swallowed slowly as an image of his father formed inevitably in his mind. Sex *was* sin as far as his father had been concerned – 'the grand old man', 'the White Man', 'the m'zee' or wise man – as if he had been a bearded patriarch from the pages of the Old Testament. But his father had been tyrannical, a religious zealot, even omnipotent in that little place he had made his kingdom. Once a precocious Samburu girl, painted red and wearing only a calf-skin apron, had reached up to touch Jamie's cheek with a wide inviting smile, and he had suddenly found himself paralysed by confusion and the beginnings of desire as her young, underdeveloped breasts grazed his skin and soft brown fingers came to rest on his arm, until his father's voice had roared in protest across the small dry compound and the girl had run in terror.

Jamie had obeyed him in everything because he had not known how to do otherwise until he was sent when he was thirteen, to the Jesuit school near Nairobi which had prepared him for the seminary. There, the invisible shutters which has been covering his eyes and his soul all his life had fluttered open just a fraction and gone on opening. After two years he had run away for the first time. It had not taken him long to realize that the rigid, unnatural life of a priest was not meant for him despite his father's dreams and hopes. He had never felt or known God, and any belief had been corroded with the passing of time, but when he told his father he had ranted and raved and beat him: that stooped and stubborn old man beating his enormous son.

The bleak, lonely lodge on the foothills of Mount Marsabit was closed up and silent now. His parents had built the lodge themselves; hauling stones from a riverbed, hoarding water in the dry season, the roof buckling in the rains, and he had lived there almost all his life, loving and hating it, bound to the mud and stones and the wood as he had been to his father.

Now his father was dead. Jamie squeezed his eyes tight shut on his terrible, secret joy; his father had been a burden, a pointing, unforgiving finger, and now the burden had gone and he was safe. There was a thickness in his throat as an unexpected wave of grief and homesickness choked him, and disbelief because he could not imagine that his father was no longer there, somewhere: brown grizzled skin in huge baggy shorts and floppy hat, feet encased in big brutal sandals.

Jamie turned his face to the wall, curling his legs up beneath him as his eyes began to prick and burn, hating himself.

'The understudy.'

Lucy looked back at Richard and said nothing.

'I thought you said the audition had gone really well . . . ?'

She still didn't reply, but her vision blurred as hot, hateful tears filled her eyes.

Richard watched her helplessly for a moment as her nose reddened and fat tears began to course down her cheeks.

She turned away from him, fighting for control.

'It did go well,' she said at last. 'Better than I could have hoped.'

But not quite well enough.

'Who got it?'

Lucy lifted her chin up and shifted her gaze to the window. 'I don't know.'

'You mean they haven't picked anyone yet?'

She swallowed. 'No, I don't mean that . . . they *have* picked someone, but I don't know who exactly. Anyway, it hardly matters now.'

'Couldn't they still be making up their minds?'

She shook her head and he watched her with growing impatience as an uneasy silence fell.

'How can you be so sure?'

She turned sharply round and stared at him. 'Because the director took the trouble to telephone me at the bloody casino of all places and *told* me, Richard – why do you think?' And Max Lockhart had loved every minute of her discomfort. Would the outcome have been any different if she had been more cooperative three years before and let him seduce her? She was suddenly touched by bitter sadness for that lost, wretched opportunity and hated herself for it.

'Even so, there's always the possibility . . .' His voice trailed off as he caught her glance.

'Don't Richard – just don't,' she snapped. 'I don't need any of your platitudes or little lectures. They simply gave the part to someone else – someone better.' Or perhaps to someone who was more willing to 'cooperate' with the director.

'All right, Luce,' he said quietly. 'All right.'

Her eyes wavered beneath his and she turned back to the window.

'Where have you been until now?'

'You weren't here when I got back, so I went to Roger.'

'Jolly Roger,' he said with contempt.

'You weren't here, Richard.'

'No, I wasn't, because I was sitting in the Indian waiting to pick up our dinner.'

'I'm not hungry.'

'Thanks very much,' he said. 'And would it be too much to ask if you could look at me when I'm speaking to you?'

She turned around. 'Look, I'm sorry – I didn't mean to sound offhand. I'm just not hungry, that's all.'

'As my meat Madras and your prawn Biriani happen to be all dried up and covered with a rather unappetizing crust after sitting in the oven for nearly three hours, that's just as well – I am such a considerate prat that I rather stupidly decided to wait for you, despite the fact that my stomach thinks my throat has been cut.'

'Richard, it's not really my fault. I didn't know where you were.'

'You didn't have to trail half-way across London to see your ex-boyfriend. Anyway, you could have telephoned.'

'I wanted to talk to someone.'

'Great.'

'Don't look at me like that – I've had a bloody rotten day.'

His head began to shake ominously and then his own hoarded wretchedness suddenly burst through.

'*You've* had a rotten day! What the hell do you think mine's been like? Glorious, bloody glorious! I suppose doing the shopping and carrying my faithful little list to dear old Tesco's day after day is particularly thrilling – or going to the laundrette, or doing the hoovering, or writing to my mother, or buttering the bread for my pathetic sandwiches, or worst of all sitting here hour after hour waiting for the bloody telephone to ring and when it finally does, it's either you or a bloody wrong number or something – not my damned agent, *never* good old Ned.' He took a deep gulp of air. 'So you see, all that is really *very, very* uplifting, my dear.'

'Stop it.'

'Stop it!' He mimicked, ' – as the actress said to the bishop. Christ, Luce! Do you know what you've been like to live with ever since you fancied yourself as Marilyn Monroe? I've sat here and listened to all of your little insecurities hour after bloody hour, gone through the songs and the lyrics with you, even had to go through that damned woman's bloody *life story* day after tedious day . . . never mind that I'm pissed off myself and that my own life is going absolutely nowhere.'

'I didn't mean . . .'

'I don't care what you meant,' he said bitterly, 'just don't come back here and throw a tantrum at me – you're not Elaine Paige yet! Do you realize just how fortunate you are to be given the understudy in what will probably be a major musical? For chrissakes, it is a job, after all.'

'All right, Richard.'

'No, it's not all right. Aren't you glad to be able to have the luxury of handing in your notice at the casino? Then you'll be able to give a big fat finger to all those smarmy businessmen and Arabs who are always chatting you up with greasy fivers lying in their sweaty palms. Think of that for a moment, will you.'

She made no answer, but it was true. The casino had been a job when she was 'resting' between acting roles and the manager had always been very good at having her back when she was out of work again, but God, how she hated it! The late hours, the smoke, her aching feet, the bribes, the unsettling little silences when the dice were rolling, and the dark temptation of sickening propositions for more money than she'd earn in a month.

Lucy had allowed herself to be tempted once, but it had been before Richard, even before Roger and when she dared to let herself think of that wretched time in her life there was a sort of blackness over all of it.

She had been part of a 'casting couch' set-up simply to obtain a coveted Equity card and become part of the exclusive actors' union, because without an Equity card a would-be actor couldn't get an acting role and without an acting role the would-be actor couldn't get an Equity card. Catch 22. Unless you were extremely lucky, a member of a theatrical family, or knew someone in the right place when a few strings could be pulled. Most actors and and actresses could only claim to have stars in their eyes.

Eventually she had become desperate and agreed to sign with Jim Nicholson, a silver-tongued publicist who had introduced her to Silks Club in Mayfair and then the Limelight where she had met some of Jim's famous and wealthy friends. Lucy had been persuaded to give a particularly influential executive 'a good time'. Four bleak weeks later her Equity card had arrived in the post.

Much later the casting couch scandal became public when other girls talked to the press and there had been quite a furore followed by sad shaking of hypocritical heads, but at least she had escaped without detection and sometimes, even now, she could still see that 'influential executive's' grin when she had reluctantly agreed to sleep with him and the wooden smile on her own face as she had looked into his sixty-two-year-old bespectacled eyes.

'And I don't doubt that you've also been given a singing part in the chorus or something on top of the understudy – haven't you?'

She nodded feebly as Richard's words broke harshly in on her unhappy thoughts.

'Lucky old Luce,' he spoke so softly that she could barely hear him.

A silence fell between them again and suddenly Richard felt soiled and depressed and he realized with a sense of bewilderment that his anger was rapidly slipping away. He sighed heavily. 'And did you really think I'd jump for joy knowing that you'd seen Roger?'

'It was nothing – just a drink.' But that wasn't quite true, because Roger had made a clever pass at her and she had found herself almost giving in to it. She closed her eyes for a brief, uneasy moment, wondering at her own weakness.

'And a talk, don't forget, just because I wasn't sitting waiting here as usual . . . Mad-am's captive audience.'

'That's not fair,' she said quietly.

'Nothing's fair, Luce.'

'He asked how you were.'

'Dear old Roger,' he retorted dryly.

'He's not all that bad.' But he wanted her back.

'Obviously.'

'I just needed to speak to someone . . .' And she had done nothing to encourage Roger's arms circling her, bringing her too close. Nothing.

'So you said.'

'Richard, please.' She looked at him very carefully, wishing

54

that she could call back all she had said because she was tired and miserable and he had made her feel guilty and ashamed.

'I'm sorry.'

He searched her face for a long moment, feeling his resistance begin to crumble. He didn't care any more how it had all started, he just wanted it over. The anger had finally been dissipated and he felt bleak and lonely as he looked into her unhappy face. Wanting her.

'Come here.'

Lucy slowly walked the few steps which separated them and Richard held out his hands. She let him pull her into his lap and fold his arms across her body as she buried her face in his shoulder and was relieved to find the spectre of Roger's closeness slipping away.

'Sorry,' she whispered, 'sorry.'

'You don't need to say it twice.' He kissed her brow, her nose, her ear. 'Once is enough.'

'I wanted the part for both of us.'

'I know.'

'It's worse this time, somehow . . . knowing that my best wasn't good enough.' And knowing that she had only been a hair's breadth away from fame and all that that would have meant for her.

'Save it, Luce. Don't agonize, or you'll eat yourself up.'

'I thought with the extra money we could have . . .' She started to cry. '. . . Now it's back to one hundred and ninety-nine pounds and twenty-six pence – and a bit for the understudy, all of twenty quid.'

'Ssssh,' he soothed.

He rocked her gently, one of his hands winding itself into her hair.

'As the understudy you'll have to make sure that you're damn good anyway . . .'

She sniffed in response.

'After all . . .' he continued stubbornly, 'whoever she is could fall down and break a leg, or get a sore throat, etcetera, etcetera, and it is a very strenuous role, you said so yourself.'

'You sound like Roger.'

'God forbid.' He glanced at her and she was smiling. 'I suppose he's still playing the handsome doctor in that pathetic soap?' But he knew, Richard saw it almost every afternoon because he couldn't help himself.

She nodded.

'*And* they've asked him if he wants his contract renewed?'

She nodded again. 'He gets a lot of fan mail.'

Richard closed his eyes in exasperation. 'Naturally.' He swore softly. 'Smooth bastard.'

'Richard, don't . . .'

'It's okay,' he said wearily, 'I'm only jealous.'

'He said they're re-casting for the hospital chaplain . . .'

Richard looked at her sharply. 'Me?'

'I don't really see you as a chaplain, somehow,' she said doubtfully, 'but it's worth a shot.' And Roger had promised her that he could 'get Dick the part'. He had been so nice about it, so understanding. She kissed the top of Richard's head, but there was something unsettling about that niceness. Lucy sighed softly, pushing the thought down, away, to think of later.

'Anything is worth a shot, my dear,' Richard said with forced jollity, 'even a lousy slot on an afternoon soap.' He shut his eyes tight with distaste and then felt her fingers gently tracing the curve of his mouth, as if she would save him from himself.

'Let's go to bed,' he said softly.

'I thought you were hungry.'

'I've suddenly lost my appetite.'

Jackie's eyes flickered open and immediately she felt the pressure of Drew's body beside her.

She turned and gazed at his sleeping face and then the naked rise of his shoulder, felt her pulse begin to race and her cheeks burn with desire and remembered pleasure. He was so good at that pleasure and the heat of the moment which grew hotter and hotter as he touched and probed so that she thought she might go out of her mind. But afterwards, when the fleeting ecstasy of their climaxes had died there was a gap, an awkward empty space because Drew was not very good at affection and holding and hugging and that warm voice-tone which comes with love. She shrugged, realizing that she had not met many men who were.

Jackie leaned her head back in exasperation, wondering why

she could not just accept what had happened and be happy. Happy. She smiled wryly and began to push back the bedcovers because she was already late and any more thoughts of Drew would have to wait.

'Where are you going . . . ?'

'I thought you were asleep.'

'I was, but I'm not now – come back to bed.'

'I'm late.'

'Come back to bed.'

'No, Drew,' she said, 'I mean it. I have a very busy day ahead.' And tomorrow, and tomorrow, and tomorrow.

'Okay, okay.' He searched her face as she slipped her arms into her robe. 'You don't have any regrets, do you?'

'What do you mean?'

'About last night.'

'Not yet.'

'Thanks.'

'What do you expect me to say?'

'Forget it.'

'I need some more time, Drew,' she said. 'It's happened so fast.'

He watched her carefully; after their lovemaking he had fallen asleep like a baby, sure in the knowledge that everything would work out just the way he wanted it.

'Do you want me to leave?'

Jackie seemed to pause.

'No, no – of course not.'

He sighed softly with relief.

The edges of her mouth tilted upwards into a hesitant smile. 'It's just that I've had a lot of time to think over these last six weeks.' She had even started to believe that she was getting over him.

'That's your privilege after what happened; you're entitled to some time to think things over. I can't blame you for that.' He wondered if his easy reply sounded too slick, too practised. 'But I mean it; if you want me to go, I will.'

'No,' she said, 'I don't want you to go, but we'll talk tonight.'

'Anything you say.' He watched her as she moved into the bathroom. 'Maybe I could keep you company today?'

'I don't think so, Drew.'

'Why not?'

'It's going to be a pretty hectic day.'

'How about lunch?'

'I'm not even sure I'm going to have time for any.'

He frowned as the shower began to run, shutting him out. She was playing it cool which surprised him, and perhaps he would do the same under similar circumstances, but he didn't have to like it. He had made Angela eat humble pie once because she had tried to mess him around, made her really sit up and beg, literally. As a penance she had knelt in front of him and slowly, very slowly he had opened a lavish box of Turkish Delight and then pushed tiny, floury pieces of the soft sweetmeat into her mouth, one after the other, then pushed her on to her back – naked, of course – and taken more tiny pieces of the Turkish Delight, and this time he had knelt in front of her and had succeeded in making her squirm quite a bit more . . . Drew's eyes narrowed. It had been different then.

He switched on the television from the bed and plumped up the pillows with clenched, angry fists. His eyes flicked to the screen: there were a man and a woman sitting behind a news desk talking about current affairs.

'Assholes . . .'

He switched channels until he came to a cable channel showing an old Beatles concert from the Sixties; as he watched the camera zoom in on the audience which was mainly made up of semi-hysterical screaming teenage girls leaning hopefully towards the stage with their arms outstretched.

'Oh, man . . .' Drew muttered wistfully.

The picture changed to Woodstock and legions of flower people in various stages of undress as they writhed to the music and the dope in their veins.

'Oh, man . . .' Drew muttered again.

He had been about nine years old when all that had been happening, and still living in Crenshaw, North Carolina, the back-end of nowhere – a crappy little hole of a town with three thousand inhabitants just on the edge of a national park and an Indian reservation. Crenshaw had a two-mile-long main street with a few dried-up backstreets tagged on to it. There were a couple of gas stations, a motel, a drug store, a movie-house, Arlene's Shopping Mall, a few junk food and ice-cream parlours and a whole half-mile of old, paint-peeling trailer homes, and if you turned off the main street at the end of town that was where you found the Indians selling trash and gen-u-ine souvenirs. On a bad day you didn't need directions to get there because you could smell the bourbon and the Indian stink half-way down the street. Yet his mother had met his father there, a Cherokee. When she had finally told Drew years later, he had put his hands over his ears because he hadn't wanted to hear any more, but she had even produced a photograph – as if he should be proud of a man who had screwed her a few times and whom he could not even remember – a flat-nosed, flabby-titted Indian in raggedy-assed war dress who had charged two dollars for a photograph. She had carefully run one pallid hand over that dog-eared snapshot as if she could feel the man through the paper, his skin, as if she really were touching that old Indian. He remembered her body growing rigid, her breathing becoming shallow and heavy and then she had pressed the goddamned thing to her loose, skinny little breasts and reached out for him, a nine-year-old kid. She had loved him, but not in the way a mother should love her son.

Drew clamped his eyes shut, his hands clenching and unclenching as the memory rose up inside like a noxious gas.

'Are you all right?'

He jerked his eyes open and felt his face burn red as if Jackie had just read his mind.

'Fine . . . just fine,' he said quickly and then added as an afterthought, 'Well, if you want the God's honest truth, I was really thinking that I have rushed things – that maybe I should leave you alone to get your head together.'

She sat down on the end of the bed and from the expression on her face he knew he had said the right thing.

'No, don't do that, it wouldn't solve anything.' She sighed heavily. 'I'm sorry if I'm not reacting in quite the way you wanted, but arriving out of the blue last night was a bit of a shock.'

'I know,' he said. 'Maybe I should have called first.' Drew grinned then, beginning to feel safe. 'But I always thought that you liked surprises.'

Jackie was undone by that grin, by the warm open mouth which promised so much.

'You know I do,' she said softly.

'Then let me come with you today, just for a few hours . . .' He took her hand. 'I promise I won't get in the way.'

'You'll be bored.'

'I've always been interested in your work,' he lied, 'you know that.'

'I don't know – it's going to be quite a day.' She searched his face and then smiled slowly. 'All right, but I'll see you at the studio because I have to leave now.'

'Studio?'

'Rehearsal room,' she explained, 'I've got a meeting with Aldo and Max at nine and then an interview at ten, plus an audition.'

'Where do I have to go?'

'I'll leave the address by the telephone.' She stood up. 'Now, I really do have to leave.'

He looked at her and thought of Angela, wishing Jackie were Angela. He hardened just thinking about it and then quickly buried the wish; he would make a mistake if he weren't careful. 'Come here for a moment.'

'I haven't time.'

Drew pushed back the bedcovers. 'Then I'll come to you.'

Jackie felt air catch in her throat, even now, at the opulence of his nakedness, but laughed despite herself as he moved towards her and his arms slid up her back. He began kissing her again and again, moving his mouth across her face and neck and she closed her eyes the better to appreciate the sensation as her hands slipped slowly around his neck and across the muscles in his upper back, pressing him against her, marvelling at the dusky perfection of his skin.

'It must be your hot Italian blood . . .' she murmured, almost to herself, as if she needed an excuse for the intensity of her desire and that practised trick he had of seduction, of making her believe in him.

Drew did not respond. He was remembering the unhappy image of his father and he wondered what Jackie would think if he were ever stupid enough to let his rancid secret, any of his rancid secrets, slip. And Angela – Angela most of all – she would really blow her mind. Oh, she knew he had no money, that he was not related to the bloody high and mighty Carocci family and she had come to terms with that, but she would never come to terms with the knowledge that his dear old daddy was some cheap drunk of an Indian with a big flat nose and flabby tits selling his half-baked photograph for two fucking dollars. No, sirree.

Rose Lyle had chosen to sing a first act 'Norma Jean' song, 'Dreaming the Hardest', in simple denim jeans and check shirt, and then asked if they would mind if she changed again. They agreed and she emerged from the dressing room in a white-blonde wig, skin-tight sequined gown, teetering on high heels and sang the show's Madison Square Garden number, 'Thank you, Mr President', almost perfectly.

'She is definitely the one,' Max said after letting out a long breath of admiration, as Rose returned to the dressing room.

'What do you think, Aldo?' Jackie turned to the musical director who was sitting quite still behind the piano.

'After the interview I still would have gone for Lucy Wilding who struck me as having an edge on the sort of commitment and discipline we need for the show,' he said cautiously, 'plus the fact that physically Lucy is almost perfect for the role . . .'

'You mean that Rose is somewhat lacking in the boob department?' Max interjected crudely.

'If you must put it like that . . .' Aldo responded.

'Easily remedied from a cosmetic point of view,' Max said with a small smile. 'A couple of very large sponges will do the trick.'

'Please go on, Aldo,' Jackie said turning deliberately to her musical director.

'As I was saying – in many respects Lucy is perfect for the role . . .' he paused with a sigh, 'but the minute Rose started to sing, particularly when she acted the part, I knew we'd found our Monroe. She projects so beautifully the vulnerability.'

'I was sure you'd agree,' Max said smugly.

'And we'll give the understudy to Lucy Wilding?'

'It makes sense.'

Aldo got up from the piano and walked across the room towards them, a big grin on his face.

'I feel like opening a bottle of champagne.'

Max nodded in agreement. 'By the way,' he said lightly, looking at Jackie, 'I told Lucy there would be something in the chorus for her as well.'

'*You* told her?' Jackie frowned. 'When?'

'Saturday, after Madam Jo Jo's – I was only putting the poor girl out of her misery, after all we both agreed that Rose tipped the balance.' And Wilding would be kept neatly in the background and he could even have a clear conscience about the way things had worked out.

'I wanted Aldo's opinion first, Max.'

'I assumed that was just a formality.'

'Formality or not – I wanted to be the one to tell Lucy.'

'Does it really matter, Jackie?'

'I think it does, very much.' Her eyes darkened with anger. 'You do realize that I could have made an additional call to her which would have made us look like a bunch of incompetent fools.' She paused. 'You should have discussed it with me first.'

'Okay, okay . . .' he held his hands up in mock fear. But it wouldn't have made any difference; once the girl's initial disappointment had faded she still would have been begging for a slot in the musical, no matter how clumsily they may have played it.

'And you called her after I left,' she continued with disbelief, 'at one o'clock in the morning?'

'She works at a casino most nights until the early hours.'

'You must have really made her day.' Max had known something that she didn't and that irritated her even more.

'All right,' he said uneasily, 'point taken.'

'I hope so.'

Sometimes she had the distinct impression that Max felt he knew much better than her, and not just about directing. Was it because she was a woman and Max had never worked with a female producer before, nor with one as young?

'Here's Rose . . .' she looked away from him, brushing the exchange aside, sensing that he would find out soon enough how things really stood.

'Let's talk over some coffee,' Jackie said, as the girl approached, 'but you should know that we're unanimous in offering you the part.' She smiled. 'Congratulations.'

'Oh, my God . . .' Rose exclaimed, 'thank you, thank you!' She shook her head, almost in bewilderment. 'That's fantastic – I can hardly believe it!'

'Believe it,' Max said, 'because we start rehearsals next month.'

'And there will be quite a lot of work between now and then with regard to publicity and also going through your songs with Aldo, but we'll talk about that in more detail in my office.' Jackie pushed her chair back and was moving towards the door when she saw Drew.

'Hi,' he said and stepped forward out of the shadows.

'I didn't realize you were there.'

'I thought I'd surprise you.'

'You certainly did that.'

She found herself irritated and a little embarrassed by Drew's 'Malibu' look – dark glasses, white jacket, crisp new jeans, but she smiled, making a real effort not to let the irritation show.

'You met Max and Aldo in Cape Cod, but not Rose, of course.'

'Definitely not,' Drew said with a grin, 'I just saw your audition – almost Marilyn Monroe incarnate . . .'

'Almost,' Rose responded and dropped long dark lashes demurely over her eyes.

Drew shifted his gaze quickly to Jackie's face. 'It's really coming together.'

'After five years it should be,' she said wryly and turned to the others, indicating that they should go on ahead of her.

'I'm afraid I won't be able to make lunch, Drew.'

'A team meeting?'

'Sort of.'

'Can't I sit in on it?'

'Not this time.'

She was still not sure of him and needed space and time. It definitely wouldn't help matters if he was constantly breathing down her neck.

'Okay.'

But it wasn't okay; he didn't like the way Jackie was blowing hot and cold, shutting him out when it suited her, even if she felt she had all the reasons under the sun.

'Maybe we could have dinner out this evening?' she offered. 'You choose the venue.'

'Fine.'

'You're angry.'

'No.'

'Look, it's my fault. I should have given more thought to you coming here this morning.' She sighed. 'This is Rose's meeting, Drew, we're talking money and PR and Marilyn Monroe.'

'I said it was okay.'

She gave him a searching look because all at once she felt unsure of her ground and a little guilty.

'You're going to be late for your meeting.'

'It can't start without me.'

He forced his mouth into a smile, the sort of smile that he thought she would find irresistible.

'I didn't mean to get in the way.'

'You're not,' she protested. 'Look, I'd better go . . .'

'I know.'

'I'll see you about seven.'

Drew nodded and then watched her carefully as she walked away.

He lunched early at a café directly across the street from the studio because he could think of nothing else to do. After a mediocre steak with French fries, apple pie and cream and three cups of black coffee Drew was beginning to feel a little bored. He sat facing the window looking out on the people in the street and the traffic clogged with black taxi cabs and huge red double-decker buses. London was not his city, it seemed small-time compared with what he was used to, just like the rest of Europe; he felt more at home in somewhere like LA or New York. There was something comforting in the miles of soaring concrete and apartment buildings and the incredible neon lights which blinked and rippled for blocks at a time pressing people to buy and buy, and the crazies, the hustlers and strip joints. Drew thought of Angela; missing her.

His gaze returned to the door across the street which led into the studio just as it opened and Rose Lyle stepped out into the cold October sunshine. He watched her as she stood at the kerb waiting for a break in the traffic and then as she walked through the lines of vehicles until she was standing only a few yards from the plate glass window of the café, so close that he felt he could almost reach out and touch her.

Drew studied her unobserved as she smoothed back her short dark hair and moved the long strap of her bag further up her shoulder. Rose was a little on the slim side for his taste, not enough real curves, but she had a pretty, almost child-like face and a beautiful mouth, and at that moment the mouth was smiling with barely concealed excitement. He was suddenly envious because she was happy and the happiness was like a gloss on her skin – a glittering future filled with promise and hope which at that moment seemed guaranteed; something he had never had, never would have.

Drew tapped on the glass. She turned round sharply and smiled with recognition. He beckoned her to join him and was rewarded by the nod of her head as she moved towards the doorway of the café. He signalled to a waitress and then looked over his shoulder as Rose approached, still smiling.

'You were terrific in there . . .' Drew said softly, his voice tinged with deliberate admiration.

'Thanks.'

'I told Jackie that as far as I was concerned you were the only one for the part.'

'Really?' Rose replied, blood rushing into her face.

'Oh, yeah,' Drew said easily, 'the others were just nothin' compared to you. I mean that.'

'You've been to all the auditions?'

'Only the important ones,' he lied. 'I'm sort of on the US side of things.'

'I could tell you were American.'

'That's right.'

'An advisor to the show?'

'Something like that.' Drew glanced at the waitress and the two coffees she was placing at their table. 'Jackie and I are old friends.'

'I really admire her – there aren't that many female producers in this business and certainly not so young.' Rose chuckled. 'She must be brave as well, I don't think I'd want to risk the sort of money and effort she must be putting into this show, but please don't tell her I said so, this is a really big break for me!'

'Ah – but Jacqueline Jones has friends in high places, Miss Lyle,' Drew mocked. 'Don't forget her father is *the* David Jones, Oscar-winner *extraordinaire* and her mother. . .' he swallowed deep in his throat '. . . is Angela Cassini.'

'Rea-lly?' Rose caught an audible breath with something like awe. 'I didn't know that.'

'Let's face it . . .' he said a little meanly, 'with those sort of connections she shouldn't fail.'

'But having friends in high places didn't help most of the makers of near disasters like *Children of Eden* and *Matador*,' she said nervously, 'and look at *King* – it lasted five weeks and lost three million!'

Rose grimaced as he nodded his head in what she thought was agreement, but Drew had never heard of musicals that hadn't made it because he had never been inside a real theatre until he met Jackie. Putting it crudely, he knew sweet F.A.

'After all,' she continued, 'you've got to be realistic, and with the incredible price of theatre tickets these days a successful musical has to have spectacle as well as a special kind of magic in order to have staying power *and* make a profit.' Her eyes grew bigger. 'You know, sometimes I wonder why I'm in this crazy business at all, it's so damned insecure. This time last year I was waitressing and if this show goes down the pan I'll be back where I started.'

'Hey, with you in the lead, it can't fail,' he said silkily, 'trust me. Anyway, Jackie's been working on *Marilyn* for years, it's her pet project, her baby – she's even arranged for the music to be out on tape and CD for Christmas. If anyone can get this thing right, she can.' He thought of the summer in Cape Cod when she had eventually finished the final draft and driven him almost crazy in the process because he had had to keep up a constant pretence of believing in her and her precious work: listening, reading, watching, kicking ideas around, picking holes in it – practically eating, sleeping and breathing the goddamn production. If it hadn't been for Angela he would have left the East Coast and gone back to LA there and then, but if he had done that he would have been left with nothing, not even a straw to cling on to.

'The songs *are* beautiful . . .' Rose remarked wistfully, bringing him back to the present, 'I can tell that much.'

'It's the way you sing them . . .' Drew said softly, but he was beginning to feel bored.

Her eyes lit up. 'Really?'

'Really.'

There was an odd little silence as Rose looked into Drew's face, at the same time she felt her stomach turn and her pulse begin to race.

'Will you be staying in London – in England, that is – long?' She swallowed. 'For the show, I suppose . . . ?'

'For as long as it takes.' And he stared at Rose for a deliberate moment.

She blushed and Drew's mouth slanted upwards and outwards into that dazzling grin which seemed to win him any prize he ever wanted. Except one.

'Why are you so dead set against the idea?' Jackie asked reasonably. 'Give it a chance, Max.'

'A narrator – for want of a better word – would be clumsy, obvious, crass.' He waited for a moment before speaking again, then, 'Shall I go on?'

'I don't think you've really listened to anything I've said regarding the approach.'

'The show should be able to do it on its own – there should be no need for a stuffed dummy standing at the side of the stage telling the audience what's going to happen next!'

'That is not what I meant, or how I see it,' she said so quietly that Max paused and examined her face sharply.

'If you two don't mind, I've got some work to do . . .' Aldo said and began pushing his chair away from the table.

'Okay, Aldo,' Jackie responded, 'I'll give you a call later.'

'Fine,' he said, 'because I still need to discuss those lyric changes in the first act which Max mentioned this morning.'

She nodded quickly and he gave her a dry, knowing smile before moving towards the door. As he closed it softly behind him Jackie switched her attention back to Max. 'I would just like you to think about it.'

'I don't need to think about it, Jackie.'

'It's not a gimmick. The woman I have in mind would provide a complete contrast to Monroe, a parody if you like . . .'

'A woman,' he said flatly.

'Yes, a woman – is there something wrong with that?'

'Of course not,' he said quickly. 'I just don't like the idea, full stop.'

'Don't you think there were – and, indeed, are – thousands of women out there who would give their right arm to be someone like Marilyn Monroe – the Love Goddess, the greatest sex symbol of modern times and every man's dream apparently?'

'What has that got to do with it?'

'I want someone up there, on stage, reasoning with the audience, actually *saying* that Monroe messed up all her God-given opportunities, that the girl who finally seemed to have everything she had ever wanted lacked one basic ability, and that was simply to survive the fame and adoration she craved.'

'Everyone knows that.'

'Do they?' She shook her head. 'I don't think so, Max; I think it needs spelling out because I believe that whatever Monroe may have done with her life it was inevitable that she would mess up, particularly when it came to the opposite sex.'

'We're making a musical, not a documentary – and in case you had forgotten, times are tough for musicals.'

'Bear with me just a little while longer,' Jackie plunged onwards. 'Imagine a woman without obvious good looks and sex appeal, but with a strong charismatic personality – someone, for instance, who resembles Bette Midler – who talks us through the dubious parts of Monroe's life. Maybe she would say something along the lines of "Now that wasn't very smart", or "I don't care if that guy *is* going to be President, she must be crazy falling for a line like that . . .'

Max closed his eyes. 'You might just drive the audience crazy with interruptions by this charismatic character of yours.'

'If it's done exactly right they won't seem like interruptions, besides I don't intend there to be many,' she said, 'and it could give the show an interesting edge.'

'I still don't like it.'

She stared at him. 'Well, I'd like to try it.'

'That's your prerogative.'

'If it doesn't work the idea can be dropped,' she said, 'after all it will hardly affect any of the scenes in a real way – Monroe's "alter ego", shall we say, will literally be on the sidelines. Rehearsals can go ahead as planned.'

'You obviously have someone in mind for this "alter ego".'

'Perhaps you remember the rather tall brunette who auditioned for Monroe's mother?'

'No – I don't.'

'Her name's Pat Goodall. I worked with her in Edinburgh on my *Wuthering Heights* production. I know she could do it.'

'If you say so.'

'Max . . .'

'All right, Jackie, all right – have it your way,' he snapped, 'now can we get on with something else?'

'I told you that if it doesn't work, the idea can be dropped.'

'And I said all right.'

Jackie looked at him for a moment, longing to deliver a sharp retort. 'What else did you want to discuss?'

'The design meeting – can you be available for tomorrow morning about 9.30?'

'That's fine.'

'I'm already late for a quick word with Yvonne about the costumes.' He stood up. 'Naturally she'll need to spend some time with us and Brian so that the colours, etcetera, of the costumes won't ultimately clash, or be lost against the sets.'

'I've talked through some ideas with her, but we're trying to stick as closely as possible to Monroe originals and I don't want that changed too much if it's at all possible.'

'We can discuss that tomorrow morning,' he said impatiently. 'Right now, as I said, I'm late and I'd like to pick up a coffee on my way because my throat feels like a piece of leather.'

'Okay.' She spoke with more ease than she felt. 'If you need me after you've seen Yvonne, I'll be in my office, or back at the hotel.'

'Fine,' he said flatly and started to walk away.

'By the way . . .' she added quickly, 'I now have twenty copies of the Jordan biography of Marilyn and as agreed these should be distributed among the cast and read before official rehearsals begin.'

'They'll love the homework . . .' he remarked sarcastically as he opened the door.

'It's essential reading, as we've both said on various occasions.'

'Just one of my little jokes.'

'It's reassuring to know that you still have a sense of humour . . .' Max smiled. 'One needs it in this business.'

He closed the door behind him and Jackie found herself gazing uneasily at the space where he had stood.

She walked slowly back to the table and scanned her open draft, the dog-eared pages criss-crossed with lines and notes and names and likely changes. This show was the culmination of a dream which had begun to take shape so long ago she could not accurately remember its beginnings.

Years before, after leaving stage school, she had walked the rounds of the London theatres until she landed a temporary job as a dresser, or general dogsbody and factotum to three bit-part actors at the Aldwych theatre. Her father had refused to give her any help because he had said that 'doing it on her own' would be 'character building' and he had been right in a way because it had been bloody hard work, yet she had loved every minute.

Nothing had changed since then except growing ambition and a certain toughening-up process against bruising times and people like Max who could often make life very difficult, but she had been lucky to get a director with his experience and talent for *Marilyn*, particularly as this was her first venture into the West End. When she first contacted him, Max had been working on another production also destined for the West End, but it had been jinxed from the beginning: the leading man resigned, one of the main backers decided to opt out, costs escalated and when it closed, the director, Max, came up for grabs. Unlike two of the other directors she had approached Max had been convinced by her belief in *Marilyn*; she had also offered him a salary he couldn't refuse.

Jackie closed the draft and trailed her fingers gently down the front cover as she thought about Max; disagreements were part of the business of theatre. It wasn't possible that she and Max

70

would get through the all-important next three months without them, but surely they were both professionals and mature enough not to let such things get in the way of the production and their working relationship? Nerves cruised in the pit of her stomach for a moment, but then she shrugged and shuffled her papers together, packing the draft quickly into her briefcase because she had forgotten to give Max the notes she had prepared which explained in detail what she had in mind for the narrator. He could read them tonight and then perhaps he would find himself more amenable to the idea by the time they met again in the morning.

The studio seemed almost too quiet as she walked the length of the corridor towards the wardrobe department, but it was past six and most of the small crew of people who were already working full-time on the production had probably gone home. Jackie pushed back a loose strand of hair and smiled softly to herself as she thought of the transfer to the Adelphi they would make at the beginning of February when everything would suddenly seem real and the opening would be looming up to greet them.

The door to Wardrobe was just ajar. She pushed it open, puzzled by the solitary lamp left switched on as the room seemed empty. Part of the L-shaped room was roughly partitioned off by pieces of tired oriental screening where Yvonne had her desk, a sewing machine and a narrow *chaise longue*. Jackie moved towards it and realized, too late, that Max had indeed kept his rendezvous with the costume designer.

Yvonne sat astride him, her black buttocks rising and quivering with the ferocious strength of his thrusts. It was an incongruous sight and would have been almost comic in other circumstances; Yvonne was a big woman and her massive thighs seemed capable of engulfing Max's white, almost hairless legs, which protruded unkindly from beneath her body. Jackie took a silent step backwards and another and another as Max began to groan and his breath to quicken, his voice rising and rising in a gush of ecstatic obscenities as his climax whirled and crashed out. There was one final, guttural cry and she knew it was over.

Jackie backed out of the door unnoticed and then closed her eyes with disgust as Max spoke again, 'For God's sake – get off! You're nearly crushing me to death . . .'

FOUR

Drew blew a slow cloud of smoke through his nostrils and then two perfect rings from his mouth. He leaned back on the bed and stared at the hotel ceiling, waiting for Jackie.

He could have had sweet-smelling Rose that afternoon – seduced her with tedious ease, but he had not been in the mood and besides it wouldn't have been a very intelligent move to take the risk, not yet. He rolled on to his stomach and crushed the cigarette out in an ashtray. His thoughts returned to Jackie and he smiled thinly because he was remembering how much she liked champagne and how easy it had been during the long hot summer to please her with a nice, chilled bottle – only Krug, naturally. Just like her mother. He wondered whether she realized that at least they had that much in common.

Drew lifted the telephone receiver to call room service, but his fingers hovered above the numbers. He began dialling.

'Good afternoon,' a very English voice said, 'Mrs Cassini's residence.' He recognized her imported butler, the one who walked as if he had just crapped himself.

'Is she there?'

'Who is calling, please?' The voice sharpened, as though it had been offended.

'Drew Carocci,' he said, 'tell her it's urgent.'

'I'm not sure – sir – whether . . .'

'Just tell her it's urgent,' Drew snapped, 'like I said.'

The receiver was put down and he could hear the sounds of feet walking, people calling and laughing nearby, music. She was having a party.

'What do you want?' she hissed.

He didn't mind her barely hidden fury, at that moment it was simply good to hear her voice; he could almost imagine she was in the next room.

'I thought I'd just call and say hello.'

He heard the sharp intake of her breath and smiled.

'And I asked a question – what do you want?'

'I was thinking about you . . . that's all . . . the last time,' all the times, 'when you did that strip for me . . .' Oh, and afterwards – and afterwards.

'Now now, Drew.'

'You're having a party.'

'A *lunch* party.' One of her more important lunches in aid of the foundation she had created herself, The Lloyd Shriver Memorial Trust to the Arts; she had even managed to persuade Baryshnikov to attend, but she wouldn't expect Drew to understand what that meant to her among the glitterati of the charity circuit.

'Same thing.'

'What do you want, Drew?' She sighed, running a leisurely hand over the bodice of a Bill Blass favourite and then down and across her flat stomach which cost her so much damned effort. 'Money?'

'No, I don't want your goddamn money . . .' he said, '. . . you know what I want, or have you forgotten all our erotic little meetings in Cape Cod and all the very hot things you said when we were rolling in the sack together?'

Angela gave a start and her hands clenched because his bluntness both surprised and disturbed her. She didn't want to hear any more; it was over between them and there was too much at stake to re-open an affair.

'I have to go – there are people waiting, this is very important to me – I was in the middle of a conversation . . .'

'I don't give a horse's ass.'

'Drew, don't do this.'

'Speak to me – say something nice,' he said slowly, 'something *hot* and nice.'

'I said *don't* Drew.'

'I want to see you . . .' his voice sounded strangled, thick in his ears, '. . . I want back that afternoon in your apartment.'

Angela stiffened, but as the memory returned she could see his face very clearly and imagine that beautiful dangerous mouth closing over hers. A thrill of desire unfurled in her stomach, between her legs, and she wondered with something akin to astonishment how he had the power to do this to her.

'We finished it, Drew.'

'*You* finished it,' he protested.

'I had to.'

'Bullshit.'

She cleared her throat. 'I can't talk now.'

'You bitch.'

'I have to go, Drew.'

'No.'

'Yes.' She rubbed her forehead and it was slick with sweat. 'I'll send you a cheque.'

'Keep your fucking money.'

'Goodbye, Drew.'

Angela's hand was trembling as she put down the receiver and her heart was a hard knot in her chest. She would still send him the cheque because she knew he had no money of his own. Perhaps it was a way of salving her conscience. Her eyes closed for a second and she took a deep breath before realizing that she didn't even know where he was, but there was a box number somewhere, some place, wasn't there?

She smoothed down her dress again, her gaze shifting back to the safety of the luncheon party and the sea of faces that chatted and laughed and sipped champagne. Her heart was pounding and there was a sour taste of doubt in her mouth as she walked away.

Drew slammed down the receiver in frustration.

'Bitch, bitch, bitch . . .'

At that moment he wanted revenge, good and sweet, something that would make Angela wish that she had never dropped him as if he were something that didn't smell right. He lay back on the bed and squeezed his eyes tightly shut because he was once more back in her apartment and she was standing wickedly on that little table taking off her clothes.

'She used me . . .' he murmured, 'just another toy-boy, just another fuck . . .'

Drew could not understand why he was unable to shrug off the memory of Angela with the cold control he had used for the countless other women he had known. It had always been he who had had the upper hand – the women who had endlessly phoned him, begging him to take them to bed – he who had called almost all the shots. But he didn't know himself, not deep down, because in all his life he had never loved anyone, until now.

He brought his arm up and let it fall across his eyes, shielding him from the light of the room. She would regret what she had done and said, of course; he would make her regret it. He thought of Rose Lyle, her eager smile, that 'puppy-dog' look which made him want to hurt her, and Jackie. She was more cautious and had made that plain, but he would bring her round. And then Angela would come to him eventually because he would work it out that way. After all, she had a jealous streak a mile wide and definitely didn't want him anywhere near Jackie. The corners of his mouth began to turn up a little. And she would beg just like before, he would make her, for what she had made him suffer, but even then, in the blackest part of his heart, he knew that he would never forgive her.

His thoughts returned to Jackie and the present as he lifted the telephone again and ordered a bottle of her favourite champagne on ice.

'Put it on the bill,' he said tightly, 'yes, that's right, Jacqueline Jones – I'm her fiancé.' Almost.

Drew made another call to a nearby florist and ordered two dozen red roses. Finally, he put the receiver down and trailed a hand languidly down the length of the thick ivory plastic. His fingers came to rest on the small bedside table and he made them dance and tap to the music he had suddenly switched on in his head. He looked at the clock on the wall; Jackie was late.

It was dark and rather bleak by the time she closed the studio door behind her. Jackie quickened her step and pulled up the collar of her coat against the rain as her eyes scanned the street for a vacant cab. She turned into the Charing Cross Road and immediately saw one coming towards her from the direction of Shaftsbury Avenue. Automatically she hailed the cab and sighed with relief as it U-turned in the road and drew up swiftly beside her.

'Jackie?'

She jumped, startled by the voice behind her.

'Jamie,' she said, 'what on earth are you doing here?'

'I thought it might be a good idea to call in and have a look around before starting officially on Monday, but I took a wrong turning somewhere and must have got to the door of the studio just after you left.'

It was not quite true; he had deliberately wandered around the old theatre streets and seedy back alleys, staring with fascination at the lights and the people and the shop windows. Quite by accident he had stumbled into the outer realms of Soho and seen the garish posters outside the girlie bars offering promises and pleasures (apparently beyond his wildest dreams) if he took a step inside and allowed himself to be tempted.

A life-size cardboard cut-out of a scantily clad woman had grinned at him through a window and in an instant his eyes had travelled over the cartoon size of her breasts, the beckoning red mouth and the plump mound at the apex of her thighs over-emphasized by a lacy black G-string.

An old man leered at him from behind the cash booth as if he had looked into his mind and discovered his virginity: perhaps it showed, like sweat on his skin.

Virginity, chastity, purity had been qualities he was supposed to cherish in the cloistered confines of the seminary. At least, that was the theory. Now, all that had been turned on its head and wherever he looked the world seemed alive with seduction; he could only wonder when his turn might come. He had known all along what his father would never admit, that his son would have made a very bad priest.

Jamie walked on, the words and sacred vows he had once tried to keep playing uselessly in his head. When he glanced at his watch he realized that he had wasted an hour and then had to retrace his steps in order to find the studio. He had finally turned into the right street some thirty minutes later afraid that the building would be shrouded in darkness, closed up, but the lights had still been blazing.

' – and then I saw you walking down the street.'

She had opened the door of the cab.

'You should have telephoned,' she said, 'I could have saved you the trip.' Jackie gestured towards the waiting vehicle, 'you'd better hop in, or we'll both get soaked if we stand here any longer.'

'This was a bad time to call, then . . .' he ventured, sitting next to her, smelling the dampness mingled with perfume on her skin and blushing in the darkness as a vivid picture of the cardboard woman slipped into his head.

'In many respects it hasn't been the best of days.' An unlovely memory of Max with Yvonne lingered and she closed her eyes. 'And I suppose I'm tired.'

'You can drop me off somewhere, if you like – if this is inconvenient for you,' he offered, 'really,' wishing now that she would agree.

'No,' she smiled with an effort, 'don't be silly. Come back to the hotel and we can talk over a drink.'

'Not if you're tired.'

'If I was too tired, I wouldn't offer – believe me.'

She sat back and he darted a glance at her profile, half-hidden in shadow. The lights of the city fled across her face and over the windows in bursts of colour as the car sped through the streets and all at once he wondered what he was doing there, with her, in London, apparently taking a job in a theatre production – a musical of all things – a business he knew nothing about. For a brief moment he imagined himself as one of those tiny motes of dust which turned aimlessly in the air – he had watched them so often at home in brilliant shafts of sunshine. Jamie looked out of the window at the mass of people surging across the choking junction of Piccadilly Circus. Would he ever get used to this?

Jackie was glad of the silence, it gave her time to think in peace. She thought of Max and Yvonne, disappointed by what she had seen, or was it disillusionment? She knew of Max's reputation, so what she had witnessed shouldn't have come as that much of a surprise, but it had left a nasty taste in her mouth. Yet there was nothing she could do about it and she could not allow it to get in the way of their working relationship. After all, it really wasn't any of her business and Yvonne was old enough to take care of herself.

With an effort she thought about Drew, but was not greatly comforted because he had been angry when she left him at the studio that morning, no matter what he had said to the contrary. Now it was past seven and he would be waiting, she had almost forgotten – a month ago, even a week ago, she wouldn't have believed that possible. The Ritz loomed up on their left and then the cab sped past Green Park and into Knightsbridge. Sometimes she wondered if she knew herself at all.

Marilyn was beginning to take up every moment of her time and there was still so much to discuss, so many details to iron out and then try out . . . at that moment it seemed like chaos. Jackie cursed softly as she realized she hadn't remembered to call Aldo and he would be out now, attending a preview at the Barbican. Damn. Drew couldn't expect her to drop everything because he had decided to come back into her life – he, of all people, knew what this production meant to her. She shifted uneasily as the car drew up outside the hotel.

Drew had come half-way across the world just to be with her and of course she appreciated that. She was still in love with him. Wasn't that why her stomach did somersaults even as her eyes lifted involuntarily to the window of the hotel room where he waited?

She turned to Jamie as she climbed out of the cab.

'I have a friend waiting in my room. . .' She blushed and wished she hadn't.

'If this is inconvenient . . .'

'It is *not* inconvenient, I told you,' she smiled, and began rummaging in her bag for the fare.

'No, let me pay – I insist – it's the least I can do.' He moved her gently aside as if she weighed less than nothing.

'It's all right, Jamie – really,' but he had dropped the money into the cab driver's open hand before she could say anything more and she found herself strangely touched by the gesture.

Jamie followed Jackie past the uniformed doorman, Harry, who smiled and said good evening to her as if she were an old friend, and then into the entrance hall, dazzling with its gilding and crystal chandeliers. She took him up the impressive marble staircase and into the shadowy elegance of the hotel bar. Jackie slipped off her coat and inevitably Jamie's eyes were drawn to the outline of her body just visible beneath a black cashmere sweater and superbly cut jeans.

'I have to make a quick call – I won't be a moment.'

He watched her walk away, hips swaying gently, and he took a deep gulp of air.

'There was nothing I could do about it, Drew.'

'Tell whoever he is to go take a run . . . I've arranged for us to have a cosy dinner in . . .'

'I can't.'

'Jackie – come *on* . . .'

'It will probably only take half an hour at the most,' she said. 'Join us.'

Drew was gripping the phone so hard that his knuckles showed white. He looked around the hotel room with growing fury as his gaze darted from the vases of red roses to the champagne bucket.

'I'll wait for you here.'

'I have to come up anyway, there's a book that might be useful to him . . .'

'Who is this guy, anyway?' he persisted. 'Why is this such a big deal?'

'Because he's starting at the studio on Monday, because he turned up at the door in the pouring rain, because he's my step-mother's godson . . .'

Now he understood.

She drew a sharp breath. 'Okay?'

'Sorry, hon', sorry . . .' he said quickly, 'I was just looking forward to seeing you – alone.'

'We'll have the rest of the evening, Drew.'

'I know, I know.'

'See you in five minutes.'

Before he could respond there was a soft click as she replaced the receiver.

He swore and then realized it was the second time that day he had had the telephone put down on him by a woman. It was definitely not his day. Maybe it wasn't his year.

The lift doors slid soundlessly open and Jamie found himself in an opulently furnished foyer – wedgewood blue and ivory carpets, antiques; like a stately home. He was reminded of a photograph he had seen of his father taken in 1920 at the old family estate in Gloucester: a small knock-kneed boy in a sailor suit standing beside a massive Victorian bureau. The only time he had ever seen his father looking dwarfed and lost.

'Do you like living here?'

'I've been coming to the Hyde Park a long time. My father always brings me here for lunch when he can and has done so for more than ten years. Some of the staff are almost like old friends.' She smiled. 'Normally I hate staying in hotels for too long, but somehow it's different here, relaxed despite its grand appearance and also convenient – I have a large suite which gives me extra room, but unfortunately I'm going to have to forego such luxury because of an unforeseen financial hiccup.' She thought of her mother. 'I'm now in the middle of negotiating the lease on a house.' She smiled again. 'Such is life.'

He followed her into the corridor beyond the foyer.

'Where is this house?'

'I wanted Hampstead, overlooking the Heath – near Clare and my father, but it's not practical from a working point of view, so I've opted for a small mews in Half Moon Street – close to Green Park.' She looked back at him as they approached the hotel suite. 'And what will you do when you decide you no longer want to live under the guiding eye of Clare?'

'I don't know,' he said, but he had been wondering as much himself. 'I seem to have been living under the guiding eye of someone all my life.'

'You're only twenty-four, Jamie,' she said gently, 'you have your whole life ahead of you.'

'Like you.'

'What do you mean?'

'Well you're not much older than me.'

'Six years.'

'You make it sound more like sixty.'

She looked at him quizzically as she opened the door of her suite, but then Drew was standing in front of them with a bottle of champagne in his hand.

'Thought I might as well open it now – it would look pretty stupid just sitting there in that ice bucket.' He looked from Jackie's mildly surprised face to the boy who stood just behind her, although 'boy' was probably not the right word. He was big, this boy, at least a head taller that Drew – thick neck, powerful shoulders. A good-looking dude. Drew was touched by an irrational jealousy because Angela had been with just such a 'boy', a big macho beach bum – laying him – when he had first got to know her. 'And this is . . . ?' he continued, smiling with an effort.

'Jamie – Thurley,' Jackie replied quickly, 'Drew Carocci – Jamie starts as a trainee production assistant with me on Monday.'

'Glad to know you,' Drew said and walked over to the glasses waiting to be filled. 'You're a beginner in this business, then?'

'Yes.' Jamie was looking at the red roses which were displayed about the room. Was this man a boyfriend? A lover?

'Champagne, Jamie?' Drew was deftly pouring as they slipped off their coats.

'Thanks.'

'What were you up to before this?'

'I studied for a while, then gave it up.'

'What sort of study?' Drew probed, instantly reminded of the smooth, privileged preppies of his high school days.

'The priesthood.'

'Pardon me?'

Drew stared at him.

'The priesthood.' Jamie watched Drew's mouth fall open.

'Well, I'll be . . .' Drew gulped, 'but you're *not* the actual genuine article?'

Jamie shook his head. 'No.'

'Jamie's making a fresh start, Drew.' Jackie interjected, 'he was living in Kenya until very recently; this is his first time in London.' She shot him a glance. 'Now can we have a glass of that champagne? I'm dying for a drink.'

Drew nodded and handed round the glasses. She wanted him to shut up and naturally he would oblige, but he wanted to laugh out loud. He had not known much about 'show business' before meeting Jackie and had only come into contact with a few bums from the seedier side of things, like out-of-work snake charmers and one-time actresses turned call-girls shooting up, but his opinion hadn't changed much; they were all weirdos, alcoholics, faggots, or self-conceited smart-asses. He presumed Jamie Thurley would fit into the 'weirdo' category, or maybe he was a fag as well. Priests were, weren't they?

His mother had been Catholic, but the priest who was supposed to look after good ole Crenshaw had made it his business to live miles away, in a neat little white clapboard house beside a neat little white steepled church, and had shown his reluctant face once a month when it had been Crenshaw's turn to hold mass in a converted mobile home set between two scrawny trees. Father Connor's round red face had lit up when those cute little altar boys had come on stage; he actually came close to looking human.

'Are you in the theatre?' Jamie asked.

'Not really, but you could say I take an interest.'

'Have you been in London long?'

'A couple of days,' Drew smiled and flashed a glance at Jackie. 'You could say I came to give Jackie moral support.'

Jamie drank some champagne.

'And you lived in Kenya?'

'All my life.'

'The big city must be some change.'

'I enjoy change.'

'That's good,' Drew said smoothly. 'Maybe I could show you around some time – hit some of the hot spots . . . ?'

'I'd like that.'

'I'm not sure you would, actually,' Jackie said.

'Why not? The kid's over twenty-one.'

'London isn't Kenya, Drew, and Jamie's used to a more reclusive life.' She smiled anxiously at Jamie: she didn't want to sound like a nanny, but God knows where he'd end up with Drew as tourist guide.

'Not that reclusive,' Jamie said. 'I imagine Nairobi is not so different from any other big city in the world. It has its dark side.' He had discovered that for himself when he left the seminary for the last time and deliberately explored beneath the sleek and shining surface of the city, wandering through forbidden back-streets, among the beggars, pimps and prostitutes. Some of the girls who approached him were the most beautiful he had ever seen, but his nerve had failed in the end.

'You see, Jackie,' Drew said, 'you're being over-protective.'

'Perhaps.' Jackie shrugged: she had enough to do without playing nursemaid to Jamie.

'You really don't need to worry,' Jamie said.

Drew took a mouthful of champagne and regarded the boy

with silent amusement over the brim of his glass, but the amusement faded as he caught the intensity of the brief glance Jamie darted at Jackie. So he wasn't a fag, after all. He put down his glass, suddenly wanting him gone.

'I thought you wanted a book that's lying around here somewhere?'

'It's on the desk,' she said, 'I'd almost forgotten.' She turned to Jamie. 'It's just some background reading, really. I would concentrate on the second half of the book rather than the first, as that will take you through the last forty years of the American/ British musical . . .' She crossed to the desk and started rummaging among the heap of books and papers.

Drew switched his attention back to Jamie, his gaze growing watchful and sardonic as the boy's eyes followed Jackie.

'The Seventies and Eighties are particularly interesting . . .' Jackie continued '. . . when the British musical really began to shrug off its somewhat parochial image and emerged on to the international scene.'

'I think it might be a little beyond me.'

'No it won't,' she said gently, 'you might even find it interesting, and once that happens, the rest is easy.' She took another book from a stack which sat beside the telephone. 'Take this, as well, it's a biography of Marilyn Monroe – you'd better learn something about our subject. Oh, yes . . . and it will also be useful to have a copy of the current script and detailed scene-by-scene breakdown of the proposed action . . .'

'Hey, Jackie, slow down – ' Drew draped his arm casually around her shoulders, 'don't you think you're giving the kid more than enough to go on? The stuff will be coming out of his ears.' He ruffled her hair and kissed her playfully on the nose and stared at Jamie. 'She always gets like this once the word "musical" enters the conversation.' He was bored, he was hungry, he wanted another drink, but above all he wanted 'the kid' to leave.

'I think Drew's right . . .' Jamie said, forcing a smile, and making a clumsy gesture of looking at his watch, 'and it's really getting late – I promised Clare I'd be back for dinner,' he lied.

'Telephone – I'm sure she'll understand,' Jackie said.

'No,' he responded too quickly, 'I'd better go.'

She looked at him, a little startled by the abruptness of his response.

'All right.' She was boring him before he had even started on the production, perhaps Drew was right and she did have a tendency to go over the top when she got on to her pet subject. 'Well, call me if you have any questions between now and Monday.'

'I will.' He moved towards the door.

'Don't forget your coat . . .'

'Of course.'

'And the books, kid,' Drew prompted, raising his eyes to heaven.

'I'll put them in this carrier bag for you,' Jackie offered.

'Thanks for everything.' He lifted his hand in an awkward gesture of goodbye. 'See you Monday.' He opened the door and closed it softly behind him.

Jamie walked back along the lush blue and cream carpet towards the lift, embarrassment slowly giving way to unexpected anger. His hands clenched and unclenched as he pictured Drew's face. Drew didn't like him. Perhaps they didn't like each other, and he didn't like the patronizing way he called him 'kid', either. Most of all he didn't like the way Drew's arm had draped itself around Jackie's shoulders as if he were marking out his possession.

Richard stood outside an Italian delicatessen and thought of Lucy – they could have a celebration, just a small one. His eyes returned to the tempting magnum of Dom Perignon which even had a thin layer of dust covering its beautiful dark neck. His thoughts switched to his bank account which had very little in it, but he had actually got a job today, an *acting* job, and would even sign the contract on Monday . . . that was worth celebrating, wasn't it? After all, he would soon be receiving his first proper pay packet in months. And Lucy needed cheering up.

He had taken up her suggestion of trying for the part of the chaplain in the hospital soap, despite the fact that he would be working alongside Roger whom he loathed, but when it really came down to it he had no choice. Lucy would think him unprofessional and, he supposed, childish if he refused the job because he would be working with her ex-boyfriend. Besides, he simply could not afford to turn it down.

Richard shrugged; granted it was only a small job, six appearances in an afternoon soap, but it was a job. *St Winifred's* was almost a household word, although not yet quite in the dizzying realms of *Coronation Street*, or *Knots Landing*, the top US soap now that *Dallas* and *Dynasty* had bitten the dust. There was something of a chummy feel about *St Winifred's*, as there was with *Neighbours*, the nauseating Australian soap. Very comforting.

And it had been good to have the scent of make-up in his nostrils again. After the make-up girl had finished greying his hair and adding a few more wrinkles he had been instructed to ape a Scots accent and really didn't think that he had succeeded very well until Roger had winked at him from across the studio. He had hated that wink.

It was only later, after the audition was over, that Roger had said, 'I've put a good word in for you, Dick – no probs . . .' Richard closed his eyes, cringing inwardly; he hated being called Dick, hated more that it was Roger.

He took a deep breath and pushed open the door of the delicatessen. Immediately a bell rang and his nose was assaulted by a score of different smells, from garlic to salami to cheddar cheese; his mouth began to water and his stomach to rumble. By the time he walked out of the shop with the bell ringing in his ears he was laden with a large brown paper bag containing Stilton, coarse duck *pâté*, plump queen olives, two French bread sticks, a cold cooked chicken and a bottle of cheapo plonk. It had been the thought of Roger and his sickeningly handsome face which had turned him away from the champagne and even the tempting 1982 red Bordeaux.

He had never seen anyone with a perfect jaw-line like Roger's. Square and perfect. He was also taller than Richard and blonde, and tanned. The ecstatic make-up girl had told him that there was very little she needed to do to improve Roger's 'amazing face' – just a touch of powder to take off the shine. She had said this during the course of developing his own, rather ordinary, face into a series of unappetizing cracks and crevices. When he had finally looked at himself in the dressing-room mirror he thought that he resembled a cross between Elia Kazan and the Pope.

Richard sighed and tightened his hold on the brown paper bag. Maybe next time he would splash out, when he got a decent part and when he didn't have to thank good old jolly Roger for it. Anyway, he couldn't afford the champagne, or the red Bordeaux, it really was as simple as that. At least that is what he told himself.

He thought about Lucy. She seemed to have got over the disappointment of not getting the lead in *Marilyn* and had even looked forward to a few publicity shots with the girl who had actually got the part, but last night when he had cuddled up against her, trailing a hand down her thigh as a prelude to making love, she had pretended to be asleep. There was a pattern to Lucy's 'sleep-breathing' – heavy, rhythmic and slow. He knew that, just as he knew there was a mole on the back of her neck and a scar behind her left knee.

Richard could only remember her rejecting him once before and now he couldn't even recall the reason why. Rejection seemed a strong word, but he couldn't think of her turning from him in any other way, not without an explanation. In the morning she had slipped out of bed before he was awake and when he turned over to find that she was gone he had rolled on to his back and stared unhappily at the ceiling wondering what was the matter, what he had done, what she was thinking. It had been his idea to meet her from the studio this evening and she had agreed readily enough.

He saw her as he turned into the street: she was already standing outside the studio doors, moving slowly from one foot to the other as if she were cold.

'Sorry I'm late.'

'Doesn't matter.' She smiled, slipping her arm in his and he felt better.

'Would you like to go for a drink before we go home?' he asked and tapped the brown paper bag. 'I've got supper.'

'I'd like that.'

'You seem a bit subdued,' he glanced at her. 'Bad day?'

'It was all right.'

'How did the PR shots go?'

'Fine,' she said. 'The *Mail* is going to give us almost half a page.' There was some consolation in knowing that she photographed better than Rose, but that was all. Despite the fact that Rose did not have the obvious charisma Lucy had expected, as soon as the girl opened her mouth to sing her whole appearance seemed to change, and it was difficult to look away from her and not be drawn totally by the quality of that remarkable voice.

'How was "Marilyn"?'

'You mean Rose Lyle,' she replied, 'and the answer is that she's very good. I don't think there's much doubt that Jacqueline Jones and Max Lockhart chose the right girl.' Lucy had vowed to herself that she would not be bitchy or jealous, but it was hard and she could feel a little coil of bitterness curled tightly inside waiting to spring.

'Time will tell,' Richard said and squeezed her hand.

They crossed a busy street and into the outer realms of Covent Garden.

'Aren't you going to ask me how I got on?'

She looked up. 'Oh God, Richard – I'm sorry.'

'Well, you're now looking at the Right Reverend Angus Fraser.'

'Really?' But she already knew, because Roger had telephoned and told her; he had also told her that it had been 'touch and go', but with 'a few words in the right ear' he had 'got Dick through in the end'.

Richard would hate that. She swallowed slowly because now Roger had persuaded her to have lunch with him and it had been very difficult to refuse after what he had done. If it was possible, Richard would hate that even more.

'Yes, really.'

'Congratulations!'

'Don't go mad, it's only for six episodes and I have to look about one hundred and three.'

'Really!'

'Really.'

She laughed, and he was glad, suddenly, that he had to look 'about one hundred and three'.

Drew closed the door behind them.

'That was a lovely meal, Drew, thank you.'

'My pleasure, Jackie.'

'We could invite Jamie next time, he doesn't know many people here.'

'I'm sure he'd like that . . .' Drew said and crossed the room to pour himself a Scotch.

'Do I detect something in your voice?'

'Don't tell me you didn't notice?'

'What?'

'He's hot on you.'

'I don't think so, Drew.'

'*Come on*, Jackie.'

'He probably sees me in a big-sisterly sort of way.'

Drew laughed. 'Oh, no . . . not at all.'

'He's not much more than a boy.'

'Some boy!' He raised his eyebrows and laughed again. 'Anyway, a little healthy competition never did anyone any harm.'

'All right, joke over – now let's talk about something else; I've got enough problems as it is.'

'Have it your own way.' He shrugged. 'Like a drink?'

'Please.'

'You haven't said thank you, yet . . .' he gestured at the flowers which decorated the room.

She frowned and then her mouth moved into a sheepish smile. 'Sorry . . .'

'No big deal.'

'They are beautiful, Drew.' She leaned down to the nearest vase of red roses.

'No smell, hon'.'

'Doesn't matter . . .' she said softly, taking her drink from him, 'they're still beautiful. And you didn't forget the name of my favourite champagne, either.'

'I could never do that,' he grinned and thought of Angela. 'Seems like it's been a long day.'

'Too long.' She smiled ruefully at him. 'I'm sorry about this morning and for the hiccup this evening.'

'It's okay,' he said, 'not your fault.'

He took the glass from her hand and placed his hands on either side of her waist.

'And we still have the rest of the evening – and the rest of the night . . .'

Her mouth tilted upwards into a dry smile.

'I do have to work in the morning, Drew.'

His hands slipped inside her sweater. Upwards.

'I know, I know . . .'

'And I have to make a phone call later . . .'

He made no answer as he found her breasts, was immediately rewarded by the parting of her lips, her head falling back so that he was able to caress her neck with his mouth.

'That big blonde kid's hot on you . . .' he murmured, and she felt the mocking curve of his grin against her throat.

'Don't . . .'

'I bet right now he's thinking about you – us – ' Drew pulled the sweater over her head and slid his hands across her back and round to the opening of her jeans, 'trying to imagine what I'm doing . . . except that he can't.'

'Stop it . . .'

But he didn't want to stop now, he was enjoying himself too much. He liked her protest and her discomfort, he liked the erotic image he had painted in his head of the beautiful boy and Jackie. The image took him back, back . . . to Angela, because that was what he wanted. Oh, sweet Jesus, more than anything.

He kissed her deeply, squeezing his eyes tight shut and moving against her, creating a delicious friction.

'That big boy would like to do this, wouldn't he, hon' – wouldn't he?'

She pushed him abruptly away. 'I said *stop*.' Jackie's eyes were over-bright and she was looking at him with hurt and anger, as if asking why he wanted to say such things.

Drew felt his erection die and he swallowed uneasily. 'What did I do?'

'You don't know?'

'Hey – it was a joke. I was kidding.'

She watched him in silence for a long moment.

'I'm sorry.' He took a step towards her and gently gripped her bare shoulders. 'Okay?'

'It wasn't funny,' she said quietly.

'I said I'm sorry, and I meant it.' He took off his jacket and draped it around her.

Jackie looked up into his face: he looked wounded, as if she had done the hurting and she wondered tiredly if she hadn't overreacted. Her gaze moved to the roses and the champagne and she wondered how the day had gone so bad so easily. That vivid picture of Max and Yvonne slid unhappily into her mind and she felt soiled and depressed.

An oppressive feeling from the past with her mother crept over her, and she saw again the black and white photograph of a rotting apple her mother always pinned up on top of a newspaper cutting of her father in each dressing room they ever occupied. The image of that rotting apple suddenly loomed too large and she felt a little sick. Jackie leaned her head against Drew's shoulder and closed her eyes. She didn't want to think about that any more.

FIVE

The table was laid, the candles lit, the Krug Grande put on ice. Angela took a step back and surveyed the scene, then lifted her head to look at her reflection in the ornate mirror on the wall opposite. When Dougie arrived he had practically swooned into her arms with relief and lust. And she did look good; good enough to eat.

She was wearing her latest favourite: a long, lush, semi-transparent sarong by Donna Karan. As soon as she had seen the blue-on-black vibrant material floating towards her along the catwalk she knew she must have it. Naturally she was buck-naked underneath. Her hands moved to her breasts and she touched them gently, lovingly, reassuring herself of their firmness, their uplift which had been aided considerably by a little 'nip and tuck' of surgery two months previously. And there was Dougie, her lover of six long years – flabby and paunchy with a set of varicose veins like a road map. Not a pretty sight when he was in shorts. Angela frowned; even when she closed her eyes it was getting difficult to imagine that he was Tom Cruise or Patrick Swayze as Dougie huffed and puffed on top of her, trying to tuck his little old thing inside her.

She smiled then, but not with kindness and Drew's face slid inevitably into her mind: it was Drew she imagined, Drew's body, no one else, simply Drew.

Angela reached for a forbidden cigarette. She had met him at a girlfriend's party and it had been like David all over again, crazy irrational passion, but Drew was dark where David had been fair, and she loved that darkness, that beautiful combination of Italian black hair with dusky skin – flesh that drove her wild, except that Drew was no Italian and had no connection with the wealthy Carocci family as he had claimed. Drew was in fact almost stone broke. She had found out soon enough, after all – she checked everything – but it hadn't mattered in the least at the time, actually it had amused her and there had been reluctant admiration for the very clever fictitious background he had woven for himself. And she had thought that he would be another minor affair, another beautiful boy to entertain her for a brief moment in time, but Drew had turned out to be different.

There was no future with someone like Drew, a nobody, not forgetting that he was years younger than she was. She would be laughed out of Virginia, let alone the Knickerbocker Club and, no doubt, the committee for the April in Paris Ball. After all, she was a doyenne of American society, *the* darling of the society gossip columns and her name literally shone in the annals of charity – all ninety-seven of them. The large sums of money she had dropped into the coffers of deserving trusts over the years were not only tax deductible, more important, they bought her social status and a place on the exclusive charity circuit of galas, openings and exhibitions. A match with Dougie could only enhance her position, but Drew . . . no, it was impossible.

Angela squashed her cigarette out in the nearest ashtray. She would make sure Dougie gave her the best when Miriam, his sickly wife of thirty years, died. He was afraid to divorce her – afraid of the scandal and the ruin of his political career, if so much as a breath of his affair with her should reach the press.

She poured herself a large martini and thought of her proposed marriage, because Dougie had promised her marriage one day and she would make sure that's exactly what she got.

She swallowed a mouthful of the ice-cold martini and turned her thoughts reluctantly to her daughter; once she was married to Dougie, Jackie could have her precious money and produce her precious musical because it wouldn't matter then, even if her new husband was a Democrat, lover of the Kennedys and hero-worshipper of those brief, Camelot days of JFK. Now was not the time to let Jackie push the legend and naturally the dubious life – and death – of Marilyn Monroe once more into the glare of publicity and embarrass the Kennedys. Not again.

Besides, no one had ever made a musical on Monroe's life work. She was doing Jackie a favour by not releasing the trust-fund money.

Angela drew a deep breath; she had never liked hurting Jackie, it just happened quite naturally, her daughter seemed to

have that effect on her. Jackie had always been in the way somehow and nothing had changed that over the years.

'Won't be a moment, sugar . . . ' Dougie's nasal tones called
to her from the confines of the bathroom; he was still freshening-
up and supper would be ruined if he didn't show his round little
face soon. So much for home-cooking.

She had never pretended that she had been a good mother,
perhaps any sort of a mother, simply because she was too selfish.
There was a lot of garbage talked about motherhood bringing
happiness and fulfilment; she had not wanted to be a mother and
had never experienced the pangs of longing for a fat little bundle
of joy. Having Jackie had brought her no joy, only trouble and
grief, and from the very beginning. Her daughter was too much
like David, she even looked like him – tall, fair, lovely in a cold
sort of way, a little like Grace Kelly in her heyday. No wonder
they got on so well, no wonder that she really didn't like either of
them – love, perhaps, but her love was of the other kind, the sort
that ran parallel to her old friend jealousy, and possession –
something akin to hate. Not a nice way to love.

She heard Dougie's footsteps drawing closer and she glanced
at the doorway, waiting for the right moment to fix a broad,
dazzling smile on her face.

'It's perfect, Brian.' Jackie grinned at her stage designer. 'And
no real problems?'

'I fiddled with the model a long time until I got it right.' He
flicked a switch. 'It turned out not to be as complicated as I'd
originally thought and, after all, it doesn't have to be three-
dimensional, which makes it easier. I hope you don't mind about
the introduction of the sliding doors . . .'

'Not at all – I wish I'd thought of it myself.' She turned enthusi-
astically to Jamie. The planned dais would propel Marilyn
Monroe gently forward at the scene of the Birthday Salute at
Madison Square Garden. 'Do you see, Jamie? Monroe will be
behind these doors which will be black, merging invisibly into the
background. She will stand several feet from the stage floor on
the long dais, which will move slowly forward towards the audience once the doors slide apart.'

Jamie nodded. Fortunately he had read the biography Jackie

had given him and realized the sort of impression she was trying to create at that particular moment in the dead film-star's life: a very drunken, humiliating, but nevertheless glittering moment.

'I also want the nearest box, A, stage left, to be made out of bounds to the public and anyone else because that will become "the presidential box" . . .'

Brian smiled. 'Are you going to find yourself a John Kennedy lookalike?'

'As near as damn it, although it won't matter too much as the lights will be dim. You know that he was unescorted that famous night, the First Lady was in Virginia – horse riding – unless you want to count Robert Kennedy and his wife.'

'Nothing like playing gooseberry . . .'

'Now that, Brian, was something the president *never* did. Besides,' she added, 'it's a widely held view that Robert Kennedy was also having an affair with Monroe and probably at much the same time as his brother, or at least the affairs overlapped. If anyone was playing "gooseberry" that night, it was Ethel Kennedy.'

'I had heard something like that, but it's hard to believe that men holding such high office could be so damned foolhardy.' He shook his head and smiled, 'I have my time cut out just keeping my wife happy . . .'

'So you don't see any problems with this set-up?'

'No – the dais will be tricky, but it can work and I love the idea,' he said. 'As for Kennedy's box I expect you'll want a nice fat garland attached to the front?'

'Red, white and blue.'

'Naturally – I'll have a word with Yvonne, that's more her area.'

'Fine. But apart from that, I don't want any more colour, nothing to draw the eye away from Monroe – or Rose – and her rendering of "Happy Birthday" and "Thanks for the Memory". The doors and dais should both be in matt black and any other background – simply black.' Jackie turned to Jamie who was staring down at the model. 'The main reason I want this moment in Monroe's career particularly highlighted is because it was her last memorable public appearance – and on behalf of President Kennedy as it happens. She wore an extraordinary dress that

94

evening, especially made for the occasion: a shimmering creation embroidered with rhinestones so that she would literally shine in the spotlight, but made from extremely thin, almost transparent, material. It's obvious that she wanted the thousands of people watching, and one man in particular, to see that she wore absolutely nothing underneath.'

'She was desperate, wasn't she?' Jamie said.

Jackie shot a glance at him. 'Yes.'

'And she was taken advantage of.'

'Yes, that too, but you shouldn't forget that she was also ambitious enough to take advantage of other people.'

'If that's all, Jackie . . .' Brian said, gently interrupting, '. . . I'll get along and see Max.'

'Fine, and I'll expect a call on Friday?'

'Of course.' He smiled and gave Jamie a nod before leaving the office.

'I worked with Brian on another production,' she said, turning back to Jamie, 'and it was not only a huge bonus, but a relief to have a stage designer of his talent and calming temperament around.'

'I can see that . . .' he replied and his thoughts swept instantly backwards over his first day and the many different people he had met, the noise, the colour, the atmosphere – a world he had never dreamed existed, at least not for himself.

'I know you will probably think that the first day, the first week and probably the first month here will be like working in a madhouse, but all successful theatre – particularly the musical – depends on excellent teamwork, and despite what may seem like chaos, that is exactly what is happening here.' She smiled warmly and Jamie's gaze was drawn to her lips and rested there. She wore no lipstick but did not need to: her mouth was unusually deep in colour, and wide, the lower lip slightly plumper than the upper.

Jackie blushed as she caught his glance and was reminded unhappily of the night before, and Drew, and what he had said. They had made up finally and Drew had told her again and again that he had 'only been kidding'. Later he had made love to her sweetly and gently, as if she were frail and delicate, and at the end of the passion, and the love, she had forgiven him and he had asked her to marry him. She paused, reflecting, and took a deep gulp of air; it still had not sunk in, even now, but she had told him that they would wait until *Marilyn* opened and talk about it again. It was too soon after their reconciliation, wasn't it, to take such a step?

She found herself looking at Jamie. Of course Drew was wrong about him; he was not much more than a boy and an unworldly one at that, *and* he was six years younger than she was.

'Theatre promotion . . .' she said too quickly, flipping over the cover of the large portfolio on her desk, '. . . something I haven't even mentioned yet.' She turned a page. 'This is the *Marilyn* logo, or symbol if you like, of the musical.'

Jamie disciplined himself to study the two cleverly merged faces which looked back at him. The design had been adapted from a photograph taken of Monroe in 1954 after her breakup from Joe DiMaggio: her eyes were closed, a hand was brought up partly to shield the unhappy face, but the other face showed her laughing, head thrown back, lush red lips brilliantly set into a dazzling, provocative smile. The picture was drawn in lines of velvet black, except for the mouths which were painted with a vibrant shade of crimson.

'You're trying to convey the two sides of her life?'

'Yes.' She flipped another page. 'We're using the same design on the CD sleeve and cassette. The posters have already been printed and there are quite a few displayed in tube stations and more to come on the sides of buses, so keep your eyes peeled for them – we've also got some T-shirts under way.'

'Who does this sort of thing?' he asked, 'and where did you get the ideas from?'

She smiled at his genuine interest. 'I thought about the basic idea some time ago and then took it to a freelance graphic designer friend who polished it up and did the rest. But, generally, such jobs are given to ad agencies, like Dewynter's, who do everything – at a nice price, of course. As it is, the poster campaign alone will cost in the region of twenty-five thousand pounds.'

She glanced at her watch. 'Look, I have to meet Aldo and Max now, why don't you come along because we're on the last lap of auditioning the short list for Monroe's husbands and the other men who figured prominently in her life.' Jackie closed the portfolio. 'It can be an agonizing process, so I won't be offended if you decide at some point that you've had enough and take a break, because you just might need it!'

They walked out of the office together and down the long narrow corridor to the studio. As they approached Jamie could already hear a song being sung, but then it was halted abruptly and someone laughed. When he stepped into the studio the girl who had been singing was waiting by the piano as the musical director began the first notes again. When her voice grew and lifted into the room he could hardly believe that such power, such beauty could come from the small girl who stood in front of them.

'That's our Marilyn Monroe,' Jackie whispered, 'meet Rose Lyle,' and then as the music developed she nodded her head in recognition, 'She's singing "Late-Night Phone Calls" – the last song in the show.'

Jamie listened to the words which conjured so well the last hours of the dead star's life. Lonely pathetic hours. He found himself wondering whether it would not have been better if she had never craved the spotlight or dreamed of having the dubious honour of being famous and a sex symbol. Quite clearly it had never made her happy and certainly not content. Yet she had become a phenomenon, a legend.

By the time he had finished reading the biography Jackie had given him, he felt only pity for the 'dream girl', 'the goddess' and nothing but contempt for Hollywood and the brittle world of the film industry. He shrugged inwardly; perhaps he did not fully understand or appreciate all the complexities involved, but he realized quite suddenly that neither did he want to.

Rose finished and the few people who were in the studio applauded. Jamie took a seat at the back of the room as Jackie began talking to the musical director and Max Lockhart who stood by the piano. Rose left and Aldo disappeared through a side door, reappearing with the first shortlisted artist who waited nervously in the centre of the floor as the musical director moved back to the piano.

'Joe DiMaggio – *one*,' someone called.

He was a tall man with a long thin face and large nose who had narrowly missed being ugly. The first notes were struck once, twice, three times before the man, Ian, was able to get into the song which had been written for Monroe's second husband, Joe DiMaggio, but then he stopped again and shook his head with obvious irritation. Jamie saw Max shift restlessly in his chair and Aldo smile encouragingly as the song was begun yet again, and found himself offering up a small prayer for the painfully nervous Ian. But Ian managed it in the end and his voice was good, even very good.

Five others followed and then there was a short break and a further six men auditioned for the part of Arthur Miller, Monroe's third and last husband. Jamie watched as Jackie, Max and the two lyricists made notes and he wondered at their patience and what, exactly, they were looking for, because each artist seemed to sing well and each one, for him, needed a second hearing as their faces began to blur and their voices merge.

Finally, he stood up, feeling a little stiff, and moved out into the corridor intent on getting himself something to eat and a large mug of something hot and sweet. His coat, a sheepskin he had borrowed from David, was still in Jackie's office and he was glad of its warmth as he moved out of the building and into the busy street.

He turned right and towards the neon-lit theatres of Shaftes-bury Avenue. There was a small hamburger bar next to a news-paper stand and he stopped, caught by the smell of frying onions, and went inside. This would be his second hamburger ever. His godmother had bought him the first when she was showing him around London several weeks ago and he had been waiting for an opportunity to sample another. Jamie stood patiently by the window as he waited for his order, glancing through the dusty glass out into the street.

A man was hailing a cab on the other side of the road; he was wearing a white jacket and sunglasses despite the fact that there was no sun. Jamie watched Drew's tanned American face grin as the cab stopped, and saw how he held out his arm and circled the girl who stood beside him. Her hair was short and dark and even from where Jamie was standing he could see the glint from the huge hooped silver earrings she had worn in the studio. Rose

Lyle tilted her face towards Drew and smiled eagerly as she climbed into the back seat of the car.

'You can have anything you like.'

Rose looked at Drew and felt a delicious chill run up her back.

'I mean from the menu – naturally . . .' His mouth slid into a meaningful grin and they both laughed.

'I'll have the avocado soup with croutons to start, followed by the *tortellini della nonna*, my favourite – it's laced with lashings of cream . . .'

'I think I'll just settle for the steak Diane.'

'I don't have to watch what I eat, you see,' she said apologetically. 'Max Lockhart told me that he'd like me to put on a bit of extra weight for the part.'

'It wouldn't hurt,' Drew said, 'after all, sex goddesses are supposed to be curvy . . .'

She blushed and her eyes fell mournfully to her small breasts which hardly protruded through the thin material of her blouse.

He snapped his fingers to the nearest waiter, gave their order and asked for the wine list.

'White or red?'

'I don't mind . . . really.'

He sighed inwardly. 'How about some champagne?'

She gasped audibly with pleasure, his previous lack of tact forgotten.

Drew scanned the page and his eyes came to rest on the heading 'Sparkling Wines'. There was not much choice: Lanson Black Label, Asti Spumante, or 'House Sparkling' – whatever the hell that was. He flicked a glance at Rose; she probably wouldn't even know the difference.

'Number thirty-one,' he said to the waiter who hovered at his elbow; there was a first time for everything – even 'House Sparkling'. Angela would have known the difference, of course, but then he would never take her to a place like this, not a pseudo-Italian joint with plastic vine leaves hanging from the ceiling.

'You know, I could hardly eat a thing once they told me I'd got the part, I was so keyed up and excited . . .' Rose's words ran on, 'but now my appetite has come back with a vengeance.'

Drew smiled automatically.

'Did you see my picture in the paper today?'

He shook his head.

'No?' Disappointment flitted across her face. 'Oh, well . . . anyway – I could hardly believe it!' She smiled hugely and plunged onwards: ' "Dazzling new talent to play Marilyn" . . . it didn't seem possible that they were actually talking about me – of all people!' She brought her hand nervously to her mouth and realized just in time that she was about to start biting her nails.

'You deserve it,' he said easily, 'and I'll ask Jackie for a copy of the article.'

'You don't need to do that.' Her cheeks were pinking again.

'Why not? I'd like to.'

The waiter placed a bucket full of half-melted watery ice beside them and plunged the 'House Sparkling' into it.

'This is so nice of you, Drew.'

It had been a long, long time since anyone had called him 'nice', if they ever had – 'sexy', 'cute', 'macho', even 'mean' perhaps, but definitely not 'nice'.

'Think nothing of it.' He took a mouthful of his 'champagne'. 'Maybe we could have dinner one night, and really celebrate?' Jackie needn't know, not if he were careful, after all she was going to be neck-high in work, which would mean that he would only be in the way, more than that, he would be bored. He stared at his glass and watched as his fingers tightened around the fragile stem.

He had thought that Jackie would jump at the chance of marrying him, and she had told him to wait! Hadn't he asked her at that moment because he had felt her slipping away after that stupid scene she had made over what he had said about Jamie Thurley?

His gaze shifted from the glass to the girl opposite and he felt his mouth move into a practised smile, except that the smile felt stiff and hard as if the skin might break.

Rose flushed again as he looked at her, dropping her lashes demurely over her eyes.

Drew wanted to laugh; she was playing the innocent, but some instinct on which he had always relied told him quite the opposite. Rose was one of those girls who didn't know how to, or just couldn't, say 'no' to a guy. She was like a piece of rubber, infinitely pliable, hopelessly stretching and flexing in order to suit her man of the moment: the sort of girl who believed everything you said, the sort of girl who called *you* instead of the other way round – the pathetic 'puppy-dog' type who gave you everything you thought you wanted until you were sick of it.

A white basin filled with steaming pale green soup and sprinkled with a few over-crisped croutons distracted him as it was placed before the obviously delighted Rose.

'My flatmate has a recipe for this . . .'

'You have an apartment?'

'Well, I share the rent.'

'Where is it?'

'Kentish Town.'

He had never heard of it.

'Sometimes I say Camden – sounds better,' she said, 'but once I start getting my new salary I plan to change a few things, which includes a move.' Gingerly she brought a spoonful of the hot soup to her mouth. 'They were quite generous at Madam Jo Jo's, where I used to work, considering that my act really needed polishing up, but all I've ever wanted to do is act or sing. I was lucky Max Lockhart was in the audience that night he spotted me.'

'Fate, Rose . . .'

'Yes, I know,' she sighed happily. 'Actually, I've learnt a lot about all that tarot stuff, astrology, that sort of thing. A friend of mine can really read signs; she says you can learn quite a bit about a person just by looking at their palm.' She placed her spoon back in the pale green soup and held out her hand. 'See, I've got a very strong Fate line, runs right up the middle of my hand; supposed to be lucky . . .'

Drew took hold of the proffered hand and began spreading out her slim pale fingers one by one. 'Pretty hands.'

She swallowed as their eyes locked and he began to stroke the centre of her palm. The muscles of her abdomen jumped and she was sure a volt of electricity passed between them.

'I bet you're a Leo . . .' she said softly.

'Why do you say that?'

'Because you're warm and generous . . .' the flush was back in her cheeks '. . . and strong and sort of dangerous-looking.'

He made no answer.

'Am I right?' she probed.

'Right,' he lied. What did it matter? He was a Sagittarian, born on a cold, wet December day in good ole Crenshaw, North Carolina.

'Really?'

He nodded.

She shook her head in wonderment. 'You know, I've never done that before.' She looked at him eagerly. 'Can you guess what I am?'

Still holding her hand Drew picked up his glass and took a large mouthful of the wine. 'Couldn't begin to try, hon'.'

Her heart leapt at the casual endearment, as if it were the deepest compliment. 'I'm a Cancerian,' she said quickly, 'you know, the Crab, and I'm really typical: strong psychic feeling, creative, intuitive, fertile . . .' She giggled.

'I'm surprised some guy hasn't snapped you up by now.' He let go of her hand.

'I was engaged once, but it didn't work out.'

Drew smiled sympathetically. 'Maybe after this we could go and relax somewhere . . .' He had the whole afternoon to kill and probably a good part of the evening once Jackie finally decided to leave the goddamn studio and return to the hotel. His thoughts switched inevitably back to the night before and that irritating image of her hurt, questioning face. He had asked her to marry him and she had practically turned him down. Another spasm of disbelief coursed through him, followed closely by dislike. Jackie had humiliated him, hadn't she, and let him down?

'I'm supposed to be back at the studio for 4.30,' Rose said quickly and stared nervously into the bowl of pale green soup; she had not anticipated this would happen quite so soon. But he was older, more experienced, more sophisticated and perhaps he expected her to be as relaxed as he was about it. Her eyes shifted to the heavy gold ring on his little finger, to the carefully clipped nails and beautiful brown hands. She thought he was the most attractive man she had ever seen.

'Maybe . . .' she hesitated.

Her voice cut into his thoughts and he looked back at her with barely concealed boredom.

He shrugged. 'Some other time, then.'

'It's just . . .' she stammered anxiously.

'Eat your soup, it's getting cold.'

At Drew's elbow the waiter arrived pushing a small trolley in preparation for the steak Diane. The tender fillets of beef were sautéed in a large pan and then flamed in too much brandy and sherry. Drew felt heat on his face and wondered if the waiter carried a fire extinguisher under his trolley every time he did his little trick.

Rose felt panic as Drew fixed his attention on the extravagant performance of the waiter, as if she had lost him. 'No, really, I'd like to.'

He turned slowly back to look at her. 'Not if you have something else on your mind.'

'I won't – I mean, I don't.'

He examined her sharply for several seconds and her heart sank because she thought he had changed his mind.

'Naturally I'll make sure you're back for 4.30; after all, you know that the successful outcome of *Marilyn* means as much to me as it does to you. I'm on the US side of things, don't forget.'

'I know, I'm sorry.'

He grinned, the big white smile lighting up his handsome face and Rose felt her knees grow weak.

'I don't see how you could have forgotten,' David said reproachfully, 'the arrangements were made weeks ago.'

Jackie sighed and said lamely, 'It simply slipped my mind.'

'Clare's birthday and our anniversary?'

'I know, I know – it's just been so busy.' She pushed her hair back from her face. 'It's not only been work, but trying to arrange my move from the hotel, and personal things . . .' She thought of Drew.

'I can work all that out for myself.' He scrutinized her carefully. 'This is important, Jackie.'

She returned his gaze sheepishly. Her father looked well, a little windswept, but fit nevertheless, despite the fact that he was frowning. He and Clare had decided several months ago to celebrate her stepmother's birthday and their twentieth wedding anniversary by holding a black-tie dinner, followed by dancing at

Annabel's. The last time Clare had telephoned – ten days ago, a week? – Jackie had even discussed what she might wear.

'Yes – of course I'll be there,' she said finally.

'Good girl,' he said, 'I didn't really think you'd let us down.'

'Are you on the way to the theatre now?'

'Yes, I'm seeing the matinée again. It will be the last opportunity I'll have before the show closes and work on the film version begins.'

'You're excited, aren't you?'

He grinned and she thought there was still a trace of the boyish in him.

'Best thing I've been offered in years.' In truth he had argued and pleaded and pestered for the part until he got it. About a Scots tenant farmer who murders his neighbour over the disputed ownership of a small stretch of river, *The Wound* was a traumatic story of passion, outrage and extraordinary anger.

'What does Clare think?'

His gaze shifted uneasily to the window. 'Oh, she's pleased, naturally.'

'But it will mean hard work and long hours and she knows you're not getting any younger?' Jackie said wryly.

'Something like that.'

'And it will be very, very cold in Scotland at this time of the year.'

'Please, Jackie, not you as well.' He noticed that the sky was fading to a measureless expanse of grey as it stole into evening and he longed, suddenly, for a drink that would burn his mouth and spread warmth through his limbs.

'How's Jamie getting along?' he asked, dismissing the subject.

'Fine.'

'He's a good boy, but unlike Clare, I don't harbour any illusions about this job, at least with regard to his future.'

'Perhaps it's too soon to say.'

'Perhaps, but all this . . .' he gestured with his arm, 'is so different from what he's used to.'

'Give him a chance,' she said, 'he's adapting very well.'

'I suppose I'm thinking of his social life, or lack of it, really. He reads, talks to Clare – or me if I'm there – then as often as not takes a long, and I mean long, walk on the Heath.'

'Sounds healthy enough to me.'

David waved a hand again in exasperation. 'But there's more to life than that – he's only twenty-four, for heaven's sake. I've even tried to encourage him to join some sort of club so that he can meet some new people – you know squash, or chess, anything.'

'I think you're rushing things a bit.'

He smiled. 'I said that to Clare.'

'There you are then.'

'I don't suppose . . . ?' He gave her a searching look.

'No, Daddy.'

'Well, you are near his age.'

'Not really,' she said quickly, 'anyway, I'm far too busy, and besides I hardly have time for my own personal life.'

David's eyebrows lifted heavenwards in surprise. 'What "personal life" is this?' he probed.

'Aren't we now getting off the subject?'

'Just a little,' he grinned mischievously, 'but I am your father, after all.'

She started to laugh and then added, 'I have a meeting in exactly five minutes.'

'You're trying to get rid of me.'

Jackie slipped a file under her arm and kissed him lightly on the cheek. 'I'll see you on Saturday.'

'Seven-thirty.'

'I won't forget.'

He watched her go and was caught by a surge of pride. Twenty years ago he had met her for the first time: Jackie, aged nine, walking from customs and into the arrival hall at Heathrow. He would have known her without the name-card pinned neatly to her lapel; she had been tall even then, fair, blue-eyed, wary. Like looking at himself. He had been pierced by pity and a fierce desire to protect and save her, his child, except that it had seemed a little late for that then.

A dozen grey stone steps led up to a shabby front door. There was a small square pane of broken glass in the centre, and beneath that a brass door knocker in the shape of a lion's head which had been allowed to turn green from neglect.

'It's just temporary,' Rose said, avoiding his eyes, but wondering at the same time why she had never noticed before how tacky it really was.

Drew did not reply, but his nostrils twitched just slightly in disgust; it had been a long time since he had been anywhere near a place like this. He tried to lose his thoughts, but unquiet echoes floated out of the dusty cracks of his memory and he was reminded, unhappily, of his mother.

'It's not bad, if you can ignore all of this – ' Rose added quickly and then gave a nervous laugh as they walked into the narrow confines of a porch, over old mail and advertising garbage which littered the floor, and passed a line of empty grimy milk bottles. 'There are at least eight other people living in this house besides Babs and me – you'd think someone would bother to pick this stuff up. We tried and gave up . . .'

'Hey, it's okay.'

She looked at him for an instant with a kind of gratitude.

'We're lucky with the flat, though, it's really quite large,' she heard her voice running on as she walked up the stairs, feeling his eyes on her back. 'Babs did the decorating – she's an art student and has much more of an eye for colour than I do.' She stopped before a door with a payphone fixed beside it on the wall and patted it affectionately. 'Couldn't be more convenient, really.'

'I guess not.'

'My agent has promised to pay for the installation of a real phone once I move from here, as a sort of present for getting *Marilyn*.'

She began fishing anxiously in her bag for her keys and finally pulled them out with an audible sigh of relief. 'I'm always losing them.' She slipped the key into the Yale lock and closed her eyes with exasperation because she had turned it the wrong way as she always did. When she flicked open her eyes she made a conscious effort to still her racing heart and the nerves that were beginning to dance in her stomach.

Drew watched the white, trembling fingers and her clumsy attempt at unlocking the door and felt the muscles in his neck and jaw begin to bunch up with irritation. His gaze switched restlessly to the empty, paint-chipped stairwell; there was a faint smell of damp and he drew a sharp wary breath as an old feeling of depression began to sneak up on him.

'Got it,' she said over-brightly, as the door swung open, 'come on in.'

A massive print of Sting in John Lennon spectacles glared back at him from above a chest of drawers on which stood a small Snoopy lamp. There was an Indian rag-rug on the floor with most of the tassels missing. He followed her through a curtain of wooden beads into the sitting room where Rose quickly plumped cushions and moved a pile of magazines into an acceptable heap. She shook her head and opened her hands in a gesture of apology. 'I didn't know you'd be coming . . .'

He thought, meanly, that it wouldn't have made much difference if she had. 'You don't have a drink, do you?'

Her eyebrows came together in a frown. 'There's a bottle of Lambrusco in the fridge.'

'Lambrusco?'

'It's wine . . . well, fizzy wine, if you know what I mean?' She smiled hesitantly. 'I'll get a couple of glasses and you can try it.'

The wooden beads jangled as she disappeared through the doorway and he sat down into the creaking arms of a bamboo chair. There was a round glass coffee table in the middle of the sitting area with a two-seater sofa on one side and another bamboo chair on the other. In an alcove, near the two-bar electric fire, was a portable television set with a stereo underneath and a stack of old albums going right back to the ass-end of nowhere. Drew picked up one of the sleeves and just recognized the slick made-up face of Boy George complete with dreadlocks. He dropped it on the floor in disgust and leaned back his head and his eyes strayed to the glass coffee table and the magazines and a patchwork of ring marks from mugs of coffee. He lifted his gaze to the wall nearest the door and the multi-coloured shawl which someone had pinned across the bland yellow wallpaper. A large green plant, its leaves coated in a thin film of dust, stood underneath.

'I don't expect you'll like it . . .' Rose walked back through the bead curtains bearing two glasses. 'It's just something we keep in the flat for when we're having a night in.' She sighed inwardly because the bottle of Lambrusco had been Babs' and she would have to replace it before she returned at the weekend.

Drew took a sip of the pink liquid. 'It's like drinking soda-pop.'

'You mean lemonade.'

'Whatever you call it in English,' he said flatly and looked back at Rose, at her pretty face which was so anxious to please. 'Why don't we take it where we'll be more comfortable?'

Her heart jumped in quick and sudden panic.

'That's what you want . . .' his voice was low, intimate, 'isn't it?'

He put down his glass and held out his hand to her. She stepped hesitantly towards him and he stood up.

'You're as nervous as hell, aren't you?'

She nodded and he closed his arms around her, pulling her into his chest.

'No need to be, hon',' he said. 'I won't bite.' Not much, anyway.

The curtains were still closed in her bedroom, shutting out much of the light, but he could see the outline of the narrow, unmade bed and the dozens of soft toys, mostly teddy-bears, sitting on, and in, every available space. As he closed the door behind him he was confronted with a score or more of postcards pinned to the surface, all of them picturing teddy-bears in various shapes and sizes. As Rose switched on the bedside lamp his attention was drawn to a poster above the small ornamental fireplace: it was an old one of Ali Magraw and Ryan O'Neil with the caption, 'Love means never having to say you're sorry.'

She began to take off her clothes as he instructed, a little stiffly, but obediently, like a child. As he lifted her on to the bed her eyes focused on his and she thought that they were grave, dark, heavy with meaning.

It was over very quickly. There had been no desire or necessity on his part to prolong their sex; he had hardly heard her soft moans, or felt the caress of her fingers stroking his cheek, his neck, his back; he had hardly felt *her* at all. But there was curious pleasure in the knowledge that it had been longer than he could remember since he had been able, simply, to please himself alone.

Rose clung to him in the semi-darkness, all worries and doubts cast away: she had the lead role in *Marilyn*, she would be a star, everyone said so and now she had met Drew. With a small, happy sigh she traced a forefinger lightly through the hairs on his chest and then lifted eyes full of raw adoration into his closed face. Rose blushed and her heart pounded; she felt soft and utterly exposed and she thought she had never been so happy.

Dougie's wife was dead. Across the throng of glittering people who had come for the wake Angela could just see the top of Dougie's head. She made her way through the large, sunlit foyer and into the neo-Spanish salon which had been Miriam's pride and joy – her delightful hideaway near San Marino.

Angela was touched, suddenly, by a twinge of shame because she had longed for this moment; it had only been Dougie's wife who had stood in the way of her purpose through six tedious years of playing cat and mouse. But it wasn't her fault that Miriam had died, she told herself, no one's fault, just bad luck – which had turned out, very nicely, thank you, to be good luck for her.

She smoothed down the navy shot-silk Arnold Scaasi she had had made especially for the anticipated occasion months ago; it was superbly tailored, if a little dull. In fact she had actually hesitated over black, almost conceding that it was the least she could do under the circumstances, but it had never been her colour – and so ageing!

A faint smile of satisfaction tipped the edges of her mouth as she stood under the wide archway of the open doors because it was like looking into a sea of the rich, the powerful, the famous, or attending the Opera Ball which had been gatecrashed by a political rally: the Kissingers stood by the terrace with the Sinatras just to their right, and behind them Jessie Jackson, Ann Getty, the Schwarzeneggers, Teddy Kennedy, Dan Quayle, Michael Eisner, Paloma Picasso . . . This was what her sacrifice had been about, all the subterfuge and the boredom, and the waiting and waiting and waiting – in six months, perhaps a year, she would inherit all the 'friends', the dinner parties, the weekends, the top slot that poor Miriam had been unable to fill for so long. Well, it was an ill wind, or so they said . . .

She turned to a silver tray laden with only empty glasses and she frowned; her throat was dry and she had yet to be offered a glass of champagne from the dozen or so trays hovering about the salon – she made a mental note to discover the name of the caterers because they were obviously sloppy and that sort of thing would have to change once she and Dougie became 'official'.

A warm, comforting glow suffused her cheeks as she looked upwards at the brilliant white ceiling of the mouth-watering Spanish villa and then to the walls hung with seventeenth-century Córdoba leather panels, an idea that Miriam had copied from Rudolf Nureyev's apartment in Paris when they had had dinner there in '89, her last in Europe. Angela ran her hand across the lid of the hand-painted harpsichord which had been another 'Miriam acquisition', quite beautiful. She turned her face to an open window as the scent of oleander and jasmine poured into the salon from the tiered gardens sloping to the sea.

'Angela!'

A rotund woman in a dress which was too tight bounced up. 'How are yo-oo-u?'

'Fine, just fine, Dakota.' Privately she had always thought that 'Dakota' was an absurd name, like calling your child Twin Falls or West Virginia, and somehow it always reminded her of cowboys and chow and long-horned cattle. Dakota's eldest daughter was called Aspen, after *the* ski resort and where she had met Aspen's father, her first husband, who had killed himself two years into their marriage by jumping off the Golden Gate Bridge.

'And how is Dougie?' Her voice had become low and confidential.

'Why don't you ask him?'

'Oh, Angie – '

She hated being called Angie.

'– Don't be cute, you know what I mean.'

'No, I don't.'

Dakota's generous cheeks began to redden a little.

'I thought now that Miriam . . . you and . . .' Her words trailed off.

Angela made no answer; she had told no one about her relationship with Dougie and she was not about to start now. What people suspected, or chose to think, was another matter and something which she could do nothing about anyway. Someone like Dakota Greenbaum was the least of her worries. She drew a bored, silent breath and turned her attention to Dougie who was apparently deep in conversation with a brunette whom she did not immediately recognize. He was smiling, too warmly, and the woman was smiling back.

'How's Jackie?'

'Fine.'

'How's that musical of hers coming along?'

'It's not,' she replied, hard put to keep impatience out of her voice, 'lack of finance – it was a crazy idea anyhow.'

'But I heard from Jimmy Nederlander that it's going ahead; we had him over for dinner only a week ago.'

Jackie stared at Dakota full in the face. 'I think you're wrong.'

'He said that Jackie had called him about bringing the Monroe production to Broadway.'

Angela pressed down her anger and even managed to force a smile. 'What did he say?' Nederlander, with a chain of theatres and considerable financial resources, was, like the Shuberts, a byword for royalty on Broadway.

'Well, he said he laughed because she's so young and because he's only ever heard of a Monroe musical crashing – like it's jinxed – but he also said that he'd keep his options open.'

'He'd be wasting his time,' Angela said and reached for a glass.

'Don't you want her to succeed?' Dakota's mouth was almost hanging open in curiosity; she had heard that there was no love lost between Angela and her daughter.

'It would be like burning money, and not just her own.' And for a subject which irritated Angela more than she cared to admit – Marilyn Monroe, the blonde, dumb love goddess – which could screw up her chances with Dougie.

'I'm sure she won't do that; Jackie's a very talented girl.'

'But impulsive,' Angela added quickly, 'and musicals are always very risky, Dakota, you should know that.' Dakota's present husband, the bald, chinless Rubin, was a top producer, a big gun in theatreland. 'And I thought, unless Rubin misinformed me, that the heyday of the smash, international production is over.'

'Rubin didn't misinform you, Angela . . .' Dakota said defensively, dropping the 'Angie', and remembering, too vividly for comfort, the conversation Angela had had with Rubin over cocktails when he had been staring at Angela in a frankly speculative way, as if he were sizing up a potential mistress. Except that he would never stand a chance with Angela – he was too ugly, one of the factors which she had convinced herself would make marriage to Rubin a fairly safe bet. 'He also said that there *are* exceptions and as long as those great Broadway barns are standing, there'll always be someone who wants to put a musical in them.'

'I'd just rather it wasn't my daughter.'

'You're not being very positive – I always thought you liked crazy ideas and taking chances.'

'Let's forget it, shall we?' Angela smiled with an effort. 'Anyway, I'll be calling Jackie in a day or two – naturally I'll give her the benefit of my advice and support.' Like hell. And if she wasn't satisfied with her darling daughter's explanation, she might just book a flight to London and put a stop to this garbage once and for all.

Dakota rolled her champagne glass uneasily between her hands and then waved self-consciously at someone across the room.

'There's Marla Brinkner, Aspen's therapist. I didn't know she knew the Hicks . . .'

'It's a small world.'

There was an unmistakeable note of derision in Angela's voice and Dakota wondered what she could have done to offend her. She flushed.

'I'll catch up with you later, Angela . . .'

She watched her walk away, knowing she had been rude, but Angela didn't care, instead she switched her gaze back to the spot where Dougie had stood, but he had disappeared and she cursed silently, glancing sideways, looking for the brunette; then, as some people moved towards the terrace she saw him for a brief moment standing alone. Their eyes met and she walked towards him, noting with irritation the high colour seeping into his cheeks at her approach. Douglas Hicks the Third might be Governor of California, but he was sure lacking in the guts department.

'So sorry about Miriam, Dougie . . .'

He nodded sheepishly. 'Glad you could make it.' But he didn't sound very glad, he sounded embarrassed.

'You look tired.' Her lips moved into what she hoped was a good imitation of a sympathetic smile should anyone be watching. 'I hope you haven't been overdoing things.' He seemed to squirm and she found herself wanting to laugh.

'Lot of good people here,' he said.

'I can see that, Dougie,' she locked eyes with him, 'but too *hot*, don't you think?' Her voice was close to being husky.

'Now stop that, sugar . . .' he said under his breath.

'I only said it was hot, Dougie,' she murmured, 'just as well I didn't wear my panties . . .'

His eyes bulged slightly and she could see a thin film of sweat break out on his face.

'Can I introduce you to someone?' His voice was tight and he swallowed nervously.

'Only if you promise to come and see me – *soon*.'

'Tomorrow night?'

Her mouth slanted into a satisfied smile. 'Perfect.'

It was a beautiful speech and as her father sat down he lifted Clare's hand, palm uppermost, and kissed it tenderly. Jackie felt a lump gather in her throat; it was, she thought, more than just a touching gesture, it symbolized all she had ever wanted for her father – deep abiding contentment with one person – and almost all she had ever wanted for herself. But such a relationship, such love, was rare, even extremely rare, despite all the wishful thinking and junk that was spouted on the subject. It was, she supposed, like the chances of striking oil, or finding gold, and she smiled to herself because some words of an old song by Neil Young stole softly into her head – something about 'searching for a heart of gold . . .' Her smile faded as she thought of Drew.

It had been bad enough trying to explain to him why she was going to Clare's birthday dinner alone and she thought he had understood at first, but as the evening wore on his mood had changed and he had become sullen and withdrawn. Jackie had been tired and not in the mood to argue, and she was in the middle of trying to work on some notes. In the end she had allowed him to intrude on her concentration because he would not let the matter drop and her head had felt as if it were splitting open with the tension.

'There's nothing to it – really, Drew.'

'Then why can't I come too?'

'It was arranged months ago.'

'So?'

'It's a very formal, family thing . . .'

'What's that supposed to mean?'

'It doesn't *mean* anything.'

'Call your father and tell him I'm coming too.'

She had stared back at him for a long time. 'Why are you being so unreasonable?'

'Now *I'm* the one who's being unreasonable – Jesus-H-Christ!'

'Drew – they don't even know you exist!'

'Well, maybe it's about time they did.'

'Not tomorrow night.'

'Why the hell not?'

'Because it's Clare's night – *their* night – they've planned the guest list so that the numbers are just right, everyone is matched, the seating already arranged . . .'

'You mean a lady for every guy, don't you?'

She shook her head in exasperation and looked down at her clasped fingers.

'And who's *your* guy for the night?'

'Don't be ridiculous.'

'Oh, *come* on!'

'I'm going to finish these notes and then I'm going to run a bath because I can't seem to get through to you at all.'

A momentary shadow had crossed his face before he slumped down into an armchair to stare, unseeing, at the blank face of the television screen, but then he had abruptly stood up and walked out of the suite without a word.

The door slammed and the room seemed to reverberate with the sound of that door closing. She tried to return to her work, to ignore the silence and the empty chair, but gave up as a sense of hopelessness spread through her like a stain. He had understood none of the things she had said, refusing to come to terms with any of it.

He had returned much later and seemed calmer and in a more reasonable frame of mind. He poured himself a drink and then apologized, finally, for his impatience and lack of manners – it was a cultural difference that was the problem and the English love of formality. She had forgiven him, unable to bear his discomfort and the real sense of remorse she was sure he was feeling; it was only jealousy, after all. And he had made her feel a little guilty, hadn't he?

Drew had smiled then and kissed her greedily before ordering a lavish dinner. Finally they made love in the huge king-size bed. She could still hear his voice calling her name and touching her in all the places she loved, but she had had to close her eyes and concentrate very hard before the magic would come back.

More applause at the table cut through her reflections. She blinked and focused on the sixteen guests who sat at the glittering table; she knew most of them because they had all played some part in her father's, or Clare's, life, stepping in and out of her own at the same time over the years. Her gaze settled on Jamie Thurley, who looked back at her as if he had sensed her eyes. He matched her stare, for too long, and she felt herself blush.

She turned to her father who caught her glance and smiled, but there was something about the smile that wrenched at her heart, as if she were seeing him clearly for the first time in years and the proverbial veil had dropped from her eyes. All at once she realized that he was getting old. And she didn't want that, not ever. There was a tightness in her throat as she returned the smile he wanted, as she forced her eyes away to concentrate on the tiny champagne bubbles in her glass which rose up and up and up.

When the party reached Annabel's she tried hard to shake off the melancholia that had touched her without warning. Clare, who was a little drunk, bundled her into the ladies' cloakroom.

'Jackie, I haven't had the chance to say so – but that is a simply stunning gown!'

'After deciding I had nothing to wear, I dashed out on Thursday . . .' bearing in mind her father's timely reminder, 'and stayed out until I found something.' Thank God it had been late-night closing.

Clare looked back at her step-daughter, a touch awed by the Jackie who confronted her this evening.

'Darling, really, it's beautiful,' she said seriously, '*you're* beautiful.'

'Clare . . .' she said, 'you've had too much to drink.'

'No, I haven't!' Clare said dryly, 'Besides, haven't you learned yet how to accept a compliment graciously?'

'Thank you, stepmother,' Jackie responded, a little sheepishly, 'and before you ask, the dress is by Hidy Misawa – I picked it up in Selfridges.'

'It looks as if it could have been made for you.' And it was true, because the black lace and silk taffeta flattered Jackie's creamy colouring, the sensational shawl collar skimming the top of her arms, leaving her shoulders bare and dipping down to the pale swell of her breasts.

'Off the rail, I assure you. It's been ages since I've had a dress made. I simply don't have much time for anything these days.'

'Not even a man?'

'Daddy's been talking to you.'

'He just hinted.'

'There's nothing much to hint.' Jackie hesitated. 'Well, there *is* someone, but things haven't actually been straightforward lately.' Jackie looked back at her reflection in the mirror. 'But don't worry, I'll tell you should there be any developments you and Daddy need to know about.'

'You'd better, my girl!'

Jackie shook her head and laughed. 'Don't you think we should get back to the party?'

'Of course, of course.' Clare took her arm as they walked through the door. 'It just seems so long since we've managed to have a little talk. Can't you really forget *Marilyn* for a few hours and come and see us properly? Why don't you make just a little gesture of good will and come for lunch next weekend with this young man?'

'You are incorrigible.'

'I just thought I'd ask.'

'I'll think about it.'

They walked down the narrow carpeted corridor into the intimate darkness of the cocktail area and the dance floor beyond.

116

'That's not your father dancing . . . is it?'

David was gyrating madly in a far corner to the first of a medley of golden oldies by the Stones – 'Miss You'.

'Good God!' Clare exclaimed, 'it's been years since I saw him do anything like this.' She guided Jackie to their table. 'Let's have another glass of champagne, or perhaps we could sample one of the wonderful cocktails?'

Jackie looked at the surface of their table which was covered with an array of interesting drinks, flanked by two ice-filled buckets bearing Bollinger Reserve.

'I think, Clare, that Daddy has taken care of everything,' she said as she indicated the table.

'While you sample another glass of champagne, or whatever, I'll rescue him, because they're sure to play "Satisfaction" and I really don't want to have to take him home suffering from exhaustion so early in the evening!'

Jackie slipped into her chair and picked up a glass, softened and made happy by being with Clare; she wondered why she had left it so long since the last time they had spent some real time together. She smiled to herself in the semi-darkness, realizing her mood was passing, and looked across the table to old friends of her father's. They were holding hands, and she looked away and took another gulp of champagne, feeling a little giddy.

The music had changed and slowed. Jackie felt herself begin to relax as Barbra Streisand's 'Guilty' oozed gently through the speakers. She lent back in her chair as her thoughts began to swim and memories crowd in, and then realized with a little embarrassment that Jamie was sitting just to her left and she hadn't even noticed he was there.

'Having a good time?'

'I've never been to a place like this before.'

'It's not so bad, is it?'

'Oh, no.' He looked at her in the darkness.

'I expect it all feels very strange to you, but that's to be expected.'

'Not now,' he said. 'Everything is beginning to fall into place.'

She tilted her head on one side. 'You mean London – your work?'

'People . . .' he said, 'here they work much harder at hiding their feelings or avoiding saying what they really mean. It takes a while to get used to that.'

'And you talk "straight from the hip"?' She smiled.

'That's what David said.'

She darted a glance at the dance floor, at Clare and her father.

'It's been an awfully long time since I've been to a place like this . . . I'd almost forgotten what it felt like.' Excruciatingly lonely, she thought, unless you were with the person you wanted to be with, more so if there was no such person.

'Why don't we dance?' he said, although he had never danced in his life.

'Well. . .'

He stood up before she could say anything more. 'You'll have to show me what to do . . .'

She hesitated for a moment, then took his outstretched hand.

The music was syrupy and romantic and the floor crowded with couples clinging to one another.

'It doesn't look very difficult.'

'It isn't,' Jackie said, placing one of his hands on her waist, 'the slow ones are always easy.'

She glanced at his face and saw that he smiled.

'What's so funny?'

'It's rather primitive really, don't you think? Like a mating ritual.'

She laughed and his eyes settled on her lovely mouth.

'After all . . .' he continued, 'we only dance with people we want, wouldn't you say?'

Jackie looked him full in the eyes. 'Nothing is ever that simple.'

'Why not?'

'Life just isn't like that.'

'You can make it so.'

She sighed. 'Can't we just dance, Jamie, please?'

She leaned against him and he could feel the outline of her body through the stunning gown.

'Will you have dinner with me?' He'd been practising the invitation for over a week now.

He felt her stiffen, then she lifted her head and stared into his face. 'I don't think that's a good idea.'

'Why not?'

'Please, Jamie.'

'Because of Drew?' But Jackie didn't really mean anything to the American, Jamie had seen that for himself.

'I said I don't think it's a good idea.'

'You think I'm too young for you.'

'I don't know what I think,' she said abruptly, 'now can we just drop it, please?'

He looked down at her partly bowed head and breathed in deeply as the heavy sweet fragrance of her perfume floated into his nostrils. Like a drug.

She had turned him down, but he would have been surprised if she had said anything else. And it changed nothing for him, he still wanted her, would go on wanting her. After all, he had plenty of time and he could wait. Jamie had always been very good at that.

SIX

Drew picked up the cheque again and kissed it – five thousand dollars, enough for a while, but he would have to phone Angela again because it wouldn't last him very long, only if he was careful, and he hated being careful. As he poured another Scotch into his glass he frowned and wondered why she had sent it at all. Part of him wanted to believe that she still needed some link with him, the other, dark part, told him it was simply to keep him quiet. He lay back on the bed with a small ragged sigh, then a clatter of hooves caught his attention.

'The goddamn cavalry!' He stood up and walked over to the window as the familiar sight of the Household Cavalry resplendent in their brilliant uniforms, plumes fluttering, trotted through the park. 'Sons of bitches . . .' he muttered petulantly as a wave of envy spread through him. In a corner of his heart he harboured a secret longing to see himself in uniform, to have people look at him with something like respect and awe, to rise above all the crap he had been born into. He had seen Richard Gere do just that in *An Officer and a Gentleman* and it had been a thorn in his side ever since.

Drew pressed his face up against the glass, touched by loneliness, watching them until they disappeared from sight. He felt faint distaste because he should be getting beyond high-school dreams, but he had survived on such dreams when he was growing up and had easily explained away the lack of a father because 'Pop was in the navy'. He had almost come close to believing it himself, but lies didn't last too long in a small place like Crenshaw, and once his weirdo mother had started meeting him from school it had ruined everything and he had wanted to die. Everyone knew who *she* was. In his mind's eye he saw her again and winced: that bag-lady who had alternately beaten and slobbered over him. He felt a surge of despair, a shrinking, as if he were still that skinny kid with zits, wearing trousers two sizes too large.

He reached for the Scotch and moved into the drawing room in an effort to lose his thoughts and was confronted by Jackie's desk, her makeshift 'shrine' to delicious dead Marilyn, covered with papers and photographs and books and an old manual typewriter. Her obsession. The corners of his mouth tilted slightly into a sardonic smile; he would call Rose, get her to come over. Why not? Jackie was out enjoying herself, so what was he supposed to do – play with himself? And she wouldn't be back for hours; there was even a possibility that she might stay over at her father's. Good ol' Oscar-winning, wino David.

Immediately his eyes darted to the photograph, framed in ornate silver and sitting on the marble fireplace watching him. Famous, privileged, arrogant David who had everything; he had even had Angela once. The knowledge always enraged Drew and he felt hatred seep through his body like slow poison.

Angela had been crazy about David all those years ago in Hollywood, maybe she still was. Hot, jealous blood surged to his head because she had practically confessed as much to him the one and only time she got drunk, really drunk, and had cried in his arms like a baby. Finally she had stumbled to her feet and walked into the bathroom, teetering ridiculously on high heels, and retched and retched into the cold white basin until there was nothing left. He had caught a glimpse of her contorted, tear-stained face, and then she had closed and locked the door so that he could not see the reality of her pale, make-up-damaged features. That glimpse had changed nothing; it had only made him want her all the more.

When, finally, she had emerged the make-up had magically been repaired and she was smiling with that big lush red mouth, acting as if nothing had happened. She had made him undress, slowly, then sinking down on to her knees she had licked, sucked and touched until he thought she would drive him out of his mind. All she kept saying over and over again was, 'We can go as many times as you want . . . we can go as many times as you want.' He had never forgot ten.

Drew looked into David's blue eyes and placed the photograph face down. It was the least he could do.

He picked up the Scotch again and suddenly remembered Rose. Hesitating only for a moment before picking up the phone he began dialling, but immediately a picture of the miserable payphone next to Rose's flat door almost made him change his mind, and there was that angry little voice way back in his head saying Angela's name all over again.

'Hello?'

'Rose?'

'No.'

'Could you tell her to come to the phone,' he said and then quickly added the habitual English 'please'.

'Oh, yeah, sure.'

He listened as the girl, whoever she was, banged on the door and yelled Rose's name, and he held the telephone away from his ear.

There was a long silence before he realized that the receiver was being picked up again.

'Hello?'

'Rose? This is Drew,' he said. 'Can you come over?'

'Now?'

'Yes.'

'Where are you?'

'The Hyde Park Hotel – Knightsbridge – just hop in a cab.'

He heard the sharp intake of her breath.

'Okay.'

'Don't sound so nervous . . . you want to see me, don't you?'

'Yes – of course.' Apart from landing the role of Marilyn, she had been able to think of nothing else but Drew.

'Look – ' he paused, carefully choosing his words, 'dress up in something special – something black and sophisticated . . .' otherwise they probably wouldn't let her through the goddamn doors; not in those purple leggings and another baggy sweatshirt.

'Oh,' she said in a small, puzzled voice.

'A special dress for a special night,' he said easily, 'and once you arrive just get the elevator up to the Bennett suite.'

'The Bennett suite?'

There was only the sound of her breathing now.

'What's wrong?'

'I thought your name was Carocci.'

'It is,' he lied, but it didn't seem like a lie any more.

'Who's Bennett?'

Perhaps he should could laugh this one off, but instead he caught a weary breath.

'Bennett is the name of the suite, or the rooms, doll, not my name, or anyone else's if that's what you're worried about.'

'Oh.'

'Now, why don't you just get the cab, like I said.'

'Okay,' she said softly, happily, 'I'll be there as soon as I can.'

He put down the receiver, picked up his Scotch and sat down amongst the plump cushions of one of the sofas facing the window. It was dark outside except for the lamplight in the park and he could see the black skeletal branches of trees swaying almost in rhythm, but then pinpricks of quiet oily rain began to spot the glass and the picture blurred. His thoughts turned to the cheque he had pushed back into the safety of his pocket and then, naturally, to Angela and a never-to-be-forgotten afternoon in her apartment: her little strip – her *very professional* little strip.

He had promised himself that he would follow Angela right back to where she came from and now, as he had some time on his hands and a few spare dollars, he would really be able to get down to business; maybe hire a private dick, which would give him the sort of results he needed sooner rather than later, with the few questions he had already started asking and the few leads he had. Jackie had mentioned her mother's former agent once, a guy called Oleg. Drew chuckled; there couldn't be too many showbiz agents called Oleg. Of course, the guy could be dead now, but it was a lead, and it had given him a start.

The bottle of Scotch beckoned from the table; he picked it up and drank greedily, feeling the delicious heat burn his mouth, his throat and way down into his belly. For a moment the whole room seemed to move and he smiled slowly as the warmth spread through his limbs. Angela. He had a gut feeling that he wouldn't be wasting his time, or his money. With a satisfied grunt, he put his feet up on the coffee table and grinned again because it was an investment for the future, maybe the best one he would ever make.

The rain was beginning to drum on the window and he wondered if Rose had managed to get herself a cab. He glanced at the telephone and thought he might order some champagne, Krug Grande, naturally. Angela's favourite.

'That was him, wasn't it?' Babs asked.

'Yes.' Rose walked past her flatmate into the bathroom.

'Are you seeing him tonight?'

'Yes.'

'What time will you be back?'

'I don't know.'

'You said you wanted me to give you a call in the morning, in case you oversleep.'

'Well, maybe you won't have to bother.'

'So you won't be back?'

'I don't know.'

'Which means no.'

'I didn't say that.'

'That's what you meant.'

'What is this, Babs – *Twenty Questions*?'

'You have to be at the studio early tomorrow.'

'I know.'

Babs sighed heavily and looked at her friend, wondering why she bothered.

'I'll be okay.'

'You said that last time.'

'What are you talking about?'

'Remember Jules . . . and Frank and . . .'

'Don't start that again.'

'He's a lot older than you, Rose.'

'I know,' she said, 'and it feels good.'

'Be careful, for God's sake – you hardly know him!'

'Drew is different. Now, do you mind if I get ready? I'm going to be late.'

She closed the bathroom door and Babs stood uselessly outside.

'Don't sleep with him . . .' she said quietly, but it was probably too late for that.

'What?' Rose switched on the shower.

Babs closed her eyes. 'It doesn't matter.'

*

'Christ, that's another show for the chop.'

Jackie frowned as Max began reading from the *Evening Standard*.

' "First-night Blues for *Magic* – variously called 'feeble', 'confusing', 'ludicrous but well-intentioned' . . .".' He fell silent as his eyes greedily ate up the words. 'Fallows goes on to say, "I am bemused by the lack of critical and managerial judgement which considered the production ready to open" . . . blah, blah, blah, "the few highlights are pastiche numbers . . . the music mostly bland and lacking in inspiration . . . too much spectacle, too little substance".'

'What do the other critics say?'

'About the same, with one mediocre exception, but all basically non-selling reviews.'

'Bob must be ready to shoot himself – and he thought he had a hit on his hands.'

'Well, I certainly didn't think so and neither did you, if you're honest.' He shook his head with impatience. 'The story was bloody weak from the beginning – anyone with half a brain would not make a gigantic wind-up doll the star of a show, even if it does light up and swing from the rafters.'

'Perhaps the public will like it, after all the critics have been known to be wrong,' she responded and thought of Bob Ratcliffe, an old friend and one-time vocalist with a famous Seventies band. He had talked of nothing else but *Magic* for the previous two years and had put almost everything he had into the making of the musical. If it really went down the pan, it would break him.

'Don't be naïve, Jackie.'

She looked at him sharply. 'I'm not very good at damning things out of hand.'

'That's something which comes from experience.'

'Thank you, Max,' she said, 'you certainly have a way with words.'

'Look, darling – Bob got things just a little bit wrong,' he offered sarcastically. 'He decided to opt for the loud, aggressive laser-lights, theme-park type musical, except that the script, the score and the cast seem to have got lost somewhere amongst the tons of luminous scenery.' He shook his head in disgust. 'Now that ridiculous doll is a miracle of engineering, might even get an award – I would go as far as to suggest that it beats *Starlight Express* and *Time* hands down when it comes to mindless spectacle, because human beings don't actually seem to be necessary to the action at all.'

'I accept what you're saying, but rightly or wrongly some audiences *like* that kind of thing and if ticket prices continue climbing then they will expect even more razzle-dazzle for their money.'

'God help us all.' He closed the paper abruptly as if the subject too were closed.

Jackie suppressed a smile.

'Did Aldo mention cutting one of Marilyn's solos in the second act?' he asked sharply.

'You mean "Bennie, the Camera and Me"? We discussed it first thing, but I don't see why we need to panic at this stage.'

'I thought you wanted a three-hour show.'

'I do.'

'Then it has to be cut.'

'Not at the expense of its message.'

'I didn't say that, but it is the longest in the show.'

'And a fundamental element of the whole. In a way the song *is* Marilyn – it sums up what she was all about.'

'But it could be cut,' Max persisted, 'and if advance bookings are still slow by the time we open, overtime costs will be catastrophic.'

'That's my problem, Max.' She raised her eyebrows a little. 'You surprise me; I always thought directors had a habit of putting artistic considerations before anything else, and cared least of all where the money actually comes from.'

'The song is too long.'

'We'll trim it, as I said.'

'I also think it might be a good idea to switch it to the end of the first act.'

'Aldo said something along the same lines. Why don't we discuss it in more detail over lunch?'

'I'm busy for lunch, but I could see you in the studio at two before the team meeting.'

'Fine.' But she felt faintly exasperated and wondered, a little unfairly, whether it was Yvonne he was likely to be 'busy' with or some other female eagerly awaiting his attentions on the side-lines. Even as the thought took shape and fled he was moving towards the door.

'I'm popping down to wardrobe first; there are some notes on the sets I left with Yvonne.'

She watched him go and wondered with a trace of regret why it seemed that they circled each other warily and whether he was used to getting his way with people, or rather women, too easily.

She sat in silence for a moment. Nothing seemed straight-forward, or calm, or right in her life. A mug of lukewarm coffee sat on her desk and she picked it up and moved to the window overlooking the Charing Cross Road. The pavements were dark from the faint drizzle which shrouded everything with a mournful mist: November weather. One avenue of traffic had come to a standstill as the lights changed to red, a queue of people waited patiently for buses and a group of Krishna enthusiasts were busy trying to sell obscure albums in aid of the god Vishnu as their familiar chant of 'Hare Krishna' reverberated into the outer realms of Oxford Street.

Her eyes wandered the length of the road and then she saw Jamie weaving his way down the street, head and shoulders above everyone else. He had a white paper bag under one arm and a large polystyrene cup in his hand and she assumed that he had just bought his lunch and was on his way back to the studio.

She had seen little of him since Annabel's, at least on a one-to-one basis, which was just as well. Why in hell's name did he have to complicate her life even more; after all, she had never given him any encouragement? Perhaps it had been the champagne and all that gushing romantic music. Yet in the back of her mind lurked the image of their first meeting when he had said that she was 'quite lovely'. And she had been flattered, hadn't she? Even in the solitude of her office she found herself blushing. Shouldn't she have known then? But there was nothing she could do about it now. She wondered how she could have been so stupidly blind to Jamie's crush, because that was all it was, and how she had been sure that Drew was wrong. She had misjudged him again.

Richard watched her dress, and Lucy never minded, not like some of his other girlfriends who had been wary of his scrutiny,

127

or any man's scrutiny, he supposed. Women fascinated him: he had realized that a long time ago and it never mattered to him in the least if his lady of the moment had a few wayward hairs growing on her nipples, uneven teeth, or ample dimpled thighs as long as he found some element about her which attracted him, and he usually could find something. He linked his hands behind his head as jigsaw images floated out of the past to tease him. There was something utterly womanly about a big, round bum; toenails painted crimson; the lovely curve of cheek or breast; the taste of lipstick. He smiled sheepishly as the thin sheet which covered him peaked in a telltale area; obviously his thoughts had been swiftly relayed to his genitals and he sighed because Lucy was already sliding into her jeans.

'What time will you be back?'

'Late.'

'Like to meet for lunch?'

'Not sure I can.'

Her face was hidden behind a curtain of hair, making it impossible to read her expression, but inevitably his erection began to wither.

'Oh.'

She pulled a heavy sweatshirt over her head and then looked back at him as her face reappeared.

'Don't look so crestfallen . . . I may have to work through,' she said lightly. 'I'll call you if things change.'

He shook his head. 'Don't worry – really – we can do it another day. I merely thought that it would give the next eight hours or so some meaning and bring a little ray of sunshine into my shabby existence . . .' He wouldn't push it; things had been better lately and it seemed to him that that invisible barrier which had risen between them was was fading nicely.

Lucy threw a slipper at him.

'There is no need to resort to violence, my dear.'

'Go back to sleep.'

'I am far from sleepy after watching you swan around our bedchamber half-naked.'

'Some of us have to work . . .' The response had been automatic, but she regretted it instantly as a shadow momentarily dimmed the humour in his eyes. 'Sorry.'

'Forget it, I'm not made of glass,' he said and then added over-brightly. 'Anyway, I shall soon be joining the whiter than white cast of St Winifred's – only another week – can't wait to rub shoulders with a great professional and talent like old jolly Roger. Almost a privilege.' He stopped with forced laugh.

She made no answer, but looked carefully at herself in the mirror.

Richard stretched extravagantly and swung his legs out of bed. 'And today I intend to get on with my bestselling novel.'

'I thought you were just playing around?' she asked, glad to change the subject.

'Well, I was,' he said, scratching his head, 'but it seems to be developing a life of its own . . . anyway, it's good for me, gets rid of all my pent-up frustrations.'

'I'd like to read it.'

'No – not yet,' he said, too quickly.

She shot a glance at him, surprised by the edge in his voice.

'It's just jumbled paragraphs, rubbish . . .' he said defensively, but it wasn't *just* that. There was too much of himself written on those pages – his own Pandora's box with the lid removed – all the secrets, all the pain, all the hopes, and he didn't want to share it, not even with Lucy. There was plenty of time, after all; he would let it evolve slowly until he was ready and then he might do something with it. He didn't want another failure held up for the world to see and at least if he was rejected again it would just be on paper, through the faceless offices of a few publishers, and no one would see *his* face and no one need know. Just an anonymous envelope through the post.

'Well, whenever you're ready . . .' she said with a soft frown and then looked self-consciously at her watch. 'I'd better go.'

'Rehearsals?'

'Not exactly, I'm going through the *Marilyn* songs with Rose – oh, God, my throat spray . . .'

'It was on the side of the bath the last time I saw it.' She always sang in the tub and last night had been no exception. In one of those rare, beautiful moments they shared, Lucy confessed that in the close steamy warmth of the tiny bathroom she sang her best, her most pure notes, but no one ever heard. Oh, but he did, always. And there had been something extra in her voice the previous evening, something that had made him stand rooted to the little patch of worn carpet outside the door as she glided into tender-sad phrases, the notes climbing and climbing and then diminishing so delicately, so sweetly that it had caused a thickness in his throat.

Lucy disappeared from view and reappeared clutching an aerosol can.

'Ozone-friendly, I hope,' Richard said, grinning.

'You never give up, do you?' But she was smiling. 'See you later.'

'I'll cook dinner,' he said seriously.

She blew him a kiss.

Her umbrella was caught by a sudden gust of wind and blew inside out. Lucy swore softly and crossed the street to take a short cut through Primrose Hill. The rain had continued all night and now the ground was sodden and water dripped, dripped from the trees, denting the puddles and turning the narrow path to black mush.

Her thoughts returned to Richard and his guarded face when she had mentioned reading his 'novel'. It was not like him to be secretive and she wondered what all those closely packed lines held that he would want to keep from her. She winced as the wind tore at her hair, throwing it into her face and blinding her for a second. But she kept things from him, didn't she? There were bits of her past that she would never want Richard to know about, because they had been the result of humiliating, desperate measures which had given her very little in return.

Lucy felt a twinge of bitter shame: she was doing the same thing again by meeting Roger because she felt indebted to him for helping Richard get the part in St Winifred's. Just as with the previous times it had seemed like a good idea, but there was a little voice inside which kept repeating 'stupid', 'stupid', 'stupid'. Again.

He stood naked, watching her from the window as she battled against the wind and rain: a small dark blur, getting smaller and more indistinct as she crossed the park and water began to rage against the glass. Richard shivered and reached for an oversized sweater which his mother had knitted for him during his student days and pulled it over his head. He padded into the tiny kitchen and filled a kettle with water in preparation for a cup of instant coffee. As he went through the safe little ritual he found his thoughts running back in time to the appalling 'Vicars and Tarts' party where he had met Lucy. He had spotted her almost instantly as he came through the door and she walked down the stairs; she had been the only girl wearing a clerical collar and not showing off all the succulent gifts Mother Nature had given her. Lucy had never needed to do that. He could recall feeling distinctly hot under his own collar when she smiled back at him. Even now he felt his heart begin to beat a little faster at the memory.

They had made their exit from the appalling party very quickly. He had held her hand in one of his and with the other he had smuggled the carefully hoarded bottle of plonk he had brought to the party under his coat. When, finally, they found a cab she had been frozen and he had warmed her by wrapping her against him, plunging her icy hands into the deep pockets of his coat. And then, in the untidy warmth of his small flat in Kennington they had made mad passionate love. It had been as simple as that, at least for him.

The water from the kettle sent up a plume of vapour as he poured it into a large enamel mug and drank the scalding coffee where he stood. Nothing ever stayed the same, of course, but it was still good with them, he was sure of that and in his heart there was no room for anyone else; Lucy was all he ever wanted. He leaned against the formica kitchen cabinets and stared at the cheap patterned wallpaper they had inherited on their move to the flat. Rows of bloated tomatoes played noughts and crosses with corn cobs and cucumbers and overripe apples that looked like more tomatoes. Reluctantly he wondered whether he should do something really constructive and strip the revolting stuff from the walls and slap on some paint, but his eyes strayed through the open door to the typewriter sitting against the wall and, as if drawn, he moved towards it and sat down on the old typewriter chair which cried out as he shifted his naked behind on the threadbare cushion. He began to type.

*

Max was speaking again and Jamie looked up wearily; they were still arguing over the future of one of the songs, at least which lines to cut from where. Gordon and Joe, the lyricists, thought the song should stand without any subtractions or juggling of lines; Aldo met them halfway, but Max wanted major cuts. And Jackie – Jackie had just left to take a phone call and her chair stood conspicuously empty; when she returned he would switch his attention back to Max, or his notes, and pretend that he was actually listening to every word that was being said.

'The same message is repeated over and over again . . .'

'It's a way of ensuring that the audience understands that this moment in the show – in Marilyn's life,' Joe began, 'is of paramount importance.'

'I just don't think we need to bore them to death in the process.'

'For God's sake, Max – it's a beautiful song!'

Jamie closed his eyes, still unused to the easy blasphemy he heard day after day. They didn't realize, of course, what it meant, or what they were saying and if there was a God he did not believe that He would be so mean-minded as to damn them out of hand. He looked down at his hands which held a pad of paper and a pen to take notes on the meeting – to learn apparently – instead what looked back at him from the white paper were scores of spirals carefully and tightly drawn, one after the other, becoming smaller and smaller until they seemed hardly there at all.

He had learned little so far because no one really had the time or the patience to teach and explain. Mostly he was doomed to run messages or make coffee, or sit in on meetings like this where he was unable to contribute anything of value.

It did not help that he was not completely familiar with the legend of Marilyn Monroe, but even after reading up on her life he still could not come to terms with the fascination or attraction of a lost, emotionally disturbed woman, no matter how beautiful or seductive, who finally drowned herself in drugs.

It oppressed him – the book, the woman, the legend – there was very little to relieve the constant references to corruption, self-indulgence, vanity and sex. And the sex was ugly and empty.

Sex, the word seemed to haunt him.

Jamie recalled the waking dream he had carefully woven in the safe darkness of his room the night before: Jackie naked beneath him, smiling, inviting, sweet beyond belief. His imagination had been so strong, so vivid that he had seemed able to conjure the feel of his mouth kissing her mouth, her face, her throat, the hotness of her breasts. There had been no hesitation in the way his hand had nurtured his hardness, bringing him to a shuddering climax which left him weak and dazed, yet still wanting her.

His father must be turning in his grave.

On his seventh birthday the old man had told Jamie that this was a day of great spiritual significance because, according to the Catholic church, he had attained the use of reason and was therefore capable of committing both mortal and venial sins. The thought of mortal sin had terrified Jamie for years after that – mortal sin which 'kills' the soul by depriving it of sanctifying grace and therefore must be confessed as soon as possible to a priest before God will forgive.

He thought of the words his well-meaning – he realized that now – father had repeated to him down the years: 'A man with mortal sin on his soul will writhe in agony in Hell's hottest fires for eternity.' And now he would be damned, then, by all the rules he had broken.

The sound of voices in the corridor outside made him look up as the door opened and closed and Jackie returned.

'Sorry about that . . .' she said.

He watched her cross the studio. He found it difficult to look at her and not entertain the sort of 'impure thoughts' his father had despised. It was not something which happened with other women he came into contact with and there were many now the production was taking shape. Whatever he felt for Jackie seemed quite natural and there was very little he could do about it, even if he wanted to.

'I'm not disputing the quality of the song, Joe,' Max snapped, breaking into Jamie's thoughts. 'Despite its dramatic potential, it will come across as repetitive and disappointing,' he sighed with apparent exasperation, 'it's just too *damned* long.'

'All right, let's stop just here,' Jackie said calmly and turned to Joe and Gordon. 'I'd like you both to take another look at the song and see if there is any way you can trim it without spoiling its impact. I don't want major cuts,' she added pointedly, turning to Max, 'it's not necessary yet.'

'Christ – we start rehearsals in three weeks!'

'We still don't need to hit the panic button.'

'Despite the fact that Aldo wants changes in the lyrics to at least half the songs in the show?'

'That's a little different, Max . . .' Aldo interjected quietly, puzzled by the harshness of Max's response and his pigheadedness. He, of all people, knew that at this stage in the production of any musical there was a certain amount of chaos and that some lyrics would have to change – some words, no matter how meaningful, are neither easily sung nor instantly understood once put to the test at rehearsals. He gave Max a searching look and wondered why he was being such a pain in the ass.

'Okay, okay,' Jackie said tiredly. 'Max, I have a meeting at Thames Television shortly, perhaps you'd like to join me?'

'You mean now?'

'We should have finished this half an hour ago,' she said carefully, 'we can talk about your lyric concerns on the way.'

He did not answer immediately and she made an effort not to let her irritation show, turning instead to the others who were beginning to wrap the meeting up.

'Thanks, everyone,' she said. 'I'd like to do this again on Wednesday at about the same time.'

'I take it this Thames meeting is something to do with PR?' Max broke in sharply.

'That's right. I've got a car waiting outside, I'll see you there in five minutes.'

She did not wait for his reply, but turned to Jamie. 'I hope you got something out of today,' she said smiling and felt herself blush and her voice running on too fast. 'We'll catch up with each other later, or perhaps tomorrow morning first thing.'

He nodded wordlessly in response, noting the high colour in her cheeks because doubtless she felt awkward with him now, but he would change that somehow. Even his father had once surprised him by paying him the dubious compliment that he could 'charm the monkeys out of the trees'. But it seemed to him at this moment that his experience of worldliness was pitifully inadequate, that the solitary years with his father coupled with

134

those in the seminary had prepared him for nothing more than a spiritual bubble which floated serenely above the pain and complexities of real life.

He blinked as the studio doors opened and then closed and he realized that he was now quite alone. Outside, beyond the window, it was already darkening towards evening and he could hear traffic stopping and drawing away, the blast of car horns and screech of brakes, voices raised and the dim sound of scores of passing footsteps. The pavements would be black with quiet rain and the dampness would seep through his clothes to his skin. When he reached Hampstead he would walk up the steep hill to his godmother's home with slow, heavy steps and think of Kenya and Mount Marsabit where the world he had known was all blues and golds and breathtaking silences.

'What the hell's eating you?'

Max looked back at his reflection in the mirror of the men's room and his gaze slid to Aldo who was watching him steadily. 'Nothing.'

'Oh, come on, Max,' Aldo said. 'I've known you a long time.'

'So?'

Aldo shook his head with exasperation. 'Okay, have it your way, but don't forget, I *did* ask.' He swung round on his heels and began to walk out of the room.

Max followed Aldo's retreating back with his eyes. 'I think I've got the clap.'

Aldo turned round slowly. 'Christ – don't you ever learn?'

Max shrugged his shoulders. 'It's not easy to change the habit of almost a lifetime.'

'What about Polly?'

'What about Polly?' Max repeated.

'Well, you *do* still live with her, don't you?'

'Oh, I see what you're getting at.' He smiled in a lacklustre way. 'We haven't had sex in weeks.' Thank God. That was one problem he didn't need right now.

Aldo's eyebrows drew together in a puzzled frown.

'She's got some mechanical trouble in the old fertility works and won't let me near her.'

'I thought she wanted to get pregnant?'

'She still does, unfortunately, but until things are sorted out my rampant throbbing member remains *verboten*, which is just as well under the circumstances.' And he didn't want to ruin whatever chances he had with Polly; she was pretty, well connected and her father seemed to own half of Scotland, including substantial interests in North Sea oil. *Not* something to dismiss lightly.

'Is it serious?'

'Gonorrhoea, I suppose.'

'I mean Polly.'

'Oh, God knows, fibroids or something.'

Aldo sighed and wondered again why a nice girl like Polly allowed herself to be mixed up with someone as self-involved as Max. But Max was talented, wasn't he? And well known in the theatre world. He was not yet a Trevor Nunn or a Terry Hands, but, Aldo supposed reluctantly, he was on his way and Polly would no doubt be aware of that. Not forgetting the opportunities he never failed to miss, like the uncanny knack of ensuring his name got a mention in *Punch*, the influential *Observer*, or the *Sunday Times* review section in some shape or form. He had even managed to manipulate a spot on *The South Bank Show* a couple of months before, in spite of the nauseating, but memorable appearance he had made on one of the BBC's top arts programmes the previous year. Aldo cringed inwardly – Max had been screwing the producer's wife at the time and she had persuaded her unwitting husband how 'exciting' this 'up and coming' director was. He could still recall how Max had laughed.

Yet he was not so different from the hundreds of other *prima donnas* he had come across in his twenty-five years in the theatre: gigantic egos bestriding the stage, convinced of their titanic destinies, and ever hungry for the attention; applause and publicity which would never be enough.

'I take it you've seen a doctor.'

'Not yet.'

'What?'

'Tomorrow morning, Aldo, don't panic.'

'How long have you known?'

'Since Wednesday.'

'For Christ's sake, you could have done something about it by now.'

'I thought it might be a false alarm.' Like a fool wishing the symptoms away, but he still wasn't quite sure, because the last time he had steeled himself to urinate it had felt a little less like peeing sulphuric acid.

'You mean you *hoped* it was.'

Max squeezed shut his eyes with frustration and said almost to himself, 'Why can't a guy savour some innocent pleasure without picking up a dose?'

'Hardly innocent.'

'I don't need any sort of a lecture, Aldo,' he said, 'particularly from you.'

'Because I'm gay?'

Max had the grace to blush.

'Gay I might be, but stupid I'm not,' Aldo smiled with a flicker of distaste. 'At least not in these historic times of AIDS. I'll see you tomorrow, I've got work to do.'

He opened the door and was hard put not to slam it behind him, except that Max was just not worth it. He took a deep gulp of air, because despite what he'd said to Max he *had* been stupid, irresponsible and promiscuous, or whatever anyone wanted to call it. Oh, so promiscuous, so reckless, so ready to receive and enjoy: tasting all there was to taste, trying all there was to try – even women.

Once, what now seemed a long time ago, he had made several trips a year to Bangkok: wild, beautiful, dangerous trips. He would never go back, of course, there was too much temptation, too many memories. And Jonno was gone now, so there was little point. He could try and fool himself, like the times before, that another slender pretty boy with smooth dusky skin would suit, would taste the same, give him the same pleasures, but it was not true. In Jonno's arms he had known a healing calm he had never found with anyone else.

Aldo's vision dimmed as Jonno's face took shape in his mind and he felt that old dull ache inside. For a fleeting, hope-filled time he had thought that it could really be – that somehow he could find a place for the boy in his own world, that they could live and love together, and all the rest be damned.

Jonno had not, finally, understood or believed that he would have somehow got him back to the UK, to relative sanity and the chance of a proper life. Ultimately he had refused to come and they had said goodbye in the dirty crush of a railway station. Jonno had blown him a kiss from his perfect peach-painted lips and then simply slipped away, vanished, into the sea of olive faces, like some lovely wraith. Back to the sleazy bars and cheap sexual adventures which he undertook with such delicate expertise. Aldo swallowed, not wanting to remember, not wanting to think of all those brief, alien and sometimes brutal encounters Jonno no doubt embraced with the same, unswerving generosity. Perhaps it was he who had not understood.

Max swilled out his mouth with a glass of water and spat angrily into the basin, torn now by what he had said to Aldo, what he should *not* have said to Aldo. Basically, he couldn't give a shit what his musical director and sometime friend was, or where he put his dick; what he couldn't stand was that nauseating holier-than-thou attitude, that pious hypocritical crap Aldo had begun to adopt over the last few months.

Max snorted softly with impatience as he held his hands beneath the running cold water and stared back at his reflection in the mirror, not liking what he saw. But that was nothing new: he was short and thin with narrow shoulders and no chin, and yet his looks, or lack of them, had never stood in his way when it came to the opposite sex. It was the power thing – *what he could do for them* – he had never fooled himself about that; it was a fact of life, and he wondered if that might have something to do with the almost irrational contempt he felt for women in general. It worried him sometimes, that contempt; it got in the way, blunted his thinking, but it was always there like an iron bar in his head.

The sound of the water, still running, made him blink. He turned the tap off slowly until the water just drip-dripped, and he was caught by a sudden desire to urinate, but he repressed the impulse because he did not need any untimely reminders of his possible condition. And where the hell had he picked it up? Yvonne was crazy about him: he couldn't believe that she'd been spreading it around, and if it wasn't Yvonne then it must be Polly's sister, Nadia. But that didn't seem possible either; she was only seventeen and still doing her A-levels. Max realized that he was growing fond of her, even very fond, which puzzled him when he cared to think about it. He was not one to 'grow fond' of his women.

Frowning, he gently smoothed down his sweater and then rested a loving hand on the small mound of his trousers where his genitals lay hidden. Perhaps there was nothing wrong, after all, but his instincts told him otherwise and his stomach churned nastily at the thought of all the sordid, embarrassing consequences which would no doubt follow.

'It's getting very late.'

'Just another glass of wine.'

Lucy looked at Roger's lean tanned face and wondered whether he used a sunlamp.

'I've got to get back to the studio; I'm supposed to be in wardrobe by five.' And this 'lunch' had managed to stretch into most of the afternoon. She had deliberately arrived late hoping to make it short, but Roger had turned it to his own advantage after all, because he claimed 'they had time to make up'. Lucy sighed to herself with frustration.

'Plenty of time.' He poured more wine into her glass and then said slowly, 'I expect Dick's looking forward to starting with me on Monday.'

'Naturally he's glad to be working again.'

'Of course, and it always helps if you know someone in the right place – at the right time – don't you think?'

'You know I'm grateful, Roger,' she said with an effort.

'And Dick would be too, no doubt, *if* he knew.' He grinned.

There was a moment's odd silence as she looked into the plum coloured wine in her glass and felt sweat break out on the back of her neck at the thought of Richard finding out what she had done. She wondered with a feeling of helplessness how she had ever allowed herself to be painted into this corner and by Roger of all people.

Had it been so easy to forget why she had broken off their relationship in the first place? Or was she still so dazzled by his irresistible charms that she found him difficult to refuse? She glanced up at him and saw that he was staring back at her quite calmly, that old look which was telling her that she could trust him implicitly, that she was special. Roger had always had that trick of making you believe him.

'I know it's only six episodes and not much of a part . . .' he continued carefully, his hand still lying hotly over hers, 'but I do have quite an influence on the set these days and even assist with the script – you know, ideas, sub-plots, that sort of thing – and well, if things work out . . .'

For a split second their gazes locked and she felt blood surge into her face. 'I really do have to go, Roger.'

He let go of her hand and glanced at his watch. 'I didn't realize time was passing so quickly . . .' His mouth drooped in mock sorrow.

'I can't afford to be late.'

'I understand completely.' He was smiling broadly, invitingly, with a show of perfect white teeth. 'I'll give you a lift.'

'That's not necessary, really, I can call a cab.'

'I want to.'

'It's okay, Roger.'

'I *want* to, Lucy.'

He looked at her until she was forced to drop her gaze and then he clicked his fingers at the nearest waiter to ask for the bill.

She stood quite still on the damp pavement outside the studio. As Roger drove off in his bright-red Alfa Romeo, he tooted his horn and she cringed. Across the street a luminous orange notice with enormous black letters screamed at passersby: 'Book now for your company Christmas lunch!' It was the end of November, the festive season loomed, and she had almost forgotten. With a small sigh she made her way into the building just as Jackie and Max Lockhart were coming out. Jackie's face lit up into a smile as she passed, but Max slowed and paused and her heart sank.

'They're waiting for you in wardrobe.'

'I'm only a couple of minutes late.'

'Not good enough, Lucy darling,' he said sarcastically, 'but we will try a little harder in future, won't we?' His eyes travelled deliberately over her body and back to her face and his mouth slanted into a humourless smile. He walked away, meanly pleased at her obvious discomfort, glad to find a target for his black mood.

She didn't reply, but stared after him, yearning to say something insolent and fatal. Then she walked down the long corridor towards wardrobe and Yvonne's domain, the sounds of people talking, laughing, singing in other rooms only making her feel more lonely. If it had been possible at that moment she would have turned on her heel and gone back to the safety of the sweet shabby little flat which she always claimed she hated and where Richard waited, cooking dinner. And she would close the door on the world.

'No problems?' Jackie asked as she and Max climbed into the waiting car.

'Problems?'

'With Lucy?'

'Not exactly,' he said carefully. 'I was just checking that she was coping – after all, we both know how disappointed she was about not getting the lead.'

'I think she's taken it rather well.'

Max said nothing for a moment, then, 'I almost worked with Lucy a couple of years ago, but she struck me as being a little neurotic at the time.' A sullen shadow crossed his face as he recalled the abortive seduction; there had been thinly veiled disgust in Lucy's lovely face.

'Really?' Jackie replied with surprise. 'You've never mentioned this before.'

'I didn't think it was important,' he said quickly. 'As I said, it was a couple of years ago, maybe more.'

'And people change,' she said quietly, and the acting profession was enough to make anyone neurotic at the best of times. 'By the way, I've been wondering whether we should seriously reconsider alternating the girls on a one-night-on, one-night-off basis.'

'Not that again.'

'It's a very strenuous role . . .'

'And Rose can handle it.'

'Week in, week out – eight performances a week?'

'I thought we'd discussed this and you said you'd abide by my decision.'

'It's worth thinking about again.' She looked out of the

141

window wondering why he could not agree with her just once, or at least meet her halfway with something approaching good grace. And Rose simply doesn't strike me as having that much stamina.' Jackie had walked into wardrobe the previous day and seen Rose half-dressed and had been struck by how fragile she looked.

'She's a little underweight, I agree, but as it happens she's put on nearly two pounds since last week and I've already told her my thoughts on eating properly – extra vitamins and all that – and getting to bed at a decent hour.' He frowned. 'Besides, have you forgotten where I first saw her?'

'You cannot compare a nightly stint at Madam Jo Jo's with a major role in a musical – and a role which means she is on stage ninety per cent of the time.'

'Don't ever underestimate how gruelling a night-club act can be for a performer.'

'I'm not, I'm simply trying to anticipate possible problems and avoid them if I can. There's a lot of money tied up in this show, need I remind you, not forgetting your reputation and my own. It would be catastrophic if Rose didn't make the grade because we pushed her too hard.'

'All right, Jackie darling,' he said dryly, 'the truth is, I have never liked the "one-night-on, one-night-off" arrangement. It just doesn't have the same sort of impact for the theatre-going public. After all, this is not a star show, we don't have any big names to draw in the crowds, but hopefully it will make a star of Rose overnight. People will come just to see and hear her. The same just cannot be said of making two girls both stars overnight – particularly two unknowns.'

'We're not selling a star, Max, we're selling a musical called *Marilyn*.'

'Marilyn is Rose,' he said slowly and patiently, 'Rose is Marilyn.'

'And she could disintegrate just like Marilyn did if we push her too hard.'

'Now, aren't we being just a teenie bit melodramatic?'

She closed her eyes in quiet exasperation. 'All right, Max, all right.' She turned to him. 'Rehearsals begin in earnest very soon, and by the end of January just before we move to the Adelphi, we'll talk about this again.'

'It's only fair to give the girl a real chance,' he persisted.

'That's why I've agreed to wait until the end of January.'

'Good,' he said, 'good,' and rubbed his hands together.

'In the meantime I shall include Lucy in ninety per cent of the publicity shots leading up to opening night.'

'As a safety net.'

'You could say that.'

'Fine, fine,' he said absently, as if he had now lost interest in the conversation.

She looked out of the window at the people clogging the pavements in the street outside.

'Who, exactly, are we seeing at Thames?'

'Michael Kinsey.'

'The boy wonder.' Max smiled cynically. 'Isn't he responsible for the new breakfast channel?'

'And *Hot Leisure*.'

'Really?' he drawled. 'I didn't know.' Instantly Max found himself more than a little interested. *Hot Leisure* had only been launched at the beginning of September, but already it was topping the ratings for light entertainment. It was much more than just a chat show, there was an acceptable raunchy element to it and a 'hot' arts slot which might include anything from Pavarotti to the rippling muscles of the Chippendales. The programme was, to say the least, unpredictable, but it worked.

'He seems very keen to give us a spot provided we include a song from the show.'

'Is he taking an angle?'

'He'd *love* the Monroe-Kennedy thing casually dropped in somewhere.'

'Can we do that?'

'I don't see why the hell not. It's all been said before so I hardly think we're likely to be sued, particularly as the Kennedys have scarcely been out of the scandal sheets and the Monroe legend is enjoying a revival. It must be a little, shall we say, "awkward" for anyone who knew Monroe "intimately" because the legend just keeps bouncing back along with all those old, disturbing questions which have never been answered.'

'You mean the true facts about her relationship with both Kennedy brothers?'

'That . . .' she answered, 'and the true facts of her death. All I have read supports the conclusion that there was more to Monroe's death than "probable suicide". There was never a full or open inquiry into the way she died despite the suspicious circumstances and despite accusations of negligence or a deliberate cover-up. Kinsey wanted to know if there was reference to this in the show, symbolic or otherwise, or perhaps a song along those lines.'

' "Late-Night Phone Calls"?'

'That's the one.'

'If the show goes to the States, some people there won't like the implication.'

'I'm not – correction – we're not implying anything, or trying to make any sort of a statement about the rights and wrongs of what happened thirty years ago. *Marilyn* is a musical play of Monroe's life as near to the truth as we can get under such circumstances. Obviously men played a huge part in her life, it's been documented meticulously: she used, and let herself be used by them, for whatever reason. As far as Monroe was concerned she had "blonde hair and a body men liked" which basically got her where she wanted to go.'

'You're talking about a casting couch set-up.'

'You know as well as I do that influential guys at the studios regularly inspected starlets and even Monroe was quoted as saying "the worst thing a girl could do, was to say no to one of them".'

'Isn't that a bit of an exaggeration?'

'Oh, come on, Max, I think we both know that the casting couch thing hasn't exactly disappeared from the face of the earth, even in these so-called enlightened times.'

Max shot a wary glance at her, but made no answer.

'Once she became famous she was able to use the fame, the beauty, the sexuality to reach for the dazzling life and the rich and powerful men she thought would make her dreams reality. Fantasy, of course. Nothing and no one ever seemed to live up to her expectations, except the unattainable.'

'She was, you might say, chasing her own tail.'

'As I've often said before, Max, you have a charming way with words.'

'I'm not so far off the mark,' he said defensively. But her knowledge and conviction impressed him. 'Anyway, as far as Kinsey is concerned, we should bring in the last scene in the show. He'll go for that.'

That final stage image she had planned with such meticulous care took loving shape in her mind: a shrinking spotlight focusing on Monroe's naked body, followed by fading phone calls and voices reaching out of the darkness . . . Then silence, complete and utter silence.

'Of course, it needs a lot of work.'

Jackie stiffened. 'Naturally,' she said, 'but otherwise you're happy with the idea as it stands?'

'Oh, yes,' he said, 'it's almost a perfect ending.'

Rose lay on the floor, a handweight clenched in each of her small fists. She took a deep breath and slowly lifted her lower arms and brought the weights towards the centre of her chest, held them there for a moment, then brought them back to the safety of her sitting-room carpet. She performed the exercise ten times before rolling over on to her stomach and attempting twenty press-ups; she found that she could not push her body beyond twelve. It would come, she told herself, she was getting a little better every day.

For a long time she lay quite still on the floor, staring at the blue matted weave of the carpet which seemed to stretch as far as her eyes could see, like a secret world unto itself. She ran her tongue along her dry lips and shivered a little as the sweat began cooling on her body.

Since getting the part she had given up coke and the joints she had so enjoyed when her nerves frayed with despair and the world seemed too much. Things were different now.

Rose stood up and looked back at her reflection in the long piece of mirror propped up against the wall. She stretched her neck, lifting her chin into the air, then dropped her arms loosely by her sides as her gaze fell to her breasts, her waist, her thighs, her feet. Everything was small and neat except her eyes and mouth. If anything, the black leotard she wore made her body seem even more small, more neat. It wasn't the neatness she minded so much, but the smallness of everything. Even Yvonne, the wardrobe mistress, was having problems plumping her out in all the right places for Marilyn, but she had put on a couple of pounds in only a week, thanks to Babs and her home cooking. Except that she couldn't see it; weight never seemed to come in the places it was needed. She glanced forlornly at nipples protruding from breasts the size of button mushrooms. Drew found them wanting.

She ran her hands tenderly over her chest and felt inexplicably sad; but he loved her, she knew that, and he made it obvious with his calls, the lunches, the red rose he had slipped so casually into her blouse. He had made her promise not to tell anyone about their 'relationship', particularly anyone involved with the show. If Jackie found out she would not approve of the leading lady in her pet musical adding more emotional strain to an already strenuous rehearsal schedule which would become more so as opening night drew ever closer.

Rose smiled to herself as she recalled the delicious way his arms had circled her so protectively, so possessively, as if he were telling her in his own way that no one need worry about her because *he* would take care of her. And she loved him, oh, yes, indeed, there was no doubt of that.

Her mouth moved into a wide grin of happiness because her life had never held such promise: she had the lead in a West End musical – which meant she could pay the bills – she would be a star, everyone said so, and she had met someone as incredible as Drew who really seemed to care.

There had been many times in her life when she had wished for such things, but the wishes stopped when she found only disappointment in their wake. With a rare flash of self-knowledge Rose realized that she had always made wrong decisions or wrong choices; even at school it had been the same and nothing had changed when she entered the big wide world except that she had simply made more of them. Until now.

A song from the show began to run in her head and her voice began to rise in reckless, happy abandon. Rose sang to the empty room, to herself, from the heart, and all at once she knew that this was one of those magical moments that she would remember

forever. She thought of Drew, his face, his voice, his hands –
taking kisses from him like a drug, tasting them on her lips long
afterwards. Seeing him every day, every night.

SEVEN

'Does it have to be now?'

Drew nodded.

They walked up the curved driveway to her father's home for the long-delayed Sunday lunch gathering which Clare had suggested that night at Annabel's. Jackie lifted her eyes and scanned the blue horizon, suppressing her disappointment; the sun was shining and it was an exceptional day for the beginning of December. Even the news that the Australian backers might be pulling out of the show had not yet daunted her spirit, but now she could feel it begin to weaken.

'Business, hon',' he lied and then added quickly, 'Look, I didn't plan it this way.' Drew took her hand and kissed it as an act of contrition. 'I tried to get out of it, but my mother's people need someone in LA to discuss a new line, someone they can trust, which means family.'

'Sounds like the Mafia,' she said sourly, but a little ashamed of herself. 'Sorry, sorry . . . I just want you here.' She swallowed, surprised at the intensity in her voice.

Drew had worked so hard at making her happy over the weekend; last night he had even managed to book a table at her favourite restaurant, Le Caprice, at the last moment. He had whisked her into a cab and made her laugh almost non-stop, even over the Caesar salad as he poked gentle fun at a glittering set of film people and several young royals. It had been like the old Drew, the Cape Cod Drew and now, suddenly, he was returning to the States just as he was winning back her confidence. She walked on, hating the tiny nagging doubt inside. The 'other woman' was there, the one he had told her nothing about, but maybe it was better not to know.

'It won't be for long.' He thought of Angela and the cable he had received from the private dick in LA – her agent was still alive, that old crud Oleg hadn't kicked the bucket after all. What a break! Drew clamped his mouth shut on a smile as a pleasing sense of anticipation began to spread through him. He simply hadn't expected any news so soon, maybe he would give the guy a bonus. He stopped and turned Jackie round to face him. 'And it will be good for me to *do* something, kiddo, instead of sitting around on my butt all day. You don't really need me here – not while you're giving birth to *Marilyn*.'

'That's not true.'

'You can't just expect me to be waiting for you in that god-damn hotel room every night. I need more than that, Jackie.'

'What do you need?'

'A little commitment.'

'You mean marriage.'

'At least tell me you'll think about it while I'm away.'

She didn't answer immediately, her eyes straying to the house where David and Clare had been so happy and then back to settle on his face.

'I'll think about it,' she said, smiling.

He threw his head back and grinned and then took her face in his hands and kissed her deeply.

'I haven't said yes yet,' she laughed as he released her.

'Oh, but you will, hon', you will,' he said lightly and then fished in his pocket to produce a small box. 'Wear it, for me, while I'm away . . .'

Jackie stared at the exquisite ruby nestling amongst the plump silk folds of the box.

'I can't . . .'

'It's just a ring, it doesn't have to be *the* ring,' he said. 'Wear it on the "wrong" hand if it makes you feel any better.'

'You shouldn't have done this.'

Her voice was hushed, too gentle and low.

'For chrissakes, Jackie, don't go serious on me!'

'All right, Drew,' she said softly, caught by the infectious warmth of his smile, 'all right.'

He slipped the ring on her finger. 'You can take it off as soon as I get back if you want.'

She looked at her outstretched hand. 'It's beautiful.'

'I knew it was for you as soon as I saw it.' He leant forward and kissed her gently on the lips. The jewellers in Bond Street had gladly accepted a deposit on approval when they saw the pedigree of his credit cards, once their eyes had finished travelling over his designer clothes, his solid-gold cufflinks, his solid-gold watch, his solid-gold pen – Angela had pampered him like a baby. He felt Jackie's warm, soft breath on his cheek, saw the pleasure in her face and as he looked at her there was an instant of discomfort, even guilt, but then it was gone.

They began walking again and he took her hand with a certainty he had never felt before, and as they approached David's house, their feet crunching the gravel drive, he wondered how the ageing actor would feel if he knew that he was about to dine with a sponging bum who had hardly done a real day's work in his life. With a little more concerted effort the sponging bum would then proceed to marry his daughter, and then probably blackmail his rich and famous ex-wife. Not that David cared too much about what happened to Angela, of course. But it was a neat trick.

Drew felt the beginnings of cautious triumph, found his vision swimming slightly at the dizzying possibilities his neat trick would bring him if it paid off. After his trash-can childhood, the bad luck of years, the rejections, the never-ending shit, he might actually have it all. He licked his lips, squeezed Jackie's hand more tightly, and drew a voluptuous, mouth-watering picture of Angela in his head.

'David's having a nap,' Clare said brightly as she poured them drinks, 'he seems to be developing a taste for them just recently.'

'There's nothing wrong . . . ?'

'Good Lord, no, Jackie – it's this bloody part, I suppose, preying on his mind and all that, but he'll be down in a moment, don't worry. I expect he's lost track of the time.' She raised her eyebrows. 'And you know what he's like, he'll be furious, but anyway, let's have a little toast before he arrives, as it seems we have something to celebrate. . . ' She smiled mischievously.

'We do?'

'I'm not blind, Jackie – that's a beautiful ring.'

She made no answer, but felt the heat of a blush stealing into her face.

'It's not quite like that – yet,' Drew said quickly. 'I'm going to the States for a couple of weeks and I wanted her to have something to remember me by.'

Clare chuckled. 'Well, that shouldn't be difficult!' She noted Jackie's blush and the shadow of discomfort on her face. 'Don't worry, I won't mention anything to your father until you say so.'

'Thanks,' Jackie paused, 'it's just that with Drew going away and so much else on my mind . . .'

'I quite understand, darling.'

'Sure,' Drew said easily, 'and there's no rush.' But he was annoyed, wondering why she had to make so much of it. There were thousands of girls who would kill for a ring like that coming from a good-looking guy like him.

'Where's Jamie?'

'Another missing person – perhaps you'd like to hunt him up and show Drew the house at the same time, while I disappear into the kitchen.'

'Do you know where he might be?'

'In the pool, or was, but he promised to be here . . . ' Clare shook her head in exasperation, 'and I thought everything was so organized.' She glanced at Drew. 'I do apologize.'

'No problem, Mrs Jones.' It was a relief, the lack of organization, because it took the heat off him, and he was nervous and ill at ease despite his outward bravado.

'Please call me Clare.'

He nodded, switching on one of his winning smiles, and then turned to Jackie. 'Why don't you hunt up Jamie like Clare says, and I'll stay here and wait for your father.' Perhaps he could have a few quiet moments to collect his thoughts and another nerve-quenching drink without any hassle.

'Why don't you keep me company in the kitchen until Jackie gets back?' Clare offered.

'Fine.' Caught. He managed to smile again despite his sinking heart as he watched Jackie walk out of the room. And it was the sort of room he hated because it made him feel uncomfortable, different, just as he had imagined it would.

It was Home with a big H: soft, warm, rich. Books lined all of one wall, silver-framed photographs and some old theatre programmes littered the lid of a baby grand; the huge marble fireplace bore a carriage clock, fresh flowers, yellowing ivory

151

figurines, masses of snowy-white invitations. Great fat velvet cushions were scattered casually across three enormous sofas and an overweight tabby cat lay sprawled in front of the log fire. It was like something out of one of those cosy black and white Forties films. This was the sort of home he had secretly coveted and which had always been denied him, and when others had been happy and safe in such homes it seemed that they had closed their doors against him. Yet he would have his chance now, wouldn't he, if his luck held?

The pool was an extension of a converted cellar which stretched outwards into the garden from the back of the house, sloping down towards the Heath. It was enclosed by double-strength glass; vast plants climbed to the ceiling from some of Clare's heavy ceramic urns, and plump, sensuous cherubs filled every space so that even from a short distance the pool-house looked like a Roman bath gone wild.

Jamie was not in the water when Jackie reached the poolside and she assumed he was changing, but as she turned to go she caught the distinctive sound of her father's multi-gym in use, something she had not heard in a long time. Once her father had finished the film which had necessitated the purchase of the equipment, he quickly lost interest in the daily effort of keeping his body in shape. A long time ago.

She frowned softly as the movement finally stopped and then walked into the adjoining room housing the equipment where Jamie stood with his back to her, wiping perspiration from his chest and shoulders with a small towel.

She felt heat flood her face: he was naked and his body, still slick with moisture, was breathtakingly superb. Her eyes could not let him go, and she was appalled by a sharp stab of desire which made her heart race. She swung quickly round and called to him from just beyond the threshold, 'We're having drinks in the drawing room, Jamie . . . will you be long?'

'Oh . . . no, of course not,' he said rapidly. 'I didn't realize it was so late.'

Jackie closed her eyes, rubbing her forehead with the palm of her hand, and then slowly walked away.

*

'Drew has been telling me that he has to return to the States?' David said to Jackie as he handed her a drink.

'That's right,' she said, 'it's business.'

'May I ask what sort of business, or is it classified information . . . ?' He chuckled.

'Family business – not very hot stuff,' Drew responded carefully.

'Something to do with cars, I think . . .' Jackie said before her father probed further.

'Not secondhand cars, I hope!'

He chuckled again and Drew began to feel irritated, but this was tempered by self-satisfaction and something like relief because David Jones must have aged considerably since the photograph back at the hotel was taken; he was practically an old man. Reluctantly he admitted to himself that the lean aristocratic face must have been quite something in David's youth, but it was haggard now and deep lines, like crevices, stretched from the high cheekbones almost to the chin. The famous blue eyes had paled and the skin surrounding them was puffy and criss-crossed with tiny wrinkles. Drew laughed silently; the Brits never had believed in facelifts.

'No, Daddy,' Jackie said wryly, 'it's rather removed from that.'

'I'm intrigued – tell me more.'

'There's nothing to tell, sir.' Drew winced. The American 'sir' always made him want to puke.

'I think it must be something to do with that very interesting surname you have.' David paused. 'Carocci,' he rolled the word around on his tongue.

'Spot on, Daddy, I had no idea you had designs on playing Sherlock Holmes . . . ' Jackie said and smiled reassuringly at Drew.

'Actually,' David said, 'I'm sure I met one of your namesakes at the Cannes Film Festival a few years ago.'

'Oh, yes?' He froze a little, taken off guard.

'Only briefly, I'm afraid.'

Drew breathed a soft sigh of relief.

'Your family seems to have a lot of fingers in a lot of pies.'

'I've always tried to keep my distance, if you know what I mean. I like my independence.'

Jackie's father looked back at him carefully. 'Good for you.' He turned to his daughter. 'And how's *Marilyn* coming along?'

'Apart from a million irritations, it's about on schedule.' She sighed heavily. 'Plus one very large irritation like a couple of my "angels" opting out.'

'Ouch,' David said.

'When did you know?' Drew asked, his voice careful with concern. 'Why didn't you say something?'

'You have enough problems of your own and I didn't want to burden you with another of mine, particularly now that you're going to the States,' she said. 'Besides, I only got the fax this morning and I really didn't feel like talking about it.'

'What's the problem?'

'The two Australian backers concerned have just lost a great deal of money in property investments and they simply have to pull out.' She frowned. 'I'm still hoping that there's a chance they'll be able to change their minds, but it doesn't seem very likely. In fact, there's even a strong possibility that they might lose everything – they've been just as vulnerable to recession, Down Under, as everyone else.'

'God . . . what wondrous times we do live in.' David took a large mouthful of Scotch. 'So how much do you need?'

'Don't ask.'

'How much?'

'Something in the region of three hundred and fifty thousand.'

'Oh, Jackie,' he said with an audible groan.

'I know.'

'What will you do?'

'Think of something.' She tried to laugh. 'Raise the money myself?'

'You mean ask your mother again?'

She closed her eyes. 'I don't have much choice, do I?'

'Why don't you let me ask her?' Drew interjected suddenly, 'after all, I'll be in the States by Tuesday and she might listen to a neutral player – if you know what I mean.'

'You know Angela?' David asked warily.

'We met at one of mother's parties,' Jackie responded.

'I see.'

'An aunt of mine used to sit on one of her big charity

committees . . . ' Drew added quickly as the blue eyes scanned his face again.

'And you really would go and see her for me?'

'Why not?' He shrugged. 'It can't do any harm and it might do *you* a lot of good.'

'Watch out . . . ' David broke in, 'she bites.'

Drew didn't answer, but it would be nice to be bitten by Angela, have those sharp little teeth nip and rake his skin again like the old times.

'Lunch is ready,' Clare called as the delicious smell of roasting meat began wafting through the open doors of the dining room.

'Where's Jamie?' David asked.

'Here . . . ' Clare replied, 'he's been helping me lay the table.'

He was standing against the french windows in the dining room, removing the cork from a bottle of wine. He nodded and smiled dutifully as they sat down around the magnificent circular table.

'Come on, Jamie, sit down,' Clare urged, 'you've done enough. David can pour.'

'How're tricks?' Drew said, pulling back Jamie's chair.

'Fine, thanks.'

'And does the show make any sense to you yet?'

'It has its moments,' Jamie said tautly.

David flashed a glance at him. 'I think Jamie finds it absorbing enough,' he said, 'but I don't have the feeling that the theatre is exactly in his blood.'

'Too bad.'

'Not at all,' Jamie said, 'I'm enjoying the experience.'

'By the way, Jackie,' David said, steering the conversation away, 'how are you getting along with Max Lockhart? Clare mentioned that you'd said he was being a trifle difficult?'

'I suppose it's par for the course,' Jackie said with more lightness than she felt.

'At least he hasn't the appalling reputation for temperament of one or two others I could mention.' David's face grew serious. 'I have never been able to develop an immunity to the nastier breed of director – seeing them being spiteful and cruel to actors who can't really retaliate does something to me. Of course, it doesn't happen when you become successful . . . ' He took a gulp of wine. 'But then, I haven't always been a success. Anyway, darling, just remember all directors have a bit of the bastard in them.'

'I know, I know.'

'And what about Marilyn: how's she shaping up – if you'll excuse the pun . . .'

'You mean Rose, of course.'

'She sounds wonderful from what you told me on the telephone,' Clare added, passing over a plate of mouth-watering roast beef.

'Oh, she is . . . I'm just giving myself nightmares in case she doesn't quite have the stamina.'

'Have you seen her, Drew?' David asked.

'Great voice, but she sure needs some meat on her bones,' he said and recalled the first time he had seduced her – how meagre her hot little body had seemed.

'She's terribly pretty,' Jackie explained, 'but a little on the fragile side, so we're trying to plump her out a bit.'

David guffawed. 'I don't think Marilyn Monroe ever needed "plumping out".'

'Those were the days,' Drew said, lifting a glass of wine to his lips, 'when women were women.'

'But she wasn't a real woman, at least not the one the public was allowed to see,' Jamie said abruptly, ' – she was manufactured, like a product.'

'And one of the best products ever made, because she has never gone out of fashion.'

Jamie straightened his cutlery with great care, saw a tiny reflection of his face in the polished silver handles.

'It's a pity, then . . . ' he said, with a slight pause, 'that she's not here to appreciate it.'

'Okay,' Drew said, winking heavily, knowingly at Jackie, 'I take your point.' But the boy was beginning to play on his nerves. He forced another broad smile and Jamie thought that his grin would split his face in two if it got any wider.

'The costumes will be fabulous,' Jackie said too quickly, trying to change the subject, 'and as near to the real thing as possible.'

'And wigs, of course – luxurious and blonde, I suppose?' Clare followed her lead, a frown just visible above her big doe eyes.

'Oh, yes, out of this world . . . but more platinum than blonde. I've even tried one on myself.'

'You know, that would suit you,' Drew said, cutting in on their conversation and staring at her intently.

'What would?'

'A Marilyn Monroe look – all those voluptuous waves . . .'

'I don't think so,' Jamie said abruptly.

Drew caught a sharp impatient breath. Get off my back. 'Why not? Jackie's certainly got the face for it.'

Jamie looked Drew full in the eyes. 'It seems pointless to change something that is beautiful just the way it is.'

Drew's face darkened and there was a moment's silence before David was topping up everyone's glass unnecessarily and Jackie was wishing that somehow they could start this lunch all over again.

It was raining. Richard looked out beyond the enormous windows of the BBC bar to the world outside and wondered what he was doing there. He had spent longer in make-up than he had spent saying his lines, or rather line, and after his big moment was over the director, Conroy, had yelled something incoherent like 'brill (brilliant)' or 'fab (fabulous), darling', from some dark, murky corner of the studio and that had literally been it. Blink, and the chance of seeing Richard Wilson's amazing performance would be completely missed.

With a wry grimace he turned his attention to Roger who was weaving his way through numerous chairs and tables with their drinks, a dazzling smile fixed on his face. He nodded several times and pointed with one of the very full glasses to a fellow Thespian, some colleagues and a few girlish admirers without spilling a drop, hardly interrupting the smile at all. It seemed to stay plastered to his sickeningly handsome face as if it had been freeze-dried.

It was, in fact, Roger's ex-wife in the soap who had made it necessary to bring Richard's character, the local vicar, into the cast. The glamorous, but wildly jealous Nova was leaving the show, never to return, so the scriptwriters had decided to kill her off; after all, there was nothing like a death to beef up the ratings. Nova played Dr Mason's (Roger) possessive, obsessive ex-playmate in the series, but rumour had it that the possessive obsessiveness didn't stop when the lights turned off in the studio. The gossip went that she was actually crazy for Roger himself and that matters were getting heavily out of hand. Poor old Roger, life was a real bitch sometimes.

'I think you'll be performing the last rites next week – thank God,' Roger laughed, 'that silly cow is beginning to drive me out of my mind!' He put down their drinks. 'How did you find your first day, by the way?'

'Put it like this, I'm not exactly suffering from exhaustion.'

'Give it a chance, Dick . . .'

Dick. Richard cringed.

'And tomorrow you get to share a fairly lengthy scene with me.'

The Star. Kiss my ass.

'I know, Roger, I have read the script.'

'Good, good. . . ' Roger looked down at his Perrier water, then shot a glance at Richard from beneath half-closed lids. 'Tell me, Dick, have you ever thought of changing your name?'

'What?'

'Your name. Why not change it?'

'For God's sake, why?'

Roger played with his glass for a moment, pushing the base from side to side. 'Well, Wilson is hardly the most exciting of surnames . . .' he looked up, 'is it?'

Cheeky bastard.

'It's the name I was born with, and I can't say that it's given me any cause to complain so far.'

Roger looked at him steadily without speaking.

'Ah-ha . . . ' Richard exclaimed in a hearty unconvincing way, 'you're trying to tell me that if I change my unexciting name to something like Gielgud or Getty or Kojak, offers will come flooding in and I shall be able to turn my back forever on the low-life of soaps and the Right Reverend Angus Fraser in particular.' He gestured dramatically: 'You can see me can't you, Roger, winning my first Oscar, my first BAFTA?' He leaned back in his chair, shaking his head in mock astonishment. 'If I'd only realized years ago that simply becoming Richard – no – *Dick*

Kojak would solve all my problems, literally change the course of my destiny . . .'

'All right, Dick, joke over.'

'Christ, Roger, what do you expect? You left yourself wide open for that one.'

'I only made a suggestion, and you had to go right off the deep end,' Roger said with a trace of sullenness and then added cautiously, 'it didn't do me any harm, in fact I believe it did me a hell of a lot of good. My agent thinks that once I changed my name to St John, things really started happening for me.'

'If I'd been born with a name like Fock,' Richard chuckled, 'I'd have changed it too.'

'Foch.' Roger pronounced the name with a guttural sound.

Richard's eyebrows drew together in a frown. 'Sorry?'

'F-O-C-H,' Roger emphasized each letter with great deliberation. 'It's German.'

'Good God, I had no idea.'

'Something wrong?'

'Should there be?'

Roger breathed in sharply and took up his glass, drinking the Perrier water in one mouthful. 'How's Lucy?'

'Fine.'

'Lovely girl.'

Richard looked at him. 'Yes, she is.'

'The show's coming together pretty well, I understand.'

'Yes.'

'She must be exhausted when she gets home,' Roger said. 'Theatre can be so punishing.'

'I'm there to soothe her weary brow, Roger, so don't concern yourself too much.'

'Oh, yes, of course,' his voice was leisurely, as if he had forgotten.

'And I hear you're writing a book.'

Richard stiffened. 'Who the hell told you that?' His stomach lurched just slightly with disbelief. Not Lucy?

'Let me see now,' Roger paused, 'must have been Lucy, I think, we bumped into each other somewhere.' He stood up. 'Another drink?'

Richard nodded dumbly.

'By the way, I don't mean to discourage you, but writing's a mug's game – all that effort slaving over hot typewriter keys when you know that hardly anyone ever gets published . . .'

He picked up their glasses and began walking away. Richard lifted his eyes from the ring of moisture where his glass had stood and watched Roger's retreating back as it moved further and further away. It was quite something, that back, wide but beautifully proportioned; it was even possible to see the well-developed muscles moving languidly beneath the fine silk of his shirt and imagine how that back would look if it was naked and those muscles arching, pumping: lifting and falling in perfect time as he made love to Lucy.

A panhandler muttered an obscenity as he passed without dropping a dime into the open, grubby palm, but Drew laughed; this was New York, wasn't it? Home sweet home. It was also West Side and he could almost taste the desperation and the poverty behind the boarded-up, never-open-to-a-stranger doors.

Oleg Bergman lived in one of these run-down blocks, in an area where abandoned supermarket trolleys grew wild like weeds and old cars sat windowless and rusting on every street corner. Drew knew that if his visit had taken place in a steamy, unbearably hot New York summer his clothes would be sticking to his skin by now, no different from the blacks or Puerto Ricans who would be sitting out on the street, or the kids splashing in the turn-on fire hydrants – the poor man's Plaza fountain. Like his own childhood, but he didn't want to think about that.

There had been a dream last night, the latest visit from his creeping friend, and when he had finally dragged himself awake the hair had been standing up on the back of his neck.

The linen on the bed had stuck damply to his thighs and backside as he groped for the lightswitch beside the bed; he had wet himself. A sick feeling swam in his stomach and his temples thumped and throbbed mercilessly. If it had not been for the fold of silver foil he had purchased in a bar on Times Square he thought he might have quietly gone out of his mind in the choking confines of that tiny hotel room, but the coke had been his saviour, his little angel from heaven, whiter than white. And so-oo good.

For a split second an image of the woman, his mother, stole out of his memory . . . soft hands gliding over his chest, a sickly smell of lavender as she came too close. He walked along the sidewalk, his fists clenching in an unconscious spasm, his eyes searching for the cracks in the sidewalk so that he might avoid them.

Outside Oleg Bergman's apartment building there was a puddle of rainwater a mile wide with a plank thrown across the middle for a bridge. Drew swore as the length of wood dipped in the middle with his weight and his new loafers took on water.

'Shit!' He looked up at hundreds of grimy windows reaching to the sky and then back to the lurid graffiti on the lobby walls. 'This had better be worth it.'

The old man must have been at least seventy-five, about the same age as his apartment. The cramped room stank and Drew's nostrils twitched in disgust: stale sweat, cigar smoke, urine. Piles of old newspaper cuttings and *Star-Parade* magazines sat next to cardboard boxes and an open suitcase full of black and white photographs.

'You can sit down, if you want.'

There were two chairs, and Bergman sat in one of them, his wasted body too small for the big balding head which seemed to teeter on one side as he looked at Drew.

'Thanks.'

Drew sat down and looked reluctantly into the face opposite. He prayed silently that he would never end up like Bergman, not that shrunken mummy's face, that greyish skin seamed with thousands of ugly, broken capillaries, and folds of wrinkled flesh which left only narrow slits for his eyes to peer through. Like something out of a horror movie.

'You wanna know about one of my girls?'

Drew nodded.

'Did that private dick tell you about the fee?'

'A hundred dollars.'

'Two hundred – he didn't read the small print.'

'Okay.'

Bergman waited patiently while Drew counted out the dollars in front of him.

'What name did she use?'

161

'Jones, at least, that's what I heard.'

The old man sneered with contempt. 'Give me a break . . . ' he sighed, 'what did she do, what colour was her hair, how old . . . ?'

'Strip joints, sho-bars. Red hair. About twenty, I guess.'

'Where?'

'Maybe LA, maybe here – New York.'

'When?'

He caught a breath. 'Maybe twenty-five years ago.'

'Jesus Christ,' the old man snapped and peered sharply at Drew, 'pour me a drink.' He pointed to a small ice-box. 'There's some good gin in the bottle marked malt vinegar.'

Drew crossed the room to the 'kitchenette' and retrieved the gin, all the time trying to suppress his apprehension, the cold nervousness in his belly. A tiny glass sat on the floor beside Bergman's chair. He picked it up and gave it to him to hold as he twisted the top from the bottle.

'You're gonna spill the goddamn drink all down my pants if you don't keep your hand still . . .' Bergman swallowed the alcohol in one gulp and held the glass out again. 'Did she use any other name?'

'Maybe. I don't know.'

Bergman sighed. 'Jones, you said.'

'Yeah.'

'Big?'

Drew frowned and looked at him.

'Here . . . ' the old man said impatiently and lifted his hands up and out in front of him, '. . . the bazookas.'

'Oh yeah – yeah – definitely.'

'Take a look in that crate over there . . . ' He waved indifferently with an abrupt flick of his hand. 'The one in the middle with Pepsi-Cola plastered across it.'

The flaps of the box were not stuck down, and there was dust on the free surfaces, yet inside the contents were surprisingly neatly filed and in alphabetical order; a small full-length photograph was glued to each ID and beside it a description, personal details and a score out of ten. Drew knelt down, his mouth was dry and he swallowed repeatedly as his fingers reached for the buff and white cards, hovered for an instant, and then moved directly to the letter J. His heart was an annoyingly hard pressure in his chest as he flicked through one card after the other, but there was only one Jones and she was a diminutive Chink with a breast job. Five out of ten.

He became very still for a moment, pushing down his disappointment and despair. Painstakingly he went through the whole box, from A to Z, and again and again, just to make sure.

'She's not here,' he said thickly.

Bergman shook his head and rubbed his sandpapery jaw, then he lit a cigarette. 'I was sure . . . but maybe . . .' He shook his head again and tapped ash on to the floor.

'Maybe what?'

'Depends how much it means to you.'

Drew cleared his throat as comprehension dawned. 'How much?'

'A thousand dollars.'

'You bastard.'

'If you want something real bad, you gotta pay for it – and I can see that you're sweating good and hard for what I've got tucked away.'

'How do I know it's what I'm looking for?'

'It is.'

'That just isn't good enough, old man.'

Bergman sat back in his chair with a grunt.

'Pinkey Jones: redhead, forty double-D, good legs. Used to wear red silk stockings in her act. Handled her for about four years back in the early Sixties. One of the best was Pinkey, real cooperative, if you know what I mean; got a few nice shots to prove it . . .' He licked his lips. 'She had a kid, too, used to follow her around. I didn't like that, wasn't good for business.' He shrugged. 'Last I heard she'd gone and married some rich schmuck of a media guy.' He laughed. 'Yup, quite a girl was Pinkey.' He paused and gave Drew a searching look. 'Although she wouldn't be much of a girl now, would she, but maybe you'd know more about that?'

'Where is this stuff?'

'In a safe place.'

He believed him, he had to, and the old crud had no need to lie.

'I can get the thousand dollars tomorrow.'

'Fine.'

'What do I do?'

'Come back here at the same time and wait outside.'

'And I get the stuff?'

Bergman's big head nodded.

'No fucking around, old man.'

He looked at Drew carefully. 'Fucking around got me in this filthy shit-hole, sonny . . . took me too long to wise up and get smart.' He crushed out his cigarette in the empty glass beside him. 'You should remember that.'

There was a mist ghosting up from the turf and the leafless trees in Green Park had taken on a sombre gloomy beauty. Jackie sat down on a bench and watched a woman walking her dogs and, some way off, an elderly man jogging carefully as if it might be his first time; beyond him someone still slept blanketed in newspaper, hugging the bare shoulder of a dead tree, an empty bottle and some cans lying discarded beside the motionless body.

It was only 8.30 in the morning, but she had been up since six and now held the keys to the mews house in Half Moon Street. She could move in any time she liked. She had hoped that Drew would be around to help, but from the conversation they had had on the way to the airport he seemed to doubt that he would be back from the States before the middle of December, so she would have to manage on her own; not exactly something new.

He hadn't telephoned since the flight, and she thought that he might have done – at least just to say that he had arrived safely. Her eyes fell on the ring on her right hand and immediately she reproached herself because she had not been able to appreciate what he had done, and Drew knew it, of course. She wriggled the ring around on her finger, slipped it off and on to the other hand and studied the effect before putting it back. She snuggled her head into her collar and tried to sort her feelings into thoughts, but it was too difficult and she wondered why she had bothered to try. Her father had told her a long time before that life had a way of working things out for itself and that it was pointless to push against it, even if the picture taking shape seemed not to be what you thought you wanted, or needed.

'Jackie . . . ?'

She looked up and found Jamie standing in front of her.

'It's starting to rain,' he said.

'I hadn't noticed.'

'They said at the hotel you'd gone to the house . . . ' he offered. 'I've been looking for you.' And the looking had not been difficult, he had seen her from the top of the bus; there were not many people sitting in Green Park on a misty, mournful morning in London, particularly not blonde and beautiful women.

'Is there something wrong?'

'Oh, no – no,' he said, 'I thought you were moving in today, so maybe I could help.'

She glanced safely past him to the mild, undulating grassland of the park and the sleeping drunk.

'That's sweet of you,' she said neutrally, 'but I only collected the keys today and now I'm simply killing time, waiting for the burglar alarm people to come round – there are no locks on any of the windows. As to moving in . . . ' She smiled wryly, glad to focus on mundane matters, 'I'll do that next week, provided I can summon up the energy and the time.'

'I could help.'

'Yes,' she said. 'I know.'

There was a pause.

'Was it so wrong to ask you out to dinner?'

'Of course not.'

'You don't like me?'

'Jamie – for God's sake . . .'

'Well, do you?'

'Yes,' she said sharply. 'I like you.'

'I mean – as a man?'

Instantly she recalled that disturbing moment when she had seen him naked, and she snapped her eyes shut.

'I'm involved with someone else, you know that.'

'Drew,' he said flatly.

'Yes,' she said, 'Drew.'

The rain was fine as mist; he could feel it begin to settle on his hair, but he didn't care.

'If you like,' he said, 'I could wait at the house for the alarm people, and you could go on to the studio?'

She looked back at him warily. 'That's good of you,' she said, fishing in her pocket for the keys.

'I don't think I am good . . . ' he said, taking the keys from her, 'do you?'

'Did your father ever call you impertinent?' she said, with a careful smile.

'As a matter of fact he did.'

'I can see why.' She glanced at her watch and stood up. 'We'd better make a move.'

They walked in silence to the park gates and he waited with her until a cab came along.

'I'll leave it a week,' he said, as she climbed into the car.

'What?'

'Until I ask you again.'

He never did know what Jackie replied, because her response was drowned by the closing of the door and the roar of the engine as the cab moved away.

'Christ!' Max hissed, 'how the hell am I supposed to get this thing off the ground if half the cast is missing!'

Aldo sighed. 'I thought you knew that Ian couldn't start as Joe DiMaggio until next week; he's still got seven days of his other contract to run.'

'I do know, damn it!' he said furiously. 'I just bloody well forgot, that's all.'

'Well, Rupert – alias Arthur Miller – is having a coffee down the hall: we were going to skip the first three scenes and start putting him through his paces, if you remember.'

'I had myself geared up for *this* scene,' Max snapped, slapping the pages held in his hand.

'Are you all right?'

Max stiffened and glared at Aldo. 'What the hell's that supposed to mean?'

Aldo took a deep breath, aware that some of the cast milling around were beginning to stare.

'Forget it, just forget it, Max,' he said tightly. 'But right now I'm going to walk back to that piano and then I shall work out where we're going to begin this rehearsal because we're already running twenty minutes late.'

For a split second their gazes locked and then Max was shaking his head slowly. 'Okay, all right – sorry, Aldo,' he said, lifting his hands up in mock protest, 'I didn't mean to lose my cool; I seem to have a lot on my mind.'

'I suppose it wouldn't have anything to do with our conversation last week?'

Max closed his eyes. 'Inflammation of the bladder,' he said.

Aldo restrained a smile. 'I thought only women got that sort of thing?'

'Apparently not.' Once the very cheery doctor had finally got the results of his tests he had told him that he probably had a short urethra, the tube leading up to the bladder, which meant that he was more prone to such a condition than the average male.

'Aren't you relieved?'

'I could have been, but I panicked and with my usual subtlety broke the unhappy news to one of the ladies concerned before I really knew what was the matter.'

'Yvonne.'

Max gaped at him. 'How the hell did you know?'

'For God's sake, *everyone* knows.' Aldo shrugged. 'It also explains why she was in tears on Friday morning and why she is conspicuous by her absence today.' She had called Max a bastard – a filthy bastard, in fact, but he wouldn't tell him that. 'I hope the news hasn't found its way to Jackie.'

'I doubt it.'

'But it might be a good idea to make your peace with Yvonne, all the same . . . ' Aldo said. 'And soon – after all, we need our invaluable wardrobe mistress here . . . ' he said dryly, 'do we not?'

Max watched him walk to the piano, with his lips pressed together, almost white. Did Aldo think him a complete fool? Naturally he had tried to make his goddamn peace with Yvonne, but she kept putting the phone down on him. What the hell did she want him to do – get down on his bloody knees and beg? He promised himself that he would fade out of the affair once he had finally persuaded her to return to the studio. Max's thoughts switched effortlessly to Nadia, and he immediately felt a swift surge of pleasure, then frowned. Polly would kill him if she found out.

The sound of the piano and the opening bars of a song caught his attention and he clapped his hands, turning to the cast who were standing waiting around the studio.

'Okay, darlings. Scene four – let's get started.' He scanned them quickly with a practised eye. 'Where the hell's Rupert?'

'Having a coffee,' a girl's voice piped up.

Max's nostrils flared with barely suppressed fury and he turned to the speaker with a thin smile on his face. 'Well, I should go on and get him, sweety, before I have to – and he wouldn't like that very much, I can assure you.'

The girl's face coloured pink as she moved to leave the room, but the door swung open and Jackie walked in.

Max swore under his breath.

'How are things going?' she asked from the doorway.

'Fine – great.'

'Good,' she said, 'I'll see you at the set meeting later.'

'We'll be one short, I'm afraid.'

'Oh?'

'Yvonne,' he said, 'throat infection.'

One way or the other, the piece had come all the way from Van Cleef & Arpels in Paris, via the Duke and Duchess of Windsor, of course. Dougie had really excelled himself this time.

Angela studied her reflection in the sliding doors of the penthouse terrace and then ran her fingers lovingly along the backbone of the outstretched tiger bracelet. Wrapping it gently around her wrist she raised her hand so that the encrusted gold, emeralds and diamonds caught the lamplight and she blinked and sighed with deep satisfaction. The Duke of Windsor himself had assisted in the design of the Panther Collection because of his obsessive devotion to Wallis – America's one and only real Cinderella. She brought the exquisite tiger closer, stroking the jewelled paws, kissing the perfect onyx nose. How clever of Dougie to remember that little gasp of envy and admiration she had made when they had gone to the jewel exhibition together.

She picked up the card which had been delivered with the gift and read the inscription once more: 'A little something to keep my Tiger happy . . .' Angela walked away from the window to pick up a glass of champagne and switch on the music system. Harry Conick Junior's silky voice began to drift out of the speakers and she smiled with pleasure as the music sealed her perfect mood before sinking down into a sumptuous bank of silk cushions.

'Tiger . . .' she said, and grinned.

Immediately her thoughts turned to the next Democratic Convention in Chicago and all those functions, parties and people she would have to miss because Dougie was still 'in mourning'. He wouldn't even hear of her just being there, not even in the goddamned town. Her mouth began to droop sulkily and she scoured her imagination for ways that Dougie might make it up to her. Why not a betrothal gift for his bride-in-waiting – something fabulous and really out of this world? The doorbell chimed and with a sigh of irritation she got up.

Drew stood outside. 'Well?' he said.

She cleared her throat. 'What are you doing here?'

'I was just passing – thought I'd call in,' he smiled and let his eyes travel freely over her body, 'and I like the outfit, shows off all your best features, you might say.' It was a flesh-coloured flimsy robe, like a kaftan, embroidered with tiny black beads. Angela was naked underneath.

'I asked you what you wanted.'

'What do you think I want?'

A tiny eager thrill began to unfurl in her stomach. It was the shock of seeing him, of course, just the shock.

'I could call Security.'

'But you won't.'

His gaze beat her down. 'I'm here on business.'

She looked back at him, relaxing a little as she recovered her composure. 'Don't make me laugh.'

'It's true,' he grinned, 'by all that's holy.'

'What business?'

'Jackie business.'

Her face darkened immediately. 'I told you to stay away from her.'

'I got lonely.'

'It was over between you two.'

'Was,' he said, 'past tense.'

'Are you trying to tell me that you've been in England all this time?'

He nodded.

Her eyes glittered in the lamplight, hard and brilliant, and then she made a savage gesture of her head towards the penthouse, and stepped back so that Drew could pass by her into the room.

He prowled around the room, familiarizing himself with all her precious things, her artwork and glass; opening magazines and books lying across the enormous Italian coffee table.

'This is new . . . ' he exclaimed, 'but, man – what *is* it?' He stopped in front of a large sculpture of a double-headed eagle.

'It's a bronze – French,' she said tautly and walked over to the waiting champagne bottle. 'I suppose I could offer you a drink, but you haven't answered my question yet.'

'Now I remember this,' he said, ignoring her, and lifting the statuette from its pedestal, just as he had done once before.

'Put it down, damn you.'

'Who is it?'

'For chrissakes, Drew.'

'Who is it, I said.'

'It's nearly two hundred years old – how the hell should I know?'

'Tell me something about it.'

'No.'

'Tell me,' he repeated slowly. 'I want to learn.'

'*What for?*'

'Tell me.' There was a warning note in his voice.

He was standing with his back to her and for a moment she looked at him, at the shape of his head, the beautiful black hair, the dusky powerful hand with its fingers coiled around the statue, hating the desire which was creeping up inside her.

'It's supposed to represent Night,' she said sullenly.

He turned back to her, still studying the statue, following the curves of its classical form with a single, trailing finger.

'Beautiful,' he remarked, 'but I said that last time I was here, didn't I?'

'And I asked you a question.'

He put down the statuette and walked towards her.

'Jackie needs an advance from her trust fund.'

'Why did she send you with the begging bowl?'

'I had some other business to attend to here and offered my services.'

Angela laughed, but it was not a kind laugh. 'This is a joke, isn't it?'

'No joke. She needs something like five hundred thousand dollars.'

'At least the price has come down,' she snorted softly with contempt, 'but I told her no some time back. I'm not interested in her goddamn musical – no one will be.'

'She thinks they will.'

'Bullshit, Drew,' she smiled thinly, 'and you couldn't give a damn about her precious musical, could you? That's not why you're here.'

'It's beginning to attract quite a lot of attention,' he said mildly.

'I can put a stop to that.'

'I don't think you can,' he said with deceptive idleness and poured himself a glass of champagne. 'Why do you care so much, anyway?'

'Like I told Jackie – it's a dud – something that's been tried before and crashed. For chrissakes, Monroe is dead, long dead – I just can't see what the fatal attraction is.'

'It's not your money, Angela.'

'As far as the law is concerned, I take care of it.'

'I still don't see why you're so concerned about a musical that might, or might not, crash.' He examined her face carefully, smelling the proverbial rat. 'You've never cared a horse's ass how Jackie spent her money before.'

'That's none of your damn business – and the answer's still no.' And it would remain no until Dougie married her. There had been too much scandal associated with the Kennedys already without resurrecting another reminder. She sighed inwardly. Dougie had been having a love affair with the tedious Kennedy legend for years, sometimes she thought he would be quite prepared to bow down and kiss the ground they walked on. With a feeling of helplessness she wondered why the hell he couldn't have been a Republican.

'She didn't think you'd say yes.'

'In that case she won't be disappointed and you've had a wasted trip.'

'Like you said, that's not why I'm here.' His mouth moved into a small derisive smile.

'I think you'd better go now,' she said, 'and stay away from Jackie.'

He made no response.

'I'm expecting someone.'

'Oh, yeah?'

'*Yes*.'

He shook his head. 'I had a meeting with an old friend of yours.'

'How nice,' she said dryly, draining her glass and putting it down on the table.

'Oleg Bergman.'

He saw her hand tremble as she moved it away from the glass.

'I said you'd better go.'

'For an old man he's smart.'

'Really?'

'Had some real pretty pictures . . . there was one girl who looked just like you.'

'What a coincidence.'

'Pinkey Jones she called herself.'

'What has that got to do with me?'

'Do you really need me to tell you?'

'Get out, Drew.'

'I'm not finished yet.'

'Yes, you are.'

'Do you know when I first began to suspect?' He continued as if she hadn't spoken. 'Right here, that crazy afternoon when you did that strip – like it was straight out of one of those sho-bars.'

'Bullshit.'

'No . . . oh, no . . . I loved it.' He deliberately misunderstood her and his lips slid into a slow sensuous smile.

Their eyes locked and there was that power surge, that heat, and time seemed very slow. Angela swallowed, caught by the

172

memories she had tried so hard to keep at bay. Her gaze fell to his lips: she could almost feel that old familiar greed, that hot open mouth closing over hers. And the youth, arrogant youth in that perfect tanned body, and the wildness – like a magnificent animal. All those sensations and images flashed through her in an instant. He took a step towards her, but immediately she stiffened.

'No, Drew.'

'Don't fight it,' his voice was patient, low, almost hushed, 'we're two of a kind you and me.'

'Not any more.'

Her words struck him like a blow.

'You don't mean that.'

'I do.'

He was only half-listening because his gaze was drawn to the luxurious gift box which lay open and empty. A profusion of red satin ribbons curled across and around it; there was a small gold card with matching red edging lying beside it. Drew stepped forward and picked it up.

Angela's eyes widened and her breathing grew heavy as she looked at the partly bowed head, as he lifted his eyes and stared back at her.

'You shouldn't have read that – it's personal,' but her voice had grown small.

He took a deep gulp of air as jealousy began to rise inside and the cold control he had exercised with such care began to break out in a roaring wave.

'Bitch.'

She felt the fear press up against her stomach and glanced instinctively at the telephone, but Drew got there before her and ripped the cord from the wall.

'No calls.'

'Drew . . .'

'What did he give you?'

'Who?' She moved backwards away from him.

'Who?' he screamed. 'Dougie kiss-my-ass Hicks, that's who!' He jammed his finger at her and she jumped as nerves cruised unmercifully over her body.

'It was nothing really – nothing.'

'Nothing,' he sneered, 'you keep your lies for *him*!' He spat the words contemptuously, 'you think that pot-bellied has-been's gonna take you to the White House, don't you? From what I've heard he won't ever, and I mean *ever*, get close to Vice-President – he's a yes-man, a fat buggy-eyed yes-man.' He started to laugh suddenly, then stopped, so that the laughter had the rough rawness of a sob. 'And you let him *touch* you, that disgusting *old* man.'

'It's not like that.'

He clenched his fists and squeezed his eyes shut tight for an instant.

'Where's the "nothing" gift he gave you?'

'It wasn't really a gift . . .'

He watched her face, saw her mind search for a lie and then let his eyes travel over her until they came to settle on the bracelet. 'Tiger . . .' he said softly and caught her wrist, bringing it close to his face, staring into the exquisite emerald eyes. 'I can't give you things like this,' he said in a grieving voice, 'can I?'

She made no answer.

'Can I?'

'Let go.'

He looked at her without speaking, his eyes glazed as a thought, a certainty, took shape in his mind and he realized that he would never want anything as much as he wanted her now. Not ever.

'Pinkey,' his voice was husky. 'Pinkey . . .'

God, that name! That image rising up out of the dusty past complete with all its gaudy colours, its filthy noise. She clamped her eyes shut on the memory, but then he was bringing his face too close and she could feel his breath, smell his sweat, feel her body begin to grow limp. He caught her other wrist, pushing both hands behind her back and holding them with one fist as he began lifting her dress. It was too late, it had been too late from the beginning.

A whimper escaped her lips as his tongue begin to run down her neck and she threw back her head, her belly jerking, as his hand found the hot flesh between her legs. He sank to his knees, pulling her with him, calling her name over and over, tearing her dress, sliding young strong hands across her body so that he might find the heavy breasts he loved.

It was his fantasies and all the long lonely days and nights wanting her made real. Tears stung his eyes and he felt himself tremble as she took his head between her hands to suck feverishly at his lips, his cheeks, his eyes, pulling at his clothes, reaching for his sex and arching her back so that she could guide him inside. 'Now, Drew, now – please God, please God.' She looked at him in astonished delight, her lips stretched wide in a gasp of pure pleasure. '. . . Oh yes, oh yes, oh *yeess* . . .'

EIGHT

'Use your mouth more, loosen up . . .'

Rose nodded mutely at her voice coach, Lilian.

'In the States the voice tones are harsher,' Lilian continued, 'you English don't use your mouths that much when you talk, so we'll have to work on that.' She patted Rose's shoulder. 'Hey, it'll come, don't look so down.'

'I'm okay.'

'You could have fooled me,' she said with a smile. 'Where is the girl I saw last week, and the week before, dripping with energy and enthusiasm.' Lilian lifted Rose's chin gently and looked into her face. 'Don't lose it, Rose, it's like gold dust.'

'I'm okay – really,' she protested.

'Are you eating properly?'

Rose nodded.

'Sleeping?'

Rose nodded again, but Lilian thought otherwise from the telltale smudges, like purple thumbprints, beneath her eyes.

'Well, okay,' she said doubtfully, 'but if there's a problem and I mean *anything*, let's talk about it.'

'I'm fine, don't worry,' Rose said, feeling uncomfortable beneath Lilian's penetrating scrutiny. 'I'd better hurry,' she added quickly, 'Jackie wants me for an interview and some photographs now.'

'In that case you'd better sit still for a moment while I give your face some colour – you look as white as a sheet. We don't want our producer thinking that you can't stand the pace, now do we?'

'But the make-up guy will be there.'

'Oh, sure, I know – this is just to make you look as if you have good red blood running through your veins!'

Rose glanced at her reflection in the wall mirror and thought how large her eyes seemed rising up out of the pale cameo of her face, even her lips which were normally a pretty pink had lost colour. She surrendered to Lilian's delicate ministrations, soothed by the careful, kindly fingers which brought her features alive.

It was Drew, of course. He hadn't telephoned for over a week. He had mentioned something about going to the States, and then nothing. She had tried the hotel and they told her that he had 'left on business', leaving no message. Her forehead puckered into a frown of painful bewilderment. America had telephones – he could still call her, couldn't he? She shifted restlessly in her chair as images and thoughts began to run riot in her mind; perhaps he had had an accident?

'Hey, keep still . . . ' Lilian said softly, 'almost finished.'

Rose tensed and stared straight ahead as her eyelashes were skilfully coated with mascara. She focused on a hairline crack which ran from the ceiling to the upper edge of the mirror and was reminded of her shoddy flat which had been home to her for something like four years. Now her agent was telling her that she must think about moving in the not-too-distant future because 'it wouldn't be good for her image'. A month, three weeks, ago, when everything had possessed an exciting, dream-like quality, a move had seemed like a good idea, but now the thought alarmed her slightly; everything was suddenly happening too fast and she didn't know how, or when, she should start trying to slow things down. She stared back at herself in the mirror with a feeling of helplessness, if only Drew were here, or if she could just call him and know that he was *there*.

'Okay, finished!' Lilian said brightly and took a step away from Rose to survey her handiwork. 'You know, I don't think even a professional could have done a better job – all you need to do is give them a big smile and you'll knock them dead.'

Rose caught a breath, as if she had not heard. 'You know what Marilyn said once . . . that the biggest and most difficult thing she could imagine was making one person completely happy.'

'So you've been doing your homework? Good girl,' Lilian responded. 'But Monroe never succeeded, did she? I mean, she never made anyone happy in the end, and certainly not herself.' She shot a sharp glance at Rose. 'Hey, I've read up on her, too; it makes depressing reading, but don't let it get to you.'

Rose looked down at her clasped hands, they were cold and she shivered.

'You're not feeling well, are you?'

'It's just a headache, Lilian, nothing much.'

'Well, take a couple of these. . . ' She fished out some paracetamol from her handbag and poured Rose a glass of water. 'I knew there was something wrong.'

For a moment Rose was tempted to spill out everything she had been thinking, but she set her mouth shut on her weakness because of her promise to Drew and because she would probably say too much, too many things in a rush of idiotic embarrassing words.

'I'll see you on Friday, then . . .'

Rose looked up. 'Oh – yes, of course.'

Lilian watched her pupil move to the door, still uneasy; Rose was fragile, despite the tremendous voice, and insecure like many performers. It was a sad profession, and actors suffered for their art because it was part of the job – expected and unavoidable, but there was something about Rose that made you feel her capacity to suffer was too great.

'Perfect.'

The photographer shuffled quickly backwards, stopped, tilted the camera a little and took four or five shots. He straightened and snapped Rose again from his full height, which was considerable.

'Could we have her as Marilyn now, please? My make-up guy's already in the dressing room waiting to do the honours.'

Jackie nodded and Rose left the studio to change into the costume they had picked out from the ones that had been taking shape under Yvonne's eagle eye, but the extensive make-up would come first: the dusted white complexion, arched darkened eyebrows, black liner, glossy red lips, beauty spot on left cheek, and finally a white-blonde wig.

'While we're waiting, let's concentrate on Lucy Wilding, the understudy,' Jackie said and gestured towards Lucy who was sitting waiting a few seats away.

As Lucy took her place Max approached the group from the back of the studio with Jamie trailing behind, notebook and pen in hand. Max didn't say anything for what seemed a long time and then leaned down so that his arms were resting on the back of the chair next to her.

'You know that some of the music will have to be rewritten if we finally cast Charlie Fitzgerald as Jim Dougherty?'

'Because he's a baritone and not a tenor,' she said patiently, turning around. 'Yes, I know.'

'I just wasn't sure whether you were aware of the extra work involved.'

'We're only talking about rewriting the music of one song and a verse of another, aren't we?'

'Ah . . . ' he said, 'you've already spoken to Aldo.'

'Yes, of course,' she said, 'but you haven't changed your mind about Fitzgerald, have you?'

'Oh, no,' he frowned nevertheless, 'but it would have been nice to have a tenor, and waiting for the changes will mean more delay.'

'I suspect that if we decided to wait and find the perfect tenor, which would mean even more auditioning, we probably wouldn't cast Monroe's first husband until the New Year.'

He nodded reluctantly and then turned his attention to the photographer who was busy arranging Lucy's hair.

'Where's Rose?'

'Changing for a Monroe pose.'

'How's it going?'

'Fine.'

'Have the shots of Lucy and Rose together already been taken?'

'Yes.'

He nodded again.

'Why don't you sit down?'

'Haven't the time, but Jamie might as well hang on, he'll probably find it interesting.' He started to walk away. 'Perhaps you'll let me know when the roughs come back, I'd like to see the results.'

'Yes, Max, I'll try not to forget,' she said with a trace of sarcasm; PR was her job and she had no intention of consulting Max on the choice of publicity shots.

'Perhaps Jamie would like to make a note of that . . . ' he said loudly before disappearing through the double doors.

'God, that man . . .' she muttered under her breath.

'I think he's simply a perfectionist.' Jamie offered, with a smile.

Jackie raised her eyebrows. 'You're being very diplomatic.'

'I'm glad I'm learning something.'

'It's not as bad as that, is it?'

He said nothing.

'I see,' she said. 'It is as bad as that.'

'I like watching the interplay between the people involved.'

'I suppose that's something.'

'And I like watching you work.' He stared at her closely and was rewarded by the onset of a blush.

'Jamie – don't.'

'Miss Jones?'

She looked up with relief; it was the photographer.

'Rose is ready . . .'

She was wearing black skintight slacks and an equally skintight sweater in white heavy-knit from a picture taken of Monroe in Korea when she had visited American troops in the Fifties. Jackie was greatly encouraged by Rose's appearance; the padding discreetly placed in shoulders and breasts looked convincingly real and no one could have guessed except those who knew Rose well. The transformation was far better than she could have hoped.

'The shot would be along the lines we discussed earlier,' she said, 'something vibrant and alive.'

'This is what I want to try . . .'

The session lasted over an hour and it was only towards the end that Jackie felt that they had hit upon the perfect pose based upon a 1959 shot of Monroe literally jumping for joy. It was unusual enough to catch the eye, but also filled with movement which would mean that Rose's resemblance to the dead star could not easily be measured. The camera would do the rest.

'Wonderful,' she said standing up, 'I really think we've got something there.'

Jamie sat at the back and followed her with his eyes as she walked over to the photographer, caught by her enthusiasm and wishing he could feel the same. But he had come to terms with the fact that the only reason he was here was Jackie.

He thought of his father. He would have hated all of this – the people, the theatre, its trappings and the subject matter of this musical most of all. The 'goddess' Marilyn Monroe would have been labelled simply 'a whore', but everything had always been very black and white as far as his father was concerned, particularly with regard to the forbidden subject of sex. Curiously it had never really been discussed or analysed in depth, even by his fellow novitiates at the seminary, and it was remarkable that not even murder, the taking of life, seemed to be regarded as more sinister. He had never understood that.

'Jamie – would you mind getting three coffees?' Jackie called, not even pausing to look at him before she resumed talking.

He closed his eyes in frustration and made his way across the room to the small table on which stood a kettle, dried milk, plastic cups, but no sugar; there was never any sugar.

'I'm gasping.'

He glanced sideways; it was Rose.

'Shouldn't take a minute.'

'This is really hard work, you know, I'm exhausted.' She smiled with an effort. 'I hadn't expected all that leaping around.' She gently pulled off her blonde wig and grimaced, sliding a hand back through her own hair which had been flattened and made slick with grease.

'Jackie seems happy with the result.'

'Oh, yes, definitely,' she moved nervously from one foot to the other, 'but I thought there might have been more of a crowd here.'

'Crowd?'

'Well, you know, the team – Max, Aldo, Joe, Gordon . . . ' she cleared her throat and blushed, 'maybe that American guy.'

Realization flooded in and he found himself caught by the expression on her powdered white face, the red lips grotesque and strange suddenly; feeling sorry for her.

'You mean Drew Carocci?'

'That's him,' she said. 'Haven't seen him around lately.'

'He's in the States.'

'Oh – right.' She swallowed slowly.

The kettle began to boil and he turned to it with relief and poured the scalding water into three cups. For a vacant moment

Rose hovered hopefully at Jamie's elbow watching the steam cloud and rise up.

'I'm sorry, there's nothing more I can tell you,' he said gently, 'I don't know when he's due back.'

Something in his tone made her look up and she turned to him with eyes grown round and afraid, her anxious hand reaching up to touch his arm. 'But he is coming back?'

Jamie smiled uneasily. 'As far as I know, yes.'

She smiled back at him and the tremulous smile seemed to hang there small and alone.

'You had no right.'

Lucy could hardly bear the wounded look on his face.

'I told you,' she said, 'it was just conversation . . .'

'My writing is a private thing, you know that,' Richard said, 'and how could you discuss it with *him*, of all people?'

'I didn't discuss it at all, the subject was merely mentioned.' She looked back at him desperately. 'I was doing it for you if you like . . .'

'Me!'

'I just wanted him to know that you were busy, that you didn't spend your time simply waiting for the telephone to ring.' But it had all gone wrong somehow and then Roger had used it against her.

'I don't need you to boost my confidence in the eyes of other people,' he said harshly, 'I couldn't give a damn what they think.' If only that were true. 'And what a coincidence that you should bump so cosily into dear old Roger.'

'Oh, stop it, Richard, not that again,' she said quietly, 'please.'

'He mentioned it again today,' he retorted sharply as if she had not spoken, 'like slow torture.'

'Ignore him, can't you – he's just tactless, always has been.' But the expression on his face told her that her words were wasted. 'He thinks you're very good, you know,' she lied finally.

'Oh, don't make me laugh!' he sneered. 'The only person he has any opinion of is himself – the star.' Richard closed his eyes in exasperation. 'And please, *please* don't quote him again – I have no wish to be patronized directly or indirectly by a Dr Kildare clone.'

'Sorry,' she said meekly.

He glared at her, drained suddenly by the repeat performance of this inquisition and disgusted with himself for allowing a buffoon like Roger to come between them again. It was, he supposed helplessly, jealousy and envy, and probably a little fear thrown in for good measure. Fear of losing Lucy.

He swept a hand through his hair and took a deep gulp of air and then the faintest of smiles began to tilt the edges of his mouth and she knew it would be all right.

' – Or by a bloody Kraut with a name like Foch, come to that!'

'What?'

'So, he hasn't told you that he has another name and was in the Hitler youth?'

'Richard, Roger wasn't even born then,' she started to giggle.

'Makes no difference,' he mocked imperiously, 'because he would have been – got the makings of a good Nazi has dear old jolly bloody Roger . . .' He placed a finger horizontally beneath his nose and shot a hand into the air: 'Yes, the *Führer* would have been proud of Roger von Foch's Aryan good looks and no doubt given him top marks for sadism, I can assure you of that, *mein liebling . . .*'

'Richard,' she pleaded, 'can we stop talking about Roger now?'

He paused abruptly with a faint, foolish grin on his face. 'I can get a little tedious, can't I?'

She shook her head.

'No?' He said softly.

'No.'

When she looked at him that way he felt all doubts, worries, thoughts drift quietly away. He held out his arms and when she came to him he wrapped them around her carefully and hugged her tightly.

'I'm a hypocrite, you know,' he murmured, winding his fingers into her hair.

'Why?'

'They've asked me to do six more episodes, maybe more.'

'Don't.' She had been waiting for him to tell her; Roger had telephoned her at the studio to break the 'good news'. He had persuaded the producer to alter the script so that the storyline

Richard was involved in could be extended; he had been very pleased with himself.

'Why not?'

'I can't bear any more misunderstandings.' Or meetings with Roger.

Richard moved her a little away from him so that he could look at her.

'There won't be,' he smiled guiltily like a naughty child, 'and we need the money.'

'Not that badly,' she frowned and added uselessly, 'anyway, I thought you were only needed for a short time because they were writing someone out.'

'Well, they've decided to postpone the last rites – Dr Mason's wife is to be allowed to linger a little, it's good for the ratings apparently.'

'I thought you hated it?'

He groaned. 'I know, I know, but apart from the spectre of Roger, I'm actually beginning to enjoy getting up in the morning with a purpose in mind and somewhere *real* to go.'

She said nothing.

'It's comical, really . . .' he continued, 'I've even had a couple of fan letters from lonely middle-aged ladies. I haven't told you that, have I?' He turned around and moved to the window. 'And I know I never actually said so, but it was all beginning to get to me,' he darted a careful glance at her. 'I don't think I could have been held responsible for my actions if I had had to make one more cheese sandwich and wrap it in cling film.' He forced a laugh. 'I began to loathe this place and the damned silence hour after dreary hour, so I'd have the television switched up loud to drown out the nothingness; I watched all the soaps avidly, knew all the names of the flickering soapstars . . .'

'What about your writing?'

'That's different.'

'You won't stop, will you?'

'No, of course not,' he swung round. 'It's almost the perfect set-up, Luce, because I'm getting paid for the soap three days a week and can write the other two.'

She smiled back uneasily. 'If you're pleased, I'm pleased.' Yet she spoke with a sinking heart. 'I should have realized you were so depressed.' That was why she had asked Roger if he could help. She should have known that she would have to pay for such help in the end; it had never been Roger's style to give without taking in return.

'Why? You've been busy working – thank God, and "resting" is par for the course, isn't it? Which is exactly what we were told would happen when we were training, what we were warned would happen by our parents and friends, aunts and uncles, etcetera, etcetera, but we didn't really listen, did we?'

'I think you're being rather hard . . .'

'Perhaps,' he shrugged, 'all I know is that despite my initial reaction and despite Roger's crassness I'm beginning to feel part of the human race again.'

She wanted to tell him then, about Roger, but the words wouldn't come.

'Is everything all right?' he asked suddenly. 'I mean work – you're not bothered about anything, are you?'

'No,' she responded quickly, 'the show's ticking over and things are beginning to come together, but it's been a difficult week . . . ' She exchanged a rueful look with him. 'Hasn't it?'

He nodded and looked shamefaced, but she didn't want that because none of it was his fault; it was hers for being such a bungling idiot, such a coward. Since that day Richard had come home furious and white-faced and told her of the unfortunate conversation he had had with Roger, she had been promising herself that she would tell Roger to take a walk, but she hadn't . . .

'Why don't you let me take you out for dinner?' he said brightly. 'We could splash out and go to Zen NW3 in Hampstead?'

. . . And now she couldn't.

He walked quietly over to her. 'Hey, don't look so worried . . . ' He kissed her lightly on the nose. 'We can afford it now.'

Angela studied Drew as he walked across the room wearing only an open robe. He poured himself a drink and lay back on the sofa opposite, plumping up the cushions and then picking up the book he had been reading. She watched him silently for a long time.

'What is it?'

He looked up and she thought how beautifully young he seemed at that moment, yet how fast his face could change from sweet vulnerability to calculating gigolo.

'The book?'

She nodded.

'Art history.'

She shook her head and laughed out loud. 'You?'

'Why not, is there something wrong with it?' He *had* to learn about the things that mattered to her if there was ever going to be any chance of her taking him seriously. But there was more to it than that; for the first time in his life he had discovered a form of art that had begun to fascinate him – *he* had found it, inside himself, and that discovery was like a small wonder, like finding something beautiful in a trashcan.

'Not wrong exactly. . . .' She shrugged, but hadn't she learned the same way herself? Once she married Lloyd Shriver all those years ago he had encouraged her to read and she devoured almost any book she could lay her hands on and then proceeded to put his money to really good use. Not only did she remodel her body, but her mind as well – all the necessaries: art history, antiques, French, the works. There had been a purpose in everything she did, but Drew, where did he think it would get him?

'Then lay off, will you?' He trailed a hand across a glossy photograph of a painting called 'The Dance of Life' and would have shaken the artist's hand if he hadn't been dead long since. It was about women, and the guy, Munch, was unhappy in love. In the picture he danced with a girl in a red dress who was supposed to represent passion and they were watched over by two women, one in white, youth and purity, the second in black, representing death. It seemed to Drew that Munch and he shared a lot in common; apparently the guy had felt that, like vampires, women would eventually devour him. *A* woman, Drew thought, and lifted his head, and a shadow seemed to fall behind his eyes as he stared at Angela.

A delicious chill ran up her back and she shot him a greedy, dazzling smile because it excited her when he got angry.

'Go ahead, tell me about it . . . ' she said languidly and began

to stretch, arching her body a little, pointing her perfectly manicured toes.

He blushed and closed the book.

'Oh, Drew, don't be such a baby.'

He sat in silence; immobile, brooding, hating her for the power
she held over him and his pathetic desire to impress and please.

'The wall lights . . . ' he began.

'Wall *brackets*.'

'The wall brackets are Lalique.'

'Correct.'

'And the lamp.'

'Yes.'

'But that isn't.' He stood up and her eyes fell immediately on
his nakedness, his sex, and she felt that greed again, that eagerness, rise up inside. Once more she found herself wondering
what it was about him that excited her so much. She caught a
wary breath, but it could not go on, of course, Drew would have
to leave, and soon; she was supposed to be seeing Dougie at the
weekend.

'No, you're right, it's not.'

He stood in front of the silver and gold vase and simply stared.

'Art Nouveau?'

'Yes,' she said, 'good.'

'It's not French.'

'No, German, but close, Drew.' She started to applaud.

'Tell me about it.'

A heavy sigh escaped her lips.

'Can't we drop this now?' She was getting bored.

'I wanna know,' he said stubbornly.

'For chrissakes, not now – you're beginning to drive me crazy
with all this.'

His mouth turned downwards into a sullen frown.

'This is important to me, you just can't see that, can you?'

'I didn't realize it was *that* important – and, I mean, what is the
point, where exactly will it get you?'

'You still think I'm some low-life jerk, don't you, going
nowhere?' And she did, there was no getting away from that,
except that she wanted him, still, despite all her big-shot words.
Even now as he looked at her he knew that she wanted him.

She did not speak for a moment, glaring at him with barely suppressed anger for spoiling her mood. When he did not move she stood up finally and walked slowly towards him.

'What exactly would Mr . . . ' she paused with great deliberation, 'you know, Drew, you never have told me your real name.'

He smiled, but it was not a nice smile. 'If you tell me about the vase, I might tell you my name.'

Her eyes examined him sharply, but then she was smiling back and lifting up a finger to run one scarlet fingernail down, down, from his chin to his chest, to his belly, and slowly, slowly to the mound of hair and hardening flesh between his thighs. He gasped.

'It's by a guy called Johann Lötz,' she said softly, 'anything else?'

'When?'

She took him in her hand.

'About 1900, give or take a year.'

'The design?' He swallowed convulsively as she began to stroke him.

'The design?' she repeated and gave a throaty chuckle, 'that's easy, you'll like this because it sort of represents what Art Nouveau is all about.' She squeezed him hard, harder until he moaned. 'Sensuous lines, Drew,' she said, 'think of a woman, all those rounds and curves, think of ripe burgeoning fruit and those soft sensuous lines converging, diverging . . .' She let him go.

He fought for control, breathing heavily, staring hard at her.

'And this?' He placed a finger against a detail on the vase as if it might steady him.

'You don't give up, do you?' Her voice was low and tinged with something like admiration.

'And this?' He repeated stubbornly.

'It's a favourite design of the period, a plant called Honesty.' She became very still as their eyes met. 'Purple flowers and fragile seed pods which people once believed to possess magical qualities.'

'But it is sort of magical, isn't it?'

'Oh, stop it, Drew,' she said suddenly.

'Stop what?'

'This.' She gestured at the vase and at the book lying where he had left it. 'It doesn't suit you.'

'How the hell do you know what suits me?' he asked bitterly.

'Oh, for chrissakes . . . ' she snapped, 'you can have the damned vase as a present – a leaving present.'

'What the hell's that supposed to mean?'

She shook her head with exasperation. 'Look, we were just talking about the word "honesty". Well,' she swallowed, 'it's time I was honest with you, again, once and for all.' She swore silently; why did it always come down to this?

'I don't want to hear!' Abruptly he clamped his hands over his ears.

'This can't go on, Drew,' she said carefully.

He swung round and away from her. 'Shut your goddamned mouth – just shut it!' He walked into the bedroom and slammed the door behind him.

Angela looked at the closed door helplessly. Gritting her teeth she stalked towards the door and kicked it hard.

'And don't walk away when I'm talking to you, goddammit!'

The door flew open and he stood there, glowering at her.

'I said I want you to leave.'

'No.'

'I have a life outside this apartment – a damn good one.'

'And I'm not a part of that life,' he said tightly, 'right?'

'If you want to put it like that.'

'I could learn.'

'No, Drew.'

His face contorted, and he looked away to hide the pain. 'Why?'

'Because that's the way it's got to be.' But her voice sounded oddly uncertain.

'Why?'

She caught a sharp, impatient breath. 'And don't keep asking me, why – why – why! You sound like a six-year-old kid.'

He slammed her against the wall. 'Don't – just *don't* say that – ever!'

The force of the impact knocked the breath from her lungs and she felt sick as the blood drained from her face. Yet even as the effects of the blow began to fade there was a slow tingling, a nerve throbbing as if champagne were flooding her brain. She looked at him wordlessly, unable to speak.

'You want me to do it to you, don't you . . . ?' he whispered.

She nodded slowly.

'Say it.'

As if for an answer she caught hold of his hand, put it to her mouth and began raking the skin with her teeth.

'Say it,' he pressed up against her, 'say please.'

They looked intensely at each other and then her head fell back and very slowly she lowered herself to her knees.

He felt her mouth close around his sex and he sighed and moaned to her touch. She looked up at him as he buried his fingers in her hair, holding her head between his hands, moving it backwards and forwards, but with an enormous effort of will he backed away just enough so that she would release him, pulling her to a standing position and lifting her on to a small table which stood flush against the wall. He pushed her thighs apart.

'I said, say please . . .'

'Please,' she whispered.

There was no tenderness in their embrace as arms and hands searched feverishly for possession. He lifted her up, his fingers digging into her flesh as he pulled her against him, her greedy thighs and calves hugging his body tightly as he drove bitterly into her and they locked together in hungry, desperate union.

Much later when her mind attempted to play back the pleasure and the pain she could only remember the warm wetness of his tears as he climaxed, and the moment when she had finally asked him his name, his real name. She was cradling his head in her lap, pushing her fingers up through the beautiful black hair. Drew had slowly turned on his back, interlocking his fingers with hers, and had looked straight into her eyes.

'Tell me yours first.'

'Don't start that again.'

'Why don't you admit it – you know I know the truth now.'

'And you're beginning to push your luck.'

'I don't have anything to lose.'

'And I do?'

He took her hand, pressed it to his lips and began running his

190

tongue around and around the centre of her palm. 'Oh, yes, Pinkey,' he whispered, 'definitely.'

The Park Room had always been her father's favourite; he adored its light and space and the wonderful view of Hyde Park from 'their table' in the restaurant. For many years they had tried to keep their monthly lunch date and were only forced to miss it when one of them was not in the country. Today had already been confirmed and more than once, yet he was late, which was not like him. Jackie glanced at her watch again before turning back to the window.

Thunderclouds massed overhead and raindrops spat warnings on the glass, then the heavens opened. The trees in the park seemed lifeless, hardly moving except for the tips of the branches which trembled at the weight of the water running down and drip-dripping to flood the ground beneath.

'A penny for them . . . ?'

She jumped, then laughed. 'I was beginning to wonder where you were.'

'Nigel's decided to change the location of the film because he's worried about the unreliable Scottish weather,' David said, sitting down with a rueful grin. 'We're moving much closer to Fort William just in case we get holed up in the snow – so at least decent hotel accommodation will be available.'

'You're excited, aren't you?' she asked, knowing what the answer would be; it was written all over his face.

He nodded. 'I must say I haven't looked forward to a part in years as much as I'm looking forward to this one. I just wish it was a little nearer home.' And home was where his heart was, with Clare, especially now. Yet he was aware in the darkest part of his heart that even if the film had been set in northern Australia he would still have accepted the part, and willingly. He knew with certainty that it would be his last film and the romantic side of his nature tried to tell him that it was the intervention of Providence and not merely blind chance which had given him this gift of a part at such a time in his life.

'That's never bothered you before.'

He seemed to shift uneasily in his chair. 'Take no notice – it's probably old age creeping on.'

Yet 'old' was a word she had never used about her father; he was David Jones the actor, aged but never quite grown up. She gave him a searching look. 'Is that all? There's nothing else worrying you?'

'Good Lord, no – I certainly can't think of anything.' He smiled and picked up the menu. 'Oh, yes, I do have some very good news for you; all this talk about me pushed it right out of my mind. That's an actor's ego for you.'

'I know all about actors' egos and a lot of other people's come to that, but right now I'd like very much to hear some good news.'

'I've found you an angel,' he corrected himself, 'well, Clare has, actually.'

Her eyes grew round with disbelief. 'That's wonderful, but who?' And how much, how much?'

'An old friend she hasn't seen in years apparently,' he frowned, 'now I'm sure she did tell me his name, but it seems to have slipped my mind. How stupid.'

'And he really is interested?'

'Oh, very, by all accounts.'

'Has a figure been mentioned?'

'I thought there was only one.'

'Are you trying to tell me that he will back the production for the whole Australian loss?'

'Apparently.' And it *was* hard to believe, he would certainly concede that.

'And you can't remember his name!' She shook her head with disbelief. 'Oh, Daddy, that's crazy.'

David looked suitably chastened for a moment. 'Well, he's Canadian, I remember that much . . . but naturally Clare intends to call you and let you know all the details.'

Jackie frowned. 'Are you really sure about this – I mean, you did hear correctly?'

'Oh, yes, absolutely.' He placed a hand on her arm. 'I'm sorry, I haven't come terribly well prepared, have I? But Clare mentioned it to me rather quickly over the telephone and I was half-absorbed in a script I was reading, so probably didn't take it all in.'

'You mean you weren't listening.'

His mouth slid into a sheepish smile. 'Something like that.'

'As long as you haven't got the offer wrong, I couldn't care if it was King Kong who wanted to advance the show some money,' she said with obvious relief. 'I can hardly believe it.'

'Well, I know that I did not dream the offer up, so, in my opinion, the best thing for this rather pleasant shock is a glass of champagne. I shall therefore order some from the wine waiter who has very patiently been waiting for us to brighten his day with an exciting choice. Let us not disappoint him.'

Jackie laughed. 'I couldn't have put that better myself.'

'How's that American friend of yours, by the way?'

'You mean Drew, of course?'

'Ah, yes – Drew.'

She gave him an odd look. 'I don't think you like him very much, do you?'

'I wouldn't say that exactly.' His eyes flicked past her to the rain-lashed window. 'He just doesn't make me feel very comfortable.'

'Is that it?'

'Oh, I don't know, darling,' he said quickly, wishing she had never asked. 'Take no notice. It's your life, after all, and you are over twenty-one, and who you go out with is hardly my business any longer.'

'That's a very irritating thing to say.'

'Yes, I know.' He waited for a second, his hand playing with the edge of a napkin. 'Perhaps it was simply his knowing Angela,' he said lamely.

'A great many people know mother, Daddy; she's famous for it,' Jackie said defensively. 'Anyway, as I recall, Drew explained the connection.'

'Exactly,' he said vaguely, 'so why does it bother me?' It was Angela and her lifestyle and her *boy*friends. From what he had heard through various grapevines over the years she had developed a taste for handsome young men in between marriages – and probably within them, too – that would be quite in character. There was something decadent and unhealthy about his ex-wife and it was a matter of fact that he was uneasy whenever Jackie spent time with her. And Drew. What was it about him that he found unsettling – a feeling, an instinct – because he knew

Angela? David shook his head, but their conversation was interrupted by the champagne arriving and he sat back in relief, wondering why he hadn't kept his mouth shut.

'I don't know, Daddy.' Jackie watched tiny bubbles of champagne move up and up her glass, suddenly feeling tired as a seed of doubt began to take root. Drew had still not telephoned.

'I'm sorry,' David said in a tender rush and caught her hand, 'now let's not spoil good champagne – it's a 1970 Dom Perignon, almost your favourite.'

She squeezed out a smile and lifted her glass.

'To Marilyn – past and present,' he said grateful for the smile no matter how forced. His throat tightened suddenly as he looked at her, struck by how lovely she was, how dear and how proud he was of her.

Jackie gasped with pleasure as the bubbles exploded at the back of her throat.

'You see, I told you,' he chuckled and added more champagne to their glasses with obvious delight. 'By the way, when are you moving into the new house?'

'Friday,' she said. 'It will be hell, but the sooner it's over the better, I've put it off for far too long. Despite the discount the hotel's giving me, it's still costing a small fortune, something I can't afford these days.'

'Will you need any help for the move?'

'Jamie's offered.'

'I thought he might.'

'Oh, Daddy,' she said, 'what's that supposed to mean?'

'I'm sure you don't need me to tell you that he has a little, shall we say, crush on you?'

She blushed. 'I was afraid you'd say that.'

'Well, he made it rather obvious when you came over for lunch, didn't he?' he said. 'Now Clare keeps telling me that "we" should talk to him about it.'

'Please don't,' she said, 'that will probably only make matters worse.'

'That's exactly what I told her.'

'I can handle it.'

'It's not you I'm worried about.'

'Well – what do you suggest I do?'

'I haven't the faintest idea,' he looked at her carefully, 'but I'm growing very fond of him, Jackie.'

'Stop beating around the bush, Daddy, and say what you want to say . . .'

'Don't hurt him if you can help it.'

She closed her eyes briefly in exasperation. 'You, of all people, should know that you don't need to spell that out to me.'

'I know, I know,' he said apologetically.

'Besides, I think Jamie is quite capable of taking care of himself.'

'That's bravado.'

'Don't be so sure about that,' she said. 'He has a way of wearing one down.'

He laughed. 'What on earth is that supposed to mean?'

'I'm not sure I even know myself.'

He knew he should hurry; she would be sitting waiting in the cab outside the hotel, but he had been driven by curiosity to explore the suite where she had spent so much time with the American, Drew.

The sitting room was sumptuous and ornate, too ornate for his taste; he thought the whole effect a little pompous, yet he could understand why she had felt so comfortable here, so at home. In style, it was not unlike the interior of the house that David and Clare shared – warm wood, antiques, rich fabrics and plump, stately furniture.

Jamie walked slowly into the adjoining room scrutinizing one thing after another. He came to a halt in front of the elaborate king-size bed and stared at it for a while, noting the pencil-slim vase which stood on a table beside it still holding a withered red rose. His eyes grew dark as an unwilling picture of Drew, with Jackie, began to take shape in his imagination. And they would have done all the things that lovers do, he supposed jealously, things he had little knowledge of, things that no one had ever thought fit to discuss with him, things that other boys discovered naturally as they grew into men. But he had not been allowed to be like other boys, of course, his father and the one, holy, Catholic and apostolic Church had seen to that.

He caught a sharp breath, not liking his thoughts, or himself, very much. He sat down on the edge of the unmade bed. The coverlet was drawn back so that the dazzling white sheets were exposed to the world; they were rumpled, a little creased. He ran his hand across the cool silky surface and his eyes fell on one of the pillows, there was still a shallow indentation where Jackie's head must have lain.

He wondered what it was like to be Drew, to have the ease and assurance he must have with women, to have Jackie and yet not really want her at all. His beautiful solemn face creased into a soft frown and he thought that he really knew nothing of people, what they could do, what they were capable of, what dark complexities could live and thrive in the minds of men. But he was beginning to learn.

Jamie stood up finally and walked back to the large cardboard box which waited for him in the sitting room; it was full of her paperwork, her books, her notes, her photographs of the 'goddess' Marilyn Monroe, who had been no goddess at all.

'I was beginning to wonder where you were,' Jackie said brightly. 'Actually I used the time to make a quick call to my mother. I wanted to let her know that I did not need any money from the trust fund after all. It was a beautiful moment!'

Jamie slipped the box on to the floor of the cab and climbed in beside her.

'Has Drew already seen her about it?'

'Apparently,' she replied, 'and my darling mother practically slammed the phone down on me. I wish I knew why she was so dead set against the idea.'

'But you can go ahead now?'

'Oh, definitely, I feel almost lightheaded, but it's strange, my new backer wants to remain anonymous and I shall receive the money via Clare.' She shook her head and smiled. 'I have a sneaking suspicion that it's probably Clare who's actually investing this money and she's using this so-called long-lost friend as a blind.'

'Did you ask her?' he enquired casually, turning his face to the window and the world outside.

'Of course, but naturally she denied it.' Jackie sighed. 'It's very

196

generous of her . . . almost too generous . . . I just hope her confidence is not misplaced.'

He darted a glance at her and saw uncertainty for the first time.

'I suppose I'm a little worried about Rose,' she added. 'Max told me that she seemed to have difficulty concentrating at rehearsal – the third day in a row. I'll have to talk to her because I don't trust Max to handle the situation, if there is one, with the delicacy likely to be required.'

'Perhaps there's something on her mind?' he suggested and thought of Drew.

Jackie smiled with an effort. 'Maybe delayed reaction to getting the part.'

'I'm sure whatever it is will blow over,' he said, wondering if it would.

'I hope so.'

'Everyone's working so hard . . .'

'I know, but I'm afraid hard work doesn't guarantee anything, least of all the success of a West End musical – and the list of crashes and failures is legion. Oh Jamie, I hope Clare realizes what she's doing.'

'Well, if Clare *is* the "anonymous" investor, she obviously has faith in you.'

'I suppose so,' she said, 'but the other aspect that irritates me is that I like to be able to say, "I did it on my own", which makes me sound ungrateful – which I'm not. I simply hate any form of nepotism. Too much of that goes on in the theatre as it is. Naturally I was happy for David and Clare to have a stake since they really believe in the production, but I don't want any special favours.' She looked at him and added wryly, 'Who am I trying to kid, Jamie? I need all the favours I can get.'

'Perhaps you're doing Clare an injustice.'

'Perhaps.'

'Besides,' he said, 'there are things you can't change, no matter how hard you try, simply because *they are*, they exist.'

'So I should accept them?'

'Only if you can do so without surrendering too much of yourself in the process.'

'Like making a compromise, but with myself . . .' She smiled. 'You're a close one, Jamie.'

197

He blushed because he knew what he had said had pleased her and it made him happy.

Rose opened the fridge door and stared at the sad contents which seemed to have been sitting there for ever: a tub of margarine, a carton of semi-skimmed milk, a plain yoghurt and a small plate which held half a tomato, half an onion and a shrunken green pepper. But the bottle of wine she was looking for was no longer there. She was puzzled for a moment, then recalled that Babs had said something about a party; she had even suggested that Rose might go with her, but that was impossible because Drew might phone and she wouldn't be here, waiting to speak to him.

She imagined returning from the party, unlocking the weather-beaten front door and starting to climb the dusty flights of stairs to the flat when she would suddenly hear the telephone ring. Then she would run and run and run, hurling herself up and up, thigh muscles screaming and knees trembling with effort. Her side would ache with pain every time she breathed, like it used to do when she was a little girl. At the top she would see the telephone hanging from its fitting on the wall – vibrating with sound, shrieking at her to answer – but it would stop just as her fingers closed around the receiver.

The tears were very close as Rose closed the fridge door; a lock of hair fell into her eye and with a gesture of anguish she pushed it away and walked slowly back into the drab sitting room and sat down beside Babs' stereo. She pulled her knees up to her chin and sat for a long time staring helplessly into space. Almost two weeks, her mind cried, and still no word; but he *loved* her, she repeated silently, and if he loved her why didn't he call? With a sigh of despair she pressed her lips against her clasped hands resting on her knees and went through the possibilities all over again, but came to no satisfactory conclusion, except one, and that was something she would not, could not, accept.

The last few days had been bad, hell, even her voice had grown tight and uncertain and Max had yelled at her that morning, something he had never done before. It was unprofessional to let her emotions conflict with work, she knew that only too well, but such control was obviously given to greater mortals than she. With a sinking heart she wondered for the first time if the role as

Marilyn might prove beyond her reach. It seemed crazy, and a little frightening, that she could not project her own despair into a part which required so much of the same. Like Max said, she had not yet made *contact* with the character; she knew as well as he did that it was not enough just to sing any song well, it had to be *felt*. And she could not feel or give any more of herself because her emotions were stretched to the limit. There was nothing left for Marilyn.

When Babs had been ready to leave for the party she had asked Rose again if she would go with her, but naturally she had refused. And then Babs had been cruel, had practically screamed at her to stop waiting for the phone to ring because 'it never would'. Except that Babs didn't know Drew like she did; he would call, she told herself again, it was just a matter of time.

Rose fished into the pocket of her jeans and felt for the little envelope of cocaine she had been saving for just such a moment, but she still waited, wrapped in silence, pressing down the cold nervousness in her belly. Perhaps it would help her sing the way Max wanted, and that would make everyone happy.

The roll-top desk was hidden behind the high back of a leather armchair, squashed into a corner and therefore impossible to use.

'It just doesn't work,' Jackie said, 'does it?'

'There's too much furniture,' Jamie remarked.

She nodded tiredly. 'Most of this stuff has been in store for so long that I'd forgotten how small, big or awkward it was. I'm not even sure I like it any longer.'

She pushed aside a *chaise longue* to stand in front of the terrace doors which would not open.

'There's no key.' She could have screamed with exasperation. 'God, I hate moving and all the confusion and chaos it entails. It will take me weeks, probably months, to settle in here.' She yearned, suddenly, for the Hyde Park and its comfort, its ease, how it simplified her life.

'I think the *chaise longue* could go in the bedroom,' Jamie suggested, 'it would leave you much more space to play with here.'

She took a deep breath and spoke more clearly, 'You're right – it would.'

'Do you want me to write a list?'

'Sounds a sensible idea, particularly as some of the pieces will definitely be going back into store. Might as well organize it properly . . . ' her voice trailed off. She felt no enthusiasm for the task and stared dejectedly at the unfamiliar surroundings.

Jamie's pencil hovered over the pad in his hand and he sensed that she was wishing herself anywhere but here. He waited, watching her patiently, as his own thoughts took him back, and he wondered how often he had wished the same for himself.

Home. The word wrenched at his heart as a vivid picture of Marsabit rose out of his memory.

'What's the matter?'

'I was miles away – literally.'

'Kenya?'

He nodded.

'You'll go back, won't you?'

'I don't know, yet.' Their eyes met and she turned away.

'Look . . . ' she said in a rush, 'I'm going to unpack this case. Why don't you pop out and get a couple of coffees?'

'Okay.'

Jackie did not look at him as he moved to the door and only turned back when she was sure that he had gone.

The case was not locked and came open easily. A cashmere jacket, sheathed in polythene and belonging to Drew, lay on the top and she slid off the flimsy cover and ran her hand over the surface, savouring the beauty of the material.

The scent of perfume was very strong, rich and heady, as she took the jacket out of the case. She stood very still; it was the sort of fragrance that stirred memories, painted names and faces. Après l'Ondée. She brought the jacket close to her face and took a deep breath just to be sure, but there was no mistaking that distinctive signature. Only one person she knew wore the almost unknown perfume by Guerlain: her mother.

'I've been looking for you all over the house,' Jamie said. She was sitting in the tiny stained-glass conservatory, a bottle of wine, half-full, by her side.

'I decided I'd had enough.'

'I'm sorry I was so long, but I stopped off at a takeaway and got us something to eat as well.'

Jackie shook her head. 'Doesn't matter.' She pointed at the wine, 'I found this and thought I'd start on my own.'

'Is there something wrong?'

'No.'

'You just don't seem . . .'

'Would you like some wine?' she broke in. 'It's not chilled and I'm afraid I can only offer it to you in a coffee mug.'

He looked at her curiously, then shrugged. 'Okay.'

He sat quietly sipping his wine until she could stand the silence no longer. 'You never knew your mother, did you?'

'No, she died shortly after I was born.'

'And you wonder about her?'

'I used to a lot – but not now.'

'I wonder about my mother,' she said, 'and she's still alive.'

'You don't see her very much, do you?'

She shook her head, hardly trusting herself to speak.

'But you have your father and Clare.'

'Yes,' she said, 'so I must be very lucky.' She took a mouthful of wine. 'It just doesn't feel that way at the moment.'

Jamie looked down into his mug. 'You won't tell me what's wrong, will you?'

'There would be no point.'

'How do you know?'

She closed her eyes. 'I just do.'

'You see me only one way, don't you?'

She looked at him steadily. 'And what way is that, Jamie?'

'An overgrown schoolboy – an *idiot savant* – something along those lines, probably,' he said coolly.

'You have no idea what I think.'

'You make it rather obvious.'

'Because I won't have dinner with you?'

He made no answer and she stared at his half-bowed head, feeling mean and depressed and lonely all at the same time.

'Have you ever kissed anyone, Jamie?'

He looked at her warily. 'Not really.'

'What does that mean?'

'There was a native girl once . . .' He reddened; it had been on the only occasion his father had been absent.

'Would you kiss me, now?'

He was very still as if he had not understood.

She smiled, but there was no mockery in her look and she leant forward and slowly took his beautiful face between her hands, not caring any longer.

NINE

Jackie stood at the back of the rehearsal room and watched Max, a clenched fist resting on each hip, shaking his head at the three men playing Monroe's husbands and then he leapt on to the dais and performed a clever improvisation so that there would be no doubt as to what he wanted from them. She moved quietly over to Aldo who was standing at the piano, flicking through some notes. He grinned widely as he saw her approach.

'How are things?' she said with a wry smile, 'or shouldn't I ask?'

'Not bad, actually, we're just taking the boys through the first part of their scene and then Bella, the choreographer, will take over from there.'

'And Rose?'

'Max has given her the day off.'

'Oh, God,' she said with a groan, 'as bad as that?'

'Afraid so – she burst into tears this morning, and Max hadn't even opened his mouth.' He added quickly, 'Oh, you had a telephone call, your American friend, Drew – said he'd tried to call you at the hotel. I told him you were in the process of moving to the house.'

'Thanks.' But Drew should have known that, he was probably too busy with her mother to remember.

'He said he'd call you on the new number.'

'Did he.'

Aldo frowned. 'Anything wrong?'

'Forget it,' she forced a smile. 'Do you think I should speak to Rose?'

'Why don't you leave it until tomorrow – maybe she just needed a break.'

'We all need a break, Aldo.' She sighed. 'Well, thank God we have an understudy who is more than worthy of the name.'

'I don't think it's got to that stage yet.'

'Perhaps not, but it's only ten days until Christmas; after that we have four, maybe five weeks until we move to the Adelphi. It doesn't seem very long.'

'And we can't afford for Rose to be unreliable,' he finished for her. 'I know.'

'Everything still seems so raw, so undeveloped . . .'

There was laughter behind her, followed by a smatter of applause. Aldo smiled reassuringly. 'I don't think the cast would agree with you.'

She nodded slowly. 'Take no notice, I generally get a little nervous at this stage.'

'Well, don't lose too much sleep – it always seems chaotic and impossible at this point; maybe there would be something wrong if it didn't feel like that.'

Her eyes slid to the twenty or so actors sitting grouped on the floor and Max, now standing over them, explaining exactly what he was trying to achieve. She was surprised to see not only interest on their faces, but exhilaration and for an instant she envied them. Her thoughts switched to Clare and the huge sum it seemed she had invested in the show and for a weighted moment her stepmother, and the other backers, seemed to hang like a millstone around her neck.

'Cheer up,' Aldo continued gently, 'rehearsals have gone pretty well today, despite Rose's unscheduled absence.'

'Ignore me,' she said again, 'my mood probably has something to do with the splitting headache I've had for the last hour or so.'

'Let me make you a coffee and we'll find an aspirin or something,' he offered. 'It doesn't look as if they'll be starting up for another few minutes.'

'Thanks, Aldo.'

She took the seat next to the piano and waited until Max had finished talking. He saw her as he swung round, gave a brief final word and walked over.

'Aldo told me about Rose,' she said as he drew close.

'I wouldn't mind quite so much,' he pushed a hand rather theatrically through his hair, 'if the little darling would just say what the hell's the matter, rather than just "it's personal". Beats me.'

'Well, if there's not an improvement by tomorrow, I'll speak to her myself,' she said and then shot him a wary glance, 'and perhaps now you'll give more thought to our previous discussion regarding Lucy and Rose as alternate leads.'

'There's no need to panic yet.'

'I'd call it common sense.'

'Let's give Rose a little more time to settle into the role.'

She caught an audible breath. 'As far as I'm concerned that means next week.'

He shrugged lightly and turned his attention to Aldo who was approaching with two coffees.

'Where's our Tarzan-like teaboy today?'

'If you mean Jamie,' she said with barely concealed irritation, 'he's been helping me move.' And she had kissed him, and he her, because her guard had dropped. Jackie wondered how far things would have gone between them if the doorbell had not rung and she had come to her senses.

'Comes to something when the director has to make his own coffee.'

'If it bothers you that much,' Aldo broke in, handing Jackie two painkillers, 'you can have mine.'

'Oh, don't be ridiculous.'

'Have it, for God's sake – I have to have a pee anyway, and I can make another on the way back.'

'Well,' Max said brightly, 'if you put it like that . . .' He looked at Jackie who was gingerly sipping her steaming coffee. 'Has Aldo mentioned that we've sorted out the lyric problem for "Bennie, the Camera and Me"? Should fit nicely at the end of the first act now. I don't think even Joe and Gordon have too many complaints with the finished product.'

'Have I a copy of the complete changes?'

'Of course.'

She made a mental note to look it up and then slowly took another sip of the scalding coffee. 'You remember I said I'd let you know when I was ready to try that narration idea, well perhaps you could slide it into rehearsals some time next week.'

He shrugged. 'If you insist.'

'I simply want to see if it can work.'

'Well, you know what I think about that.'

'Yes, Max, I do,' she said patiently, 'and I know you resent my interference, but right at the beginning I told you that *Marilyn* was special to me and that I had more than just the usual producer's interest in the show.'

'You've said all this before, Jackie darling . . .'

'Perhaps, but contrary to what one well-known producer once said I'm not just "bringing a few people together around a show which I hope the punters will want to go and see" – my role means much more than that to me.'

He damned her silently because she had made that abundantly clear. 'But as director, I trust you won't deny me the right to disagree with you on any aspect of the dramatic structure?'

'I'm sure that even you would agree I haven't denied you so far,' she looked him full in the eyes, 'and I don't think I could stop you even if I wanted to, Max.'

He had the grace to smile.

'Just indulge me with this idea and give it a chance,' she said finally, 'because I'd like to know, one way or the other, before Christmas. Pat's been working really hard behind the scenes.'

'What's her name again?'

She closed her eyes for an exasperated second, hating his deliberate arrogance.

'Pat Goodall.'

He nodded grudgingly. 'Well, I suppose Wednesday could suit – but it will have to be first thing.'

'Fine.'

'By the way, did Yvonne mention that she might need an increase in her budget?' Max said casually. She had mentioned it to him first, naturally, and been persuaded that he would do everything he could to ensure that she got it. He supposed that it had been the least he could do under the circumstances, but their 'relationship' was over, his bladder infection had seen to that.

'Yes – copies of the original Monroe designs will cost a small fortune, more than we'd anticipated.' The budget might have to rise from sixty-five thousand to seventy-five thousand pounds. 'I also understand you may want to increase the cast in order to flesh out two or three of the choruses?' Which would mean more costumes and therefore more money. 'Do they seem that insipid?'

'I'm not absolutely sure yet, it's just a feeling,' he said, 'but I won't make my decision until the New Year when rehearsals will really begin to take shape.'

'If I let Yvonne have the increase and we do add to the cast, she'll have to manage their costumes inside this budget increase.'

'I'm sure she'll understand and "cut her cloth accordingly",' he said, amused by his little pun.

'As she won't have much choice, I'm sure she will.' Jackie suppressed a smile as a vivid image of Max's spindly white legs sticking out from beneath Yvonne's ample black bottom inevitably flashed through her mind. 'I want to push more money into publicity as we get into the New Year. Also Brian tells me that one or two of the stage designs will need an injection of extra cash. So January should be a fun month,' she finished wryly, suddenly more than grateful for the financial millstone which Clare had so kindly donated.

'Yes,' he agreed vaguely.

'And will you be around for Christmas if I need to get in touch?'

'Scotland, probably. Polly's – my girlfriend's – parents.' It would be excruciatingly dull unless he decided to go tramping across the family estate with Murdo, Polly's recently knighted father, killing anything that moved and with a darling old twelve-bore which looked as if it had come out of the ark.

Last year he had been persuaded to go deerstalking which had been one of the most miserable experiences of his life. He would never understand why anyone should want to half-crawl through tangled and usually wet Scottish undergrowth looking to blow the head off an unsuspecting stag and then give it the dubious honour of sticking it up on a wall.

It seemed to him that most of those long damp wearying hours had been spent with his face practically glued to Murdo's gargantuan backside, tiptoeing behind, trying not to breathe. Agonizing. Except that all that discomfort had been worth it because of Nadia. Polly's little sister was supposedly a no-go area, but he had been unable to resist and she had been sweetly willing with her pretty pink mouth and smooth schoolgirl thighs. She even laughed at his jokes. For an uncharacteristic moment he surprised himself, seeing again her elfin face, those soft, wide eyes, and wondering where she was, what she was doing . . .

*

With a smug smile Roger produced a huge bunch of keys from his pocket and approached a set of seedy double doors in an alley just off the street where they had lunched.

'*This* is my little surprise!'

Lucy looked at him and said nothing. He began unlocking the doors and as he did so some of the flaking paintwork trembled with the unaccustomed movement and fell into a waiting puddle.

'Well, aren't you coming in?'

'What is it?' she asked, hovering a few feet away.

'These, my dear . . . ' he patted the doors affectionately, 'are the stage doors of my little acquisition – a bloody theatre, can you believe it?' He made a dramatic flourish. 'Somewhat run-down and needs considerable investment, I grant you, but,' he said with pride, 'it's a beginning – and it is not beyond the realms of possibility that in the not-too-distant future Roger St John will be starring in plays of his own choosing, in his very own theatre.'

She gave him a confused look; Roger had never been much of a success as a theatre actor, his voice lacked resonance and despite his obvious good looks the scenery always seemed to have a way of swallowing him up.

He held out his hand to her. 'Come and see the wonders of the casbah, oh beautiful one.'

Lucy glanced clumsily at her watch. 'Roger – it's late.'

'Nonsense – "There is time enough and plenty" . . .' He frowned. 'Now who said that?'

'I've no idea,' she replied, 'but I can't – really.'

'I wonder why your protestations always sound so feeble, my sweet?'

She blushed because it was true.

'Lucy, Lucy,' he coaxed, 'surely you would not deny me the benefit of your valued opinion on my investment?'

'I have to get back, Roger.'

'Of course,' he said as he gazed intently into her eyes, his smile suddenly brittle.

She was aware of a sinking feeling as they looked at each other, and a soft despairing sound escaped her lips as he caught her hand and brought her to the open door, pulling her inside.

A narrow corridor with a cement floor led into another narrow corridor full of shadows and Lucy shivered because it was cold and dark and silent.

'Take next right,' Roger's voice told her, 'there are three steps, so be careful.'

At the bottom of the narrow stairwell there was a green door with a glass inset; she pushed it open and knew immediately, despite the lack of light, that she stood at the back of the stage. There was a certain depth to the darkness, like a weight, and she sensed the gaping mouth of the auditorium stretching in front of her and rows of vacant seats staring forlornly back.

Very close to where she stood and to stage left and stage right old ropes and pulleys, backdrops and curtains still hung as if they waited. She lifted her eyes to the distant rafters and the emptiness soaring way above her; in that blackness and dust and the cracks in the walls, spiders would live. There would be mice, too, hiding among mouldering remnants, crouching, watching them.

Somewhere in the warren of passageways water dripped and there was a smell of damp, musty air. She hugged herself, then jumped as Roger's hands clasped her shoulders from behind.

'Do you think it has a ghost?'

His voice, his words made her close her eyes shut tight for an instant. 'It's certainly cold enough for a ghost,' she said with an attempt at lightness.

'But there's an atmosphere – isn't there – can't you feel it?'

'I wish it wasn't quite so gloomy.'

She was dazzled suddenly by a burst of light, and Roger stood directly in front of her, torch in hand, his face an illuminated grinning mask.

'Was that really necessary?' Her heart was thudding and her knees felt a little weak.

He whirled away from her, the shaft of light spinning with him, and spread out his arms to an invisible audience. ' "Be not afeard" Lucy, my sweet, "the isle is full of noises, Sounds and sweet airs, that give delight, and hurt not." ' He swung round and towards her. 'Caliban – *The Tempest*.'

'Yes, I know.' The play in which they had met; how could she forget? She looked into his face which glowed white above the light of the torch. 'Can we go now?'

'Already? But we've hardly seen anything yet.'

'Please.'

'Why is it that you always disappoint me, Lucy?' He switched off the light, placed the torch on the floor so that it rolled across the wooden boards.

Lucy stiffened as everything was plunged into darkness, felt his eyes crawling over her, then saw the shape of him approach as she grew used to the darkness.

'We were so good together . . .' His hands came up and circled her neck, stroking the silky skin with each thumb, pulling her insistently towards him.

'Don't . . .'

'Oh, come on, isn't this . . . ' he covered her mouth with his own and brought his hands slowly down to squeeze her breasts, 'why . . . we're here?'

'Stop it.'

He began to open her blouse. 'I've always loved your breasts, Lucy,' he breathed and she felt slightly sick as his tongue, his mouth began to suck and lick.

'*Stop it* . . .' She pushed him away, fumbling with the buttons of her blouse.

'It's a bit late for that, Lucy dear,' he said tightly, 'and don't you think you owe me?'

She shook her head. 'I came in here because you asked me to see this godawful place with you.'

'Oh, no,' his voice was chill, 'let's stop fooling ourselves. You came because of dear old Dick.' He snorted with contempt. 'And he is a "dick", isn't he? Or, perhaps "loser" is a better word. Tell me, Lucy, what the hell do you see in him?'

'You wouldn't understand.'

'Is he good in bed?' There was a scornful smile on his lips. 'Does he please you in all the places you like to be pleased – like I used to?' He took a step towards her.

'You never pleased me,' she said quietly. 'You were too busy thinking about yourself.'

'Do you mean to say that not once during all our intimate time together did I give you any pleasure – not even one teenie-weenie little orgasm?' His fingers began caressing her chin and she jerked away as if the contact stung. 'You haven't answered me, Lucy.'

'Go to hell.'

'Not said with much conviction as usual.' He caught a handful of her hair and twisted it tightly around his fist so that he was able to bring her face up close to his own. 'I've done a lot for dear old Dick, you know that,' he raked his mouth against her ear, 'you also know why I did it, so don't let's play silly games . . .'

A silent scream hovered wretchedly behind her lips because a part of her was saying that she deserved this, that she never seemed to learn; that, yes, she had led Roger on. So what could she expect?

He took her silence as consent and reached for the zipper of her jeans, grunting with pleasure as he lowered it swiftly and then his hand was sliding inside and he could feel the warm sensuous vee between her legs, if only he could . . .

The scream, when it broke free, tore open the silence, shooting through his senses like an explosion and he reeled backwards as if someone had struck him.

Lucy ran, blouse gaping, jeans open. The green door with the glass inset slammed behind her making the yellowing backdrops flap and shift. Up above, on the shadowy rafters, dust shook and spiders scurried back to the refuge of cracks in the damp, crumbling walls.

Rose lay in the bath staring at her feet which peeped up above the deep green water. She had over-indulged; pouring in too much Radox so that the mountain of tempting bubbles she had already created had faded fast. The speckled green bath salts had acted like weedkiller on the pleasing white froth and now her bath was an anticlimax, like everything else.

She leaned her head back and sighed deep down, and her eyes began to prick and sting as a vision of Drew's face slid inevitably into her mind. She was letting his absence ruin her career before it had even started. Babs had said that. Rose supposed she was right, but why, then, was she so certain – why was her body so certain that he was the most important thing that had ever happened to her?

The distant ring of the telephone made her jerk to a sitting position and she froze helplessly as the sound died into silence and her eyes fell miserably to the lurid green water.

Footsteps approached the door.

'Rose!'

Babs' fist pounded once, twice on the locked door, but Rose didn't answer.

'For God's sake, don't go deaf on me now – it's him.'

Rose remained sitting in the bath, staring at the white-painted door, her eyebrows puckering into a frown.

'All right,' Babs said impatiently, 'shall I tell him you don't want to speak to him, then, which is what you *should* do? Or maybe that you've drowned yourself in the bath, which is what you *will* do if you go on seeing the thoughtless bastard?'

'What . . . ?'

'For crying out loud, Rose, it's the call you have been waiting too long for – you know, lover-boy, Mr Slick-Rich-Kid, Drew Anti-Pasta . . .' Babs started to laugh then and threw up her hands in mock horror as Rose flung open the door and ran past her with only a small towel wrapped around her pale dripping body.

Rose's hand shook as she lifted the receiver and stared tentatively into the mouthpiece with something like disbelief.

'Hello . . . ' she stammered.

'Hi,' he drawled, 'how're tricks?'

'Oh, Drew . . .' Drew. She savoured the sound of his name, her voice buoyant with relief, her heart beating wildly. 'I'm fine, fine.' Now and forever.

She had known all the time, deep inside, that he would call; she had never really doubted it and now everything would be all right. It did not occur to her to ask him why, then, if he loved her, he had taken so long to get in touch; she was too full of excitement and gratitude that he had called her at all.

Drew knew that she had not been 'fine'; even her clinging voice, laced with adoration and hero worship, only confirmed that her erratic behaviour at the studio and rehearsals had been the result of his neglect. He had learnt of her apparent 'emotionalism' from Aldo when he had called to speak to Jackie and the musical director had confessed that they had been 'having a few problems with Rose'. Drew had forgotten her during his time away, it was that simple. Was it his fault Rose was so forgettable?

'How's the show?'

'Great, great.' She paused, searching for a suitable lie. 'Although I've had a bit of a cold, but I feel much better now.'

Naturally.

'I've been busy,' he said.

'I thought you must have been.' In her mind's eye she could see him playing the role of hot-shot executive in New York or Los Angeles, and her pulse beat a little faster. 'But where are you calling from?'

He stretched and stifled a yawn as his eyes took stock of Angela's penthouse apartment.

'The States.'

'Oh.' She shivered suddenly and with one hand dragged the towel around her more firmly, her slim fingers grasping the edges too tightly. 'I miss you, Drew.'

'Yeah, I know, hon'.' He glanced at his watch, it was four in the afternoon. Angela wouldn't be back from the beauty parlour for another hour.

'Will you be back for Christmas?'

'I might if I can wind up this deal.' There was no way he was leaving New York until he had managed to get some kind of agreement from Angela, and she was being difficult, but he had anticipated that. Her face when he had shown her the stuff Bergman had dug up! The thousand dollars he had paid the old man had been worth every cent.

'We could spend Christmas together . . . ' Rose said eagerly, 'that is, if you're back.' She had visions of a lovers' Christmas, like she had read about in one of those romance magazines once: holly, mistletoe, a perfectly cooked turkey dinner eaten by candlelight, gorgeously wrapped presents around a beautiful little tree.

'That's a big "if ", hon',' he said, 'so don't count on it.' He had every intention of spending Christmas with Angela, although she didn't know it yet.

'Oh,' Rose said limply, 'I just thought . . .'

'Look, don't make any plans,' he said testily, 'because I can't make any promises.' And he hated the sense of obligation she was beginning to make him feel. After all, he didn't owe her anything and he had convinced himself that she had gone with him a few times because it had suited her, just as it had suited

213

him. Why did she, and women in general, have to dress it up all pretty and call it love? It was like being suffocated – slowly.

'I know, I know,' she said quickly and cleared her throat. 'I miss you, that's all.'

He sighed heavily and closed his eyes, wanting to put the phone down and finish it, but he couldn't because of Jackie's precious musical. Rose would cause more problems and probably drop him right in the shit if he didn't keep her sweet for a while longer. She was the 'can't live without you' type, weak, clinging and pathetic, and he wondered why he had ever made the decision to take up with her in the first place, except that he had been both bored and angry with Jackie at the time. The fact was that he still needed Jackie until he was sure of Angela, because he couldn't afford to repeat the mistake he had made in the summer and burn all his bridges.

Never in his miserable life had he ever been so close to such a potentially perfect set-up, and he was tired of the gigolo circuit, the juiceless crones, even the young bitches who expected to feel the earth move every time he fucked them. Drew stared at the mouthpiece of the telephone as he recognized the full reality of his situation – he needed Rose for as long as it would take.

'I miss you, too, hon'.'

'Oh, Drew,' she sighed dreamily, all worries, doubts stealing happily away.

'And I'll be back in January.' He paused deliberately. 'But you've got to do something for me . . .'

'Anything,' her heart leapt, 'anything.'

'I'm relying on you to make *Marilyn* a smash.'

He heard the sharp intake of her breath.

'Of course, yes – I'll work really, really hard,' she gasped gratefully into the phone.

'That's my girl.'

My girl. 'Oh, Drew . . .'

'Well, hon',' he said, 'I've got a meeting, so –'

'You have to go,' she finished for him.

'That's right.'

'Take care,' she said softly.

'You too.'

She smiled happily. 'I love you . . .'

But Drew had already put down the telephone.

Jamie peered through the partly open door of Jackie's office, but she was not at her desk, so he pushed the door gently and walked in. The room was empty. He prowled carefully around, looking at her books, picking up a framed photograph of her father and Clare, glancing at the confusion on her desk and the portfolio which lay open to reveal the production's logo – the two faces of Marilyn Monroe.

'Hi.'

He looked up, startled for an instant.

'Did you want something?'

He stared back at her, perplexed, unable to speak, but longing to say the words that would reduce the almost unbearable gap that had widened between them since that kiss, his first, a kiss which had gone on and on, inflaming his mind and body. It had seemed miraculous that the joining of their lips, touching her, could give such intoxicating pleasure, as if something mystical poured out of her into him.

'I have to work late, Jamie.'

He gazed at her with slowly mounting apprehension.

'I could wait,' he said.

'No – you go home.'

'I thought we might talk, have a drink . . .'

'I have to work.'

'Can I help?'

She shook her head and there was something in her carefully arranged face which made him afraid.

'You want me to go?'

'It's late, Jamie, and we can talk tomorrow,' she offered, but it was no offer at all.

'You don't want me here.'

'There's so much I have to do,' she continued, as if he had not spoken, and straightened some papers on her desk.

'I don't understand,' he said, 'on Friday . . .'

'Friday shouldn't have happened,' she said quickly and looked beyond him to the window.

'Why?' A light seemed to go out of his eyes.

'For many reasons.'

215

'Tell me.'

'I have commitments, Jamie, you know that.'

What she said, what excuses she used did not interest him because they were irrelevant. For him it was quite simple; they had been drawn to each other, she had wanted him. Then.

'Look,' she said helplessly, 'I'm sorry. I shouldn't have let it happen; it was my fault entirely.'

'But you wanted to . . .'

She blushed.

'I know you did.' His voice was low as he spoke directly into her embarrassment.

She closed her eyes for a second, pushing her hair away from her face. 'It was a mistake.'

He shook his head.

'Yes,' she said and tried to stare back into the piercing green eyes which watched her too well. 'The fact is that I have this production to develop and make work, and the next few weeks will be crucial.' She visibly battled against a desire to look away from him. 'And I'm older than you – and we're so different, you and I, we come from different worlds, we want different things . . .'

'You haven't mentioned Drew.'

'What I'm saying has nothing to do with him.'

'Then why did you . . . ?' he persisted mercilessly.

'I don't know,' she said quietly.

They fell silent and he seemed far away from her, not understanding.

'Don't look at me like that, Jamie.'

He did not reply immediately, then, 'I'm keeping you from your work.'

'We can still talk tomorrow . . .'

He gave her no answer and moved to leave the room.

'Jamie . . .' She touched his arm.

He turned to look at her, at the hand which rested on his jacket, at her face, her mouth.

'And what shall we talk about tomorrow that we can't talk about today?'

She shook her head, vaguely startled by the subtle change in his voice, and stepped back to let him pass. For an instant their glances held each other and they were both very still, remembering, but then the moment was gone.

There was a spring in Richard's step as he walked alongside the canal towards Camden Lock and the market, the paths and pavements drying now beneath a cool December sun. Under his arm he hugged a large brown envelope which felt comfortingly plump: all three hundred and twenty-two pages of his completed manuscript, which had become his silent friend, his little soulmate.

He planned to bisect the market and cross the main road beyond to call in at a local newsagent which offered photocopying facilities to those lesser mortals who did not have one of their own – one copy to send to one lucky publisher.

Lucy didn't know, of course, because he couldn't bear the thought of all her questions and probings and the sympathetic anguish which would surely follow should he fail. And he knew a great deal about failure, it had followed him for most of his life. The brutal rejections he had sometimes received at auditions were lessons in life he would never forget. He shook his head in black amusement because, sure as hell, there was no business like show business.

He tightened his hold on the envelope, certain that the manuscript would be returned with a negative reply because the publishing world was almost as ruthless as that of the theatre. Richard shrugged because despite the realities of the situation he did feel good about what he had written; it had flowed surprisingly well and was, he thought, rather funny.

Only yesterday on the set, Roger of all people had said 'every dog has its day'. It had been a strange thing to say coming from an almost soap-idol, but today Richard applied the phrase to himself, because by the law of averages, it was surely about time his own 'day' came around.

The canal path began to slope upwards and there were the beginnings of the market: the stalls, the bric-a-brac, the smell of sugar, spice and curry. A group of die-hard hippies sat on a low wall looking aimless but happy, and to his left, behind a small tent enclosing Rosita, a genuine gypsy fortune-teller, some Mexi-

217

can Indians were gyrating to the throbbing beat of drums and maracas.

Richard surveyed the scene with amusement and wove his way through the patchwork of craft and secondhand stalls and wondered if he would count more, or fewer, junkies than he had on his previous visit. One character amazed him: he was long and pale and ghostly, like a sickly plant that has grown too thin searching for the sun. And he was always in black – black shirt, black jacket, black jeans, black socks, black shoes. The whitest man he had ever seen.

The shop he aimed for was squashed between a vegetarian coffee shop and a showroom displaying handmade pine furniture. As he drew close he realized that the newsagent's was closed, and just above the wooden slit which served as a letterbox a notice had been pinned: 'Gone to funeral in Cardiff, open tomorrow'. It was edged in tinsel. He turned around and began walking towards the nearest tube station. There were plenty of photocopiers in and around the Charing Cross Road and if he was quick, he could copy his work and meet Lucy as she left the studio after rehearsals. Perhaps they could take in a pizza or a plate of spaghetti. The idea certainly had appeal, but there was one distinct drawback: beneath his over-large raincoat he wore the ancient baggy sweater his mother had knitted him, the one he always wore when he was writing. Not exactly designed to make Lucy swoon.

Richard pulled the jumper down self-consciously and smoothed back his unruly hair, then he buttoned up the raincoat and tied the belt in a knot, lifting the collar and lapels carefully in the vain hope that the effect might give him a touch of style, even a hint of mystery.

Apart from the few drunks who usually littered Camden Town tube, the station did not appear unduly busy, at least not in the direction he was travelling, but as he reached the platform and a train pulled in on the other side, scores of people spilled out and he realized that the rush hour was just starting. The Northern Line took him to Leicester Square, and he walked through to Shaftesbury Avenue and found an upmarket stationer with a fastfeed photocopier almost immediately.

There was a red plastic chair by the window and he sat down to wait as the copying got underway. From his seat he could just see the side entrance of the Palace Theatre which had played host to the musical *Les Misérables* for over six years. He had seen it once and only by chance because an old girlfriend worked backstage and asked him to come. It was the best thing he'd seen in years; he had even bought the cassette to prove it.

Richard stared wistfully at the theatre hoardings and the photographs of the show on display and thought of his lovely juicy-Lucy and her fabulous voice. It was a pity he couldn't sing a note.

It was already dark as he stepped into the brightly lit and busy street. All along Shaftesbury Avenue the theatres were lighting up and he felt a sneaking thrill of excitement as he imagined being there, in one of the myriad dressing rooms, plastering on the old make-up, psyching himself up . . .

He turned into a pretty pedestrian precinct, a place he had come with Lucy once or twice. Now it was adorned with Christmas trees in fat tubs, festooned with fairylights and big red bows, stationed outside the bistros and restaurants which lined the narrow walkway. He paused to study the menu in a window, moved on to the next and the next, wondering which one she might prefer. He knew that the last restaurant on the right was French, because he and Lucy had peered covetously through the glass the last time they had come. It was not just any old French restaurant, La Tante Gigi was the superior breed: outrageously expensive food and greedily marked-up wine served in sophisticated and seductive surroundings.

Richard stepped back, conscious of a noise beneath him, and realized that La Tante Gigi had a cellar bar and he was standing directly in front of its small window which fronted on to the street. He dropped his gaze to the people he could see beyond the glass, their feet, their legs, the bottom half of a pinstriped suit, a girl's legs in black fishnet tights, and behind her a brown suede boot with tassels around the rim, like Lucy's. He stared at the boot and its twin, and the brown corduroy jeans, like Lucy's.

Richard crouched down, his heart an annoyingly hard pressure in his chest as his eyes fell on Lucy's jacket, her hand holding a glass of wine, her thick honey-blonde hair and painfully familiar profile which was very still, and very beautiful to him then, as she looked back at Roger.

'You said you would be back for Christmas . . . ' Jackie said into the telephone, 'what's changed?'

'Business.' Drew was alone, standing by the picture window of Angela's apartment, looking at the breathtaking view. 'You know how it is.'

'No, I don't actually,' she said coldly.

'Hey,' he said with surprise, 'give me a break, Jackie.'

'How's my mother?'

'You know what she said about the money.'

'I don't mean that.'

He hesitated, suddenly wary. 'She was okay the last time I saw her.'

'When was that?'

'Jackie,' he said, 'what is going on here?'

'Martha's Vineyard is a short hop from Cape Cod.'

'What the hell are you talking about?'

'The summer, and your affair with my mother.'

'Hey – come on – that's crazy.'

'Her perfume was all over your jacket – her very exclusive perfume. I'd know it anywhere.'

'What does that prove?' he protested. 'Just think about it.'

'I have,' she said, 'and everything fits.'

'You are so wrong.'

'Explain.'

'That's an insult. Don't expect me to explain anything like this over the phone.'

'Because you can't.'

'Why don't you take a long hard look at that ring on your finger and remember what I said to you before I left. Then convince yourself that "everything fits".'

She blushed despite herself.

'You know I had an affair, it nearly knocked our relationship on the head, but it wasn't your goddamn mother, for chrissakes!'

'Who was it?' She had never asked before.

'Does it matter? She was someone I knew before you . . . long time.' That much was true.

220

She fell silent, suddenly feeling tired and depressed.

'Jackie?'

'The perfume . . . the smell, was unmistakeable.'

'Maybe it was my cologne?'

She said nothing.

'Come on, Jackie, start thinking straight.'

'I don't know what to think.'

'You've been working too hard – burning the midnight oil,' he said.

'I suppose so.'

'Is the show okay? Aldo told me Rose was playing up . . .'

'Yes,' Jackie said quietly, 'and Rose is fine now.' Almost miraculously so.

He breathed a sigh of relief. 'So – apart from some old cologne reminding you of your mother's scent – what's bugging you? Advanced bookings still slow?'

'Yes, as it happens.'

'That's it, then.'

'That's not it, Drew.'

'Look, Jackie . . . I'm not gonna listen to any more of this bullshit about your mother. Okay?'

'Is it bullshit?'

'Jackie, Jackie . . . ' he said wearily, 'I'm not into older women and she's not even my type.' The biggest lie he would ever tell.

'There was just something . . .'

'I said I wasn't gonna listen any more,' he said, 'or maybe you're not being honest with *me*?'

'What do you mean?'

'Like, this is your way of letting me down gently.'

'No.' She sighed heavily. 'No, that's not it.'

'Well, what the hell am I supposed to think?'

'I don't know,' she said, 'maybe it's the time of year; maybe I *am* tired.'

'Get some rest over Christmas – I mean real rest.'

'Maybe I will.' The festive season shone like a brilliant light to which all dark thoughts seemed irresistibly drawn, except that usually she didn't feel like this, usually she was like a child glorying in all the old familiar rituals. 'I thought you were going to be here.'

'Yeah, I'm sorry about that,' he said softly, able to be generous now. 'When I get back I'll make it up to you. That's a promise.'

'When will that be?'

'I'll call – soon – and let you know.'

She made no answer.

'Hey . . . ' he added quickly, 'and stop dreaming up whacky ideas. Okay?'

'Okay.'

'Bye, hon'.'

'Bye, Drew.'

He hung up and stared at the telephone.

'Shit,' he said softly, and quickly poured himself a Scotch and drank it down in one.

The drawing room was wonderfully inviting. Clare had excelled herself with the decorations and the tree, and the punch which still sat warm and inviting on a nearby table. The few special guests who had been invited for Christmas Eve drinks had gone home and Clare was in the kitchen preparing hot chocolate for David who had gone to bed.

Jackie walked over to the tree and gently edged a fat piece of tinsel back into place and then ladled more punch into her empty glass cup.

'Aren't you coming up now?' Clare asked from the doorway.

'Yes, I'm rather tired – but I just wanted to drink my last cup of punch quietly by this fantastic fire.'

'Well, don't fall asleep.'

'No, Clare – and thanks for a lovely evening.'

'I enjoyed every minute, as I think your father did, but it obviously proved too much for him in the end!'

'I thought he looked pale. Is he all right?'

'Yes, but he's been overdoing it, and worrying about this part.'

'I thought he was happy about it?'

'Oh, he is, he is . . .' Clare looked thoughtful. 'But it's become terribly important to him somehow, almost disproportionately so.'

'Well, you know how he gets when he's really involved with a role – impossible.'

'I know, but I can't help feeling how unhealthy this immersion in a part is.'

'The point is, Clare, that he loves it – they all love it, otherwise they just wouldn't do it.'

'Sometimes I think they must all be a little mad.' Clare shook her head. 'But thank you for those comforting words, Jackie, I think I needed them.'

'You're also probably very tired and it's been quite a day.'

'And your father's hot chocolate is getting cold,' she said with a grin. 'Now I'll leave you in peace and see you, not *too* early, in the morning. Goodnight.'

'Goodnight.'

'Oh, by the way . . . ' Clare added, 'Jamie's locking up, so you don't need to worry about that.'

'Right.'

The door closed and the room was very quiet. Jackie drew close to the fire and lifted her hands to the lovely heat. For an instant she wondered where Drew was, what he was doing, except that she knew. He would be with her mother, she was very sure of that now.

After their call she had gone back to the jacket, but the scent was fading now it had been exposed to the air and she was no longer certain that she was right. She went through his pockets, but found nothing, then turned her attention to the small case he had left behind and went through each item with painstaking care, loathing doing it, but driving herself on because the need to know was too great. In the end she resorted to telephoning the Hyde Park Hotel to see if he had given his home address when he signed in. And he had. Even now she could not make up her mind whether it was arrogance or stupidity which had compelled Drew to write down such incriminating details in black and white – it was a penthouse address in Manhattan. Her mother's, of course.

'Jackie?'

She closed her eyes for a moment at the sound of Jamie's voice.

'I'm having a nightcap,' she said.

'I didn't mean to disturb you. I only came in to say goodnight.'

'Why don't you join me in a glass of punch?'

He watched her for a second, not knowing what answer to give, but then she smiled at him. 'Please.'

He poured himself some punch and stood a little apart from her.

'I want to apologize.'

'I think you already did that.'

'No, Jamie – I did it all wrong.'

'Is there a right way?'

'Perhaps not,' she said, 'I don't know. I seem to be a bit short on right answers lately.'

'You've got a lot on your mind.'

'That's a generous thing to say, considering how ungenerous I have been to you.'

'It doesn't matter.'

'It *does* matter.'

He looked at her carefully.

'And does it matter so very much that I am younger than you?'

'You really don't give up, do you?'

'My father once told me that "persistence is all", and for once, I think he was right.'

She sat down and looked up at him. 'I'm almost too tired to argue.'

'Don't then.'

She didn't say anything immediately, but only stared at him. Then, 'I wouldn't be good for you.'

'Can't you allow me to decide that for myself?'

'You push and push until you get your way – don't you, Jamie?'

He had the grace to blush.

'All right,' she said at last, 'all right.'

'You mean . . .'

'I'm not sure what I mean,' she said. 'Perhaps that's a chance you'll have to take. A price you pay for your persistence.'

'And Drew?'

She shook her head slowly and stood up. 'I don't want to talk or think any more – least of all about Drew.'

'If that's what you want,' he said softly.

She looked him full in the eyes. 'Kiss me like last time, Jamie, and drive all the bad thoughts away.'

TEN

Lucy stared miserably out of the window. She could hear her sister playing the piano in the next room, a bad version of 'O Come All Ye Faithful'. Her father was asleep, snoring softly in a chair behind her as his stomach battled with the enormous Christmas lunch her mother had prepared. Voices still emanated from the kitchen where her mother was drinking ruby wine with Aunt Sylvia, her widowed sister who always came to them for Christmas. Outside, in the garden and beyond, nothing stirred, as if everything living was sleeping like her father, satiated with too much turkey and Christmas pudding.

She wondered what Richard was doing and a lump came into her throat. He had not even called. Her thoughts returned to Friday and the note she had found on her return, saying only that he had to 'go home early'. Home was where his mother was, a tiny village halfway between Bath and Bristol where she lived alone; perhaps she was ill.

Lucy sighed and watched the window mist up with her breath. She drew a circle with her finger, then two eyes, a nose and a half-smiling mouth, so that the circle became a face and, ludicrous though it was, reminded her of Richard. Her eyes began to prick and burn.

She moved away from the window, deciding to take a walk in the garden, but as she closed the sitting-room door behind her she was confronted by the telephone which stood in the hall. She paused helplessly, then reached for the receiver before dialling the number which she had written down carefully on a piece of paper for just such a moment. It rang and rang and she was about to give up when his voice broke the ringing tone and she sighed with relief.

'Richard?'

'Oh . . . Hi.'

She waited for him to say something more, knowing in advance that he would not.

'Why haven't you phoned?' she asked in a small voice.

'I've got a bug – flu – or something,' he lied.

'You didn't mention that in your note.'

'It started almost as soon as I got here, probably picked it up on the way down.'

'Would it have exhausted you so much just to call and say "Happy Christmas"?'

'I thought you would call me.'

She took a deep, patient breath. 'How's your mother?'

'Fine.'

'I thought she was ill.'

'I never said that.'

'I just assumed, from the note, that she was.'

'No,' he said, 'you can speak to her if you like.'

'Then why the need to leave "early"?' she asked, ignoring his remark.

There was a moment's tense silence before he spoke again. 'I wanted some time to myself.'

'Richard, what's going on? Why don't you simply tell me what's the matter?'

Oh, he wanted to, he really did, because there was a part of him that wanted to scream down the phone why was she seeing Roger, despite all the promises she had made, and yet he was afraid to.

'I'm tired, Lucy.' In his mind's eye he saw Roger, all six foot and more of his Aryan good looks and longed to throttle him, slowly.

She looked at the telephone, confused and bewildered, a little fear stroking her spine.

'That's not an answer, Richard,' she said, 'and how can I help if you won't tell me what's wrong?'

'Did you find your stocking?' he said abruptly, avoiding her question.

'Oh, yes, yes,' she said quickly, recalling the bright-green woollen stocking. It had 'Ho, ho, ho, ho' embroidered in red, the words spiralling around and around, right down to the heel. They had one each in different colours and it was understood that every year each stocking should be filled to the brim with gifts, no matter how small or silly. Richard was particularly good at the silly and the sentimental. 'It was really sweet, everything . . . ' she said a little unsteadily, 'but I wasn't able to give you mine, was I? You could have waited for me to come home, at least.'

'What time did you get back?'

'When?'

'On Friday.'

'Just after seven,' her face pulled into puzzled lines, 'why?'

'I must have left just before you arrived.'

'I wish you'd waited,' she said again, 'it was horrible coming home to an empty flat.'

'Did you have a nice weekend?'

'If going to rehearsals on Saturday and spending the rest of the time alone is your idea of a nice weekend, then, yes.' She stared into the mouthpiece with growing annoyance. 'And you?'

'I went for a couple of very long walks.' In huge Wellington boots, he had followed the paths he had taken so often as a child. Some of the old high hedgerows along the narrow lanes had gone, cut down to widen meadows and field crops, so that the familiar places no longer looked the same. 'Nothing is bloody sacred any more,' he had snapped to the empty air. There was little hope now of finding a bird's nest or mice, or catching sight of an unsuspecting rabbit in some of those secret childhood places.

Outside the window in the hall, Lucy saw the rain begin to spit and fall, flooding the surrounding grass and turning the garden path to mud. 'I thought you were ill.'

Her voice broke into Richard's thoughts and he sighed softly because he had never been a very good liar.

'I was.'

'So ill you could take long, exhausting walks, but not find the strength to pick up the telephone and call me.'

'It wasn't like that.'

'Well, what *was* it like then, for God's sake?!'

'You tell me!' He retorted sarcastically, but suddenly felt slightly foolish.

He heard the exasperation in her voice as she spoke again. 'I think for the first time in our relationship I really don't understand what you are talking about, Richard.'

He said nothing because there was a sour taste of doubt in his mouth.

'And there was something I wanted to say to you, actually,' she continued, and his anxious, coward's heart began to beat a little faster. 'But I suppose it should wait until I can speak to you properly.'

He waited a second, then inhaled deeply. 'Can't you tell me now?' Praying that she would not, dread pulsing through him like pain.

'I'd rather not.'

'I see.'

'I planned to talk to you on Friday, or over the weekend, before we left for Christmas . . .' She thought reluctantly of Roger and all that he had said, what he had tried to do, wanting it over.

'But I wasn't there.'

'No.'

'And you want to wait until you actually see me?' How very thoughtful.

'Yes.'

'When will you be back?'

'For rehearsals on Wednesday, the day after Boxing Day.'

'Right,' he said quietly.

'Will you be back then?'

'I don't know.'

'Oh.'

'I'm not needed on the set of St Winifred's until Friday.'

'I suppose I'll have to wait until then,' she said unhappily, 'particularly if you still feel that you need "time to yourself".'

'Fine.'

She caught a sharp breath. 'Just "fine"?'

'I don't know what you want me to say, Lucy.'

'Happy Christmas would be nice, Richard!' she retorted hotly, but the tears were very close. 'Actually, anything would be better than this strange, monosyllabic conversation we've been having.' For one savage moment she was tempted to spill out everything she had done, and almost done on his behalf. And even the other things, the stupid shaming things when she had surrendered herself to the Max Lockharts of the world.

'I didn't mean . . .'

'Oh, just forget it, Richard.'

She slammed the telephone down and he winced. For a moment he stared blankly into space, slightly shell-shocked. Somewhere in the course of the last few minutes his self-righteousness had neatly turned in on itself, because very little of what had been said was as he had expected, and he realized with something approaching disbelief that Lucy had managed to leave him in the uncomfortable situation of thinking that it was some-how his fault.

Drew whistled. What was it about having lunch with Angela which left him languid and luxurious and wanting, more than anything, to take her to bed afterwards? He shook his head and smiled to himself as he approached the gleaming glass and bronze doors of the apartment building.

It had been her idea that they go shopping together because she wanted to 'buy him a few things' and then go on to a long and delicious lunch at Petrossian, one of her favourite restaurants. The place had nearly knocked him out – all pink Art Deco with wall sofas of soft leather edged with mink. They had eaten lovers' food: oysters, scallops and caviare – red and white – washed down with plenty of chilled champagne.

Later he had left her outside Ora Feder's on Madison Avenue because she insisted that she needed some new lingerie. He had chuckled to himself nearly all the way back to the apartment because Angela had drawers full of sensational silk underwear, chemises and bustiers, but hardly wore any of it, or at least not for very long.

Drew gave a familiar wave to the doorman and passed through the foyer to wait for the elevator. Clutched in his hands and tucked under one arm were several parcels which contained more gifts from her. On Christmas Day she had given him a solid gold Rolex and matching initialled lighter, she had cooked a fat goose and all the trimmings for them both, and they had got drunk and made love all over the goddamn suite. Later they sat up in bed eating cold cuts and pickles and watching old movies until the need to make love came around again. It had been that sort of a day, the best of days.

Today she had clothed him, like she had in the past, from head to foot: ties and shirts from Bijan, Italian shoes from Ken Cole, a fabulous white silk suit from Go Silk and several pairs of tuxedo pyjamas which had wowed him nearly out of his mind. With a happy sigh he hugged the gifts tighter and realized that he felt good, and better than he had ever done in his life. He was also coming around to believe that he really meant something to her, because there had been no mention of the data he had on her, all that Pinkey stuff, and he assumed that she was beginning to see sense and would therefore find some way to include him in her future. A shadow momentarily dimmed his eyes. She must.

He pressed the button of the private elevator to the penthouse with his free hand and immediately the doors purred open and he stepped inside. It still amazed him how quickly, how silently the elevator made it to the top of the building, Angela's palace in the sky. He was humming by the time he reached the penthouse, the doors sliding neatly apart so that he was able to move quickly into the vestibule, only a few feet away from the actual door of the apartment. Drew placed his parcels on the blood-red carpet and fished in his pocket for the keys, finding them easily enough. But when he tried to open the door with the first key it wouldn't turn, nor would the second, or the third. He tried again, then looked at them carefully, turning them over in his hand before pushing each one back into the locks once more and trying again, and for the last time, because an eerie feeling of panic and dread was stealing over him by then. He stepped back and stared at the door as comprehension dawned. She had changed the goddamn locks! Oh neat, oh beautiful! He shook his head in disbelief. She had deliberately taken him out, wined and dined him and bought him clothes, so that behind his back she could find time to have the fucking locks changed!

He slammed the door desperately with the flat of his hand, kicked the skilfully polished wood until it shook under his onslaught, then used his fists in rage and humiliation, cursing her because she had done it to him again – used him, made a fool of him, treated him like a piece of shit.

Drew squeezed his eyes shut tight and pressed his forehead against the unyielding door in misery and frustration. He moaned softly as anger gave way to grief and he saw all his dreams and hopes shrink to nothing.

The husbands of Marilyn Monroe, Jim Dougherty, Joe DiMaggio and Arthur Miller, were placed in strategic places on a revolving stage and other members of the cast, some twenty men representing Monroe's many lovers, filled the spaces left in the rest of the revolve. Rose as Marilyn stood outside the circle as it turned slowly to the sultry music of 'Itch, Itch . . . Which, Which?', pausing only as the spotlight fell on Dougherty, DiMaggio and Miller, at which point she sang a duet with each man, coming close and dallying with each of them in slow, melting movements. The lighting grew dim and the men in her life withdrew, leaving Monroe with no partner at all as the music faded, except for a big black Fifties telephone which waited for her, centre stage, like a sentinel.

Jackie caught a soft breath of satisfaction; the scene was not right yet, but its potential was obvious. She stood quietly at the back of the rehearsal room, fingers crossed, as Pat Goodall took her place as narrator and proceeded to wreck the mood which had been created by the last scene. Jackie shut her eyes tight for an instant. It was no one's fault, she told herself, least of all Pat's. After all, it had been her idea, and even Max, in the end, had been fair and suggested they wait until after Christmas when the show would be in better shape.

She watched him closely as he made Pat go through her paces again, making a few subtle changes, but cringed inwardly as the same, inescapable feeling came over her, that it just did not work. All that time and effort she had wasted on the idea, even creating more friction between herself and Max to no purpose. At that moment he turned to look at her and she shrugged as he made a throat-cutting gesture which said everything.

'Thanks, lovey,' he told Pat, and Jackie noticed that he even managed to give her a smile, no doubt with some effort, but nevertheless it surprised and impressed her, because so many directors she had come across were capable of being mean and brutally critical. There was that old, old story of an actor who left an audition with an ego so savaged that he shot himself. Oh, but she could believe it, she really could.

Max stretched and stood up and walked slowly towards Jackie, just as she had expected.

'All right, don't say it . . . ' she said.

'I thought I already had.'

'It didn't work and I accept that,' she said, 'so we don't need to have a post mortem.'

He nodded. 'Good.'

'Pat's got a fine voice; maybe we could slide her in to fatten up one of the choruses.'

'Why not? As I suspected, we'll need to hire a few more players to flesh out certain parts of the show.'

'That means that the cast will shoot up to thirty-five people, in all probability.'

'That's about right.'

She fell silent, calculating numbers and figures in her head – six or more players would mean an extra thousand pounds per week at least. The budget seemed to stretch a little more each day.

'Bookings still disappointing?'

'I don't think you need ask . . .'

'But you plan a publicity blitz this month, don't you?'

'Oh, yes,' and it was costing a fortune. The advertisements planned for the national dailies had already notched up thousands of pounds, not including the T-shirts, the hoardings, the cost of more poster locations in all the major cities – and the preparations for the cast album which would be recorded at the end of the month. The concept album had sold only moderately well, but she had high hopes for the cast album once the musical opened. She felt a sudden and welcome surge of optimism because the songs and the music were something special, wonderfully melodic tunes, irresistible.

'I feel that it's beginning to come together,' he said cautiously.

She nodded.

'And Rose is really taking the part on now, so I don't think we need have any more worries on that score.'

'I hope you're right.'

'Jackie, darling – lighten up – I have a good feeling about our little creation.'

'Not quite so little, Max,' she said dryly, because the enormity of the task she had taken on had only recently really hit home.

None of her other productions had come close to the size and cost of *Marilyn* and sometimes, just sometimes when she was tired or unable to sleep, she could feel panic begin to jostle in her chest.

'Well, big, little, what's the difference? I still have a good feeling about it,' he said loftily. 'Remember that when you next have producer's cramp, my sweet.'

She shot a cool glance at him. 'Oh, I will Max, I will,' then looked at her watch. 'Now, if there's nothing else, you can contact me at the house should you need me: there are some calls and a mountain of paperwork I have to deal with.'

'Fine,' he said, 'and you'll be at the team meeting in the morning?'

She nodded and turned to go. 'I haven't missed one yet . . .'

There was a light already on in the sitting room. Jackie could see it from the street and as she climbed the three narrow steps Jamie opened the door.

'You're early,' she said smiling, 'I didn't expect you until after six.'

'I'm here only by a margin of eleven minutes.' He came towards her and lifted the files from her arms and stood back to let her pass through.

'Sometimes, Jamie,' she said softly, 'I think you read my mind.'

'I try,' he said simply.

She shot a careful glance at him because it was true – the trying, the truthfulness, and how he could unnerve her with such innocent ease. Even on Christmas Eve he had surprised her by not losing control, sensing that she was not ready for more than kisses and caresses. Yet part of her had wanted more.

'Shall I open a bottle of wine?'

'Please.'

She slipped off her shoes and padded upstairs to the bathroom to shower and change. She picked out a black and white silk kimono, something Clare had chosen for her on one of their rare shopping trips together.

Jackie stared at herself in the mirror and realized that she looked tired, which was not entirely surprising. She pulled a comb through her hair and gave herself an artificial glow by brushing some rouge gently across her cheeks. Tonight she would not take work to bed and fall asleep over her notes and papers, but switch the light out at a civilized hour. Maybe after the opening she would take a holiday, a short one, just to get herself back together. And Jamie . . . ? The doorbell rang cutting abruptly through her thoughts and she jumped, but moved quickly to the top of the stairs. 'I'll get it, Jamie.'

The door was very secure, locked and bolted. She was always careful about things like that, something she had inherited from her mother when they lived in New York. Automatically she put her eye to the tiny spyhole and saw Drew standing outside. She watched him for a long moment as he walked to the edge of the steps, only to turn and pace back.

There was something in the rigid set of his face which made her uneasy. He rang the bell again and the sound jarred on her nerves as she released the two bolts and opened the door.

'Drew . . .'

'Hi, hon',' he said lightly, 'couldn't stay away any longer.'

'You should have telephoned.'

'I wanted to surprise you,' he said, dropping his luggage and letting his eyes travel over her.

She stiffened as he hugged her, pressing his cold mouth against her neck.

'Jamie's here,' she said, but too quickly, so that his eyes darted to her face and then beyond her to the doorway of the sitting room where she knew Jamie stood, watching them.

'Hi, kid.'

'Hi,' Jamie responded flatly.

'Doing some homework?' It was only too clear to him why the boy hung around; it was there in his eyes – calf-love, big and round and mooning.

'Something like that, Drew,' Jackie broke in, 'we were just about to eat.'

'Cosy,' he said.

'Maybe you should start, Jamie,' she said, 'I'll be a few minutes yet.'

Drew followed her, his eyes scrutinizing her new home, the paintings, furniture, *objets d'art*. 'Nice place.' He thought about the cocoon of the penthouse where he had lived with Angela for a short precious time and his throat contracted with despair, hating her.

'Would you like a drink?'

'Thanks.' He waved disparagingly at the space where Jamie had been standing. 'Is he staying in the spare room or something?'

'Of course not.'

'Seems to have made himself at home.'

'It's work, Drew.' Almost true.

He looked at her sharply and she recalled all he had said and implied about Jamie only a matter of weeks ago, but it seemed much longer than that now.

'*You*,' he pointed a finger at her, 'might think it's work, but does he?'

'That's really none of your business.'

He gaped at her. 'What the hell's that supposed to mean?'

'You don't know?'

'No.' But he could guess.

'Have you *ever* been honest with me, Drew?' Even in the beginning?

'Oh, Jees-sus . . . we're back to that crap about your mother aren't we?'

'It's not crap, Drew.'

Her face was closed against him and he was aware of a sick feeling in his stomach, and panic, because if he should lose her too, he would have nothing, no one, nowhere to go. And he could not go back to prowling the beaches and upmarket bars of Miami, or LA, or picking up rich middle-aged ladies in Saks and Bloomingdale's. Never again.

'You've got it all wrong,' he pleaded, 'I told you.'

'The only thing I've had wrong is you.'

'For chrissakes, Jackie, what have I done?'

'Oh, stop playing the innocent; I can't stand it.'

'I *am* innocent, for crying out loud!'

'Not you, Drew,' she said, and so softly that he almost strained to hear, 'not when you've been screwing my mother.'

'Bullshit!'

'You knew her address.'

'You gave it to me, goddammit, before I left.'

'I could have saved myself the effort, because you had it already.'

'This is crazy.'

'Good try, Drew,' she said coldly, 'but if you remember, you gave it as your bloody home address when you signed in at the Hyde Park.'

He just looked at her.

'And you tried to tell me that you flew halfway across the Atlantic just to see me? My darling mother threw you out, didn't she – got bored, like she always does?'

'It wasn't like that.' He spoke through gritted teeth. 'I love *you*, goddammit.'

She shook her head slowly. 'Don't say that any more.'

'Jackie . . . for chrissakes.' His eyes darted to the ring on her finger and she saw.

'You can have it – I don't want it.'

'Keep it.'

'Give it to *her*.'

'I don't want it.'

She looked at him wanting to rage, but her fury was tinged with sorrow. 'Finding out that you had her address just confirmed what I knew already. It was the perfume, you see . . . I don't suppose you can understand that.'

'Look, I can explain . . .'

'Get out, Drew,' she said bleakly.

'You don't mean that.'

'Oh, yes,' she said, 'I do.'

The yacht was moored just beyond a massive shoulder of coral, in a small inlet off Petit St Vincent; one of her favourite places in the Caribbean. Angela could see hundreds of colourful reef fish swimming in and out of the red and blue coral and once again she found herself amazed by the clarity of the water and the vibrant wilderness which survived beneath; never changing, simply turning over and over on itself. She lifted her face to the warm breeze blowing from the tiny island of grass and palms and closed her eyes, trying to rid herself of the lingering reflective mood which had stayed with her since New York.

In the end it had been so easy to change the locks and trick Drew into lunch and the shopping expedition, too easy, and to her vague discomfort there was not the slightest sensation of triumph, only an empty feeling as if something had gone wrong somehow. For chrissakes, he only wanted her money, after all, and she wasn't in the business of toy-boy husbands, no matter how beautiful, or how good it seemed to be between them. That was for fools, wasn't it? Old fools.

From the airport she had called the apartment building to be told that both the security man and the doorman had seen Drew off the premises, which was exactly what she had asked them to do. Now the penthouse had been cleaned, thoroughly, so that nothing of his presence would remain and his few things had been put into storage. She did not expect to return there for some weeks, maybe months, and by the time she did the memory would be gone.

She had planned this trip with Dougie long before Drew appeared on her doorstep with his pathetic attempt at blackmail. He would never have understood that she considered a private cruise through the Grenadines with the Governor of California and his closest friends as an unmissable event. These were important people, very important people, who understood and accepted Dougie's relationship with her. What could Drew know of such things? And did he really expect her to believe that he would actually have that sordid stuff on her published? Not a chance – not while she still paid his bills and not if he ever wanted to see her again. Because he would still want her, whatever hate he might be feeling now.

Naturally, it had unnerved her a little when she had seen what he had found out about her – that filth, that garbage – the debris of her early life which would damn everything she had ever done or achieved since. Heat flooded her face at the memory of the photographs he had shown her. Bergman had paid her one hundred and fifty lousy dollars for those shots, which had been taken at a very private stag party on Riverside Drive. All those years ago and she remembered as if it were yesterday.

A vivid, never-to-be-forgotten image rose up out of the years. Pinkey Jones. There was no real shame in her, only dusty excitement because she had enjoyed it, the stripping and the strutting, at least that crazy, delicious moment on stage when she had paraded her stuff around: moving and teasing in just the right way . . . moving, teasing . . . moving, teasing . . . when the men were hooting and hollering, thumping the tables and making her giddy with their dirty talk. Wanting *her*.

'Hey, Angie, I've been looking all over this goddamn boat for you.'

Angela swung round, a smile fixed on her face. 'Just looking at the view, Dougie. You were sleeping like a baby last time I saw you.' He was wearing shorts, knee length khaki Bermudas and she cringed inwardly, loathing them on sight. Dougie had short legs, bulbous calves and an almost identical varicose vein running from the knee of each leg to the ankle. On the occasions when he felt able to make love, which seemed to her to be getting fewer and fewer, her fingers would sometimes find the ridge of a vein, like a thick pencil lying just beneath the skin, and disgust would flood through her, so that she would try hard to think of another place, another time, someone else. And it always came back to Drew in the end.

'We're having dinner ashore, at the Resort.' He rubbed his hands together and looked at her greedily. 'You're looking lovely, sugar.'

'Do you want to go back to the cabin?' She switched on her siren look, the one that told him he was the most desirable man she had ever known.

He reddened and chuckled. 'Not right now – later, later – I'm not as young as I was.'

That was an understatement. For the first three days he had slept practically all the time and no afternoon went past without his 'little nap', which excluded her, of course.

'This would be a beautiful place for a honeymoon, Dougie.'

He followed her gaze. 'Sure would.'

She shot a careful glance at him as he joined her at the rail.

'*When*, Dougie?' she said suddenly and with exasperation. 'How long are you going to keep me waiting?'

'As long as it takes, sugar, you know how these things are.'

Angela sighed impatiently. And every day she was getting older. She was beautiful, she had been told that all her life, but it didn't last forever. A woman with everything except youth and a husband.

It didn't matter that she had wealth and respectability, it wasn't enough. In the circles she mixed with, a single woman was a nuisance without an escort, and an embarrassment with one who was found to be wanting. Besides, everyone *expected* her to be the next Mrs Douglas Hicks the Third; it was practically written down in stone. She felt that familiar fear in the pit of her stomach. After all, she had to be realistic, there were not too many seriously rich, eligible men of her age group around who would settle for a woman near their own age, no matter how beautiful. And if their current wife wasn't already dead, they would probably have every intention of trading her in for a younger model sooner or later.

Angela closed her eyes as the ghoul of old age reared its ugly head again, because in all the world her worst nightmare was the thought of withering alone, dying alone. She would rather kill herself first.

'We've got to think of my career,' his voice ran on, 'the future, what it could do to us both if we rushed things and with Miriam, God rest her soul, hardly cold . . .' He cleared his throat. 'Democrats just don't do things like that, sugar.'

She thought of the Kennedys and wanted to laugh out loud.

'Dougie . . . honey,' she said patiently, carefully emphasizing every word, 'I've been waiting six, nearly seven long, long years for you . . .' She took a deep breath because it suddenly became very important to her then. 'Can't we at least set a date – just between us – make it our little secret?'

And before he found out about Jackie and her damned musical, because the show was really going ahead by all accounts and there was nothing she could do about it now. Once Dougie knew he would no doubt use it as another reason for delaying any real commitment because of damn-fool sentiment and misplaced Democratic loyalties. Surely he owed some loyalty to her, for chrissakes – surely he could see that?

'I'd like to do that, sugar, you know I would, but . . .' He shook his head and shrugged his shoulders at the same time.

She darted a sideways glance at him, snapped her mouth shut on a sharp, damning retort and instead let her beachrobe fall

partly open. 'You know how I feel, how generous I can be . . .'
She inhaled deeply so that her rib-cage lifted her chest up and
out.

Even as she watched Dougie's mouth falling open, somewhere
inside a memory stirred as she spoke the skilfully practised
words, a little scene she hadn't thought of in years: David trying
to leave her, his beautiful face pale, almost haggard, because
their lives were falling apart. She felt a tiny shrinking, a dull
twisting pain in her chest. Even then she had thought that she still
had power over him, that she could seduce him all over again and
make him stay.

'Oh, Angie,' Dougie wheezed, and she closed her eyes.

Because of Jackie, David had always remained in her life
somewhere. An unsettling memory. He would have given Jackie
the money, of course, or saintly sickening Clare with her pricey
works of art and very substantial private income.

'Oh, sugar . . .'

She swallowed deeply. Hating them both.

Dougie's mouth settled on the round swell of her breast and
her attention was drawn to the top of his head and the grey,
thinning hair, but automatically she began running her practised
fingers along the back of his neck.

'That's right, honey . . . ' she coaxed, 'that's right . . . now,
why don't we set a date? Why not? Then we could celebrate . . .
just the two of us?'

He was silent for a few seconds, then slowly lifted his head.
There was a stupid coy smile on his face as he took her hand.

'I tell you what I'm gonna do.' He patted her hand and nodded
twice as if he had given what he was about to say a great deal of
thought, 'I'll think about it. How's that, sugar?'

Jackie stood with her arms tightly crossed as she waited by the
window, staring unseeingly at the people and the traffic swarming
up the Charing Cross Road. One hand rested on her upper arm
and she began moving it gently up and down, up and down as if
her unconscious were endeavouring to soothe away the hurt.

She had arrived at the studio before anyone else because she
hadn't been able to sleep. The scene with Drew had dragged on
and on. He had pleaded with her, of course, begged her when he

realized the magnitude of his mistake. Those pleadings had been breathtaking, as had the lies which followed the other lies; lie upon lie upon lie. Jamie had made a reluctant exit because she had told him to; the whole evening had been spoiled. Drew had left, finally, but only because she threatened him with the police.

She started as the door behind her opened and Brian, her stage designer, walked in bearing a small tray with three coffees.

'Yvonne's on her way down,' he said, offering her a coffee.

'I'm afraid Max won't be able to make the meeting for at least another half hour,' she said and reached gratefully for one of the hot plastic cups.

'What do you think of my idea?' he asked, and then nodded in the direction of the scale model which stood on his desk.

Once more she studied the set carefully; it was a model which Brian had made to help make it easy to choose the right permutation for certain scenes. The mobile dais was being specifically built for the Birthday Salute at Madison Square Garden and was proving to be an expensive piece of design, and she felt very much that, if possible, it should be made use of elsewhere in the production.

Brian had suggested that the dais could be hinged at one point and made into a ramp for use in another scene and a show number Monroe had actually sung during her career – 'Diamonds are a Girl's Best Friend', the only song in the production that was not original, but could not, in truth, be left out in a musical play about the dead star's life.

'It could be great, if it can be made to work.'

'I've dealt with more complex designs.'

'Well, I would rather this particular design were not too complex because it could leave us wide open for problems cropping up, and maybe even during a performance.' She shook her head. 'I don't think I could stand the strain.'

'Don't worry, don't worry . . . ' he laughed, 'it'll be all right on the night, as they say.'

'God, I hope so.'

'That doesn't sound like you, Jackie.' He looked at her. 'Nothing wrong is there?'

'Tired, Brian,' she said quickly, 'that's all.'

'Hi,' Yvonne said, with a big grin on her face as she looked around the door. 'Sorry I'm late.'

'That's okay, we've hardly started,' Jackie said, glad to be snapped out of her unhappy thoughts. She looked at the blank page of her working pad, at the pen in her hand. God, her own mother.

Yvonne drew up a chair. 'Brian seems to have this thing about black and white . . .'

'Our divine costume designer means,' he said, sighing with mock exasperation, 'that an idea Max and I discussed would take the form of one or two sets being all black, or all white, and the costumes relating to those scenes would be white and black respectively.'

'The first and the last,' Jackie said, looking at them both with a determined effort. She would keep her feelings well and truly inside and think of them later if she must. Between them Drew and her mother had done enough damage without allowing them to intrude on her work and the musical as well.

'Max has already discussed it with you?'

She nodded. 'The white set for the opening scene when Monroe's mother, Gladys, is confined to a mental hospital – don't forget the revolving stage comes in at the end here, Brian, after the young Norma Jean, or Monroe, is parted from her mother . . .'

'I take it that this is where the foster parents make their entrance – six couples,' Yvonne pointed out. 'They stand in appointed places on the revolve, which actually represents time passing, and as it moves around young Monroe literally passes through their hands. Right?'

'Right.'

'And the costumes revert to 1930s style in colour and design?'

'Yes.'

'Fine.'

There was a tap at the door and Jamie looked in.

'Yes, Jamie?'

'Telephone call.'

'I thought I said no calls.'

'It's the third time he's telephoned; nothing I say seems to make any difference . . .'

243

She knew instantly who he was talking about.

'Excuse me,' she said, glancing swiftly at Brian and Yvonne, 'this won't take a moment.'

'Babe,' he gulped, 'I am so sorry . . .'

Even the sound of his voice made her skin crawl. 'Don't call me "babe".'

Silence.

'Can't we talk? For chrissakes, Jackie.'

'I think we said all we had to say last night.'

'You are wrong – you are *so* wrong.'

'I have work to do, so don't call me here. Ever.'

'Look, you don't understand . . .'

'I understand too much.'

'No, you don't, that's just it.'

'It's over, Drew.'

'Jackie . . . ' he begged, 'Jackie.'

'Stop this.'

'I love you, Jackie.'

She made no answer, but there was an unpleasant prickling sensation at her cheekbones as tears cascaded silently down her face.

'Jackie?'

The large brown envelope lay on the grubby bristled mat just inside the door. Even before Richard picked it up and ripped open the flap he knew what was inside and he sighed desolately because it was the second rejection he had had since returning from his mother's. Sure enough, he found the usual photocopied letter inside with the standard reason why they were not willing to publish. 'Not suitable for our list.'

He had always wondered what exactly that meant and imagined a long table of names and titles written on a piece of paper lying on someone's desk somewhere in the heady, rarified air of a publishing executive's office. Except that his lovable lines would not, of course, rise that far. In all probability it had not got beyond what he knew in publishing circles was called 'the slush pile', something that was generally dealt with by an office junior or someone of that ilk who usually had neither the confidence nor the experience to know a good manuscript even if he or she saw one. Relegation to the slush pile meant nowhere, man.

He sighed again and walked back into the sitting room, hugging the envelope unconsciously against his chest. He slumped down into an old armchair and stared around the room which seemed very empty just then.

Lucy was refusing to speak to him, at least properly. She had left his Christmas stocking for him to find on his return, with a note pinned to it telling him that she would be back late, 'so don't wait up'. Roger, no doubt. There had been no deep, meaningful conversation when they finally met up as she had promised and he had no idea if that was a good or a bad thing.

Misery flooded from every pore as he pictured her again with the devastatingly handsome Roger St John, alias Herr Foch. And why not? After all, what did he have to offer a girl like Lucy? Oh, sure, he did have an acting job now – a small part in an afternoon soap as a temporary stop gap: a narrow-minded, bearded bigot of a Scottish parson who was so much of a caricature and so over-written that he could only come to the conclusion that the script-writers and the viewing public must be desperate, or brainless, or both.

Richard snorted softly with contempt and then fell silent. He wondered if she would move out, leave him, and go and live with Roger in his lush pad in Holland Park. He wondered if he could bear it.

A mood he knew of old began winding its oppressive arms about him. It always got him in the end, that creeping spectre of depression – tailing him faithfully for months, weeks, days, waiting for this, the most unbeautiful moment of all, to pounce.

He sat there immobile, brooding as the minutes passed, his hands resting on the arms of the chair, the imitation cuckoo clock on the wall tick-tocking too loudly so that he felt he wanted to scream, but suddenly the telephone shrieked at him and he jumped up instantly thinking of Lucy as his manuscript spilled from his lap on to the floor, page after page after page. Yet when he placed the receiver against his ear he only heard his mother's voice and her sweet innocent questions about his health, his happiness, and had he found himself a literary agent yet? He gave her all the right answers, even made her laugh and then pretended he was going out so that she would ring off.

As he put the telephone down he turned to see his work lying scattered across the rug in erratic white heaps. He swore softly and bent down to pick them up just as the phone rang again.

'For God's sake!' he hissed, and still on his knees leant across the island of paper to grasp the receiver.

'Yes.'

'Richard?'

'Yes.'

'Ned.'

'I thought you'd died.'

'Very droll, my boy, so glad you haven't lost your touch.'

Richard caught a sharp breath, at the same time calculating how long, exactly, it had been since Ned, his agent, had bothered to call him. It seemed like years.

'How does a tasty little commercial grab you?'

'After such a glorious wait, I thought at least it would be a slot on *Jonathan Ross*, or maybe even *Emmerdale Farm* as Joe Sugden's long-lost brother.'

'Joe Sugden doesn't have a long-lost brother.'

'Someone could dream him up, perhaps . . . ?'

'That only happens on *Dallas*, Richard, in case you didn't know.'

Richard sighed heavily.

'Okay, spill the beans – what is it this time – American Express again?'

'No.'

'To tell you the truth, I didn't mind that too much. At least it paid well.'

'Three grand, wasn't it?'

'Yup,' Richard said, 'three lov-er-ly big ones.'

'Well, this one isn't *quite* in that league . . . and remember there were several repeats.' So Richard had raked in a few unexpected shekels as a bonus.

'What is it?' Richard asked with a sense of foreboding. 'Come on, Ned, tell me.'

'It's a Government Health Warning ad.'

'You mean it will pay bugger all.'

'There's always the standard Equity fee . . .'

'If we're talking about the standard ninety-five pounds, just forget it.'

'One hundred and fifty pounds actually.'

Richard grunted in response.

'A series of six – that's nearly a thousand pounds.'

'Before tax.'

'Christ, Richard – I'll give it to someone else if you like.'

'All right, all right.' He groaned softly. 'What is it exactly, what do I have to do?'

Ned cleared his throat. 'I told you it was a Government Health thing . . . well, prevention of disease is the object.'

'What sort of disease?'

'You must have read about it in the papers . . .'

'God,' Richard exclaimed, 'you're talking about AIDS, aren't you?' He paused and said wearily, 'Condoms, that's what this is all about, isn't it?'

'Christ, no,' Ned snapped, 'I'm talking about cockroaches.'

'Cockroaches?'

'There's been a plague of them this year. Some of the ugly little buggers are continental cousins and plan on staying, by the sound of things.'

'Perhaps you should be talking to someone from Immigration?'

'Very funny,' Ned answered crossly. 'Well, are you interested?'

'Cockroaches . . . ' Richard sighed, 'brilliant, Ned, just brilliant.' He closed his eyes and wondered why he didn't take a long walk off a short pier. 'What do I have to do?'

'You act the expert as far as I can tell – give advice on hygiene, pesticides, that sort of thing.'

'How thrilling.'

'The ad agency want you at their studios on the twenty-third.'

'That's less than a week away.'

'Sorry, but it's all been rather last minute.'

'You mean I wasn't first choice.'

'Just be there, Richard,' Ned said. 'I'll get my secretary to send you the details in the next couple of days.'

'Thanks.' For nothing.

The telephone went dead and Richard stared at it resentfully, then looked at the sad pages of his manuscript still lying in white heaps over the floor, waiting patiently to be picked up and put in order all over again.

'Come to Daddy,' he said tenderly and crouched down.

As he placed each sheet in sequence he thought of the next publisher he had decided on and the next rejection slip which would no doubt be pushed through the letterbox. He thought of his mother and what she had said about a literary agent, but he was afraid, wasn't he, of what they might tell him once their beady eyes had scanned his words? That he was wasting his time.

She made a soft sound, like a gasp. Fingers stroked him, naked legs rubbed against his as she rolled on top and her hot meagre limbs slid greedily across him.

'I thought you'd never come back,' Rose sighed. 'Sometimes I thought you could be a fantasy I'd conjured up in my head, like a dream or something.'

'No dream, babe,' Drew said.

'You can stay as long as you like.'

'What about your friend?'

'Babs?' She lifted her head and looked into his face. 'What do you mean?'

'She doesn't like me.'

'She does, Drew – really, she does.'

'Uh, uh.' He shook his head.

'It doesn't matter anyway,' she said with a trace of newfound disdain. 'I'll be moving into my own place at the end of the month.'

'Great,' he said. 'Can I come visit you there?'

'Always,' she gushed, 'but you can stay here too, it's okay.'

'I couldn't do that.' Yet he would, because it suited him and he had no intention of breaking into the cheque Angela had given him by paying two hundred pounds a night for a decent hotel room. It wouldn't be for long, not if he managed to speak to Jackie again, face to face, convince her that she was wrong, that she had misunderstood. Of course, he could not fool himself that it would be easy, but it was still worth a try. Yet the uncertainty, the cold dread that had plagued him since New York and Angela, still clung, hovering just out of sight like impending calamity.

'Well, until you fix yourself up somewhere.'

He grinned ruefully.

'That was dumb of me.'

'What was?' She began tracing the outline of his mouth with one finger.

'Not booking myself in somewhere,' he lied. 'I was in such a goddamn rush to get back that it totally slipped my mind.'

'It doesn't matter.' She smiled slowly, sweetly. 'I love having you here, it's what I want.'

'I should have called you more often.'

'Some people just aren't much good at making telephone conversation – I could tell that was the way with you.'

'You could?'

'Yes, oh, yes . . .'

'You're smart, babe.' He moved his mouth into a big dazzling smile. 'And cute.'

'Oh, Drew,' she said helplessly and laid her head on his shoulder, running her fingers prettily through the mass of dark hair on his chest.

As she looked away from him he relaxed the smile and let it die on his lips. In the semi-darkness of the room he could still see the scores of soft toys she had collected crowding every shelf and corner, even tiny ones perched on the ornamental fireplace and a giant Paddington Bear filling the windowsill and smothering any light which might have filtered into the room.

What depressed him most was the poster above the fireplace and that ancient pain-in-the-ass message from *Love Story*, a film that had climbed to new heights of schmaltz in the early Seventies. He had been twelve and his crazy mother had made him go and sit with her through it nine times as she shuddered and wept and blew snot into those little cellophane packs of Kleenex. Every day until it left town.

He closed his eyes shut tight on the memory because now the words of the caption hurt; that sickly motto about love and being sorry only reminded him of Angela and what she had done to him, twisting a knife in the wound. Oh, but she would regret it, she sure would. Angela had risked kicking him out of her life because she didn't think he had the guts to spill the beans on her. Well, she was wrong about that, just as she was wrong about everything else, and more wrong than she could ever know.

Drew thought of the cheque she had left him – paying him off, as if he were a whore. Hate was spreading through him like a stain and he could feel himself losing control. But he didn't care any longer.

He felt Rose's mouth move on his skin, her tongue begin to play and tease, but he remained still, the sudden and overwhelming hunger for Angela making his lips quiver, his limbs stiffen. It seemed to him then that his love was agony and that the pain didn't fade as each day, each hour passed, but grew worse, more hopeless, more ugly.

'Drew . . . oh Drew . . . ,' Rose breathed and the feel of her hot little cheek against his flesh made him cringe inside himself. Yet he permitted her kisses and caresses, her feverish adoration of him because she was simply there and he had no one else. In his mind's eye Rose was Angela, just as Jackie had been, and in his imagination she was sorry, so sorry for what she had done and the cheap way she had humiliated him. His vision dimmed and his hands found her head, pushing it down, down, holding it hard and tight, forcing her to take him in her mouth.

The world swirled, his face contorting as he gave himself up to his fantasy and the searing tormenting pleasure – making her take it all, filling up her throat as lust entwined itself with waiting rage and began to rise and crest in a heated rush. He threw his head back, his body arching and convulsing as the climax smashed through, shooting into his brain, exploding and wiping out all pain, all loneliness, all memory.

Rose was not there at all.

There was no reply. Jackie looked at the telephone and her eyebrows drew together in a quizzical frown. Since David had left for Scotland Clare was always at home in the evenings, taking advantage of his absence to concentrate on her own work, sometimes not leaving the studio until the early hours of the morning because there was no need, she had the house and time all to herself. During such periods she refused any invitations, hardly socializing at all except with immediate family.

Feeling vaguely unsettled, Jackie put down the receiver, shrugged and shifted her attention back to her desk, but caught a weary breath because suddenly she felt enormously tired and lonely, longing to speak to Clare and unburden herself about Drew and her mother, despite the promise she had made to herself that she would not. Clare would only worry.

The evening stretched ahead of her, but she had plenty to do she told herself; the production transferred to the Adelphi in two weeks so there was a great deal of organizing to be done, except that she knew she was trying to drown herself in the show in order not to think too much about what had happened. The bitterness was beginning to bite deep, sinking into her slowly, and hurting. Jackie blinked and moved her gaze to the black windows, feeling soiled and depressed. The sound of voices outside in the street made the room feel isolated and withdrawn.

There was a tap on the door. She took a deep breath, knowing in advance who it was and as Jamie walked in she looked carefully back at him.

'Still here?'

'I thought we might . . .'

'I would be bad company tonight, Jamie.'

'Not to me.'

She closed her eyes for a moment. 'I think I'll finish this and have an early night.'

'It's Drew, isn't it?'

'Part of it.'

'And your mother.'

'And my mother,' she repeated bitterly, 'international hostess with the mostest – Angela Cassini.'

He said nothing, then, 'He was never good enough for you.'

'I suppose that's a very nice thing to say.'

'I'm simply stating a fact,' he said.

'Take no notice,' she said, 'just give me a few days to come to terms with this and I'll be fine.'

'It might take more than that.'

'Do you always have to say exactly what you think?'

She looked at him. There was an engaging half-smile hovering on his lips and she was caught by a sudden stab of desire. She wondered if he knew, just then, how much she wanted him.

'I've tried to call Clare,' she said, turning away, 'but the telephone just rings and rings.'

'I should have mentioned this earlier: she's joined David in Scotland.'

'When?'

'She caught a shuttle to Glasgow yesterday morning.'

'But why? She has to work towards her next exhibition, she told me. Besides, there's been no mention of her joining him.'

'I just found the note she left when I got home last night.'

'How odd.'

'Perhaps she wanted a break.'

'Not so soon . . .' she said thoughtfully. 'She didn't say in the note that there was anything wrong?'

He shook his head.

She picked up the phone, flicked her address book open to the right page and began dialling.

'It is Inverlochy Castle, isn't it?'

Jamie nodded.

Her attention was drawn back to the telephone as it was answered. 'David Jones, please.' She paused. 'Yes – it's his daughter.' She shot a glance at Jamie before turning to the mouthpiece of the receiver. 'Clare?'

'Jackie . . . this is a surprise.'

'Why didn't you let me know that you intended to see Daddy?'

'It was a rather spur-of-the-moment decision.'

'I thought you were supposed to be working?'

'Yes . . . well, I . . .' She stopped abruptly.

'Clare?'

'She's got a migraine, darling . . .' David's voice took over.

'Just a migraine? She sounds terrible, Daddy.'

'Don't fuss, she's really fine – or will be, once she has a lie-down.'

'Are you sure?'

'Jackie – Clare is perfectly well, believe me. She's been over-doing things and probably needs a change of air.'

'It just didn't seem like her at all,' she replied. 'Are you all right?'

'What do you think?' he said patiently. 'All this bracing Scottish air works wonders for everyone, including me. We even took a turn in these gorgeous grounds this morning: they run right down to the loch. If it wasn't so damn cold I would have taken a quick dip.'

'Even in summer the waters are freezing, Daddy.'

'All right, darling, point taken.'

There was a moment's silence.

'And you are both fine – really?'

'Of course.' He said lightly. 'I think your stepmother required an injection of inspiration as well as good clean air, and she's certainly come to the right place. Quite awesome, the beauty.'

'I was worried.'

'No need,' he said swiftly, 'everything is going well here, including the filming. We're only four days behind schedule which must be a record.' He paused. 'Are *you* all right?'

An ache sat in her throat and inexplicably she thought she was going to cry.

'Jackie?'

Suddenly there was that old longing for her father, from her childhood, when she had had nothing of her own.

'Jackie?'

'Sorry,' she said thickly, 'sorry – I'm just tired.'

'Is that all?'

'It's been one of those weeks.'

'Can I do anything?'

'No, it's okay,' she said. 'I'm going to have an early night.'

'Make sure you have a decent holiday once the show gets off the ground.'

'I will.'

'Are there any problems in that quarter?'

'Only the usual.' She took a deep breath. 'Look – I'll let you go now, I expect you're about to have dinner.'

'I'll give you a call at the end of the week.'

'Please.'

'And don't worry about us, you have enough on your plate.'

'But there's nothing *to* worry about, is there?'

'No,' he said firmly, 'and again, *no*.'

'I'll speak to you Friday, then,' she said, 'don't forget.'

'Have I ever?'

253

No, her father was very good at not forgetting, at just being there, especially when it concerned her.

'Now go and have a stiff drink,' David continued, 'and an early night. That's an order.'

'Give Clare my love.'

'I will.' He paused. 'Take care, my sweet.'

'Bye, Daddy.'

ELEVEN

'She's not here.'

Drew stared intently at Jamie. 'Don't I get to know where she is?'

'Jackie's with Max, and Brian Wells, the stage designer, at the Adelphi. I don't think you'll be able to see her.'

Drew's expression grew stoney, his foot tap-tapping on the polished wooden floor, and he glanced past Jamie into the studio beyond as if he doubted him.

'She's not here,' Jamie repeated, 'really.'

'And you wouldn't lie about that, would you, kiddo,' Drew said resentfully, 'being an actual real-life holy Joe.'

'Perhaps you could call her,' Jamie said, ignoring his remark.

'Oh, sure . . .' he said dryly, 'and when I do, I either get her goddamn answerphone, or she gets some flunky, like you, to tell me she's too busy.'

'I'm not her flunky.'

Drew had come here out of desperation because all his carefully made plans were going wrong. Angela, it seemed, had disappeared from the face of the earth and despite the fact that he had left several messages for her to contact him, she had done nothing. He would give her another week, which was more than she deserved, and then he would spill the beans. It was as simple as that.

He turned his attention back to Jamie and felt bitterly envious. He had been comforted in the knowledge that Jackie was there, no matter what, but he had slipped up and she had got wise at last. Now the field had been left wide open for the golden boy and almost ex-priest, Jamie Thurley.

'No?' he said, 'but you run around after her a helluva lot, don't you? Glued to her very nice, very neat ass.'

Jamie said nothing.

'We have a lot in common, you and I,' Drew persisted, 'we both want the same thing.'

'I don't think we have anything in common.' Jamie locked gazes with him. 'Nothing, in fact.'

'Why don't we have a bite to eat together, and I'll prove it to you?'

'I have work to do.'

'Oh, come on . . .' Drew said in disbelief, nodding in the direction of the quiet corridor beyond them. 'Sounds to me as if they've all checked out.'

'I still have work to do.'

Drew shook his head. 'I make you nervous, don't I?'

'No.'

'Well, come and have a bite with me – have some fun, let yourself go, for chrissakes!'

'I don't think so.'

'Maybe I need your advice,' Drew continued, deceptively smoothly. 'I bet you didn't think of that, did you?'

'What sort of advice?'

'Advice about Jackie.'

'No.'

'I've messed things up,' he said, 'you know, don't you?'

Jamie nodded.

'I just want to say I'm sorry, is that so much to ask?' Drew deliberately hung his head, bent on acquiring Jamie's sympathy. 'I let her down, badly, and I want to make it up to her.' He darted a glance at Jamie. 'Do you have any bright ideas about all this?' Good ole holy Joe wouldn't breathe a word, of course, because he had the hots for her himself. And Jackie? It would not be so hard to understand why she might be attracted to Tarzan the Virgin. Hadn't he read somewhere that it was every woman's fantasy to seduce a young, good-looking son of a bitch like Jamie Thurley?

'I don't know what you think I can do.'

'At least join me for a bite. Come on, give me a break, I'd really appreciate it.'

'I don't know what time I'll finish,' Jamie said hesitantly, but it wasn't real work, only filing, sorting out bills and making up a list of correspondence for Jackie on Monday morning.

'Hey – I know you don't like me, you've made that clear, and maybe I don't deserve anything more, but right now all I'm trying to do is stretch my hand out to you and be friends. Or bury our differences, at least.'

Disquieting echoes floated out of Jamie's memory, old words like ancient charms: 'I love my neighbour as myself for the love of Thee. I forgive all who have injured me, and ask pardon of all whom I have injured.' Still there. 'This is my body and this is my blood.'

'Look,' Drew pressed, 'see that café across the street? I'll wait for you there and we can talk over coffee, or pizza, or something when you finish. How about it?'

There was a light on in the flat and for a moment she saw the black silhouette of a man, Richard, come to the window and then disappear again. Lucy knew that he was looking for her because she was late home again. It was becoming a habit, this lateness, and she was not sure why except that she and Richard seemed unable to talk to each other any longer and so she avoided him. Yet she loved him, didn't she? At least she could not imagine her life without him, so it was weird, wasn't it, that she was avoiding him?

Lucy watched her frozen breath pouring into the chill air, then stopped and paused just across the street from the house, on the path overlooking the canal and Camden Lock, staring into the narrow stretch of water. It was so cold she wondered that it had not iced over. She swung round finally and was about to cross to the other side when a speeding car turned into the street and she stepped back, waiting for it to pass, but instead it slowed and drew up by the kerb. The driver was Roger.

She moved to walk around the car, but already he had opened the door and caught her as she reached the driver's side.

'For God's sake, can't you leave me alone?'

'You didn't turn up!' He was outraged and she wondered whether it had ever happened to him before and if he was still recovering from the shock.

'I told you at La Tante Gigi I wouldn't. The only reason I agreed to meet you at all was to tell you exactly what I thought of you – face to face – so that you knew there could be no mistake.'

He started to speak, but his voice faltered.

'You didn't believe me, did you?' she said and felt a small glow of triumph. Once upon a time she would never have dared defy him, or almost any man come to that, because she lacked the courage.

'I don't know what you expect to gain by this.'

She shook her head in amazement. 'And what did you expect to gain, Roger – sex when you felt like it?'

'I apologized, didn't I?'

'Only because you were afraid I might make a fuss and sully your whiter-than-white image.'

'That's not true.'

'Oh . . . just go away, will you,' she said in exasperation, 'and leave me alone.'

She began walking across the street, but he followed.

'What about Dick?'

'I'm going to tell him everything.' Could she?

'I doubt that very much.' He glanced up to the top of the building, his eyes drawn to the tacky flat where she lived. Staring down at them from the window was Dick.

She kept walking until she felt his hand on her arm. 'Take your hands off me, Roger, or I'll scream. I mean it.'

Reluctantly he let go, hating her for the humiliation, making him crawl. His eyes darted back to the window, Dick was still there, and they seemed to watch each other for a moment, but then he was gone. Roger felt meanly pleased somehow, as if he had just scored a point against him.

'I'm crazy about you, you know that.'

'Only because I'm not crazy about you.'

'That's ridiculous.'

'And in case you hadn't noticed, I'm living with someone whom I happen to like very much.'

'That's why you've been seeing me, I suppose.' The corners of his mouth tipped upwards into a sardonic smile.

'Yes,' she replied, and almost to herself, 'that was rather stupid of me.'

'Do you think he doesn't know?'

'He can't.'

'God, you're naïve!'

'Don't do this, Roger.'

'He implied as much on the set . . .' He jerked his head savagely in the direction of the flat. 'And that's why he's up there pretending that he hasn't seen us together, all because he needs the bloody job!'

'If I didn't know Richard like I do, I could almost make myself believe your cheap little piece of acting.' She paused and then added sourly, 'Why don't you save it for your precious soap.' She turned away, speaking to him over her shoulder as she quickened her pace. 'One more thing you should know – and this may sound like a cliché – if you were the last man on earth I wouldn't let you come anywhere near me.'

'You don't mean that, Lucy.'

'Oh, I do.'

'Can't we even be friends?'

Lucy didn't reply.

'Not even good enough for that.'

'Roger – you don't even know the meaning of the word "friend".'

He became very still as the anger he had been containing began to surge out and he took a step towards her.

Instinctively Lucy moved back and slipped into the high hedge behind her as Roger came too close. He leaned over her, his arms sliding around her body, his mouth pressing hard against her face. His weight pushed her further into the undergrowth as he rubbed his body greedily against hers. She tried to scream, but the only sound that emerged was muffled and pathetic because his body gagged her, and there was the stifling smell of his cloying skin, the taste on her lips as she squirmed helplessly trying to push him away.

Yet the warm soft flesh of his cheek pressing against her face was a gift; so easy to open her mouth and take that unsuspecting flesh between her teeth and bite down hard, harder. Then there was that old trick her father had told her always to remember, years ago, when she had been in her teens, something she had never done and only dreamt of doing in belated anger and shame.

Her hand found his erection with ease, even through the fine wool of his trousers, and she squeezed and pulled and twisted and dug her fingernails through the fabric until she heard him shriek.

259

Richard was sitting in an armchair as she let herself into the flat, a drink in his hand.

He let her take off her coat, but then she stood quite still in the square space between the closed door of the flat and the entrance into their sitting room.

'How was Roger?' he asked without expression, unable to make himself wait any longer.

She leaned her head against her duffel coat which was now hanging on its usual peg, cold and snagged with twigs and leaves from her little tussle with Roger. She swallowed hard, aching and bruised and tired and cold.

'You mean you saw?' She turned to him with disbelief.

'It was difficult not to, my sweet,' he said sarcastically, 'perhaps in future you shouldn't make your liaisons quite so, shall we say, public.'

'And you just sat there?'

'What else was I supposed to do?' He lifted his eyes reluctantly to her face. 'I half-expected you to bring him up for a drink.'

'Are you quite mad?'

'It's all right, Luce,' he said wearily, 'I've known for some time.'

She sank down on to the sofa opposite and stared at him.

'What have you known?'

'About you and Roger.'

She closed her eyes and wondered whether to laugh or cry.

'Would you get me drink, please.'

Richard got up mechanically and poured her a glass of red wine from the bottle he had almost finished.

'We don't have to talk about this now,' he said quietly, trying to be reasonable. 'You look pretty beat.'

'So would you after what I've just been through.'

'Spare me the details, Luce.'

'Oh, Richard . . .' She sighed heavily. 'You really don't understand, do you?'

'I'm not sure I want to.'

She smiled tiredly. 'I think Roger's plumbing is feeling rather sore at this moment; I'm surprised he was even able to drive off into the sunset.'

'For God's sake – do you think I need to know that?'

'I thought you might be amused.' It was wonderful the relief she was beginning to feel, and there was laughter too, bubbling just out of sight, tinged with the raw edge of hysteria.

Richard's face was white, hurt and white. 'I expected more from you, Luce . . .'

'Come here, you idiot,' she held out her hand, 'and give me a long, tight, cuddly embrace, or I might do something nasty to your plumbing too.'

His face was weary, but he knew what she was saying, even if a great deal of it did not make sense. A terrible burden of doubt was falling away, leaving it safe to love her again.

'Of course,' she continued, 'you'll probably be no longer required on the set of St Winifred's.'

'What the hell are you talking about?'

'It's a rather long and not particularly nice story, I'm afraid,' she said quietly. 'Don't stand there like that staring at me, Richard. Come here – please.'

He drew close and looked down at her. 'You've got leaves in your hair.'

'I don't care, I really don't,' she said with frustration, 'just sit next to me and hold me, will you?'

'Okay, okay . . .'

He sat down and slipped his arm around her shoulders and she snuggled up against him, pressing her face into the comforting, familiar smell of his tired old sweater.

'You don't have to tell me this "not particularly nice story" now, you know.' He gently kissed the top of her head. 'After all, we have plenty of time – don't we?'

She nodded, unable to speak as tears too heavy to hold back began to course down her cheeks.

Beneath half-closed lids Rose snatched a glance at the alarm clock on the mantel shelf. Babs was watching her carefully.

'He's not coming.'

'You don't know that.'

'He said 7.30, it's now nearly nine o'clock.'

'I learned to tell the time when I was six years old, Babs.'

'He could at least call you.'

'He's probably tied up in a meeting.'

'Oh, God, Rose – you're priceless.'

'Well, it's possible.'

'Anything's possible, even finding a telephone, or getting someone to call you on his behalf.' She paused deliberately. 'Well *you* would, wouldn't you?'

'Why do you always have to be so bloody negative about Drew?' Rose said suddenly. 'What has he ever done to you?'

'It's what he's done – no, sorry – is doing to *you* that bothers me.'

'He's not doing anything to me.'

'You're back on coke, aren't you?'

Rose shook her head.

'I *know*, Rose – anyway, you leave the evidence lying around.'

Rose blushed. 'It was just some stuff I had left.' Drew had a stash; they were taking it almost every night.

'He gave it to you, didn't he?'

'No.'

'Oh, Rose . . .'

'He really cares, can't you see that? I mean – for one thing, why would he stay here if he didn't want to be with me?'

'Maybe he hasn't anywhere else to go.'

'Don't be crazy, he's loaded.'

'Has he given you any money to help out?'

Rose took a very deep breath. 'I really don't think that's any of your business.'

Babs laughed unkindly. 'So, he hasn't.'

'Actually, he has,' she lied and blushed again.

'Look, Rose,' Babs said more gently, 'I'm not deliberately being mean minded or anything . . . there's just something about him.'

'You've hardly given him a chance.'

'Why should I? He's living in this flat rent free, using it like a hotel,' she said. 'And why do you need him – or any guy come to that – so much? For God's sake, look what's been happening for you! Probably the biggest break in your career you're ever likely to have and yet you seem to put him above everything else.' She shook her head. 'I just don't understand it, that's all.'

'I'm not asking you to understand it,' Rose said defensively, 'and besides, it won't be your problem much longer, will it, once I move out?'

'I don't want you to move out, Rose, you know that.' Babs paused and looked hard at her friend. 'And I don't want you to be hurt either.'

'Why should he hurt me?' Rose snapped. 'Why are you so certain?'

'Because you never seem to see it coming . . . even when it's staring you in the face.' And she had a horrible feeling that this would be worse than all the times before, but she couldn't tell Rose why because there was nothing to put into words, only a feeling.

'That's not fair,' Rose said quickly. 'Sometimes you just have to be unlucky in love to realize the real thing when it comes along.'

'But where is he, Rose? If he cares about you so much why doesn't he call? He knows you're sitting here waiting for him.' Babs shook her head. 'All dressed up and nowhere to go. My God. How many times do you need to go through this, Rose?'

'I know what you're trying to say, but perhaps you just can't see what's been happening.'

'What do you mean?'

'Well,' Rose said, a trifle uneasily, 'Drew and I, what we have together . . . perhaps you're just a little jealous.'

Babs almost choked. 'I don't believe this!' She closed her eyes in exasperation. 'And if *you* do, then I've been wasting my breath, haven't I, Rose?' She stood up. 'Right now I'm going to have a long hot bath and an early night, because it's getting really uncomfortable sitting here.'

Rose stared miserably after her friend, and wondered how she had let things go so badly wrong. She pulled up her legs and curled them beneath her, wishing Drew would hurry up and come because she wasn't sure she could stand the waiting much longer, and, more than anything, she wanted to prove to Babs how much she was wrong.

There was something on his mind, she had guessed that much; he had hardly said a word to her before she left for the studio that morning and when she had leaned down to kiss him goodbye he had pretended to be asleep. And it had been her idea, not his, to eat out this evening and have 'a romantic dinner for two'.

She crouched further into the chair, resting her chin on her knees like a small child, listening for the sound of his footsteps.

Jamie preferred London at night; all the blemishes were hidden and it was difficult not to be impressed by the beauty of the floodlit buildings and the busy streets, still full of light and life, as if everyone had a purpose and knew exactly where he or she was going.

Not him. He darted a glance at Drew who sat silently beside him in the black cab, leaning forward, hands clasped, caught up in his own thoughts. Since leaving the café he had exchanged perhaps two words; he had not even told Jamie where they were headed.

The cab turned off and into Bond Street, then right and into a London square which it circled before disappearing down a side street, and another side street and another, before finally stopping outside a large Georgian house painted white with black railings at the front and a blue and gold striped awning over the entrance.

'This is it,' Drew said. 'Do you have any spare cash to pay the man?' He nodded in the direction of the driver. 'I've only got credit cards.'

Without a word Jamie fished in his pocket and pulled out a five-pound note which was quickly swallowed up in the cab driver's hand.

'Now we go in,' Drew gestured towards the open doorway 'and don't worry, I'm a member.'

Jamie followed behind him into a small crimson foyer. To their left was a desk behind which sat a woman, probably in her fifties and behind her stood a very large black man, arms folded immaculate in black tie.

'This is Ethel, Jamie,' Drew said, 'now say hello nicely.'

Jamie nodded slowly, his eyes drawn to her thin mouth which stretched into a flat, fixed smile.

'We go this way, James, my boy.' Drew caught his arm and tugged him towards a darkened stairwell and the dull throbbing strains of music several feet beneath them.

At the bottom of the stairwell another, equally large man stood staring into a small room of padded wall sofas, beaten copper tables and dimmed lighting. At the far end was a narrow bar, and on the bar stools lined up in front of it sat several girls, each girl wearing very little: only a tiny body stocking, fishnet tights and very high-heeled shoes.

'Come on, boy,' Drew's voice ran on, 'I want to show you how to live, what it *really* means to feel good.' He shifted his gaze from the inviting grins of the girls at the bar back to Jamie's blank face. 'But maybe all this is just too much for someone who has lived in a pretty little bubble all his life . . .' His mouth moved into a slow smile of barely concealed contempt. 'And I can understand why you might be nervous, or even afraid, believe me. Some men try for years to really understand women, to know what they want, when they want it and never succeed, poor bastards.' He paused with great deliberation. 'And you're a virgin, aren't you?'

Jamie said nothing.

'Well, you would be,' Drew continued, 'wouldn't you, being an ex-priest?'

'I was never a priest.'

'As near as dammit.'

Jamie shook his head; he had never even come close. There had been no calling and never any real desire on his part to put on the sacred vestments of a priest. The whole charade had been his father's dream.

'Have it your own way,' Drew said with a trace of sullenness, 'but it shows, anyway.'

Jamie stared at him, puzzled. 'What does?'

'That you're not a regular guy,' Drew said meanly, 'but what the hell, takes all kinds to make a world.' He grinned, the same grin he used for Jackie, like a white slash lighting up his face.

'Are you . . . a regular guy?'

'What the hell's that supposed to mean?'

'You prefer *older* women, don't you?'

Drew reddened. 'Sometimes – there's no law against that, is there?'

'No,' Jamie said innocently, 'it was just an observation.'

Drew looked at him sharply, then relaxed. 'Come on, let's get

265

a drink.' He gestured in the direction of the girls, 'And they won't bite, Jamie, honest.' At least, not unless you ask them to.

Jamie studied the line of girls for an instant. They were not so very different from the girls he had seen in the back streets of Nairobi: ready and waiting to please, eager for money.

They sat down on the sinking velour sofas. In the semi-darkness the cheap furniture might have seemed faintly luxurious, the hard, highly patterned carpet clean, but in the morning Jamie guessed that the cold light of day would shine through, shaming everything.

'We only drink champagne here, James, my boy.' That was a house rule, that and the fact that each bottle cost a hundred smackers. Even as Drew spoke one of the girls was bringing over an ice-bucket and several glasses.

Jamie watched her as she minced over to them, an Asian girl with olive skin, huge eyes and black hair falling below her waist; behind her trailed a blonde with hair not unlike Jackie's, but there the resemblance ended because this girl was short and stocky, with big round thighs, and breasts to match spilling out of her skimpy costume. She looked back at him and the edges of her mouth tipped into a wide smile of invitation. She sat down beside him as the other girl arranged the glasses around the table and gave the bottle of champagne to Drew to open.

'What's your name?' the girl asked.

He was aware of her legs which she had crossed, a well-rounded calf swinging gently in the confines of the fishnet tights, almost touching his knee. He was not quite sure what he should do, what expression to wear.

'I'm Lauren,' she said easily and picked up a glass of champagne, her small mouth only brushing the bubbles bursting at the rim. She was not allowed to drink too much, just enough to keep the clients happy and encourage them to order more bottles of the same.

'Jamie, Jamie . . .' Drew's voice echoed, 'you're not drinking. Don't you think it would be nice to lift our glasses to these two charming young ladies and start enjoying ourselves?'

The girl moved against him, placed a hand on his arm. He flicked a glance at Drew and saw that the Asian girl was whispering something in his ear, then they both turned to look at him nd the girl began to giggle, a small sallow hand coming up to over her lips as if there was some secret held in that moist red mouth.

'You're shy, aren't you?' Lauren said, one finger stroking his wrist. 'The average guy who comes in here is loud and drunk, with a pot belly and greying hair. You're not like that at all.' She paused and lit a cigarette. 'Jasmine always gets the good-looking guys, if there are any – she tells them she's Polynesian which sounds sort of romantic and interesting and a hell of a lot better than Bangladeshi, I suppose. I usually end up with the fat and forties or the chinless wonders. Not tonight, though.' She nodded in Drew's direction and blew out a cloud of smoke. 'Oh, he's nice all right, that's obvious, but not like you . . .'

He was surprised to hear the admiration in her voice, felt her eyes examining his face and then she squeezed his arm tightly as if she were trying to convey an intimate message, but he knew that if he turned to look at her he would be confronted by those thighs, those breasts. He took a deep gulp of air and tried to concentrate on his surroundings: the pink lampshades fixed to the walls, the heavy flock wallpaper, and the tiny dance floor with revolving ball above it coated with pieces of mirrored glass.

Jamie watched the ball turning and turning, sending off narrow shafts of light to every part of the room. He could see motes of dust turning endlessly in the stale air. An appalling wave of homesickness rose up inside him and he wondered how he could bear it. He reached for his glass and drained it and said nothing as Lauren filled it once more.

'Drink it down . . . all at once,' her little voice said.

The gassy liquid hit the back of his throat making his eyes water and he coughed and thought he would heave a stream across the table, but managed to save himself. The girl handed him a napkin and out of the corner of his eye he could see a smirk on Drew's face and the Asian girl, Jasmine, giggling again.

'Your baptism of fire, Jamie . . .' Drew laughed loudly.

'Let's dance,' Lauren said.

He felt detached from his body as she took his hand and tugged him gently in the direction of the tiny piece of wooden flooring where their bodies would meet and touch. She was so short that the top of her head only reached his chest and as she lifted her chin to look up at him he glanced down and saw the plump shel of her breasts exposed and naked, pressing and straining agains his shirt.

Blood soared into his face and he felt dazzled and giddy and a little out of control. She was speaking to him and he tried to listen to her ceaseless chatter, but only caught jigsaw pieces of what she said – a word, a phrase – and he knew that it did no matter at all.

Jamie closed his eyes and then stiffened as Lauren's arms crept around his waist, slid up his back and then she was telling him to 'relax, just relax', and he did, and it was easy because he fel lightheaded, weightless, wonderfully removed from the darknes of his thoughts, as if he were not drunk at all, but curiously wise.

She began to move against him slowly, skilfully, and the flesh between his legs began to catch fire.

'We can go in here . . .'

He stared at her, his vision swimming slightly, and he shook hi head, not understanding.

'There . . .' she pointed to a closed door, 'it's more private.'

He frowned and thought that she sighed in exasperatio because abruptly she took his hand and guided him to the doo which she opened, pushing him gently inside. It was a narrow cubicle with a wall sofa covered in red vinyl; the opposite wa was mirrored and the pink light fitment above them was dim an tarnished. It was about the size of a confessional box.

'I should charge you for this, but I won't,' Lauren said softl and began to unbutton his shirt.

Her round heated face began to play against his skin. She lifte his hands to her breasts and let them rest there as her own foun the opening to his jeans. He jerked and gasped as her finge released him, cradling him, hardening him and bringing him s quickly to a pitch of feverish want that he thought he woul explode, or die, or both, but to his astonishment and horror sh sank to her knees and took him into her wet warm mouth. H was appalled yet able to do nothing because his own bod seemed beyond his control. He groaned helplessly and shud dered as the fleeting pleasure soared and died abruptly. And was over. He parted his lips and tried to speak, but failed.

'God . . .' she exclaimed softly, 'you're a virgin, aren't you?'

God in this little cubicle?

He stared fixedly into her simple face, a doll's face with odd pouting lips, thick make-up shining white in the curves of her nostrils and her mouth slightly open revealing small, uneven teeth. For an instant his eyes fell to her breasts, but they were only pale unappetizing flesh now, blue-veined and sad.

His gaze shifted away from her, drawn inexorably to the mirror; there was a crack in one corner, fingermarks on the glass, a fat layer of dust on the door lintel. He was aware of his limp penis lying against the stark whiteness of his underpants. He reached mechanically for his jeans and pulled them up.

She was still on her knees even as he brushed silently past her to open the door, and in his mind's eye there was a mean echoing image, as if she waited for absolution.

He wanted to tell her to get up, but he couldn't speak. There was only the touch of her hand on his leg and her little voice telling him that 'it was all right, it didn't matter'.

The need to say something in return, something which would make everything all right was very great, but nothing would come.

It was one of the larger theatres, perfect for a musical. The red plush seats stretched down to the orchestra pit sitting just beneath the stage. On each side of the Adelphi's auditorium two boxes were positioned directly above one another and almost overlooking the stage itself. One allocated for JFK, of course, Jackie mused and caught a deep, satisfied breath.

It had taken her five and more years to get here, but she had made it, despite everything, even her own mother.

'Feels good, doesn't it?'

She swung round and there was Max, and a much more amiable Max of late.

'Oh, yes.'

'There's an indefinable smell about a theatre, particularly an old one – something intoxicating. Don't you think?'

'Provided that the seats get filled, yes,' she laughed.

'A producer friend of mine always lights a candle at Brompton Oratory and prays to St Jude,' he looked at her, 'patron saint of lost causes.'

'I hope we're not that desperate yet.'

'It's been a bad year for the West End.'

'It's been a bad two years.'

'But not as bad as New York.'

'True,' she said, 'at the last count twenty-one out of a total of thirty-seven Broadway theatres were dark.'

'This is a filthy profession, darling, no matter where you live, but we both know we wouldn't be in anything else.' Max shrugged. 'Anyway, I can't stand all the cries of doom and gloom when we're probably only talking about seasonal dips.'

'Batten down the hatches and wait for the spring . . .'

'What?'

'Something someone said to me once.'

'We're opening our hatches in two weeks in case you'd forgotten,' he said dryly.

She smiled. 'So I believe.'

'And I've already had several complaints about the size of the dressing rooms, particularly from Rupert.'

'He of the silk scarves and fragile vocal chords?'

'Our Arthur Miller, no less.' Max sighed. 'Yet another *prima donna* and his voice is no more fragile than anyone else's as far as I can tell. He knows he'd be looking at an understudy role if it was.'

'Anything else?'

'A general moan about the lack of a greenroom, but otherwise there's a nice juicy feeling of excitement building up among the cast.'

'Good. As for the lack of a greenroom, we're not the only theatre without one. Anyway, there are at least two decent pubs within shouting distance.'

'Just for your information, Bob, the stage-door man, told me that The Peacock, a few doors down, is where Adelphi inmates usually gather.'

'I understand that we need two or three more dressers, too, but I've had a word with the theatre manager and he's seeing to that.'

She fell silent for a moment, her gaze drawn back to the stage where the cast congregated. 'And Rose?'

'I thought she seemed better this morning.'

'That isn't good enough, Max.'

'I know – it's rather like dealing with a human yoyo. I've rarely come across an artist with such extremes of mood.'

'Will she say what's wrong?'

He shook his head.

'What do you suggest we do?' And he would know what she meant.

'Consider your original idea,' he said, 'alternating Lucy and Rose each night has to make sense under the circumstances.'

She looked at him in surprise. 'I thought I'd have a fight on my hands.'

'I'm not a complete fool, Jackie darling,' he smiled, 'a mite stubborn at times, I admit.'

'I hope you don't mind if I quote you on that?'

'Not at all.'

She shook her head, perplexed. 'There's something different about you, Max.' She smiled. 'And I wish I knew what it was.'

'I'm sure I don't know what you mean,' but he reddened just perceptibly, then looked at his watch. 'Have to go, I'm afraid.'

'So early – it's only five.'

'Dear producer, I have paperwork in my briefcase and right now Aldo is about to take that lot – ' he nodded towards the stage, ' – through their paces. So, with your permission, I shall now leave the premises and see you first thing in the morning.'

She watched him go with a smile on her face, but curiosity drew her eyebrows together in a soft frown. Max was beginning to act like a changed man, and there had to be a reason.

The sound of the orchestra tuning up caught her attention and she turned back, slipping into one of the stalls to watch and savour the 'christening' of *Marilyn* in a theatre. She had waited a long time for this.

Max could not remember when he had felt this way. Not for him the soft, sweet memory of a first love tucked away in his youth – something he could take out from time to time and examine like a dog-eared snapshot. There had never been for him 'a grand passion' or, as some romantics said, a craving, a hunger for another's skin. Only lust, really.

But Christmas at Polly's parents had done it for him because her sister, sweet little Nadia, had simply been there. It was something he was still trying to come to terms with because he hardly understood it himself. He would even find himself listening raptly to the sort of music he had once categorized as 'sentimental crap' as if he had suddenly discovered that he could tune in to a new wavelength he never knew existed.

Max smiled to himself as he walked down the Strand; they had actually held hands when it was possible to do so, and kissed, of course, when no one was around, but that was all. He shook his head slowly, amused and surprised at himself, but he was happy, wasn't he – inside, where it mattered?

Nadia was meeting him for tea at the Savoy, then she would take the train back to school in Sussex where she boarded, so it was a very brief meeting. It was something they had both made plans for, but naturally he had made no sort of commitment, no promises because there was still Polly to consider, not forgetting their father, the all-powerful Sir Murdo who would probably want to throttle him once he heard the good news.

Max stopped at the kerbside opposite the familiar entrance to the Savoy. She would be sitting there waiting for him, he knew that; Nadia was always early, an eager flush on her face. He supposed she was the nearest thing to angelic he had ever come close to. He took a gulp of air as the lights changed and a flicker of doubt made his heart jump in sudden panic.

Young, angelic and the sister of his fiancée; it would not take a great mind to figure out that the odds were stacked against him. He must be out of his mind.

Richard shivered under the shower; the water was beginning to grow cold which meant that the central heating was too, and he swore loudly. How often had he asked the landlord to send someone around to check the boiler and the old sod consistently did nothing?

He turned off the tap and stepped out of the bath, water dripping on to the floor. He opened the airing cupboard where the boiler hid and flicked the power on and off, then from 'Constant' to 'Timer' and back again, but the pilot light refused to cooperate and remained irritatingly lifeless. Richard repeated the ritual, silently begging the boiler to be kind to him and to his surprise the machine suddenly roared into life.

As he stalked triumphantly across the bathroom floor he imagined himself a man with a mission who had just successfully defused a bomb, and the press and half of London were waiting outside to give him a welcome fit for a hero. With a smug smile he swung one leg over the edge of the bath and turned on the tap, yanking up the infuriating little knob which would make water cascade from the showerhead instead of the tap if he was lucky. Everything seemed to be going smoothly and the water was just getting warm when the telephone rang.

'Christ . . .' he muttered and wrapped a towel around his waist and shoulders: the flat was never warm even when the central heating was supposedly working.

He padded across the carpet to the table where the telephone sat. 'Hello?'

'Dick,' the voice seethed, 'where the hell are you?'

'Why, Roger,' Richard simpered, 'what a pleasant surprise.'

'Never mind about the pleasant surprise. Why aren't you here?'

'Where?'

'At the studio – where else?'

'I'm busy.'

'What the hell do you mean "busy"? You're needed here, on the set, for rehearsals.'

'I'm busy rewriting the script, Roger.'

There was silence for a second.

'Is this some kind of a joke?'

'To be frank, I found the Right Reverend Angus Fraser a bit of a pain in the arse, so I decided to write him out.'

'Don't be bloody stupid.'

'Or, put more simply, I resigned before you could do it for me.'

'You can't do that, you signed a contract – remember?'

'Too bad.'

'We could sue.'

'I don't think you'll do that, Roger.'

'Or make your name mud in television circles.'

'Oh, come on, get back down to earth – you're in Shepherd's

273

Bush not LA. And anyway, I think you have far more to lose than me when it comes to spreading mud.'

'What is that supposed to mean?'

'Lucy was *very* upset the other night . . .'

He could sense Roger gritting his teeth.

'. . . She told me *everything*.'

'Really.'

'So you will understand, I am sure, why I have no intention of working with an arrogant, underhanded, slimy pervert like yourself. Actually, you should count yourself lucky that I didn't appear on the set today because I wouldn't have been responsible for my actions,' Richard said with relish, 'so perhaps you will also understand why I may be tempted to tell all to a certain low-life tabloid newspaper, should you not behave like the gentleman the misguided public think you are.'

'I haven't the faintest idea what you're talking about.'

'You can deny it all you want, to whom you want, but mud sticks, Roger, even you know that – and especially to a super soap hero like yourself.'

'What a vivid imagination you have, Dick,' Roger said smoothly, 'and strange as it may seem, I was actually calling you to tell you that your services would be terminated sooner rather than later.'

'Oh, what a surprise, and I bet you were looking forward to that,' Richard sneered. 'No doubt you've decided that the nubile Nova should snuff it at last, then? How very bloody convenient.'

'I am not in the business of petty revenge.'

Richard burst into laughter. 'Is that a line from the soap?'

'It's a pity you've never been able to put your rather dubious wit to more profitable purpose, don't you think?'

'Do I detect more than a hint of sour grapes in that syrupy voice of yours, Roger?'

'I'm the one who has a career and star status, in case you'd forgotten.' Roger paused. 'Of course, you do have Lucy, but there are names for girls like her.'

'You bastard.'

'Face facts for once in your life, Dick . . .'

'And don't call me Dick.'

'. . . the truth is you're a loser, always have been, always will be . . .'

'Is that another line from the soap?'

'The two of you belong together.'

'Go to hell, you prat.'

Richard slammed the phone down and stared at it, wondering at the trick Roger had of making him feel such a hopeless clown, such a fool for all his brave words. He crossed the room to the letter which lay open on the table. It was about his writing, an agent was interested in meeting him and discussing his work.

The towel which he had draped across his shoulders fell to one side and goose pimples blazed trails up his arms. Richard turned around, towel trailing, and padded back into the bathroom, praying silently that the boiler was still working.

Jackie stood at the window as the cab drew up. There was a shallow mist clinging to the road and as Clare climbed from the car it seemed to Jackie that she could be stepping out of time past with her long flowing skirt and wool cape wrapped tightly around her narrow body. She moved to the door and held it open as Clare approached and immediately she knew something was wrong.

'Did you have a bad journey?' she asked, placing a protective arm around her stepmother.

'Not exactly, I'm just very tired.'

'Come on in and get warm. I've got something hot waiting in the oven, but would you like a drink first?'

'Please.' Clare shook herself free of her cape and walked slowly towards the fire, stretching her hands out to the flames. 'Make it a brandy, darling, I feel chilled through.'

'Are you all right?' Jackie asked. 'You look more than just tired.'

'The brandy should help,' Clare replied quietly, then glanced quickly at Jackie. 'Why don't you have one?'

'Me?' Jackie frowned and smiled uncertainly. 'I was going to have a g and t.'

'The brandy's wonderful . . .' Clare added lamely, 'So warming.'

Jackie sat down, scrutinizing her stepmother carefully with slowly mounting apprehension.

'What is it, Clare?'

She made no answer and remained standing, but there was something about the calmly arranged face that made Jackie's heart lurch.

'I promised him I wouldn't say anything,' Clare said in a small voice. 'I promised.'

Jackie swallowed. 'Tell me.'

Clare stared down into her brandy glass, then fixed her eyes on her step-daughter's face. She took another drink, then rubbed her forehead with the palm of her hand and made a soft, despairing sound.

'He's ill.'

Her stepmother's eyes seemed to glisten and grow larger all at once.

'But what's the matter with him?' Yet already there was a tightness in her throat, fear in the pit of her stomach.

'His liver.'

As if that would explain everything. Jackie sat there woodenly, staring back at her.

'He was warned two years ago about his drinking, but he didn't really take any notice . . .'

'I thought he'd cut down?' Jackie said, and there was almost a plea in her voice.

'A little – for a while – but nothing in real terms.' Clare took a deep breath. 'Until September I was still finding the odd empty vodka bottle under the bed, and that was when the old problems started playing up again, but he kept quiet about it because he wanted this bloody part so much.'

'But he doesn't drink vodka!' Jackie protested, as if there must be some mistake, knowing there was not.

'He does if he doesn't want me to know he's been drinking; he thinks I can't smell it.' She paused. 'And sometimes I didn't know . . . I really didn't. I thought he would use his common sense, you see. I thought he would realize, but I have sometimes wondered if your father really did think he was one of the immortals and would live forever.'

Jackie looked at Clare's face in bewilderment, unable or unwilling to comprehend immediately. 'What are you saying?'

'Oh, Jackie,' she whispered, and somehow that whisper was worse than anything she could have said.

'No.'

'His liver's packing up,' Clare said slowly, 'and there's a growth, something called a hepatoma – a complication of his condition.'

Jackie's face seemed to drain of blood. 'I don't believe this – and there's nothing they can do?'

Clare shook her head.

'What about a liver transplant, for God's sake?'

'Jackie,' Clare squeezed her eyes shut tight as if from a blow, 'your father is sixty-two years old and he has never taken proper care of himself, as we both know, consequently his general health is not good. Moreover his heart is affected and it is extremely unlikely that he would survive any sort of major operation, let alone a transplant.' In a vague part of her mind she was seeing the pathetic picture of all the vitamin supplements she had ever given him, most of which he had never taken because he said he 'didn't need them'; the hearty meals she had cooked and which he had only picked at; all those times she had almost asked him to seek some help for the alcohol problem which had plagued him all the years of his adult life, but she never had.

'A doctor I saw in Glasgow told me that patients with alcoholic cirrhosis are usually rejected for transplant surgery. Experience has shown most of them return to drinking after treatment.'

'So that's it?' Jackie said with disbelief. 'I mean – are you trying to tell me that there really is nothing *anyone* can do?'

Clare looked at her without speaking, unable to speak, the empty glass beginning to shake in her hands.

'And why doesn't he want me to know?' There was no expression now in Jackie's voice, only a sort of dullness.

'He made me promise not to tell you because he doesn't want any fuss and, more than anything, doesn't want to upset your life right now.'

'That was why you went to Scotland so suddenly, wasn't it?'

'He collapsed on the set.'

'And now?'

'He wants to finish the film,' she said, 'and he will.'

'Even if it kills him.'

'What would you have him do – take to his hospital bed? I think he'd shoot himself first.'

They fell silent until Jackie spoke again. 'Why did you tell me?' And the coward part of her was wishing that Clare hadn't, that she could have been left in ignorant bliss, like a child who was thought too young to face the cruel facts of life.

'Because I'm a coward. I didn't think I could get through the next six months on my own.'

Six months.

'And because I was afraid of what you might say to me if you ever found out that I had kept the facts from you.' Clare smiled with a trace of pity. 'You must have heard of those people who say things like "if only I'd known", or "I wish I could have told him how much . . ." ' Her voice trailed into nothing.

Jackie jerked her eyes away. Six months. I do not think I can bear it.

'Would you like another brandy?'

'Only a small one.' Clare flashed an uneasy gaze at her. 'He's calling me at nine to make sure I arrived home safely, so I must make a move soon. Why don't you come with me – stay the night.'

'No.' She spoke almost in a whisper as she walked across the room to the brandy bottle. 'I think I'd rather be alone.'

'I should have waited,' Clare said abruptly. 'It was thoughtless to come out of the blue like this. I'm so sorry, I should have at least made myself wait until the show opened.' Her eyes brimmed and her mouth began to quiver ominously.

'Oh, Clare, please – it's all right.' Jackie walked back, crouching down beside her chair and placing the brandy balloon in her stepmother's hands, folding her fingers carefully around the glass. 'And, for God's sake, don't blame yourself for anything – nothing, do you understand?' She swallowed. 'Daddy wouldn't want that, would he?'

Daddy.

She bowed her head and felt Clare's hand on her hair, found herself sitting on the floor beside her chair, her face resting against Clare's knee.

'There's something else, too,' Clare said at last, 'and I wish I could say that it was good news.'

Jackie sighed. 'Just tell me – it's better.'

'Your boyfriend, Drew: David checked a few facts and found out that he's not who he says he is; he's not even Italian.' She paused. 'For some reason your father took a dislike to him. Don't be cross, he was only trying to protect you.'

'It doesn't matter.' Jackie lifted her head and turned to look at her stepmother. 'And how could I be cross with him now – how?'

'Ssssh . . .' Clare soothed, 'I know. He was thinking of the future, because I'm sure he knew, even then.'

'He had a right to dislike Drew. I just wish I could have shared some of his perception sooner rather than later.'

'Do you want to tell me what happened?'

Jackie closed her eyes for a moment, aware suddenly of how trivial it seemed now, all that time and emotional energy she had wasted, when the cause was lost even before it was begun, and on someone who had obviously cared very little for her in the first place.

'It seems so unimportant now.'

'Please, Jackie.'

'Apart from the lies . . . too many to count, really . . . he was having an affair.'

'I'm so sorry.'

'With my mother.'

'*Angela?*' Clare said incredulously.

Jackie nodded.

'Oh, darling . . .'

'Don't tell Daddy, for God's sake.'

'No, no, of course not.'

'It would send his blood pressure up, or something . . .' Her voice sounded tight, almost strangled, in her ears. Daddy. An eerie feeling began to steal over her, something like fear and dread, beginning to twist and turn, suffocating everything.

She got up slowly and walked out of the room to the hall cloakroom where she retched into the white toilet bowl.

Clare was standing just outside the door as she emerged, panic written all over her face.

'You see, I shouldn't have come.' Her eyes darkened with

tears. 'Look what I've done – there probably couldn't have been a worse time to tell you. He will never forgive me for ruining this moment that you've worked so long and hard for.'

Jackie's face crumpled as she put her arms around her stepmother. 'No time would have been the right time. How could it be?'

'Try not to let him know,' Clare whispered, 'please, for me.'

Jackie said nothing, but nodded helplessly into the warmth of her stepmother's shoulder. At that moment she thought that she would cry, but there was only a little anguished sound of disbelief as she clung to Clare and she recalled that image of her father, the last time she had seen him, waving to her from the steps of the Hampstead house; tall, almost handsome, the fading blue eyes still so deceptively alive.

The house seemed unnaturally quiet. Usually when she bathed or even worked, music would be playing in the background somewhere. Not tonight, and she could not imagine how, or when, she would ever feel like listening to music again, or laughing or just being normal. But laughing most of all.

Jackie glanced at the time. It was ten o'clock and Clare had been gone for almost two hours. During that time she had taken a long bath and even attempted some work, and all the time she was aware of no real feeling at all. She seemed to be going through the motions of living and breathing, but precariously, as if she walked in her sleep.

When the doorbell rang she jumped and shivered at the same time, pulling her robe more tightly about her, thinking of Drew. She relaxed when she saw who it was standing outside.

'Jamie,' she said.

'Clare told me,' he said simply.

She opened the door wide so that he could come in.

'You shouldn't have come,' she said, 'I'm all right.'

'She was worried,' he said and added softly, 'and so was I.'

'I'm all right.'

He walked past her into the sitting room, his eyes travelling around the room, coming to rest on the open gin bottle which sat on the bureau.

'I've had two.' There was an edge to her voice. 'Large ones.'

280

'You didn't have to tell me that.'

'You may as well take your coat off and join me.'

He did as she said and then watched her as she crossed the room to pour him a drink; she seemed angry, almost brittle, as if she might break at a touch.

'It was kind of you and Clare to think of me, but as you can see, I haven't cut my throat or stuck my head in the gas oven. Anyway, it's something I can only get through by myself.' She handed him his drink.

'Sometimes people can help at times like this.'

'Is that what you've found?' she asked with unfamiliar tightness.

'There was never anyone there when I needed someone.' He looked into his glass, then brought it to his lips.

She flushed, taken aback by his response.

'And I didn't say that to gain sympathy,' he added, 'it's just a fact.'

She looked away from him. 'Did Clare speak to my father? Is he all right – is she all right?'

'He said he was feeling fine, of course, but after the call Clare went to the studio. She was still there when I left.'

'Throwing herself into her work.' Jackie lifted her chin a little unsteadily as if she were focusing on something high up in the corner of the room. 'Poor Clare.'

'Why don't you sit down?'

'I don't want to sit down, Jamie.' She swallowed hard. 'And I don't need you to mollycoddle me.'

'Do you want me to go?'

She made no answer, then shook her head and looked at him. 'I didn't mean to be rude. I'm sorry.'

'It's all right, I understand.'

'I don't think you can.'

He reddened. 'Why, because I'm younger than you – because I come from a different world?'

He was throwing back the words she had said to him weeks before. She stared at him, and for a long while she did not move.

'Will you stay tonight?'

'That's what Clare wanted.'

'Do you?'

He opened his mouth to speak, and then his stomach was turning over as understanding dawned.

'The guest room . . .' he said clumsily.

'With me.' She locked gazes with him.

'Why now?' His heart was hammering.

'Why not?'

'Are you sure it's what you want?'

'Yes.' And it was, because she could drown herself in him, dulling the pain, and the unendurable sense of loss would not fall on her in the lonely darkness of her room. And deep down she wanted him, she always had and that was lust, wasn't it? Yet she did not care any longer what her motives were, because her caution was almost entirely gone and all the rules and regulations she had tried to live by suddenly seemed pointless and irrelevant against the huge sorrow she harboured at her centre.

A small lamp burned at the side of her bed and he stood waiting, listening for the sound of her.

She closed the door and he took a deep gulp of air as she moved towards him, her robe skimming the carpet as she drew close.

'Jamie?'

He turned and looked at her, and for a long instant she seemed to study him, but then her hands reached up and she caught his face between them just as she had done once before, drawing his mouth down to those dizzying lips which had haunted him through too many long, restless nights. And the soft mouth dissolved into hardness, mutual desire shooting through their veins.

She withdrew slowly, her fingers moving to the buttons on his shirt, carefully undoing each one before pushing the shirt from his shoulders and letting it drop to the floor. For a moment she seemed to hesitate, but then her hands came up and rested upon his chest, sliding up and over his shoulders, so that he shuddered, and continuing down his arms to the tips of his fingers which she lifted and brought to the belt of her satin robe. It was already loosened and came undone easily in his clumsy hands so that the robe fell open and he saw silky white skin.

Heat flooded him again as her eyes looked back, deliberately resting on his mouth, so that he moved towards her and their lips met, parted, tongues touching, her tongue passing into him. And he could feel her soft hands peeling away his jeans, yet her mouth hardly left his, hardly disturbed the heady momentum she was creating.

She drew him to the bed, made him sit down and slowly, carefully removed his shoes and socks, placing them neatly beside the waiting bed. Still on her knees she began to massage his feet, her hair falling down around her, hiding her face so that he could look at her freely with quiet wonder: at the shape of her head, the outline of her body still sheathed by the thin material, and her hands – strong and warm and lovely all at the same time. It staggered him to have those hands caress his feet, to feel the knowing firmness of her fingers trigger tormenting sensations in other parts of his body.

He thought of Drew suddenly, and the girl at the nightclub, cringing inside himself, but as he looked at Jackie's patient hands, her golden head, the images faded effortlessly away, and he was free.

She rose slowly and stood only inches away, leaning forward and running one finger slowly along the line of his lips, then she shook her robe from her shoulders and gently brought his face to the small roundness of her belly. He heard her gasp then, as his mouth opened to taste her flesh, felt her belly jerk as his hands came to rest on her waist. Ecstatic shock of naked skin, the first time.

Wordlessly she climbed into his lap, circling him with her legs, and it was all his dreams, all his imaginings come true as she locked her hands around his neck and began raking his face with hard, hungry kisses. He felt her warm swollen breasts press against him, at the same time she pushed her hips down, closer, so that he would feel the warmth and the moistness, the secret place. He groaned and closed his eyes, lips quivering, his body charged and craving.

He was aware of her voice suddenly, a soft whisper of words encouraging, loving, guiding him as her hand found his sex and she gently lifted her hips to take him inside her. And all the time she was looking at him and he was looking at her. But then her eyes closed and her head fell back as she sank down on to him, giving her whole body and catching his thrust in one soft, desperate union. Delivering them both.

The telephone blasted her out of sleep, so that she jolted forwards, startled and disorientated.

'Hello?' Her eyes darted to Jamie beside her, then to the clock on her bedside table which told her it was only 7.15.

'Jackie – it's Aldo.'

'What's wrong?'

'I'd just got to the theatre when the telephone rang. It was Breakfast Television: apparently Rose hasn't arrived yet for that morning slot and they're getting rather concerned, to put it mildly.'

'Oh, my God . . .' she said with disbelief, 'and you've tried to call her?'

'Of course, but the telephone just rings.'

'Maybe she's on her way.'

'Well, she's cutting it fine, to say the least.'

'Have you managed to get hold of Max?' She asked. 'He's supposed to be there too.'

'Yes, I've already spoken to him and he's been in touch with Lucy. She's trying to get to the television studios so that at least she may be able to sing the number from the show, even if she can't make the interview in time.'

'When did you last go through the song with her?'

'Only Friday actually, both Rose and Lucy rehearsed the ballads together.'

'That's a stroke of luck . . . and one of them *must* sing that song, Aldo, it's the heart of *Marilyn*! I've worked hard and pulled a lot of strings to get us this slot so near to opening night.' She groaned with despair. 'Look, if I don't hear from you that Rose made it after all, I'll call in on her before I get to the theatre and find out what the hell's going on, once and for all.'

'Okay.'

'Thanks, Aldo.'

She put down the phone and took a deep breath. 'Not the best way to start the day.' She looked at Jamie and pushed a lock of hair away from his eyes.'

'I'll have to get up . . .'

His hand slipped around her waist. 'It doesn't sound as if you can do very much, except pace the floor.'

She smiled with gentle amusement despite the shadow of misery which waited just out of sight. 'I should thank you for last night . . .' He had let her cry, said things that helped. She traced his beautiful mouth with the tips of her fingers. 'It made a difference.' Her eyes still felt sore from the weeping which their love-making had triggered; cracking open her guard, making her bleed, letting her grieve.

'Don't go yet.'

And she couldn't refuse. She slid down beside him finally and he brought her against his chest so that she was cocooned by his body.

'Do you know what you did for me?' He asked.

She kissed him.

'You released me.'

'Are you still thinking of the past, your father, the seminary . . . ?'

'I'm not sure.' He began stroking her hair, aware of the delicious softness of her breasts squeezed against him. 'That seems a world away now.'

'You ran away – was it so awful? Wasn't there anything about it you liked, or could respect?'

'I loved the silence of the church, the small bare chapel with its starveling wooden Christ. I liked the peace, the old books and the library. I even came to like Latin . . .'

'You haven't mentioned faith.'

'I didn't have any – at least, not the sort of faith that was required. I was brought up, almost from the day I was born, to believe that my vocation would one day be that of a priest.' He paused. 'That sort of brainwashing happened a great deal in the old days, probably still does in places like Italy, Ireland and Poland – having a priest in the family was thought almost as good as marrying into royalty.'

'You're very cynical for one so young, if I may say so.'

'That's often said of people who have only recently lost their faith, except that I'm not sure I ever had mine in the first place.' He inhaled deeply and glanced down at her lovely face. 'I suppose I came to hate the ritual, the unnecessary pomp and

285

ceremony, the rigid hierarchy, but probably – more than anything – it was the inhumanity that the idea of 'mortal sin' can sometimes involve, particularly when it makes the ignorant afraid and creates poverty and hunger because the superstitious are too frightened or ill-educated to stop having children they cannot feed. It simply occurred to me that God – any god – had nothing to do with it.' He lay on his side and looked at her. 'The Church is out of step with the modern world, and seems far more interested in blind obedience than anything else.'

'My, my – still waters run very deep,' she said gently, 'and did you ever mention your somewhat heretical views to anyone?'

'No one who mattered.'

'Why?'

'It was too late.'

They lapsed into silence and then Jackie propped herself up on one elbow.

'So, what do you want now?'

'To go back.'

'You mean Kenya?'

'Yes.' He trailed his fingers along her upper arm. 'I think about it almost as much as I think about you.'

'But not yet.'

'No.' It would be impossible for him to leave now; he simply wanted her too much and even at the thought he was hardening again. He slid his broad hands across her body, found the silky softness of her inner thighs. It seemed incredible to him that he had had no real idea of the astonishing pleasure her body could give, and as he began to move beneath her he wondered at this newly discovered power his own body had to want and need and couple with a woman, this woman, so that the power and the drive obliterated everything.

He pushed her gently over on to her back as the drive took control and it seemed to him that he was only aware of her: every curve, all the warm close holding of their lovemaking which would wipe out any need for thought, but even as he moved to enter her he was struck by all the things she had given him, even her grief.

There would be other things, too, countless, undiscovered details which he would learn and love as time passed, and all at once he knew that he would remember this moment always; the room, her warm breath against his cheek, the taste of her mouth – the release and flight from his loneliness.

And this was joy, was it not, and rapture? A gift from the gods.

TWELVE

Angela stifled a scream. The daily papers, all of them, were scattered across the penthouse floor, and three of them had a story on her, *the* story: *News Daily*, *The New York Post* and *Woman's Wear Daily*. The *Post* had a photograph of Pinkey Jones lined up against one of Angela Cassini, a very recent picture taken at the Metropolitan Opera House standing next to Mikhail Baryshnikov and Nancy Reagan, followed by a few well chosen words: 'Watching the mighty and arrogant fall is a new all-American sport.'

'I am going to die . . .' She looked at herself again to see if there really was a noticeable resemblance. She winced, then cursed because she had never been able to fool herself. Of course there was a resemblance, a striking one, even after thirty years. She should be flattered. The photograph of the topless girl, breasts tactfully covered by a black rectangle, squirming on a satin sheet, might have been taken only a few years previously. There was some text, too, confirming that Bergman had crawled out from under a stone and contributed his own juicy piece on 'one of his ex-girls'.

With an anguished whimper she tore the page up into tiny pieces, then wondered if she could sue, or issue an official denial, except that 'they' would have covered their backs very carefully and checked everything before going to print. The horrible truth was that no one would believe her.

The telephone rang and she swallowed, turning her head to stare at it with something like dread as the noise persisted, driving her crazy, because she hadn't switched on the answerphone. Very slowly she crawled on all fours across the newspapers to the sprawling Italian coffee table where the telephone sat. She picked it up.

'Yes?'

'Is that Angela Cassini? This is the *Boston Globe*. Could I have your comments on the exposé in the *Post*?'

She slammed down the phone. 'Bastards . . .' For an instant her hand hovered over the receiver because she was desperate to talk to Dougie and try and explain her way out, but he was in Washington on business and staying with friends, so by the time he called her this evening the cat would be well and truly out of the bag.

Angela looked at her fingers, watched them tremble. God! She would become a joke, a big fat joke – standard dinner party talk for the next six months. Heads would shake knowingly, as if they had always sensed that Angela Cassini had a few sordid skeletons hidden in her designer closet, but hadn't they all? Every god-damn last one of them, probably. The difference was, of course, that she had been found out.

She clamped her eyes shut tight against inescapable reality. A stripper, a nudey, a soft-porn queen. She shivered as fright washed over her again.

But Dougie . . . to lose him after all her efforts. She clenched her fists in anger, all her dreams shattered at one stroke. Her head went back in silent agony because she could not believe it, not really, not *everything* gone up in smoke. For a blissful moment she imagined herself persuading Dougie that it was all a mistake – or that she had been blackmailed, or innocently led into vice and show-girl bars because she had only been a simple country girl way back then. Bullshit; even he would realize that.

What about her friends? What about them – a cheap little voice sneered from the back of her mind. She didn't have any, not in the real sense of the word, because she had never really needed anyone, so there was no one she could call for solace, even if she wanted to.

She recalled Dakota Greenbaum at Miriam's wake in San Marino: plump, generous Dakota had tried to be friendly in a high-school girl sort of way and she had cold-shouldered her. Angela sighed; people like Dakota practically asked to be cut dead and unfortunately she found herself always ready and willing to oblige, and with the ease of flicking a rather tiresome insect from her sleeve. Yet, at that moment Angela would have sacrificed a considerable amount of her precious pride just to talk to someone as uncomplicated as Dakota because she was honest and kind – a good woman. Something she could never be.

Her eyes focused on the telephone again, feeling sick as the extent of the damage Drew had done began to sink in. And she had thought that he would not dare do it! A misjudgement she would probably regret for the rest of her life, whatever sort of life would be left for her. She jerked her head up in a flash of rage and at the same time her arm swept the telephone from the table so that it catapulted across the floor and came to a jangling stop. She moved to stand up, but slipped on the scattered newspapers, slamming her elbow against the corner of the table so that unbelievable pain made her eyes sting.

She sat on the floor, waiting for the pain to subside and let her gaze drift to the wall opposite, the lighting and the paintwork she had grown tired of. Sister Parish, New York's doyenne of decorators, had agreed to redesign the penthouse and that was an honour in itself, because it was well known in the right circles that she chose her clients with crushing ruthlessness, selecting them on the basis of their connections, properties and snob appeal. Angela's eyes blurred; she had so looked forward to ridding herself of the Parisian theme and starting afresh once Dougie named the day. She had set her heart on English, probably eighteenth-century, and could picture all the loving details she had decided on: a marvellous black lacquer table, distressed gilt . . . She had even toyed with the idea of adding a few Elizabethan paintings sold off by impoverished dukes to confer instant pedigree and lineage.

From somewhere high above her she could hear the sound of a plane and she blinked. There was a mirror standing on the table, and she caught a pale, gaunt glimpse of herself in the glass. It was a pretty mirror, she thought resentfully, if a little odd, and Drew would like it, no doubt, with its weird voluptuous mermaids caressing the rim, all silver-gilt and sensuous swirls. Perhaps she would smash it over his head if she ever saw him again. No, perhaps she would kill him, except that that would be like shooting herself *twice* in the foot from a social point of view, and she could just see the headlines: 'Society Hostess Scandal Deepens with Murder of Gigolo'.

Rage erupted again, bursting through her cold control, and the mermaid mirror went the way of the telephone; it did not break, but turned over and over on itself and landed face up, the glass at its centre reflecting an uneven circle of light on Angela's perfectly painted ceiling.

Lucy shrank into the back of the car, still trembling from the nerves which had plagued her since the telephone call from Max that morning, except now she was also exultant because her voice had soared effortlessly, almost faultlessly, and the song, the beautiful song, had silenced everyone in the studio.

'If "Late-Night Phone Calls" doesn't have them grovelling in the aisles for more, I shall resign.'

Lucy darted a wary glance at Max. 'That's a little drastic.'

'Perhaps I jest, but I'm betting more than money on this show – my instinct and reputation.'

'The first time I heard Rose sing it,' Lucy said, 'I felt a lump in my throat. It has the sort of tragic feeling of Fantine's solo in *Les Misérables*, "I Dreamed a Dream", don't you think?'

'When did you see that?'

'I auditioned for the part in '85.'

'But you didn't get it.'

She shook her head; she had been too young and still in the process of trying to attain a coveted Equity card. Neither had she had the confidence or experience to project herself well, and her voice had croaked and died on her lips before it had the chance to soar. In any event the other voices at the audition seemed to dwarf her own and she had left with the unwelcome thought that she was a very mediocre fish trying to swim in an incredibly over-populated pond.

'Of course, there's always the chance that you may get your big break with *Marilyn*.'

She looked away from him to the window as the car passed into the traffic.

'A chance – yes, I know.'

'Rose has been very unreliable on several occasions.'

She didn't reply because she was beginning to feel uncomfortable, and trapped. Max was leading up to something and she had a horrible feeling that she knew exactly what it was; at any moment she expected to feel his hand crawling on her knee.

'I'm sure we could come to some arrangement . . .'

'Rose was chosen for the part, and I think she should be given a fair hearing.'

'That's very charitable of you, darling, but in case you'd forgotten we open next week.' he sighed. 'And even if sweet little Rose had the vocal chords of Maria Callas she could still find herself kissing goodbye to stardom because she seems unable or unwilling to behave like a professional. As a matter of fact Marilyn Monroe herself was heading for a slippery slide when she met her untimely end, and some of that had to do with sloppiness and an attitude problem.'

'Really,' she said coldly. 'Well, perhaps there's more to it than that.'

'Maybe, but why the hell doesn't Rose say so? After all, we can't read her mind, for God's sake.' He looked at her sharply. 'Has she said anything to you?'

'Not a word.'

'Silly little cow,' he said with exasperation, 'which brings me back to the whole point of this conversation . . .'

'Shouldn't we wait until we find out the facts?'

He shifted restlessly. 'What is it with you, Lucy – don't you want a God-given opportunity? Anyone else would be fighting tooth and nail to be in your shoes, and more than ready to push Rose off her rather unsteady little pedestal.'

She felt angry all at once, hating him for pinning her in a corner, in this car, when she had been so happy, so removed from the nasty, seedy little games he was talking about it.

'I suppose it depends on what you want,' she swung round and stared him full in the eyes, 'doesn't it?'

His face puckered into a frown and she was reminded of one of the gnomes she had seen in her father's garden. And he would not touch her, ever; she would not sacrifice her self-respect again for an arrogant creep like Max Lockhart, or any man, who wanted her for all the wrong reasons. She supposed her outrage at such treatment had come a little late and she should have started protesting and putting up a fight years ago when the first boy pinged her bra strap at school.

'For chrissakes . . .' his eyes lifted skywards, 'this isn't a proposition.'

'But it does have a familiar ring about it,' she said scathingly.

He spluttered with surprise: 'Look, Lucy darling, I would rather forget our last, shall we say, 'intimate' encounter, but unfortunately it is indelibly printed on my brain and not something that I would be anxious to repeat.'

She blushed furiously. 'It wasn't exactly my idea if I remember correctly.'

'But you didn't refuse – you didn't *do* anything.'

'What the hell was I supposed to do?' she said, hating him and the tears which were making her eyes brim. 'All I wanted was a bloody part in that God-awful play!'

'It wasn't a God-awful play as I remember it.'

'It closed after three weeks.'

'I didn't realize you had total recall, my dear.'

'Oh, go to hell,' she said quietly, but stunned and a little afraid suddenly that she had allowed herself to say so much.

'Touché,' Max said dryly, 'but I don't know what you girls expect when you make it so damned easy. And has it ever occurred to you that you should stop playing the victim? Let's be honest, if you didn't want something – a part, a job, a favour, a man – you wouldn't leave yourself wide open, and please excuse the metaphor, to such advances. Anyway, as we both know, there are some people in this business who try to use sex as a weapon or a legitimate bargaining tool.' He caught a breath which smacked of boredom. 'Perhaps if you'd told me to piss off, you would have got the part anyway.'

'Like hell.'

He had wounded her and not much cared at the time, or even recently when he bothered to think about it, but inside there was a change, something had blown free, and he realized that at the core of the change was Nadia. Wonder of wonders.

'All right, I concede that you may have a point, but you do seem very big on hell, Lucy darling, if I may say so . . .'

It was, she supposed, the nearest thing to an apology she was ever likely to get from him. Her fingers still itched to slap his self-satisfied face, but she suppressed the desire, realizing that this was as far as the situation should be allowed to go. There was also the echo of a mean little voice in her head whispering that there was truth in what he said; a distasteful image of Roger formed in her imagination and she blushed with humiliation.

'. . . and I suspect that you are having a hard time at the moment. Right?'

'I *was*, actually,' she said, looking at him in surprise, 'but I don't intend to any longer.'

'Congratulations,' he said with sardonic amusement. 'In which case I'm sure you are more than ready to work with Rose on a one-night-off, one-night-on basis, plus matinées on the day in question.'

She nodded slowly as realization dawned, feeling angry and foolish, but nevertheless did not intend to apologize for what she had said, and Max would not expect it. He knew that her belated protest was genuine and although he would never say so, he had exploited the casting couch situation whenever it had suited him.

'But I don't open?'

'Afraid not, Rose still has the icing on the cake despite what has happened this morning. Jackie and I are still willing to take the risk for opening night, and she won't let us down,' he said with certainty. 'I'm sure that even Rose is aware that there will never be a chance like this for her again.'

Lucy took a deep breath and turned silently to the window because his last words had stung, but it was something, wasn't it, to play the lead fifty per cent of the time, sing those beautiful songs, *be* Marilyn Monroe for four performances a week? And it was pretty close to having the part all to herself, just like she had dreamed for so long.

The car passed the junction of New Oxford Street and swung into the Charing Cross Road, and Foyle's, the bookshop, came into view. She thought of Richard, her own sweet Richard who patiently, determinedly tap-tapped away on his old Olympia typewriter. He was practically jobless again and she felt a little ashamed that she could find fault with her success and the opportunity she had just been given.

It should be enough, Lucy told herself, because it was tempting Fate to wish for anything more.

Rose had moved to a little house off Kensington High Street and Jackie almost missed the narrow roadway into Adam and Eve Mews, a pretty cobbled mews hidden behind the noise and crush of shops and traffic. She stopped outside a tiny white-painted door and could hear the muffled sound of music filtering through the wood. She lifted a heavy brass doorknocker in the shape of a horse's head and let it fall heavily so that the noise seemed to reverberate down the narrow road. She waited, but nothing happened, and she was surprised and irritated to hear the music still playing, so she brought the brass knocker down again and the sound boomed. Eventually she caught the shuffle of feet coming towards her. Rose opened the door.

'Jackie,' she said, her eyes growing wide and round with surprise.

'I thought you might be expecting me?' Jackie replied, with a sharp intake of breath, because the star of the show looked white and haggard. 'May I come in?'

'Of course – yes.'

'Haven't you been well?' she asked, stepping inside.

Rose's mouth fell open a little and Jackie saw her mind search quickly for a lie.

'A headache,' she stammered, 'a bad one – probably migraine.'

'Why didn't you telephone? Or had you forgotten that you were expected at Breakfast Television this morning?'

Rose gasped and her face reddened immediately.

'How *could* you forget, Rose?' Jackie asked in disbelief. 'You knew how important this was to the show.'

'I don't know . . . I haven't been myself, you see . . .'

'No, I don't see,' she said, 'and do you think we could find somewhere to sit and talk about this?'

'Oh, I'm sorry, of course.'

Jackie followed her as she passed into a tiny wood-panelled room with a staircase spiralling upwards at its centre.

'The sitting room's up here,' Rose said and stood back so that Jackie might go ahead of her.

When Jackie emerged at the top, she stepped into chaos. Clothes and papers seemed to lie across every piece of furniture, radiating from partially unpacked boxes, ashtrays overflowed and stained drinking glasses and coffee cups took up any extra space; there was a smell of alcohol and marijuana. In a corner a small mountain of teddy-bears and soft toys sat in a jumbled heap.

She turned to Rose. 'Could you turn the music down, please?'

Rose did as she was asked then set about clearing a space so that Jackie could sit down.

'Would you like a coffee?'

Jackie shook her head. 'No thanks.'

'I'll have one, if you don't mind.'

Jackie waved a hand impatiently at the unwashed cups. 'Seems to me you've been living on coffee lately . . .' And God knows what else.

Rose gave her an embarrassed smile as if she had been found out and then sat down.

'Well?' Jackie asked. 'Are you going to tell me what's wrong?'

Rose looked down at her clasped fingers.

'You do realize how much there is at stake, don't you, Rose? You literally carry the show – so the whole cast and everyone involved is relying on you.'

She nodded.

'So what is it?' Jackie persisted.

'I just haven't been feeling myself, like I said,' she responded feebly.

'We open in *nine days*, Rose!' she said sharply. 'That just isn't good enough.'

'I'm sorry.'

'You've got to pull yourself together, otherwise I simply can't risk you opening.' Jackie gestured to the chaotic room.

'Just look at this place – have you seen it lately?'

Rose lifted her head and let her eyes travel across the disorder, the dirty cups, the overflowing ashtrays . . . Drew's shirts and a brightly coloured silk tie she had bought him lying in a mound on the floor.

Jackie followed her glance to the silk tie and tensed, but then felt a sudden relief. Man trouble. Why the hell hadn't Rose said something?

'Who is he?'

Rose jumped. 'What do you mean?' she said stupidly.

'The man who owns that tie, those shirts?'

Rose blushed, but said nothing.

'All right,' Jackie said, 'I know it's not really any of my business, but if your personal life is affecting the outcome of *Marilyn*, I have a right to know, don't you think?'

'It's not like that,' Rose said defensively.

'How can I know what it's like when I don't know the facts?'

'It's just difficult right now.'

'You mean – he is.'

'He's got a few problems.'

'Does he live with you?'

'Yes,' Rose said quickly, but she had not seen him for three days.

'Whatever problems he may have, I'm sure he wouldn't want you to mess up your career because of them, would he?'

Rose shook her head.

Jackie sighed inwardly and let her gaze rest on the partly bowed head. She always tried to make a point of being lenient towards actors with problems, whether they were drink, drugs or sex, because sometimes they only needed to talk, or a chance to improve, and then somehow, against all odds, a mind-boggling performance would rise out of indiscipline and chaos. Could she take the chance that Rose would react in this way?

'Rose,' she said gently, 'look at me. That's right. Now, I want you to shower and change and come back to the theatre with me. When we get there you will go to rehearsals and I will arrange for someone to come round and clean the house and put everything in good order.'

'I don't think . . .'

'At this stage,' Jackie broke in, 'I'm not going to listen very much to what you think, Rose. You want to keep this part, don't you?' She looked deliberately around the room. 'And you want to keep this pretty house, don't you?'

'Yes,' Rose said meekly.

'And you want the glittering prize of opening, don't you?'

'Yes.'

'Well, don't throw it away. You have a marvellous voice, and a marvellous future if you keep hold of yourself. There must be thousands of girls out there who would sell their souls to step inside your shoes.'

'I know,' she said softly and all at once she thought forlornly of

Babs, what she had said to her before she left the flat, but they hadn't spoken since. 'I'm sorry, Jackie.'

'As long as you mean it.'

'Oh, I do, I do – really.'

'And I'm sure your boyfriend is a wonderful guy, but he isn't your whole life, no one is, no matter how much your heart flips when he walks into the room.'

Rose smiled sheepishly and Jackie shook her head and said, 'That bad, is it?'

Rose nodded.

'And you're twenty?'

'Yes.'

'Well, you may not believe this right now, but I've got ten years on you and my heart has flipped dozens of times.' She paused, carefully choosing the right words. 'And when things went wrong, as inevitably they do, there was always my work – my faithful old friend waiting to prop me up – something no one could ever take away from me.' There was a little collapsing pain inside as she realized that now it would be called upon to do the impossible and help her through the next six months, and the grieving, and then the unimaginable – learning to live with the great void in her life where her father had been.

Rose was looking at her with something close to awe, but her nail-bitten fingers twisted and turned nervously in her lap. 'Are you sure you don't want a coffee?'

Jackie shook her head impatiently, then cleared her throat. 'You understand what I'm saying?'

Rose nodded.

'Okay, then,' Jackie said, forcing brightness into her voice, 'now go and get changed, otherwise Max will be pulling his hair out by the time we get there.'

'Thanks, Jackie.' Rose stood up, feeling better than she had done in days, oddly optimistic and free.

She walked determinedly across the room, picking up Drew's things on the way and clutching them possessively against her chest. It was silly worrying about him, he was a busy guy and not good at keeping in touch; he had told her that often enough, but it did hurt her a little that he would not discuss his 'problems', no matter how much she pressed him, even when he awoke her whimpering and crying out from the nightmares.

She shrugged and moved into the bedroom she was supposed to share with him, stopping on the vast sheepskin rug to look down and gaze lovingly at the shirts in her arms, lifting them up to smell his scent. Her eyes drifted dreamily to the bedclothes, the sheets and pillowcases she refused to change. Despite what Jackie had said she could not imagine her heart flipping or pounding the same way for anyone else – it just wasn't possible. Drew loved her and she loved him and they would get through their problems, even his unsettling dreams, together.

Her pretty face grew solemn all at once as a line from the show floated into her mind: 'Without love what can life mean? It's the one immortal thing about us.' Marilyn Monroe had said that, or something like that. The words warmed Rose; her mouth slanted into a smile and she started to hum.

The neons were almost up. Jackie took a few steps back to the kerb and watched as the last letters of *Marilyn* were put carefully in place, big and golden and bright, making her pulse race as nervous excitement began to spread through her. She clung on to the moment for as long as she could, but then it slipped inevitably away because her thoughts came back to settle on her father. He would not play in the West End again; he would be lucky if he even managed to complete his precious film.

More than that, he had told Clare that he would not attend the opening of *Marilyn* because everything was against his travelling, particularly the probably savage Scottish weather which was usual for this time of year. She made herself move back into the theatre, afraid that the telltale trembling of her lower lip would betray her into tears. Of course, he would not come; the journey would probably help kill him a little more swiftly.

The room which she was using as a temporary office was soulless and spartan, but at least there was a decent chair, a telephone and a small window overlooking Maiden Lane at the back of the theatre. On the windowsill lay the notepad listing all the things she had to check that afternoon, all the people she had to telephone, and she had not had time for lunch, not that she was hungry, but she longed for a coffee.

The telephone rang and she jumped.

'Jacqueline Jones.'

'Where is he?' her mother's voice hissed at her down the phone. 'Say something, goddammit!'

'You're talking about Drew, I presume?' she answered coldly. 'I assumed he was with you.'

'Don't get smart, Jackie.'

'I'm not getting smart, mother! I don't know where he is, and I don't want to know; he could be in hell for all I care.'

'*Bull-shit!*'

'You're drunk.'

'What the hell do you expect?'

Jackie said nothing.

'Have you seen the New York papers?' Angela sounded hysterical.

'I don't know what you're talking about.'

Silence fell and she could only hear her mother's breathing.

'He did it,' she said abruptly. 'I didn't think he'd have the guts, but he did.' There was a ragged sigh before she spoke again. 'He's blown it – everything. All gone.'

'What's gone?'

'My life – my beautiful, glitzy, glamorously public life.'

'I don't understand.'

'Oh, for God's sake . . . read the papers, try *The New York Post* for starters and see a juicy shot of your mother.' Angela started to laugh, but stopped so suddenly that the laughter had the rawness of a sob.

'Are you all right?'

'You remember Pinkey Jones, don't you, Jackie? We travelled a long way together. Remember?'

Jackie drew a sharp breath. 'Someone's found out.'

'Drew found out . . . and Drew told.'

'What are you going to do?'

'Do?' she repeated and stiffened with rage as the call she had made to Dougie came back to her, every cheap humiliating word.

It was fabulous really, the irony, the fact that he had not even seen the goddamn papers and didn't even know . . . He had stuttered and stammered while she had put on her teasing little-girl's voice, pouring cream down the goddamn phone, and all he time her knees were turning to jelly waiting for him to say omething, *anything*, about the smut she was sure he must have ead about her. But Dougie said nothing, nothing real anyway, ıntil the end when he blurted out the incredible truth like a pume of vomit, the words hitting her in a rush, spinning and rashing, finally getting through to her brain and exploding there. Dougie had found someone else. Even now she could hardly elieve it.

'The view from the penthouse is quite something; maybe I hould take a closer look . . .'

'Melodramatics don't suit you,' Jackie said, the thought of leath inevitably reminding her of David. 'Am I supposed to feel orry for you? Because I can't.'

'I've never wanted anything from you.'

It shouldn't have hurt, but it did, like all the other times; her nother never failed to act true to brutal form.

'I have work to do.'

'Your goddamn musical.' Angela sighed, suddenly weary of it ll. 'Oh – and you can have the money now.'

'Money?'

'Trust fund money.'

Like giving a child a bag of sweets.

'Are you serious?'

'Just believe it, because I'm tired.'

'May I ask, why now? It doesn't make sense.'

'Your lack of understanding is beginning to drive me crazy. Does it matter "why now", for chrissakes? You can have it, very last cent for all I care. It's just not important any more.' If t ever had been. Dougie's pot belly and varicose veins were ading fast.

Deep in her heart she wondered whether her objection to *Mar-Iyn* was more personal, something to do with a certain greeneyed nonster and the fact that her own daughter had unwittingly seen t to dangle 'the legend' right under her nose. Jackie always got n the way.

Angela had never learned how to come to terms with her own veakness. She harboured grudges and hoarded bitterness like a niser; she would feel the pain of a memory as if it had happened

301

only yesterday. Even after years she had not been able to accep what could never be changed.

'Does that mean that you'll be coming to the opening?' Jacki asked dryly, unable to resist.

'Do me a favour,' she retorted, 'and I can see where you ge your sense of humour from . . .' Her father.

'Just thought I'd ask.'

'You can be sure of one thing: I won't be in New York. It' burned out, boring . . . I can't wait to get away from dinne parties and receptions full of hams spouting New Age garbage karmas and all that bullshit,' she said sullenly and unconvinc ingly. 'I'm leaving before the vultures come round to gnaw at m carcass.'

'It will all blow over – people have very short memories.'

'Not in the circles I move in, they don't. Anyway, I don't war to talk about it, it's over,' she said sharply and shuddered, look ing down at the bottle of champagne lying in the crook of th chair, the solitary glass on the table. 'I'm renting a place in Sout Beach for a month or two – or three; maybe no one will notic me among the gays, wannabees and Cuban housewives.'

'Oh, come on. I've heard that South Beach is rapidly gaining i social cachet – *Tatler* and *Elle* do their fashion shoots there Jackie knew that her mother would not set one of her perfectl manicured feet down anywhere she considered unacceptable 'It's really hotting up, even buzzing, so they say.'

'If you like photographers and tanned armies of G-strings c Sylvester Stallone lookalikes.'

'I thought you did, mother.'

'Not funny, Jackie,' Angela said icily, 'and don't call m "mother".'

Jackie heard the click at the other end as her mother slamme down the phone and almost smiled, but found her thoughts turr ing unhappily to Drew; it seemed that he had not returned t New York after all, and the knowledge unsettled her, because a far as she knew there was nothing for him in London and she ha been his only real connection.

She glanced out of the window and into the narrow stree below. But he was a free agent now, so perhaps he had foun someone else – perhaps there had *always* been someone else because that was the sort of guy he was. How could she know? And who was he really? He had proved himself a consummate liar, he had undoubted charm, was very good-looking and capable of amazing deception – 'gifts' that had allowed him to travel and party a very long way. But he had no money, that was clear, which would explain why he had persisted so hard with their relationship. And Angela? She closed her eyes as an ugly image of her mother and him, together, having sex, obtruded relentlessly.

Someone knocked on the door; she swung round and Jamie walked in. Like something fresh and sweet and clean. She sighed inwardly with relief and looked at him in fascination, still surprised at the want in her and the way he had responded to that want. She could never have guessed the depths of his sensuality, or the ease and strength with which he had taken her again and again. There had been delight, too, in all that he did, and innocence and warmth and an adoration for her that she had neither earned nor deserved.

'Hi,' he said.

'Hi.'

For a long moment their eyes held each other.

'Max would like to see you,' he said finally. 'He's in the auditorium – he wants a final decision on the filmclips.'

'Right.' They had yet to pick the six slices of film from the shortlist they had made of Monroe's major pictures for a scene in the second act. All the chosen filmclips would be edited so that they flowed into one another smoothly and would be shown without sound on a massive backdrop, while Rose stood in the foreground waiting to sing as the clips faded.

'And would you remind me to mention to him that the advance bookings are beginning to pick up at last, even the matinées.' But they were still disappointing. She comforted herself with the interest which was likely be generated by the Breakfast Television slot, and at the weekend the Sundays would be running full-page ads. There was an article in *You* magazine on the show, and the *Standard*, *Express* and *Mail* had each promised an article plus photograph of Rose and Lucy which was supposed to appear sometime during the following week.

'But you're worried, aren't you?'

'Well, we've only just tipped our first hundred thousand and that's over several weeks. The momentum has got to pick up.' She drew a breath, trying hard not to think too much about the money the backers had entrusted to her care. 'To give you some idea of what I mean, when *Joseph and the Amazing Technicolour Dreamcoat* opened, the cash advances were around a hundred grand *per day*.'

'There's still more than a week to go . . .'

She smiled. 'I know. One thing I've learned from my somewhat limited experience in this business is to have faith – and tides do turn, after all.'

'I nearly forgot,' he said, 'Yvonne would appreciate it if you could drop into wardrobe sometime today.'

Jackie nodded; she knew what Yvonne wanted, more money, and despite what she had said to the contrary she would give it to her. Now that it was agreed Lucy was taking some of the responsibility for playing Marilyn from Rose she would need the appropriate costumes, two of which were almost perfect copies of Monroe originals and incredibly expensive to make. Moreover, Lucy was not only taller than Rose, but bigger-boned and curvaceous, and the Madison Square Garden dress, in particular, was skintight, semi-transparent and exceedingly delicate. It was becoming rather obvious that, in most instances, each girl would have to have her own costume, and they were running short of time.

'You've got that worried look again – are you all right?'

'It's been a bit of a day,' she admitted. 'I've got nagging doubts about Rose, but I've persuaded myself that she'll "be all right on the night", as they say . . . and just before you arrived I had a call from my mother who was drunk, I think. Apparently Drew has dug up some unpleasant reminders from her past and sold them to the national dailies over there. She's devastated although she won't say so, of course.'

'Did it bother you?'

'Her call? I suppose my mother will always "bother" me in some way; she has that effect,' Jackie said, with a trace of bitterness. 'Of course, it doesn't help that she was sleeping with my boyfriend and almost-fiancé. That takes some beating.'

'I'm sorry.'

'I was, but for different reasons. I'm not sorry any more.'

'Will I see you tonight?'

'Oh yes,' she said softly.

'Aldo is staying late tonight, with Rose; he's trying to make up some time.'

'He won't need me for that.' They gazed at one another. 'Come here.'

He took a step towards her, then another and she was able to reach out her hands and interlock her fingers with his. She rose up on tiptoe and brushed his mouth with her lips.

'That will have to satisfy me until this evening,' she smiled, 'and now to work.'

As he opened the door for her, he said, 'Rose seems fine, by the way, her voice sounds as beautiful as ever.'

'Thank God.' But Jackie frowned. 'It's not so much her voice that worries me, it's the problems she thinks she has. She's a sweet girl, but not the strongest of characters – yet she did seem more resolute after our little talk.'

'She hasn't told you what's wrong?'

'It's like getting blood out of a stone,' she sighed. 'I spoke to her this morning and am pretty sure that whatever it is, it involves a man, but she won't say anything more.'

Jamie fell silent, thinking of Drew, and what he guessed about his relationship with Rose.

'She was friendly with Drew,' he said abruptly, 'but it might not mean anything.'

She stopped and stared at him. 'How do you know?'

'I saw them get into a cab together, but that was some time ago, October or November, and she asked me about him one day at rehearsal. It was during that period when he was away over Christmas; she wanted to know when he was coming back.'

'My God,' she said softly. Even then.

'That's all.'

'It's enough,' she said, and wondered helplessly about Drew, the person she thought she had been in love with. He had duped her so well – and she had believed every word, which surely made her as gullible as Rose. 'He's still around, must be . . .'

'What will you do?'

She shrugged. 'What can I do? I can hardly demand that she

stop seeing him and she would probably deny that she was anyway.'

They were standing outside the door and she lifted her head with exasperation to the distant ceiling and a skylight which sent a shaft of light through the warren of passageways leading to the dressing rooms. There were sounds coming through the walls and up the narrow stairwell: the faraway notes of the orchestra and the rise and fall of voices.

'What is it about some people, Jamie,' she said, 'those who stroll into our lives, wreak havoc, and stroll out again? Like there's no guilt, no remorse – nothing.' She turned, puzzled. 'It's almost as if they were born with something missing.'

'My father told me once that he believed we are all born angels.'

'And?'

'We sin.'

'Some more than others, apparently.'

He smiled.

She took his hand with a sort of gratitude. 'You really will go back, won't you?'

He nodded slowly. 'I don't belong here, Kenya's my home – I've found out that much.'

'Perhaps you haven't allowed yourself enough time.'

He shook his head. 'Come with me.'

'I can't.'

He smiled with an effort. 'I didn't really expect you to say anything else.'

She fell silent, touched by sadness and longing. 'We'd better go,' she said softly, 'Max must be getting impatient.'

He followed her glance, heard the sound of a beautiful voice rise up from the auditorium. 'And what will you do about Rose?'

'Wait.'

It started to rain, but Rose had no umbrella so she ran the last hundred yards to the house. There was a light shining in an upper window and she felt her heart leap. She began fishing frantically for the keys in her jacket pocket and when, at last, she managed to open the door, she pushed it open impatiently and slammed it

306

behind her, running through to the spiral staircase and up the stairs.

'Drew!'

Her eyes quickly scanned the empty room, then she moved towards the open door of the bedroom and there he was, lying across the bed, a bottle of Old Grandad bourbon clutched in his hands.

'Hi,' he said flatly.

'Oh, Drew,' she gushed, 'where have you been? I've been so worried.'

'Business,' he said, 'it's always business, isn't it?'

'I know, but it would just be nice to know where you are sometimes – I could call you, we could talk.' One of the pretty little scenes she had made up in her head; weaving him into her life.

'So you think it would be nice to know where I was . . .' His tone was intimate and unpleasant. 'I don't think you would.'

'Try me,' she said coyly, failing to note the warning in his voice. She sat down beside him on the bed and stared into his face with round adoring eyes.

Drew lifted his gaze from the bottle of bourbon and looked back at her, struck by how much she irritated and bored him.

'Do you know the Lux Club?'

Rose shook her head.

'It's a night-club – a girly club.'

She frowned, not comprehending immediately. 'I've never heard of it.'

'I decided to stay there on Thursday night,' he continued as if she had not spoken, 'in one of their cute little back rooms.' He took a long swig of the bourbon. 'I mooched around on Friday, then went back to the club and went home with one of the girls, a real hot piece called Jasmine. Polynesian. I stayed with her the whole weekend, until I got fed up wearing the same pants, so I came back.'

She sat there staring at him, one of her small hands resting nervously on his leg.

'I don't understand.'

'What does it take to get through to that tiny brain of yours, Rose? I've been having myself a good time. A good fuck, in fact.'

'This is a joke, right?' She smiled at him tremulously.

'No joke, Rose.'

Her mouth opened, then closed.

'I'm getting my stuff together and going back to the States.'

'But I thought . . .' Her voice faltered. 'You came to me, we're living together.'

'Oh, sure,' he said, 'I forgot.' He slammed the bottle of bourbon on to the bedside table and swung his legs off the bed. 'I needed a place to stay.'

She watched him cross the room with shocked eyes.

'Why are you doing this, Drew? What have I done?'

He hauled out a suitcase from the wardrobe and threw it on to the bed.

'You don't mean it . . .' she stood up, 'not really.'

He began gathering up the shirts she had left neatly folded, the silk tie, shoes, the tuxedo pyjamas he had never worn, the white silk suit Angela had bought him, still wrapped in tissue paper.

'Drew – please!' Rose reached across and took hold of his arm, clung to it, pressed her face up against him.

'Look,' he said, with chilling indifference, 'I don't want you. Get it?'

'Don't go, Drew,' she said brokenly, 'please.' Tears too heavy to hold back began to force themselves from her eyes. She moved towards him again. 'I love you.' She took a deep shuddery breath. 'You love me.'

He stopped what he was doing and turned towards her.

'What did you say?' His face seemed to narrow and the features to sharpen and grow dark.

'I love you.'

'Say the rest.'

She gulped and said in a small voice. 'You love me.'

He seemed to shake his head for a long time before he spoke again. 'Love you? I don't even *like* you. In fact, Rose, you are quote unquote "pathetic", and the real funny thing is that you don't even know it.' He pushed his face close and into hers, his lips curling upwards, emphasizing every word. 'And I'll tell you something else – you give me nightmares, you know that? Big, greasy, slobbery nightmares that make my skin crawl.' The stored-up hate and bitterness of the last months seeped out from wounds years deep. 'And when I wake, I find you lying there all buggy-eyed . . . and I feel sick.'

That was the real and continuing nightmare, the cold sour dread he felt every morning because Rose wasn't Angela; never would be Angela.

'And I look around this shitty room and I see teddy-bears, fucking *teddy-bears*!' He prodded her hard with his forefinger. 'You should still be in diapers, you know that?'

He could not remember having a teddy-bear, or a train set, or one of those little cars like for real – the ones kids sit in and pedal with their feet. He had never had fuck all.

Drew blinked and realized with disgust that tears were rolling down his cheeks. He turned his face to the wall, his fists clenching and unclenching.

Rose sat on the edge of the bed, whitefaced and stunned, feeling sick. 'Don't go, Drew,' she whispered desperately, 'maybe we can work something out.'

He made no answer and the silence seemed to stretch and stretch.

'I won't get on your nerves any more,' her voice pleaded. 'I promise I won't.'

'I DON'T WANT YOU!' he screamed and swung round at the same time. 'I NEVER wanted you.'

Her body jumped and she froze with fright, her stomach churning so that she thought she might retch.

'Look at my face, Rose,' he seethed, 'watch my mouth move: I don't want you. I want someone called Angela, an American lady who has more style in her little finger than you have in the whole of your sad little body.'

He jerked away from her and moved to the open suitcase which he slammed shut. His jacket hung on the back of a chair; he reached for it, slipped his arms quickly into the sleeves, then picked up the suitcase and moved wordlessly past her.

She heard his feet draw away from her, then across the floor of the sitting room and down the wrought-iron staircase, the suitcase clanging and banging as it fell against the black railings. An anguished sound escaped her lips and she stood up, panic stricken, and ran through the open door. 'Drew . . .' she sobbed, 'Drew . . .'

She moved to the top of the stairs and panic turned to dread as the main door banged shut behind him. She felt herself sway then she was running down the spiral staircase and into the grey wet streets. All her pretty, silly dreams strewn about, shattered like broken glass.

Richard studied the letter again and his heart beat a little faster. He put it down very carefully and smoothed the creases out as best he could, so that it would lie flat against Lucy's place setting. On the side plate beside it he had placed a red rose which contrasted very nicely with the crisp white tablecloth and the green candles which had been the only ones he could find in the murky depths of a kitchen drawer.

He stepped back and examined his handiwork, then glanced at his watch because he expected her home at any moment. With a little whistle he turned to the fading cassette player and the unruly columns of cassettes piled next to it. He ran a finger down the titles until he found an album which would suit the occasion, something romantic and moving perhaps, but not mournful or tragic, he was tired of tragedy. Usually he left such choices to Lucy, but this time the choice must be all his, because this was his moment and he was determined that everything should be ready and waiting when she walked through the door.

How long had it been since he had had some good news, really good news to give her? He sank to the floor and crossed his legs, leaning his head against the armchair and lifting his face dreamily to the ceiling only to note with disgust the map of lines and cracks permeating the yellowing plaster. Immediately his thoughts settled on the question of a move, and a new flat, but he let the idea fade because he was a little afraid, just yet, to allow his dreams to become reality.

Richard sighed heavily and turned his attention back to the cassettes, finally deciding against Elton John's *Love Songs* and settling on *The Essential Pavarotti*, because despite any inner reservations, he was feeling expansive and jolly and longing to release himself in a burst of song like '*O sole mio*!', which always made Lucy giggle, or '*Nessun dorma*' which always made him want to cry. Just as he switched on the power and was about to

lide the cassette into its pocket he heard the click of her doorkey
nd she walked in, redfaced, windlashed and beautiful.

'Guess what!'

He shook his head. 'You know I'm not very good at guessing.'

Lucy took a deep breath. 'I'm opening.'

Richard's mouth dropped open. 'Repeat that for me, please.'

'I'm opening!'

'That's bloody marvellous! But why? How?' He walked over to
er, kissed her rosy lips and began unwinding her scarf. 'Tell me,
or God's sake, girl!' His own news would wait.

'Well, it's not the way I would have chosen for it to happen,
ut I suppose it's an ill wind.'

'More trouble with Rose?'

She nodded and slipped off her coat. 'She's had a sort of break-
own – drugs were involved, too . . .' Lucy moved to the neatly
et table and poured herself some wine. 'No one seems to know
hat exactly happened.'

'Well, I suppose it was on the cards.'

'Everyone's running round like mad things.'

'You must have had quite a day.'

'It started off quietly enough, but finished with a bang.' She
ook a long sip of wine. 'First thing in the morning I've got
ublicity shots – Jackie's trying to make the best of it and rake up
s much interest out of the story as she can – then it's wardrobe
nd refits and finally I'm left to the tender mercies of Aldo and
Iax.'

'You like Aldo.'

'Yes, he's sweet.'

'But not the poisoned dwarf?'

'To be fair, he's been much more reasonable lately. I think he's
urned over a new leaf, or at least become more human.'

'He's probably been unnerved by your fatal charms, my
weet.'

A shadow momentarily dimmed her eyes because Richard had
o idea how close he was to the truth. She put her arms around
m and took a deep breath.

'Nervous?'

She nodded.

'You'll be fine – fabulous, in fact.'

'You know that I do the last scene naked as the day I was born don't you?'

'I hadn't given it a great deal of thought, actually, but Monro did die like that at least, so history and her thousands of biogra phers tell us. Does it bother you?'

'Does it bother *you*?'

'As long as it's necessary to the action of the story and no gratuitous . . .' he began pompously, but then smiled.

'I'm covered mostly, so it's not quite as risqué as it sounds Lucy lifted her chin and looked at him. 'I lie like the original stretched out, but not quite straight, and face down on the be with only back and shoulders exposed. My head is on a pillow right cheek down, eyes closed. Telephone clutched tightly in m right hand.'

'Sounds like someone's got their facts straight.'

'It's a musical with facts.'

'How is her death portrayed?'

'It isn't, because no one knows how she really died, whether was suicide or murder, and Jackie and Max prefer not to mak any assumptions.' Lucy paused and reached for her wine. 'She simply lying dead in the final scene. The stage is black, no light except for one – a spotlight, and it's aimed directly on her body. watched Rose play it in the run-up to the first dress rehears and it seemed incredibly effective, and the lighting was handle brilliantly . . . a bright beam of light slowly narrowing nothing.'

'Like Monroe.'

'Yes.'

Richard looked at her serious expression, the full sad mout the neat pretty nose which made him feel like Cyrano de Ber erac.

'You haven't noticed *my* surprise.'

'What?'

He gestured towards the table.

She glanced at Richard, then walked over to the sheet of pap lying on the table. His surprise – something he had waited ago izingly to tell her since the post had arrived that morning, all t long day.

Lucy shrieked, waved the letter in the air and threw herself at him.

'How could you let me rabbit on and on about myself when you had this to tell me?' She kissed him again and again, held his face between her hands and repeated the onslaught until he was gasping for breath. 'Oh, Richard . . .' she shook her head in disbelief, 'I'm so pleased for you.'

'Not half as much as I am.' He grinned. 'Five thousand smackers for my feeble effort. Can you imagine a publisher paying me, actually paying me for regurgitating my frustrations and paranoia on paper? Amazing . . .' he said, in quiet wonder.

'Oh, don't knock it, you're always doing that – just accept that it's fantastic news.'

'Of course, I don't get the money all at once. My new, *literary*, agent, Tamsin – Ned can go and take a dive – tells me that I shall have two thousand up front and fifteen hundred on publication of the paperback and hardback respectively.'

'It's still fantastic . . . to get published at all is fantastic!' She threw herself at him again.

'Well, it's a start.'

'Don't be so damned miserable.' She squeezed him tightly. 'You'll be a *published* author, and it's more than just a start, it's positively a new beginning.'

And he needed that, for so long he had needed that. His eyes twinkled and he tilted his head on one side as if he were savouring what she said.

Richard smiled and kissed the top of Lucy's precious head, aware of a delicate and tentative sensation of belief and happiness trying to unfurl somewhere inside. Perhaps it was finally time, after all, to start believing in himself.

'How are you feeling?' Babs said and placed some flowers and a bag of plums on Rose's bedside cabinet.

'Okay.'

'How long are you in for?'

'Four days.'

'You're going to be fine.'

Rose nodded slowly.

313

'And you know you can go back to the show as soon as you're well again, don't you?'

Rose stared at her tightly clasped hands. The nails were bitten down to the quick. 'Why don't you say it?'

'Say what, Rose?'

'That you were right.'

Babs sighed. 'I didn't come here to gloat. Believe it or not, I'm really sorry about what happened.'

'You never liked him.'

'No, I didn't.'

'He was lying all the time . . .' Rose said quietly, 'about everything . . .' She began plucking at the coverlet of her bed.

'Don't think about it.'

'I can't help it,' she said, 'it all keeps running over and over in my head like a bad film. Like all the other times, I never saw it coming – just like you said.' Her nose reddened and her eyes darkened with tears.

'You've still got the show to look forward to.'

'I know,' she said, and then added miserably, 'but they say I should have therapy or counselling first . . .'

'Maybe that's for the best.'

Rose shook her head. 'It's all such a mess . . .'

Babs stared at Rose helplessly. 'By the way, an old friend of yours called . . .'

Rose sniffed and looked up. 'Who?'

'Jules.'

'*Jules*?'

'He's been away apparently – with the band.'

'What did he say?'

'Not a lot,' Babs said. He'd seen the story about *Marilyn* and Rose's apparent collapse in the paper. 'But he'll call you.'

'When?'

'Soon, he said.'

'That was nice of him.'

'Yes,' Babs said and looked back at her friend with resignation. 'I suppose you could say that.'

The atmosphere backstage was electric. Apart from a horrible moment's hesitation by Ian, playing Joe DiMaggio, Monroe

314

cond husband, everything had gone extraordinarily well in the
st act. The cast from the last scene streamed off the stage as the
rtains closed, hot, weary, but exhilarated.

'Was I all right?'

Aldo patted one of the anxious chorus on the shoulder. 'Fine,
e.'

'They like it, though, don't they? I lost my balance – God, I
ought I was going to die!'

'Poor bloody Ian, I bet he feels a right prat . . .'

'Shut up, Rupert.'

'Can you believe it, the dam zip's broken on my flies.'

'Where's Charlie? He's got my fags and I'm desperate for a
oke . . .'

'I heard that, Rupert darling,' Max broke in, 'and I'd rather
u saved your fag until after the show. We don't want your
lcet tones spoilt, now do we? Where's Lucy?'

'She passed me a few moments ago – probably in her dressing
om. She's got a big change now.'

Max nodded, then stepped back to survey the stage as Brian's
ectacular dais was brought into play. The Madison Square
arden scene opened the second act; it was the turning point in
e show, but if Brian's complex machinery loused up, as it had
ne in rehearsals, the whole scene would be damned to hell. He
ok a deep breath and moved a few paces towards the closed
rtain. Behind it sat a packed auditorium and Britain's glittering
eatre establishment and he found himself unable to resist peek-
through a chink in the curtain.

'Look at those bloody vultures,' Max murmured to no one in
rticular as he stared at the critics sitting comfortably in their
ont-of-house seats.

'What?'

'Christ, you made me jump!'

'That's naughty, Max, peeping through the curtain . . .' Aldo
ghed.

'Even brilliant directors have weak moments.'

'So I see.'

'But it's going well . . . don't you think?'

'Near perfect.'

'Thank God,' Max said with relief. He glanced at his watc
'Where's Lucy?'

'Behind you.'

Max swung round and his mouth fell open. Lucy was weari
an identical version of the dress Monroe had worn to celebra
President Kennedy's birthday. It was a dazzling, almost trar
parent creation which shimmered and clung to every curve. I
one had seen it before because Yvonne had refused to ri
damage to it by letting Lucy wear it during rehearsals.

'Fabulous . . .' someone said.

Max just stared, stunned into silence because Lucy's reser
blance to Monroe suddenly seemed uncanny.

The words of the song echoed, seeming to rise to the rafters, t
notes climbing strongly then plunging into caressing sadness. T
pit orchestra fell silent as the song almost died, but then the nc
swelled again to full volume – soaring, diminishing and soari
again until it stopped abruptly. 'Late-Night Phone Calls', Ma
lyn Monroe's last song.

A telephone rang in the darkness for the final time as t
voices which had played so much with her life began to fade, ur
there was only one left, a man's. It seemed to float in the bla
void, questioning and irritated, and then abruptly ceased.

The naked body sprawled across the bed lay completely st
the beautiful back and the blonde head seemed luminous a
dazzlingly white, made more so by the penetrating spotlig
which hovered over the scene for several seconds and then beg
to shrink and narrow until all that remained was a tiny beam
light which froze, blinked and then died.

There was utter silence for a moment, the curtains ca
slowly, soundlessly together and then the applause started.
rang from all quarters, booming, gathering momentum as peo
began to stand, some with tears in their eyes. Everyone there
audience, orchestra, cast, stagecrew – felt the extraordinary bi
and believed they had just witnessed the opening of a smash.

'I don't *believe* this,' Max gasped, sifting through the first two
three reviews. 'Two of them are bloody awful, killing, in fact.'

Jackie took a deep breath. 'I know, but let's not panic yet, a for God's sake have a glass of champagne, we're supposed to be enjoying ourselves.'

Despite the bad news she forced herself to smile across the milling crowd which had gathered for the lunch party at the Hyde Park to celebrate the opening of the show the previous night. Inside she was beset by doubt and disappointment, her ragged nerves coiling and uncoiling in time to the cast tape which was being played in the background. And it's good, she thought fiercely, bloody good, whatever anyone might say to the contrary, and she had not spent the last five years and more trudging steadily towards this point to be slapped down at one stroke by a batch of critics.

'Listen to this,' Max hissed stubbornly, '*The Times*: "the cast tries hard to give this melodramatic production some life, but the score is unoriginal and the lyrics overly sentimental." '

'And what about this one . . .'

'Max, please, do you have to?' She had read them already and didn't want, or need, to hear a repeat performance.

' "Insensitive at times, this adaptation of Monroe's legendary life is sometimes like a return to the sordid low-life of *Dallas*, but on the West End stage." Christ! I think I'll go somewhere and quietly kill myself.'

'But that's Roland Vickery – he's always a bastard,' Aldo interjected. 'I've just got hold of the *Mail* and it's rather good: "bristles with wonderful songs . . . irresistibly moving . . ." '

'What? Let me see – ' Max grabbed the paper.

'Thank God,' Jackie said, with obvious relief.

'The *Standard*'s not bad, either, says something about "melancholy expertise", and Lucy gets a good mention too.'

'I think I might just be able to sleep tonight,' Max said, then proceeded to read the article again.

'Perhaps you should read it to the cast,' Jackie said.

'Good idea.'

He jumped on a chair and clapped his hands – as if he were conducting a rehearsal, Jackie thought with amusement, and his announcement was naturally received with tumultuous applause. The cast and guests had that flushed look of success and now she could share in it too.

Any criticism was a blow, but too much could kill a show stone dead. Yet the audience had loved it, there was no mistaking that, even the critics themselves and the glitterati of the theatre establishment could not deny that – standing ovations were not exactly commonplace.

'If you guys would excuse me.' She cut a path through them and into the lobby.

Max followed her with his eyes. 'I bet you a fiver she's phoning the box-office.'

Aldo shook his head. 'It's so obvious, Max, I won't waste your money.'

'Just let it break even . . . please,' Max prayed and drank some champagne.

'Whether it does or not, I plan to take a holiday when it's feasible to do so.'

Max raised his eyebrows. 'Bully for you, darling.'

'Bangkok,' Aldo said quietly.

'Isn't that a bit frayed round the edges these days?'

'I don't know, I haven't been there for some time.'

'Why Bangkok, anyway?' Max snorted softly. 'Or shouldn't I ask?'

'An old friend of mine lives there.' And Jonno had once, perhaps he still did, haunting the old places, the seedy bars like some beautiful wraith.

'Well, I hope the glories of condoms have reached Thailand's exotic shores . . .'

'That's rich coming from you,' Aldo said sharply.

'Okay, okay.' Max lifted his hands defensively. 'Sorry I spoke.' He turned impatiently to the doorway, wondering where Jackie was, what she was doing. His eyes travelled to the lobby and down the marble staircase. At the bottom a girl stood, young and fresh-looking; she looked up and his heart began to beat a little faster.

Nadia had said that she couldn't come . . . Max swallowed hard. She had made every excuse under the sun why she couldn't come and he had thought that she was avoiding him, because the cat was out of the bag and Polly and her parents knew about them. All hell had been let loose. He had tried not to think about it, what he would do if he did not see her again, how he would bear remembering her when he was alone.

He watched her upturned face with something akin to awe, and she looked back at him, her lovely mouth moving into a smile that said everything. Wonder of wonders.

Aldo lifted his glass again, considering whether he should get quietly drunk or not, but then his attention was caught by Max as he wordlessly put down his champagne and walked towards the lobby. There was a young girl standing there alone and he saw her face literally light up as Max held out his arms and quickly wrapped them around her.

It seemed to Aldo that they stayed like that for a long time: he watched them, Max, with astonishment and envy and a lump in his throat.

'Aldo?'

He turned, startled to find Jackie standing behind him.

'Where's Max?' she asked.

Aldo nodded in the direction of the lobby.

'Good God.'

'That's what I thought.'

'I'd tell him the good news, but he seems otherwise engaged.'

'Good news?'

'I telephoned the Adelphi box-office and things are really picking up – we've sold over thirty thousand tickets in twenty-four hours.'

'Thank God for that.'

She grinned with relief. 'Exactly.'

'Shall we break the news to Max?'

She shook her head. 'I think he has other things on his mind at the moment, don't you?'

Even Max. There must be something in the air. Jackie turned automatically, her eyes scanning the room until she found Jamie, talking with Lucy, lovely Lucy who had carried the show with such sensitivity and skill, and despite all that had happened. The two of them made a beautiful couple. She stared fixedly at them and was appalled to feel a sharp stab of jealousy, but then Jamie's head began to move, slowly, and he was looking at her across the sea of faces as if he had sensed her eyes. A hot rush of desire made colour flood her face and her knees grow weak so that she thought she must be going quietly out of her mind.

'Will you be taking a break once things settle down?'

Aldo's voice seemed to come from far away and she turned towards him with a remote look on her face.

'Sorry, Aldo, I was miles away.'

'I just wondered whether you might be taking a break at some point . . .' he sighed inwardly because Jackie's attention was obviously still elsewhere, '. . . when the show settles down?' Out of the corner of his eye he saw Jamie approaching and he shot a curious glance at Jackie.

His question remained unanswered because she took a step forwards and away from him, toward Jamie. Aldo watched them as they came together, and as far as he could tell, nothing was said, yet they moved into the lobby where Max had been and stood there for a moment framed in the doorway – two lovers anyone could see that.

Aldo stood alone, just beyond the fringes of the party, feeling exposed and awkward. Jackie and Jamie had slipped away, just as Max and his pretty young thing had done. Love, lust passion . . . how long had it been for him? His eyes dimmed fenced in by regret and longing, and he closed them for a brief burning moment thinking of Jonno. In his mind's eye he could see the boy who would be a man now and his heart began to beat a little faster.

There had been few real loves in his life, one perhaps before Jonno and none since, and he knew with a certainty he could not have explained that there would be no more.

Angela smiled, but not with kindness. 'I knew you'd come sooner or later. How did you find me?'

'There's a guy I know . . .' His face reddened.

'You mean a private dick, don't you – the same one you used to dig the dirt on me.'

Drew felt discomfort and shame, like a little boy, and he looked at her helplessly. 'Do you know what you did to me?' Even now she could not understand that she had left him no choice.

'Do you think I care?'

Her gaze beat him down and he looked at his feet, at his one piece of luggage standing outside the door.

'I get it,' she said, 'you think that now you've ruined my life

320

you can come crawling back because I'm off-limits to the guys who count – like the ones with money, power, influence. You think I'll want you because there's no one who wants me.'

Immediately her mind filled with a reluctant picture of Dougie, but she would have lost him anyway, the two-timing, cheap little bastard. The hardest part was that 'his new gal' was younger than she was and she wondered if she could stand the humiliation. Except, of course, that it really didn't matter any longer.

Drew shook his head and said brokenly, 'It's not like that.'

'What the hell is it like, then? What do you want me to say, for chrissakes? That I'm glad to see you?'

He was unable to speak. He could feel perspiration breaking out on the back of his neck, between his shoulder blades, and he rubbed away the gloss on his forehead with the palm of his shaking hand.

'But you are, aren't you?'

Angela stiffened. 'What are you talking about?'

'You knew I would come, you said so.'

'What has that got to do with anything?'

He looked at her full in the eyes. 'You've never stopped wanting me.'

Her eyes opened wide and blood soared into her face. She wanted to rage at him, scratch and slap the handsome face again and again, bring him to his knees for all that he had done to her. Instead she caught a deep breath and her shoulders drooped as if her resistance had flagged.

'And what have you wanted, Drew?' she said. 'Money? My glamorous lifestyle?'

'I knew a lot of ladies, and they all had money and glamorous lifestyles.'

'Not like mine,' she said proudly.

'I could have had Jackie, if I'd really wanted, you know that.'

'I don't want to talk about Jackie.'

Maybe she would tell him one day about the short, un-sweet note from her daughter; a few abrupt lines on Jacqueline Jones (Overseas) Limited notepaper 'returning' a ruby engagement ring. Jackie had finished by adding, 'it was never really mine in the first place.' How true.

He shrugged. 'Okay.'

They fell silent and he shifted uneasily from one foot to the other, afraid to speak.

'If I let you in . . .' she said suddenly, 'it's got to be on my terms.'

'Sure.' His heart began to pound.

'And legal.'

He made no answer because he did not understand what she was saying.

'I mean marriage, Drew; I don't need that gigolo scene any more.'

He gaped at her.

'There will be a marriage contract, naturally, and you won't get a cent if you mess around.'

He nodded dumbly.

'And you'll have a different name and a different history with the help of my money, maybe even something aristocratic.' She paused. 'You know, you can buy one of those tinpot titles in Europe for a few dollars.' She could become a baroness, maybe even a countess. Perhaps she would write her memoirs and give Dougie a heart attack.

Drew stared at her with disbelief and tried to speak, but nothing would come.

'Say something, goddammit,' she said and her voice was soft and low and almost happy.

'I'll do whatever you want.'

She watched him for a long moment and then her mouth moved into a cat-like smile.

'You'd better come in then.'

He picked up his suitcase and walked through the door, heard her close it behind him. She made him wait a moment so that she could examine the initials printed on his luggage.

'What *is* your name, Drew?' she asked. 'And tell me the truth.'

He sighed softly, unhappily, as a vision of an old raggedy-assed Indian took shape. No way.

'Smith.'

She laughed and helped him remove his jacket. 'You can do better than that.'

'It really is Smith,' he lied.

'Really?'

He nodded and began unbuttoning her blouse. And he would never tell her the truth, not in a million years. He cringed inwardly as the memory came back to haunt him: 'Little-Horse'. The kids at school had called him 'giddy-up', or 'horse's-ass' on the really bad days. Drew closed his eyes as Angela's mouth found him. No way – she could have everything he could give, the rest of his life, but not his name.

A pale sun was shining through the glass so that the water in the pool had turned to silver. Jamie sat at a small table next to the massive picture window overlooking Hampstead Heath. Throughout the last few months, when he needed time on his own, he had found himself drawn to this spot.

He heard the sound of someone's feet and turned to see Jackie coming down the steps bearing two coffees. She wore jeans, boots and a white silk shirt; her hair hung loose, full and blonde and all he could think as she moved towards him was that he wanted her, that he had always wanted her.

But she had been right all those weeks ago when she said that they came from different worlds; he would never be happy here, not in the real sense of the word, and not in London, or any big city; neither would he ever have the love for the theatre which she had. It held no illusions or glittering dreams for him and never would, no matter how much he tried to convince himself otherwise, and he had tried, for his own sake as much as hers, but inside his homesickness had grown too large to bear and the only real solace he found was in her arms.

For all his youth he knew such solace would become a burden as time went on, making her unhappy, pulling them slowly apart and wearing them down. Jackie knew this as well as he did and there had been no real talk of persuading him to stay, but for all his wisdom and foresight there was a part of him that wished she had tried a little harder.

'What are you thinking?'

He looked at her carefully. 'In sum, that I don't want to go, but I don't know what else to do.'

She reached for his hand and he took it and folded it carefully between his own, turning it over and caressing the fingers and the soft white palm.

'You could stay,' she said.

'What would I do if I stayed?'

'I could find you something else.'

'I'm almost unemployable; I hardly know anything that would be of any use to you.'

She had no answer because it was true, but he looked at her, willing her to say something more, yet knowing in advance that she would not.

'Anyway,' he looked back to the window and the view beyond, 'there are things remaining from my father's estate which must be cleared up, and there is still the lodge at Marsabit. I shall have to make a decision on that soon, I suppose.'

'And I still have a great deal to do here.' Her voice faltered a little. 'And my father . . .'

'I understand all of that.'

'But you have never told me what you really want,' she said with a trace of exasperation. Even his investment in *Marilyn* had been for all the wrong reasons. Jamie was her mysterious 'Canadian backer' and she had promised her stepmother that she would never let him know that she knew, but it was one of the hardest promises she had ever had to keep.

'I'm not sure myself, but I want to see and feel those wide open spaces again, find my roots as they say, then maybe, maybe I'll sit down and write something.'

'Write?'

He smiled sheepishly. 'Sometimes I've wondered whether I haven't been homesick for Marsabit all my life. When I should have been studying I found myself making notes, even rough sketches of the mountain rising out of the desert, the foothills, the wild life – that sort of thing.' He spoke with obvious enthusiasm. 'It's a strange, beautiful place: a long extinct volcanic mountain capped by mist forests. There are crater lakes, one in particular called Lake Paradise and from there you can see for hundreds of miles.'

'No wonder you want to go back.'

'Part of me does, just for the beauty of the place.' He glanced at her. 'But there is real work to do there, as well; it's always been heavily poached and the elephant population has suffered particularly.'

'So there is a serpent in your Garden of Eden.'

The corners of his mouth turned up a little. 'I think you'll find that there are serpents in everyone's garden if you look hard enough.'

She gave him a searching look, touched by regret. 'Why don't you let me come to the airport?'

He shook his head, but wouldn't meet her eyes. 'I don't want a long goodbye . . . it's not fair, on anyone.'

She looked helplessly down at their hands and the fingers which interlocked so perfectly. They sat there for a long time in silence until Clare called them from the house. Jamie glanced at his watch and realized that she was waiting, that David must be here now, because that had been the plan all along.

The cab began to move off slowly, wheels crunching on the gravel drive. Jamie lifted his hand to them from the window and it seemed to hang there, small and alone, before he let it drop. Jackie focused on his blonde head as it became smaller and smaller, but he did not look back again.

When the drive was empty she still stood there, clutching her father's hand as slow tears began to roll down her cheeks.

'Come on,' he said gently.

She shook her head, unable to hold back her tears any longer.

David looked at her lovely contorted face, thought his heart might break, and pulled her against him because it was the only thing he could do. He let her weep, stroking her hair, repeating her name, and through her anguish she listened to his beautiful voice, and her mind somersaulted back to her childhood and the first time she had seen him. A tall, handsome giant with a beautiful voice.

'It's only a question of three more weeks filming, and that's it.'

Jackie took a sip of the large brandy David had insisted on pouring for her when they returned to the house and watched him closely as he moved across to the window, his favourite place. He was thinner, if that was possible, and his skin was sallow and jaundiced-looking. She swallowed and switched her gaze to the view beyond him and watched a bird float across the sky.

'What would you like to do then, after it's over?' Clare asked too brightly.

'I usually ask *you* that question at this stage of the game,' he said quietly, then sighed. 'Don't pamper me, darling, I know why you're doing it and you mean well, but I don't want that.'

Jackie looked swiftly into her glass, felt her swollen eyes brim again and took a large slug of brandy.

'Anyway, I fancy Kenya.' He looked at them both, his women, pleased at their obvious surprise because curiosity would defea their misery for a time. 'I'd really like to go and see Jamie in hi natural environment, as it were. He knows I've enjoyed listening to him on the joys of his father's house, so he won't be surprised.'

'It's a long way, David.' There was a warning note in Clare' voice.

'I am perfectly aware of that,' he said quickly, 'but it's some thing I've made up my mind to do.'

'Your treatment . . .' she began.

'Bugger my treatment!' he said harshly. 'I'll take it with me if have to.'

Clare hung her head in the heavy silence which followed knowing that it was pointless to argue even if she had had th strength to do so.

'Sorry,' he said, shaking his head and waving a hand at then both in a gesture of apology. 'Sorry.'

Clare stood up and moved over to him and he slung an arn around her fragile shoulders and leaned his head gently on hers.

Jackie felt a choking sensation, grief, rising up into her throa and wondered how she would bear it, how they would all bear it but then David was pushing Clare gently to one side and lookin at them both.

'I want to go to Kenya, that's all, then I'll come back and the can do what the hell they want to me because I shall probably b past caring by then, anyway,' he said quietly. 'Now, as I love yo both, please bear with me because I won't dwell on this again. He paused, the pale blue eyes watching them carefully, 'I've ha a good, full, rich life, which is much more than most poor, blood people can say – so I don't want, or need to be smothered b kindness. Do you see? And I couldn't express my wishes bette than in the famous words of a Spanish civil war revolutionary: "

326

is better to die on your feet than live on your knees . . ." So Kenya, here I come.' David swung round and poured himself a minute brandy. 'And now, my darlings, we will drink to that.'

Kenya – Six Months Later

The desert road seemed to tremble and waver in the heat. Salt-white dust billowed into the air and fell back, only to be dispersed by hot winds. Up ahead, rising from the heat haze, a dusky thumbprint lay on the horizon. The guide lifted his arm and pointed, 'Marsabit.'

Jackie inhaled deeply and wondered why it had taken her so long to make the decision to come. As day followed day and week followed week the disquieting urge, the desire, had grown steadily and relentlessly.

Her direct involvement with the show had finished long since and the advance bookings had grown and snowballed. International reaction had been very favourable and there had been several enquiries about producing *Marilyn* abroad. It was ironic that she had her mother to thank for some of the show's success, because the British papers had lifted the story on Angela Cassini from the States and it had hit the scandal sheets with almost perfect timing. Naturally it had drawn upon her famous ex-husband, David Jones, and his producer daughter, Jacqueline, 'who was currently wowing the West End with a fabulous new production based on the life of Marilyn Monroe.' She couldn't have put it better herself.

Max had married his Nadia and was working on other things; Aldo had started a music workshop in Bangkok of all places; and Rose had finally returned to join Lucy in the show, older and perhaps a little wiser.

A few days before her father had died there had been a cable from Angela telling them that she had remarried, and to an Austrian count. Drew, of course.

Jackie turned her face to the window and the desert beyond as her eyes began to brim. Her father had never made it to Kenya, after all; four weeks after filming had been completed, he had been in the midst of packing for the trip with Clare, when he collapsed with a massive haemorrhage.

She took a deep breath: it was his birthday soon and Clare would come, and together they would scatter his ashes on the mountain up ahead, over Lake Paradise . . . which was what, in a sense, he had wanted.

She leaned her head back to look at the immensity of the blue desert sky. In the distance a group of birds rose and fell, then swooped and dived as one toward the mountain – Marsabit – where Jamie was.